Kirov Saga:

Paradox Hour

By

John Schettler

A publication of: *The Writing Shop Press*
Paradox Hour, Copyright©2015, John A. Schettler

Discover other titles by John Schettler:
The Kirov Saga: *(Military Fiction)*
Kirov - Kirov Series - Volume I
Cauldron Of Fire - Kirov Series - Volume II
Pacific Storm - Kirov Series - Volume III
Men Of War - Kirov Series - Volume IV
Nine Days Falling - Kirov Series - Volume V
Fallen Angels - Kirov Series - Volume VI
Devil's Garden - Kirov Series - Volume VII
Armageddon – Kirov Series – Volume VIII
Altered States– Kirov Series – Volume IX
Darkest Hour– Kirov Series – Volume X
Hinge Of Fate– Kirov Series – Volume XI
Three Kings – Kirov Series – Volume XII
Grand Alliance – Kirov Series – Volume XIII
Hammer Of God – Kirov Series – Volume XIV
Crescendo Of Doom – Kirov Series – Volume XV
Paradox Hour – Kirov Series – Volume XVI

Award Winning Science Fiction:
Meridian - Meridian Series - Volume I
Nexus Point - Meridian Series - Volume II
Touchstone - Meridian Series - Volume III
Anvil of Fate - Meridian Series - Volume IV
Golem 7 - Meridian Series - Volume V

Classic Science Fiction:
Wild Zone - Dharman Series - Volume I
Mother Heart - Dharman Series - Volume II

Historical Fiction:
Taklamakan - Silk Road Series - Volume I
Khan Tengri - Silk Road Series - Volume II
Dream Reaper – Mythic Horror Mystery

Mailto: john@writingshop.ws
http://www.writingshop.ws ~ http://www.dharma6.com

Kirov Saga:

Paradox Hour

By

John Schettler

"Mother Time is a dressmaker specializing in alterations."

— Faith Baldwin

Kirov Saga:
Paradox Hour

By
John Schettler

Author's Note:

For readers who might be dropping in without having taken the journey here from book one in the *Kirov Series*, this is the story of a Russian modern day battlecruiser displaced in time to the 1940s and embroiled in WWII. Their actions over the many episodes have so fractured the history, that they now find themselves in an alternate retelling of those events. In places the history is remarkably true to what it once was, in others badly cracked and markedly different. Therefore, events in this account of WWII have changed. Operations have been spawned that never happened, like the German attack on Gibraltar, and others will be cancelled and may never occur, like Operation Torch. And even if some events here do ring true as they happened before, the dates of those campaigns may be changed, and they may occur earlier or later than they did in the history you may know.

This alternate history began in Book 9 of the series, entitled *Altered States*, and you would do well to at least back step and begin your journey there if you are interested in the period June 1940 to July 1941, which is covered in books 9 through 16 in the series. That time encompasses action in the North Atlantic, the battle of Britain, German plans and decisions regarding Operations Seelöwe and the attack on Gibraltar in Operation Felix. Action against the French fleet at Mers-el-Kebir and Dakar is covered, along with O'Connor's offensive in North Africa, and the coming of Rommel. The little known British campaigns in Syria and Iraq get a good deal of attention, and other events in Siberia occur that serve as foundations for things that will happen later in the series.

To faithful crew members, my readers who have been with me from the first book, this volume stands as the sequel to the *Grand Alliance* Trilogy and also concludes the second eight volume "Altered States" saga in the series. It will take the action to the eve of that fateful day and hour on July 28, 1941, when *Kirov* first displaced in time.

-J. Schettler

Part I

Escape

"You cannot escape the responsibility of tomorrow by evading it today."

— Abraham Lincoln

Chapter 1

Karpov stood on the gondola bridge of *Tunguska*, riding the turbulence of the angry skies in the largest craft ever to fly above the earth. Everywhere on the ship, men were standing in taut readiness at their battle stations, the gunners behind the long steel barrels of their recoilless rifles, the flight engineers at their stations to watch speed, buoyancy, elevation and the trim and cut of *Tunguska's* massive tail rudders. There was still a stunned silence on the bridge, and Captain Bogrov could still feel the sting of Karpov's gloved hand on his cheek. They had all seen the agonizing death of Big Red, the awful searing fire of the explosion when Karpov launched every RS82 rocket that remained into the tail of the ship to ignite his terrible fire bomb.

The flagship of the enemy fleet was caught in that explosion, her sides rent open, canvass shell burned away, gas bags serrated by the fragments of Big Red's shattered duralumin tail frame. Both ships had been struck a fatal blow with Karpov's merciless order, and both would die in those last terrible minutes, suspended in the fires until the weight of their own twisted airframes overcame their buoyancy, and started the long plummeting fall to their doom. Down they went, like two massive smoking comets in the sky, crashing to earth with a thunder that challenged the storm above in its fury.

Yet out of that calamitous moment, a few souls were lucky enough to escape, leaping for their lives from the burning airships, and the men on the bridge of *Tunguska* watched in horror. Parachutes bloomed in the sky, and something fell like an evil seed from the deep underbelly of the *Orenburg*—a small metal sphere.

Karpov saw it fall, and immediately knew he was seeing the desperate retreat of his enemy, Ivan Volkov. His hard voice had broken the stillness on the bridge, the biting barb of orders forcing life and movement into hands, arms, and legs again, setting the crew to the task that was now uppermost in his mind—get Volkov. Get him before that seed fell to good ground and could sprout again in the Devil's Garden he had made of this world. And so the

Rudderman was hard on the wheel, then engines roared, and *Tunguska* lurched about in the sky, turning north by northwest, and riding the wind in feverish wrath.

Ports opened on the smooth brow and chin of the ship, and the concave *Topaz* radar dishes deployed, ready to search the grey lines of clouds for any sign of the enemy. Up ahead, Karpov could see a smaller silver fish diving into a cloud, the *Abakan*, slowly taking up position in the vanguard of his formation. This was all that remained of his fleet at the moment, unless *Talmenka* could hasten up from the south, or he could get help from his last two battleships to the east, *Irkutsk* and *Novosibirsk*.

Volkov believed he would destroy my entire fleet, thought Karpov. Instead he got a nasty little surprise here again. The tables are turned! *Orenburg* is a smoking wreck down there, and I've already killed or beaten off eight of his ships! Yes, we paid a heavy price for that. It was not easy for me to do what I had to do just now and sacrifice Big Red. So now I must be certain Volkov suffers. He's down there somewhere, and if he managed to survive that fall, then he will be scrambling to make contact with his men on the ground and get to another airship as soon as possible.

Good, let him try.

"Topaz stations, report!" His voice was hard on the voice tubes, the thin reply barely discernible over the noise of *Tunguska's* engines.

"*Contact bearing zero-one-two degrees true. Large signal. Speed and elevation unknown.*"

Rodenko would come in handy at a time like this, thought Karpov. But even he would have difficulty reading the signals from this antiquated equipment. Four enemy airships remained, and this could be nothing else than what it seemed. Volkov was planning to get there on the ground and gain the protection of those airships. His signalmen had been listening to the enemy on radio as orders were called out, ship to ship. In the heat of combat they had foolishly resorted to use of the open airwaves, instead of coded Morse signals. He knew he might now be facing these four enemy airships, and last reports had three at good elevation, at least 5000 meters, somewhere to the north. Now he finally had a good read on where they were.

They have two S-Class ships out there, *Sarkand* and *Samarkand*, and they'll have no more than eight 76mm guns each. The other two ships were reported as A-Class, the *Armavir* and *Anapa*—eight guns each again, though they will have a single 105 on the main gondola. That's 32 guns in all for the enemy. I've got 24 on *Tunguska* alone, and half of those are heavy 105s. Throw in the eight guns on *Abakan* and we match them easily enough. It will all come down to tactics and air maneuvers, and let them try to best me if they dare. One look at *Tunguska* will probably send them scattering like a flock of frightened birds.

So there you have it, Rudkin!

He spoke now to the unknown author of that precious little book Tyrenkov had inadvertently picked up on that trip up the back stairway at Ilanskiy. *When Giants Fall—The Death of the Siberian Air Fleet.* Well you can tear all that to pieces now, can't you, Rudkin— just like I tore Volkov's fleet apart here. Yes, this isn't over yet. We've another good battle to fight, but I have little doubt as to the outcome. And one day, where ever you are, Rudkin, you'll settle into a library chair and find out that everything you based your stupid little story on has been turned on its head! It will not be Ivan Volkov you glorify with that flowing prose. You have a good deal of editing to do. Try to write me out of the story? I don't think so. No! I don't go down so easily. So this time get it right. Remember my name—Vladimir Karpov. I'm going to re-write your entire book!

He smiled, his thin lips tight as he gloated inwardly at his victory. Now to make that victory complete. Now to get up north to those last few ships and finish them off before Volkov could get to one and escape. Three at good elevation... That will mean they are standing on overwatch, while that fourth ship goes to ground to lower a cargo basket and haul up Volkov's sorry ass. If I try to descend to get that fourth ship, the other three will all be well above me, and *Abakan* will not have the guns to hold them off. So I must send *Abakan* down after Volkov. It's the only way. Only *Tunguska* has the firepower to stand with their top cover. Yes, I hate to hand off this task to *Abakan*. I'd much rather be the one to get down there after Volkov, but tactics first.

"Signal *Abakan*," he said calmly. "Tell them they are to bear on that enemy contact, but begin a gradual descent. They are to look for any enemy ship near ground level, and destroy it. We will hold elevation at 5000 meters. After that, get word to Tyrenkov on the ground. Tell him I want a flying column assembled as soon as possible. Get them north to the coordinates of that contact. As to our remaining ships. They are to make for Ilanskiy, and stand on overwatch there. One ship may descend for ground support fires, but only one. I want at least two of the three ships up at 4000 meters, preferably *Irkutsk* and *Novosibirsk*, if they ever get here."

Those last two ships were both good battleships, 16-guns, and in the same basic size class as old Big Red. They were aging, but still had the firepower for a good fight. Once they arrived, Karpov knew he would have complete air superiority here. Yes, there were still twelve more airships in Volkov's fleet, and two others that were detached after that first fight with *Yakutsk*. But many of those ships will be far away, some as far south as the Caucasus where Sergei Kirov's troops were struggling with Volkov's 6th Army. So in Karpov's mind, the situation was looking very good here, very good indeed. He had a firm rein on things now, and was convinced that final victory was also within his grasp.

Yet he did not have command of all the facts. Those two ships that had been detached because of damage sustained in that first fleet battle had returned—*Pavlodar* and *Talgar*—and with them was yet a third ship, another 8-gun heavy cruiser, the *Krasnodar*. Of the three, the best of the lot was *Pavlodar*, a 160 cubic meter lift battlecruiser with twelve guns. And Ivan Volkov was not heading north to try and reach the four ships Karpov now had on his radar screens. Yes, the reports had been accurate. There were three ships on overwatch, and one at low elevation, the *Armavir*, but that was only because the ship had been fighting a bad tail fire suffered in that hot ambush when *Tunguska* had first come on the scene and nearly destroyed Admiral Zorki's entire four ship division.

The grey skies and limited range of the radars had all conspired to hide the arrival of *Pavlodar* and *Talgar* to the west, where they had also brought in two much needed companies to reinforce Volkov's ground force. As such, they were both at low elevation to land those troops, and not seen by the rudimentary *Topaz* radar systems.

Volkov, his devious mind still sharp enough to read the situation, knew he would be a fool to try and reach the airships to the north. The land was broken with stands of trees, and occasional marshy clearings, and he would never get his motorbikes through all that in any good time. But he would get west on the good road to Kansk where *Pavlodar* was still hovering low, if the Siberian Tartars did not get him first.

* * *

Volkov looked up to see the massive shape of *Tunkuska* high above, a dark blight in the skies, slowly swallowed by the thickening clouds.

I have one great advantage, he thought. I can see that bastard easily enough when he's up there lording about in that monstrosity, but the inverse is not true. He knows I may be down here—at least he must assume as much. Now he'll be trying to read my mind, and he knows I'll want to get airborne again as soon as possible. In that he will be correct. I cannot take the chance of lingering here like a common soldier. I can see now that the decision to detach *Pavlodar* and *Talgar* was premature. I was overconfident, too brash, and I underestimated that son-of-a-bitch Karpov yet again. Now there is no further room for error.

He looked west, along the road to Kansk where the situation on the ground still remained very confused. Some of his men had landed there earlier, thinking to surprise the enemy at Kansk and quickly seize that town. There they were to have set up a blocking position to stop any rail traffic from the Ob River line front from reaching Ilanskiy. But the situation in the main battle had compelled Colonel Levkin to recall those troops, leaving only his motorcycle platoon astride the road as a rear guard. They had been surprised by squadrons of Karpov's Siberian Tartar cavalry, and those who could, fled east along the road.

All this was happenstance, thought Volkov. All of it—Kymchek's failure to read the enemy strength on the ground, the cavalry ambush that sent those motor bikes to me here, and now that decision to detach those two airships pays me an unexpected dividend! So I head west, right down this road. I should find two companies up ahead, and *Pavlodar* waiting for me at ground level. No sense wasting any further time here. I must get to that airship!

"Sergeant! Lead the way!"

There were no more than twelve men left from the Motorcycle Platoon, but they would have to do. It seemed a feeble escort for the General Secretary of the Orenburg Federation at that moment, and the noisome bikes would be easily heard by any Tartars still lurking in the woodlands flanking the road ahead. This was going to be very dangerous, perhaps the most dangerous thing Volkov had done in many years. A man in his early sixties, he was still fit, and his mind was as sharp as ever. Now the thrill of danger seemed to catalyze him, and his eyes gleamed as the column started off.

Sergeant Beckov led the way, with three bike-mounted troopers. Then came the only sidecar bike in the squad, where a gunner was manning a DT-28 'record player' machinegun. Behind this went Volkov, flanked by a man on either side, with the last section of four men following. The motor bikes were quick and very agile, and easy to ride on the good road surface. They roared off, leaving a thin trail of dust behind them, and Volkov glanced up warily, thinking he might see the dark shadow of *Tunguska* looming above him at any moment.

It was only his fear whispering to him. That airship was far too high to spot him here on the ground, and the heavy cloud cover was providing a good cloak against observation from the air. They sped down the road, until Sergeant Beckov raised his right arm, fist clenched, bringing the column to a halt. He looked over his shoulder, shouting back to Volkov.

"Cavalry up ahead. Not many, but they are blocking the road."

"Well don't just sit there, Sergeant. Clear them off!"

Beckov waved at the MG mounted sidecar, wanting it to come forward, and then gathered together five men with SMGs to make his attack. They gunned their engines, speeding forward in a mad charge, firing as they went. There he saw that they were greatly outnumbered, as there had to be at least twenty Tartars up ahead all wearing black overcoats and heavy woolen Ushankas. His squad engaged, their sub-machineguns spitting fire at the enemy, and the DT-28 hacking away from the sidecar. The horsemen had not expected this bold attack from the same men they had recently sent fleeing east on this road, and they were surprised.

The gunners shot seven dead in the first wild seconds of the duel, with three others falling from stricken horses and running for the cover of the nearby woods. The rest thought to mount a counter charge, with their leader drawing his sabre and shouting out deep throated orders. His horse reared up as he waved the flashing sabre overhead, until the DT-28 shot his mount right out from under him and he tumbled to the ground in a hard fall. This sent the remaining ten men scattering in all directions, vanishing into the treeland to either side of the road. Beckov had cleared the way and waved for the remaining bikers to surge ahead. They rode forward, SMGs still spitting out cover fire to make certain the enemy could not reorganize for an attack, and soon the squad was well away, speeding down the road.

They rounded a bend, elated, thinking the way was clear, but they were wrong. The twenty men they had surprised were just an outlying squadron of the Tartar formation. A large group of enemy cavalry was assembled up ahead, the men quickly mounting their horses when they heard the sound of the firefight to the east. Now they were shaking out in to a long line, many with bolt action rifles, and others with those cruel sabres. They saw the commotion up ahead, their leader grinning balefully when he watched the small squad of motorbikes come to a sudden halt, shrouded in their own road dust.

"What now?" Volkov shouted, but Sergeant Becker had only to point. Now they could hear the sound of rifles in the distance, and a machinegun firing.

"Damn!" said Volkov. "Is there any way around them to the south?"

The road was following the rail line here, in a wide clearing. There were heavy woodlands to their right, and a small hill that was another obstacle to any movement to the south. Volkov gritted his teeth. He had twelve men here, and there looked to be a hundred horsemen forming up ahead. He could see his men ridden down in his mind, trampled beneath the charge that was sure to come any moment now. And these barbarians would not even know who was in front of them, Ivan Volkov, a prize so great that they might all be given their weight in gold to capture him. They would roll over his little squad in a heartbeat, and leave him dead on this god forsaken road, slashed to pieces by those sabres. It was no way for the General Secretary of the Orenburg Federation to die.

He saw the horses rear up, heard the sound of more gunfire to the west, but it was not what was in front of them that concerned the Tartars now. To his astonishment, he saw the cavalry turn and charge west, away from them, leaving only a single squadron which was dismounting and taking up a blocking position on the road ahead. What was happening?

My troops, he suddenly realized! That gunfire must be the men off *Pavlodar* and *Talgar* on the road to the west. That's why they turned. We're a threat they have already sized up, and of no apparent concern to them now. But I have two full companies on the road up ahead, though we're on the wrong side of the action here. He nudged his motorbike up to the MG mounted sidecar, which also had a small field radio, as this was his reconnaissance unit off the *Orenburg*, and well equipped for their role as fast moving scouts.

"Corporal! See if you can raise the men on the ground up there. Tell them a senior officer is here, and I need to get to them as soon as possible—but do not mention my name."

"Yes sir!"

Now the sound of rifle fire and the throaty shouts of the Tartars was heard, and Volkov knew that the commander up ahead was going to have his hands full soon enough.

"Belay that order. Send to *Pavlodar* instead. Tell them to maneuver along this road and look for us here! Have them make ready to lower a cargo basket and take on ground troops. *Talgar* is also to stay at low elevation and provide ground support fire for those troops up ahead. Understand? They are not to climb under any circumstances until I am safely aboard *Pavlodar*."

That's my only chance now, he thought. The sight of an airship low over this road will hearten my men, and *Pavlodar* can give those ruffian Tartars a taste of her heavy rifles. If they stay low, then it's likely Karpov won't be able to spot us here. He's off north to my diversion, and let him deal with my Admirals. If Gomel and Zorki can buy me a little time, then I can turn this situation around.

A little time…

I thought I would have eternity within my grasp by now, and look at me here, counting on a few hot minutes, and these twelve men, to save my skin. Heads will roll after this. Yes, heads will roll when I get back to Orenburg and pull together the rest of my fleet.

This is far from over.

Chapter 2

Colonel Levkin could see that his battle for Ilanskiy was not going to end well. After three hours of hard fighting, they still had no support from the airship fleet, and the Siberians out gunned them badly, with good artillery and heavy rail guns pounding his positions outside the town. The sudden appearance of armored cars and light tanks had also been a shock, as his troops had little more than old AT rifles to try and fend them off. One section had some AP rounds for one of the recoilless rifles, which they put to good use, disabling two of the nine enemy armored cars, and forcing the rest to withdraw.

He had finally driven the stubborn defenders from the farm house, and cleared most of Sverdlova. Now his men were within sight of the rail yards, but the fighting in the town itself was fierce, and his companies had taken heavy casualties. The Siberians were dug into well prepared positions, with machine guns well sighted, mortars, and squads of tenacious infantry holding buildings from the cellar to the attic. It had taken his best unit, the guard legionnaire company, all of forty minutes to take a large brick warehouse and foundry on the southern edge of the town, and now they were clinging to the position under heavy fire.

The unexpected arrival of the General Secretary had been another surprise. That meant the tumultuous wreckage that had fallen south of the town was the fleet flagship! It was no wonder the remainder of the fleet had withdrawn to the north. Now Volkov was trying to get west on the road to Kansk and reach *Pavlodar*. That was going to be dangerous, and he knew that those two companies he was expecting as reinforcements might not reach him any time soon, if at all. So what to do here?

I can't take the damn place, he thought. Even if we do push through to the rail yard, there's that damn armored train sitting there to deal with. Taking that out will be a nightmare, but suppose I do. Then what? I'll be sitting there trying to hold an old railway inn that is half demolished as it is. There will be no cover in a light wood building like that. They'll be getting up reinforcements from all compass headings, and that will be that.

He looked at his map, realizing that his only real move now was to pull out and get his men into the woodland north of the town. At least there we will have room to maneuver, he thought, and a chance to link up with our airships, assuming we still have a fleet out there somewhere. This whole operation was mere vanity on Volkov's part. We're just sacrificial lambs to his voracious appetite for power. Why he needed this place is still beyond me. We've paid dearly in blood and material here, and for what, that damn farm house?

"Sergeant Major!"

"Sir!"

"The brigade will execute a phased withdrawal to the north. We will regroup in the woodland. Get on the radio and pull our men back from that hamlet south of the town. Once they are here, wheel the line back, and reinforce the hinge on that road to Kansk. This ends now."

He strode off, looking for another radio man to get a message to the fleet. As far as he knew, they still had airships up there. Admiral Gomel was supposed to be parked right over the town, and if he was, that would put a speedy end to those damnable rail guns. If wishes were horses…

* * *

"**Ships** ahead! Watchman on the forward bow has sighted three airships. They looked to be about 500 meters below us sir. We have the advantage of elevation!"

"Excellent," said Karpov. "Do we still have rockets?"

"No sir," said his master of arms. "We expended the last of those on… in that last attack."

Karpov noted how the man stumbled with that. Yes, we fired everything we had at old Big Red, but the ship was doomed as it was. I just made a speedy end to things, and took down *Orenburg* in the bargain.

"Very well. Ahead full. Ruddermen will prepare to make a hard turn to port on my command. All gondola mounted guns to bear on the nearest ship."

Karpov stepped to the viewports, his field glasses up as he looked for the enemy ships. There they were, hanging over the charcoal cotton of a rising thunderhead, their noses up now, with the telltale drool of water from the front of the ships indicating they had just dropped ballast. Three heavy cruisers, he thought—easy prey. Each one mounted a pair of 76mm guns on the top platform. Their remaining six guns would all be on the gondolas, and therefore out of the action unless they could make a rapid ascent and gain elevation on *Tunguska*. That wasn't going to happen.

"Get the nose up, Bogrov. Match their elevation gain. Let's see how high they're willing to climb."

He would surge in at his best speed, over 120kph, and then execute his turn to bring his ship broadside to the enemy formation. That would bring all twelve of his bigger 105mm gondola mounted guns to bear on the target. All his remaining guns, the lighter 76mm caliber, were airframe mounted, two in the nose, four on each of the two top gun platforms, and two more in the tail. It was a configuration that made the ship a deadly foe at any elevation relative to the enemy.

Karpov had as much firepower topside as all the guns on one of these enemy heavy cruisers. And the fact that he had built his top gun platforms perpendicular to the long trim of the ship also allowed them to depress downward, and engage targets at lower elevation. It was a design of his own making, unique in the airship fleet. Most ships would mount their topside platforms right over the center of the long fuselage. But Karpov built in reinforced platforms on either side of the rounded fuselage, mounting his guns a few meters down the long curve of the ship to allow for this downward firing angle.

Even though they had less sheer lifting capacity, the heavy cruisers were lighter, and would gain elevation quicker than

Tunguska. But let them try, thought Karpov. I'll blast any ship that climbs right out of the sky.

They were trying, but it soon became evident to Karpov that his enemy wanted no part of a real fight with *Tunguska* here. They were already turning as they climbed, their engines straining in the wind. Yet they were rising fast, the convection of the thunderheads beneath them aiding their climb. The long years at sea had given him an uncanny sense for range. He estimated they were no more than five kilometers off now, turning tail and revving their engines for all they were worth. Even though *Tunguska* was bigger and heavier, it had six powerful engines, and could actually out-run the small airships in good air. Yet they would be some time closing to decent firing range if they ran, and now his thoughts turned again to Volkov.

He must be down there trying to get aboard that last ship. In fact, these three here may be trying to lead me on a wild bear hunt, while Volkov slips away.

"Signal *Abakan*," he said coldly. "Ask them if they have that fourth ship in sight yet."

Minutes later he had his answer. "Sir, that last ship has been identified. It's the *Armavir*, part of that same division we ambushed on arrival. *Abakan* says they've grounded the ship, but there's no sign of a loading operation underway. They're still fighting that tail fire."

A tail fire? That was always a difficult thing to overcome, as the crucial rudders and stabilizing rear fins were at stake there. Was Volkov down there? Did he scramble here only to find another burning airship that would be useless to him? If he is there, he's seen *Abakan* by now, and he'll know there's no way *Armavir* will ever get airborne. I'll make it simple for him.

"Tell *Abakan* to engage. Pound that ship to a smoking wreck, and then climb to 5000 meters."

"*Topaz* station two reporting," said the signals watchman. "contact reported west over the rail line to Kansk!"

"West? Could that be *Talmenka?*"

"No sir. That ship is still well to the south. They estimate another three hours flying time to reach us."

Karpov's eyes narrowed. Then Volkov has brought in reinforcements. Either those were the two ships he detached earlier, or they are new arrivals. Remember, Volkov has twelve more airships out there somewhere. What to do here? He knew that his enemy could not be on any of those three heavy cruisers running north. And if he was on *Armavir*, he would be having a very bad afternoon to go with the morning I gave him today. Then he thought, striding over to his map table and throwing the charts aside to get at a map of the local area.

"What's happening on the ground, Signalman?"

"Sir, last reports indicated the enemy was attempting to disengage. They've pulled out of Sverdlova, and they are falling back to the north of the rail line to Kansk."

So we've beaten them, thought Karpov. Either that or Volkov managed to make contact with them and the whole lot is forming a security perimeter around him. In any case, this attack on Ilanskiy has failed, just like the first one.

"Is that contact to the west approaching the town?"

"No sir. It appears static, and at low elevation. We only just picked it out of ground clutter returns."

That could mean only one of two things, thought Karpov. They were offloading fresh troops, or… Volkov didn't run north as I first suspected. Of course! Look at the terrain down there. It's impossible for vehicles, and can you imagine sixty year old Ivan Volkov huffing it all the way up here on foot? No. He's either down there with his troops near Ilanskiy, or else he ran west instead, along the road to Kansk!

"Helmsman, execute a hard turn to port. Steer for that new contact!"

"Hard to port!" The helmsman was heavy on the wheel, and *Tunguska* rolled with the turn as Karpov braced himself on the plotting table.

Damn you, Volkov. So you can read a map after all! You nearly fooled me, didn't you. But I'm on to you now. Of course! There was no way you could get this far north. What was I thinking? You had to run west on the road to Kansk. You knew you had ships there waiting. Well I have men there as well.

"Don't we have Semenko on that road to the west?" He said that as much to himself as to anyone on the bridge. He had three squadrons of Tartar cavalry at Kansk when this began, and they had been given orders to move east along that road and rail line. Perhaps they've run afoul of this little maneuver by Volkov. I've got to get there as soon as I possibly can.

He smiled now, realizing how desperate Volkov must be in this situation. He can probably still smell the smoke and fire from *Orenburg's* fall, he thought. Well I have news for him now, even if he does manage to slip away here. This war is only beginning. I have an entire Army up north of the Ob river line, and we've finally mended fences with Sergei Kirov over Perm. Now those troops can join the Soviets there and move south. Together we'll have enough force to cross the upper Volga and actually begin an offensive there. That will force him to abandon his campaign on the Ob and fall back west. Yet all that in good time. I'm coming for you, Volkov. I'm coming as sure as winter, and my revenge will be harder and more biting than a Siberian blizzard. Just you wait.

* * *

Ivan Volkov was waiting, feverishly pacing behind the thin screen of his small security detail, even though his Sergeant was pleading for him to get low and out of harm's way.

"We're well within their rifle range here sir!"

"Damn their rifles," said Volkov. "I'll not wallow on the ground like a common pig. Just keep them busy until *Pavlodar* gets here."

The recon squad had formed a makeshift line astride the road, actually using their motorbikes for cover as they fired at the blocking force that had been left to stop their approach. Then Volkov finally saw what he had been hoping for, the looming shape of a great airship rising over the small hillock to the south. The hard crack of a recoilless rifle split the air, and shells began to fall on the road near the enemy cavalry.

"Sergeant! Show our colors!"

His men quickly deployed a flag, emblazoned with the black eagle and red V symbol of the Orenburg Federation. The Captain on the airship spied it easily enough, and at this elevation they could also make out the dark sable uniforms of the recon section below. The heavy gunfire easily dispersed the last of the Tartars blocking the road, and Volkov smiled again when he saw there were more of his men up ahead now. His two reserve companies had made short work of the more lightly armed cavalry. Bravery aside, sabres and rifles could not stand long against the heavy machineguns his men could deploy in well practiced drills.

Already he could see the men on the airship above preparing to lower a cargo basket. Down it came, the pulley wheels squeaking, engines buzzing fitfully as the basket lowered. Then the airship above revved its smaller maneuvering engines, slowing to come to a stable hover point above the scene. The movement of the basket slowed, then it came scudding along the ground, right on the road. The shadow of the great airship darkened the scene, and Volkov strode boldly forward into that shadow, making for the container.

"Carry on, Sergeant," he said perfunctorily. Then he stepped through the open gate and into the basket, where two men saluted stiffly, their eyes wide behind their black rimmed goggles. They knew who they were saluting, and were stunned to find the General Secretary here on this lonesome road to nowhere.

"Take us up!" said Volkov sharply. "And call up on the field wire and tell the bridge to climb. Set a course west for Orenburg at once."

As to the men he left behind on the ground, they were as far from his thought now as the capitol was. All he could think of was getting safely away from this place, and back to his gilded stateroom in Orenburg. The men he left here would hang on in the woodland.

He would see about trying to pull them out later, but first things first.

I need to get back home and gather the rest of my fleet. Karpov got the best of me here, damn his soul. He was waiting there for me, hidden in that storm like he knew exactly what we were up to. It was as if he had read my entire operational plan right out of a book! Kymchek was correct. Those reports of that crash over the English Channel were a complete ruse, but he should have seen this ambush coming. If he made it to the ground, I hope he remembers what we came here to do—our little fallback plan. We shall see.

Then the weight of all that had happened that day fell on him, the sudden ambush of the enemy, savaging his Caspian Division. Then that horrific explosion when they turned to engage old *Krasny*, and his harrowing fall in the escape pod. The sound of *Orenburg* falling from the sky as a burning wreck still gored him. His jaw was tight, eyes puckered, face set and grim, smudged and soiled with the dirt and mud of this place. His trousers and overcoat were sodden and wet, and he smelled like a peasant.

But I'm so much more, he thought. I'm Ivan Volkov, and still alive, by god. And I'm going to light this whole front on fire when I get back home. It's war at long last! The Germans are crossing the Soviet frontier even now. It's general mobilization, and I'll call every man who can hold a rifle to the fight, from as far away as Turkmenistan if I have to. This little skirmish here is nothing. It was ill planned, and I won't be so stupid again.

You want war, Karpov? I'll give you one.

The long cables slowly retracted, pulling Volkov up and up, until the Sergeant below saw the basket reach the hard duralumin under-keel of the airship. It was the last time he would ever see friendly forces again, though he did not know that just then. He blinked, staring up at the hulking shape of *Pavlodar*, taking heart from the sight of the guns bristling from the gondolas. Then he turned to his men, still waiting near their motor bike barricade.

"You heard the General Secretary," he said. "Carry on. Who knows, maybe we'll get a medal for dying here."

Chapter 3

Karpov was pacing on the bridge, making everyone there more and more edgy as he did so. The Elevatorman and Rudderman were giving him sidelong glances, then watching the Air Commandant to see how he was reacting, but Bogrov stewed in silence. He was still sullen and angry over what Karpov had done, blasting Big Red like that, sending all those men to an agonizing death.

I thought he was trying to hit the *Orenburg*, but I could see easily enough that would be impossible. My god, it never entered my mind that he was targeting Big Red all along. That's why he asked about those fire bombs. He was gambling that he could detonate that wizards brew of his, and do exactly what he did. Wizard's brew? No. That came straight from hell itself, and this man is a devil if ever there was one. He didn't hesitate one second. The men on Big Red were just an expedient to him, just a means to that terrible end he had planned for the *Orenburg*. He gave them no more than a minute or two to escape before firing. Maybe the gunners got out, and the bridge crew, if they had the parachutes handy in the lockers. As for the riggers and bag men, the engineers, top gunners, cargo crews…

That wasn't all… Then he had the temerity to strike me, right here in front of the entire bridge crew! Alright, I cursed the man for what he did, and they all heard that as well. But to lay hands on me like that was wrong. He may be Admiral of the Fleet, but I'm Air Commandant, chief of all flying operations. Titles aside, I would have made him pay dearly for that little insult, and I may still find a way. Yes, I'm getting on in years, but I'm still fit, and by god I stand a head taller than that rascal. One day…

Be careful, another inner voice spoke to him. Don't judge this man by his size or the cut of his shoulders. He's a cold hearted beast of a man, this one. He's dangerous. Yes, I've held my tongue for good reason, because with a man like Karpov, you never really know what he might do from one minute to the next. He was willing to take down Big Red like that without a second thought. This man could do anything. He has no remorse, and less concern for the men he killed today. Something tells me he killed a good many more before he ever darkened my bridge with that odd uniform and jacket of his.

The man is strange. The way he paces, the way he goes off to a corner and whispers to himself, that look in his eye when the ship goes to battle stations. So what is he up to now with this maneuver? We had damn good elevation on those three heavy cruisers, and we had the speed to close on them if he wanted to engage. Then he pulls this turn hard to port, and off we go after that second contact. What's he up to? Volkov… Karpov thinks he's down there, and trying to escape. That's what this was all about from the beginning, wasn't it?

Bogrov shook his head, still trying to understand what had been happening these last hours. There we were, sitting right over Ilanskiy, though the place didn't look right. It was too small! None of the outlying hamlets were there. It looked as though the surrounding woodland had just swallowed them whole! I know this ground like the back of my hand, and there was something very wrong here. That tree line there. Why, two hours ago it was creeping right up on the rail line. Now it's well back as it should be. And where was the mooring tower at Kansk? Something is very odd here.

The Admiral has been completely phobic over this place for months now. He's posting at least two airships here at all times, and keeping a good garrison on the ground as well. The men have been cutting trees for lumber and he's brought in engineers. What is that demon up to down there? It all has something to do with that damn railway inn, the place where Volkov staged that raid earlier. And here he comes again with damn near half his fleet! We were lucky to come out of that storm as we did, and find ourselves right over those airships. I'll give Karpov one thing—he can fight. I've never seen any man so ruthless and determined in battle. We were badly outnumbered here, and look now—Volkov's boys are running for any wind they can find.

Yes, Volkov… That's what this is all about.

Karpov is dead set on making sure Volkov goes down with his

ship. Who could survive what we saw, but he's taking no chances. If Volkov was there, then he's probably lying in a pile of burning wreckage down below, but Karpov is maneuvering about like he's still in the hunt. He thinks Volkov made it safely to ground, and if he did, the man would be trying to get airborne again as soon as he possibly could. That's why Karpov pulled north after these cruisers. Now he's pulled west for that second contact.

The Signalman came in again, and this time he went directly to Karpov, speaking quietly. Bogrov pretended to be checking his instruments and ballast board, but he was keeping a subtle eye on the two men, wondering.

"You have the bridge, Bogrov. Get us west over that contact. I will return shortly."

"Aye sir."

"Admiral off the bridge," said the boatswain.

Aye, thought Bogrov. The bloody Admiral is off his bloody bridge, most likely off to the radio room for some business or another. Maybe its Kolchak this time. Maybe he wants to know why Karpov needs the entire goddamn fleet out here over this stinking little railway inn, while there's a major offensive underway out west on the Ob, and we've no air cover there. When Karpov had gone, he looked around at the other men, and finally breathed a little easier.

"As you were," he said quietly, glad for the opportunity to give an order up here once in a while. He was the goddamn Air Commandant of the entire goddamn fleet! Except when Karpov was here, and Karpov was always here, wasn't he....

* * *

The Signalman had a handle on some odd radio traffic, ship to ship, and he thought the Admiral would want to listen in. *Tunguska* had been running west at good speed, and they were very near the contact the *Topaz* Station had reported, close enough to pick up the short range ship to ship radio sets used for fleet order transmission.

"It's two ships, sir," he told the Admiral, "*Pavlodar* and *Talgar*."

"Can we break in on this channel?" asked Karpov.

"I don't see why not." The Signalman began to adjust his radio dials, and then handed the handset over to the Admiral.

"Very well. Dismissed."

The man saluted and was out the door, leaving Karpov alone in the radio room. He pressed the send and began to speak, hailing the other ships out there beneath the cloud deck. They were very close, down there somewhere, lurking like submarines, and he had the same odd feeling as he might have aboard *Kirov* whenever Tasarov reported an undersea contact. All he wanted to do is find the damn thing, and kill it.

"Good afternoon, gentlemen," he said. "This is Admiral Vladimir Karpov. Welcome to Siberia! My radar crew tells me you're running west. Not very sporting of you to leave without paying the full bill." He smiled at that, and waited, knowing that if Volkov was down there the temptation to get on the line with him would be overwhelming. He did not have long to wait.

"Greetings Admiral." The voice was unmistakable. "So you've found me at last. I thought you had taken the bait and were up north after my cruiser squadron."

"Volkov! You son–of–a–bitch! What do you think you're doing here? Didn't I teach you not to try and sneak through the back door like this? A pity I had to repeat the lesson."

"Yes," came Volkov's voice. "A pity for the men on *Krasny*, and on *Orenburg* as well. You want to play with fire, Karpov? You think I'm a fool? You think I don't know what you've been doing collecting all that coal dust? Well, let me tell you that two can play at that game. I had my service jacket on when I went down those stairs, and I've spent a good long while archiving every bit of information it contained. You hit me again with a thermobaric, and I'll lay waste to every city on the Ob. Then you can sit up there and watch them burn."

"Don't threaten me," said Karpov. "You're in no position to do that or anything else here. If you haven't noticed, a good number of your airships are missing, are they not?"

"Missing? Like *Yakutsk, Tomsk, Angara, Krasnoyarsk?* That's half your fleet, Karpov. I meant to kill them all, but I'll admit that while my intelligence is usually spot on, we missed this little maneuver you pulled here just now."

"Oh? And did you also miss the fact that half of *your* fleet is missing as well? I took down six ships here today, including your precious fleet flagship, and put damage on at least three or four others. Now I'd like to finish the job."

"Don't quibble with me," said Volkov. "Yes, we took our lumps here, but you can't trade with me. This was only half my fleet, and you damn well know that. I can come back here with twelve more ships any time I choose, and next time there will be no mistakes. I'll grind what's left of your air fleet right under my left boot, including that monstrosity you float about in up there."

"Your cruiser squadron took one look at us and ran north, Volkov. With men of that caliber at the helm, I have nothing to fear."

"Don't be stupid. They ran north because that is exactly what I ordered them to do."

"Yes? Well I wasn't stupid enough to take your bait, Volkov. I'm sitting up here at 5000 meters watching this lovely storm brewing. Why don't you come up and we'll settle this?"

Volkov laughed now, long and hard over the strained airwaves. "You'd like me to do exactly that, wouldn't you? No thanks, Karpov. We'll stay right where we are, and if you have the guts for another fight, then come on down and join me. We'll lock horns down here, and then I'll order those three cruisers to come in on top of you and put you out of your misery."

Karpov nodded, realizing that was Volkov's only play now. He had to stay low, and count on the fact that he still had those three cruisers up there to tip the scales in his favor if I drop elevation to engage here. I could call for *Abakan* to join me soon, but it would probably get here too late.

He decided to goad the man one last time, but he knew he could not indulge himself here, no matter how badly he wanted to get Volkov in another fight.

"So you're running west now, are you? Well don't wait for *Armavir*. We took care of that ship as well. And when we finish rounding up the men you left behind on the ground, the interrogations will be very thorough."

There was just enough silence on the line for Karpov to realize he had drawn a little blood with that. He let Volkov stew a moment, then pressed on. "As for that little offensive you kicked off on the Ob, you and I both know that will lead you nowhere. Face it, Volkov. It's 750 kilometers to your lines back west. You'll never take Ilanskiy militarily—*never*. I'll put three divisions here if I have to, and then you can bring every airship you have left, but they still won't be enough to land anything more than a single brigade. And while you blunder about on the Ob, I've been making other plans."

"Ha!" There was a challenge in Volkov's tone now. "Where have you been, Karpov? Yes, you were hiding in that storm up there, but have you listened to the news lately? The Germans are about to cross the frontier into Sergei Kirov's Soviet Union, or what's left of it. It's only a matter of time now. We've just been playing with you out here with a couple infantry corps, but now I'm mobilizing my entire army on the Volga. In two months time I'll raise divisions from Kazakhstan to Turkmenistan, and raise a good deal of hell with them. This business on the Ob isn't finished either. Once we shake hands with German troops on the Volga, and kick Kirov out of the Caucasus for good, then we come for *you*, Karpov."

"Tough talk," said Karpov. "You say you've archived your service jacket data files? Well why don't you read a few. Germany *lost* this damn war. Have you forgotten that?"

"Not this time," Volkov came back sharply. "No, not this time. It took every man that I can raise, and all your troops thrown in with Kirov to beat the Germans. You bet on the wrong horse, Karpov, and I'm going to enjoy these next few years as you struggle to raise troops out here. I had a good look at those Siberian Tartars you're always crowing about. My men brushed them aside easily enough on the road to Kansk. The rest of your lot will get the same treatment."

Time for the *coup de grace*, thought Karpov. Should I tell Volkov where I've been in recent days? Should I tell him I had a man staring at him from the upper window of the second floor at Ilanskiy, just hours ago? Hours, minutes, long decades. They were all the same now for Karpov. No matter what Volkov blustered about, the fact remained that he had lost this battle, and I still control Ilanskiy. That was going to make all the difference, and he decided to remind Volkov of that one important fact.

"Look here, Mister General Secretary. That was a nifty little trick you pulled with that escape pod, and yes, it looks as though you will make good your escape here as well. You and I both know I'm not giving up four thousand meters in elevation to settle this now, as much as I would love to see you leaping from another burning airship. Was the ride down comfortable last time? So, you can run your mouth all you want about the Germans. You think you can push all the right pawns, and king yourself on the back row before this game ends. But don't forget *me*, Volkov. I'll be sitting on the other side of the board now, right at Sergei Kirov's shoulder. I know the history as well as you do."

"Then let the game begin," came the challenge. "Pawn to King four! You can castle to King side or Queen side. It won't matter. The Germans will get through, in the south. They drove all the way to the Terek River, and that was with no help from me! So they'll get through, and there's nothing you'll be able to do about it."

"You're forgetting one thing," Karpov came back. "You're forgetting the very reason you tried to pull this little maneuver here again—Ilanskiy. I beat you here, Volkov, and decisively, no matter how many airships we traded. I control Ilanskiy, and that's the end of it. Do you realize what I can do when I complete the reconstruction of that back stairway? Yes, I've got all the original plans now." He let an interval of silence play on the airwaves before he finished, then spoke only one word. "Checkmate!"

No response came back for some time, and there was static on the line from the storm. Then he heard Volkov's voice again, a distant crackle on the speaker.

"See you in hell, Karpov. I'll see you in hell."

"I suppose you will," said Karpov. "Yes, I'll be sitting on Lucifer's throne down there one day, so please come and pay your respects. Karpov out."

He switched off the radio set, folding his arms and smiling. Let Volkov think long and hard about Ilanskiy. Let him wonder just what I might do when that stairway is complete again. He hasn't the foggiest idea where I was these last few weeks and days, what I can do now with this ship, where I can go when I have need. I am no longer a simple fleet Admiral here. I'm not merely Kolchak's lieutenant and Minister of all Western Siberia. No. I am so very much more now. I'm the master of time itself, and I can count the hours, minutes and seconds Volkov may have to live at my leisure. I can figure a way to put an end to that man, and a way to do the job myself instead of sending Tyrenkov. So let him raise his army here, while I raise mine.

For now, it was time to get back to the bridge.

Part II

Ghost Ship

"Nor does the man sitting by the hearth beneath his roof better escape his fated doom."

— Aeschylus

Chapter 4

Schlachtkreuzer *Kaiser Wilhelm* was a beautiful ship, fast and deadly as it plowed ahead through light swells that day. Laid down in 1937 by Deutsch Werke at Kiel, it was a design that evolved from the fast Panzerschiff models planned as successors to the *Deutschland* class pocket battleships. The Germans wanted a faster ship with 11-inch guns to better the performance of the *Deutschland* Class, but to get that speed required a longer hull and widened beam. This required more armor to cover that hull, which in turn added weight, and a vicious circle ensued. Thus only two of twelve planned Panzerschiff Kreuzers had been built, the *Rhineland* and *Westfalen*, and designers moved to a larger ship that could accommodate the armor and also get a dual propulsion system with both diesel engines for efficient long haul cruising, and turbines for high speed engagements.

The result was the *Kaiser Wilhelm*. At 35,400 tons, it was over 10,000 tons heavier than the Panzershiff, and with better armor and guns. Yet the designers had labored to give the ship the best speed possible, with four high-pressure Wagner boilers, which had a distinctive sound when they were fully fired for high speed performance. The engineers had come to call them "Wagner's Girls" when they were singing, and Chief Engineer, Otto Kremel, was fond of putting on a recording of the famous composer's *Ride of the Valkyries* when the ship ran at high speed. Designed to achieve over 33 knots, the ship had demonstrated the ability to run at 36 knots in trials, an amazing feat for a ship with a displacement equal to British battleships of the *Revenge* Class, which labored to achieve top speeds of 21 to 23 knots.

Kaiser was all of 840 feet long to achieve that speed, a third longer than *Revenge* and with a wider beam as well. Yet that gain in speed had come at the expense of both armor and firepower. While the old *Revenge* Class had eight 15-inch guns, *Kaiser* had six, and while *Revenge* had heavy 330mm belt armor, the protection on *Kaiser* maxed out at only 190mm. This had led some designers to christen the ship *Ohne Panzer Quatsch,* disparaging its lack of armor.

As a battlecruiser design, the ship was more comparable to the British *Renown* Class, where it could match or better that ship in almost every category. Kapitan Werner Heinrich had been given command, and he was well schooled in cruiser operations, having served under August Thiele aboard the heavy cruiser *Lutzow* before this posh assignment. Now he was set on putting the whispered comments about his ship to rest. As he stood on the bridge that day, he was proud to be the vanguard of the fleet flagship, *Hindenburg,* and when the order came to close on the enemy contact and engage, his blood was up.

Now we get our chance, he thought, staring through his field glasses at the smoke ahead. *Goeben* has been busy this morning. One of those hot *Stuka* pilots has already got a hit, and now we'll come in like a shark to the blood. The British don't have anything here that can match my firepower, and I can outrun any ship in their fleet. But we won't be running this time, we'll be hunting! *Kaiser Wilhelm* is the best ship I've ever set foot on, and now I get my chance to earn my keep. We were out of the action earlier in the Med, keeping a good eye on the *Goeben.* This time the ship will be put to its proper use, as an advance guard and scout ship, a hunter out to find and hurt the enemy. And my 15-inch guns will do exactly that.

"Ready for action, Schirmer?" he said to his Chief Gunnery officer.

"Ready sir."

"Good, because I intend to fight here, in spite of these orders to disengage if the British attempt to close the range. Let them try. Word is that they have three cruisers, but it is more likely that we'll see those pesky destroyers turned loose on us."

"Let's see how they like our guns, sir."

"All ahead full!" Heinrich wanted to get over the horizon and get a good look at that smoke as soon as possible. It was not long before his watchmen made the sighting, a large ship, possibly a carrier, and burning at the bow. Then the scene clouded over with heavy haze, and Heinrich knew what was happening.

They're making smoke with the destroyers, he thought. They're running, but they don't have the speed to match me. This ship is a whole new evolution at sea. Those British carriers could always outrun our heavy ships, but no longer. Now we close the range here with each passing minute, and let us see if they send anything our way to challenge us.

* * *

That challenge was inevitable. The Royal Navy was not about to allow one of its principle assets to go down here without a fight. Of the five destroyers escorting *Glorious* that day, three turned after making smoke as ordered, and now they were set to make a brave charge in the hopes of discouraging the oncoming enemy raider. *Icarus* was out in front, commanded by Lieutenant Commander Colin Douglas Maud, a barrel-chested man with a heavy black beard and his favorite blackthorn walking stick always at hand, which he tapped on the deck whenever they made their torpedo run.

Maud's fate had been strangely entwined with the long odyssey that had brought *Kirov* into this war. His ship had been in Force P under Admiral Wake-Walker, en-route to the North Cape area to attack German airfields at Kirkenes and Petsamo, though they never got there. Later, he would steam with Admiral Tovey in a hunt for another fast German raider, as that story once played out. Yet the raider was not a German ship, but a strange vessel with weapons so advanced that it managed to hold the entire Royal Navy at bay for weeks in the North Atlantic. Maud's ship had been screening Tovey's battleships when the rockets came in, weapons unlike anything he had ever seen. *Icarus* was hit and sank that day, putting Maud and his crew into the water, along with his beloved bulldog Winnie.

Rescued at sea, Maud was eventually given command of another destroyer, the *Intrepid*, a ship sailing right off his starboard bow at that moment. As fate would have it, he would meet the ship that killed *Icarus* and Winnie again in the Mediterranean, and lead *Intrepid* on a desperate attack to try and even the score. He was lucky enough to survive that encounter this second time, but not lucky enough to get his vengeance. But his story was not finished. A German U-Boat Kapitan would have something more to do with his fate, one Werner Czygan aboard U-118. It was his stealthy web of mines that would catch a fly off the Coast of Spain, a ship named *Duero*.

It seemed like a small thing, a lowly tramp steamer hitting a mine laid by a hungry, frustrated U-boat Kapitan, but it was the night that changed the entire course of history—not only of the war, but for every day that followed. For a very special passenger was aboard the ship that night, a drifter, indigent laborer, and a virtual nobody that had been taken on as cheap muscle in the fire room a few weeks earlier. His name was Gennadi Orlov.

While serving with Force H, *Intrepid* came to the rescue of that stricken ship, and Maud became very suspicious about a couple Eastern Europeans aboard, and particularly with the man named Orlov.

But all that had not yet happened. It was action that had began in a frantic naval chase between July 28 and August 8 of 1941, days that had not arrived yet. And it was action that might never occur now, for this world was strangely altered, with whole nations like Russia fragmented into warring states. Even so, details in the picture this history was painting held true, and Maud was aboard *Icarus* again. Yet the ship that had sent his destroyer to the bottom in one telling of these events to come, was no longer the mortal enemy of the Royal Navy. Instead it sailed as an ally.

Perhaps Maud would never be fated to meet Orlov like that now, though that encounter was a crucial link in the chain of events that now saw *Kirov* here in this world. If his keen eye had not spied that Glock Pistol at Orlov's side, then he would not have sent the man to

Gibraltar so British intelligence could have a look at him. There Orlov would meet and be interrogated by a man who was a double agent with the KGB, and as a result of that, he would be sent east through the med on a Turkish cargo ship, transferring to a Soviet trawler in the Black Sea.

Orlov's sojourn east, in search of his grandmother, eventually evolved into a hunt for the man who had caused her harm, Commissar Molla. It took the Chief to a place called Kizlyar, where Molla's men picked him up and sent him to a prison near Baku. Along the way he left clues in the history, particularly a journal note that a very keen eyed navigator used to find him. If Orlov had not gone east like that, then Fedorov would have never made the journey west along the Siberian rail line to try and rescue him and return him to his own time. He would have never found the back stairway of the Inn at Ilanskiy, and never met young Mironov, Sergei Kirov. It was that meeting, and the careless whisper of warning in Mironov's ear, that saw this world now shattered in pieces, altered states, skewed history that was becoming more and more unrecognizable with each turn of *Kirov's* screws in the turbulent waters of this war.

All that depended on the man now standing on the bridge of the Destroyer *Icarus*, Colin Douglas Maud. Or was it Werner Czygan aboard U-118, and his decision to alter his tactics and lay those mines instead of hunting with his torpedoes? It was that choice that sent *Icarus* and Maud to the *Duero* in the first place. Who could say where the seed of causality was really hidden in the garden? Time was tormented by these circuitous loops and changes, like unseasonable rain that caused things to grow and bloom that were never meant to be. It remained to be seen what part Maud would now be asked to play in this hour, here in May of 1941, long before he ever lived out those events that so altered the history of the world—events that he might never see now.

Out there on the grey horizon, another shadow loomed, the tall mainmast and conning tower of *Kaiser Wilhelm* becoming more prominent with each passing minute. Maud looked at it with narrow eyed respect. He knew his ships were no match for a fast German raider, but here he was, and with the fate of a fleet carrier riding in the balance.

Glorious had turned south, he knew, and now we have to buy her the time she needs to make good her escape. We're not likely to hurt that ship out there with our deck guns. They'll have us in range long before our guns can engage. The only thing we've got that matters here are those nice fat 21-inch torpedoes. Between the three of us we've all of thirty fish aboard, and that will make one mean spread for that enemy ship to avoid out there. But to launch torpedoes that will have any chance of posing a real threat, we have to get in close. The range of our torpedoes is only 5000 meters, and between here and there, it's all guts and glory.

"Well lads," he said, tapping the deck three times with his stout blackthorn walking stick. "Now we earn our grog. Make ready on the torpedo mounts, and increase to full ahead."

* * *

Kapitan Heinrich smiled when he saw the British destroyers begin their impudent charge. It was just as he expected. Technically the enemy was now attempting to close with him, and his orders stated that he should disengage and steer 300, but he saw no reason to do so at the moment.

"Schirmer, do you think you can hit one of those with our main batteries?"

"It would make for good target practice, sir."

"Then clear your throat. It's high time we gave the guns a little work."

"Very good sir! With your permission, I will open fire immediately."

Seconds later *Kaiser's* forward twin turret opened the engagement, the salvo meant to test the range calculated by the directors. Schirmer was watching closely, and when the big guns fired, he waited for the rounds to fall, seeing they were short, but much closer than he expected.

"Fire Bruno!" he said sharply, knowing that those guns were set on the same range as his spotting salvo. If he was lucky, the simple speed of the two opposing sides would close that range just enough to make this shot interesting.

And he was lucky that day. He saw the two rounds fall right astride the formation of enemy ships, so close to one destroyer that the tall plumes of seawater drenched the ship's foredeck, and shell splinters riddled the side of its hull. Now Schirmer knew he had the range, and he quickly gave orders to account for nothing more than the range that would be gobbled up by two ships closing on one another at nearly 36 knots each.

"Elevation down three! Ready…. Fire!"

This time both turrets fired at once, sending the same shell weight that *Bismarck* might throw from her own forward guns. *Kaiser Wilhelm* was no ship to be trifled with, and when the second salvo fell, the British learned this the hard way.

"A hit! My god! We got them at just under 30,000 meters!" Schirmer turned to his Kapitan, eyes alight, elated to have scored his first ever hit with this new ship, and what a hit it was.

Impulsive was the unlucky ship that day, struck aft with such force that the shell nearly broke the ship in two. The only ship ever to bear that name in the Royal Navy, she had sustained a rogue hit that would leave her crippled and wallowing in the sea. They saw the remaining two British destroyers break formation, and begin a wild, zig-zag approach, tacking to port and starboard to make themselves much more difficult targets. Schirmer knew he would probably not be so lucky again with his main guns, but in a matter of minutes he could bring his secondary batteries into play, six twin 15cm, 5.9-inch guns, the very same as those used by *Bismarck* and *Scharnhorst,* and he could get four of those in to action at 23,000 meters. After that, the eight dual purpose 4.1-inch guns would have to wait until the range fell inside 17,000 meters. That battery alone matched all the guns on those destroyers, and now the thirty torpedoes Lieutenant Commander Maud had hoped to call on had been reduced to twenty.

Yet the British persisted in their brave charge. Schirmer shook his head, realizing the maneuver was desperate, though he gave the men on those destroyers his grudging respect.

The whims of chance, however, had put Mother Time in a most uncomfortable position, for the two ships remaining had both played an important role in the long wake of the story that was still unfolding with this action. Of the two ships, *Icarus* was perhaps the most vulnerable in her eyes, for that ship had already died according to her ledger, and to find it here was the first sprouting root of the paradox that was slowly growing with each passing second.

Icarus had died. It was killed by *Kirov*, but Captain Maud must live, and *Intrepid* must live with him, or Orlov would never be found that day in 1942 when *Duero* hit Werner Czygan's mine.

Yet all this rested on a thin foundation, the assumption that this altered world was the same one that *Kirov* was destined to visit that very year, in just a few months time. How could that be possible? The ship was already there, and the world *Kirov* displaced to looked nothing like this one. For Werner Czygan and Lieutenant Commander Maud to matter at all, *Kirov* would have to have been chased across the Med by *Rodney* and *Nelson* in 1942. But how could that happen now with *Kirov* an ally of the Royal Navy?

Time was in a strange position as these events twisted slowly back upon themselves, like a mother hen fretting over eggs that had not yet been laid. On the one hand, *Icarus* and *Intrepid*, and the men aboard them, were crucial links in the line of causality that saw *Kirov* now at sea in these very waters. On the other hand, they seemed entirely immaterial, as those events were not likely to ever occur. Yet their fate would count heavily on one ledger, the reckoning of the account of one Captain Wells, and the ship he now sailed—HMS *Glorious*.

Chapter 5

Glorious was a ship of ghosts, men who had once been doomed, their names written into the ledger of time by the hand of death, and the 11-inch shells of *Scharnhorst* and *Gneisenau*. Now, like the ship itself, they were living second lives. Only 38 of the men aboard had been destined to live, all the rest were walking dead, zombies, gifted with life only because of a brief moment's delay in the telegraph room that had spared one Lieutenant Commander Christopher Hayward Wells, now the spectral Captain of this ship of fated men.

As he stood on the bridge that day, anxiously watching the damage crews fighting the fire on the bow, Wells had a strange inkling that fate was still scratching at his leg, jealous, hungry, and resentful of every breath he took. He could not know that he had been destined to die, but he could feel it, like a cold draft at the edge of an open door to a cellar. He could feel it.

Lieutenant Commander Lovell was on the bridge that day, as was his good friend Robert Woodfield, and both men seemed edgy as well. The situation they now found themselves in seemed all too familiar, for this was the second time the ship had encountered fast German raiders at sea, and few ships ever get second chances when they came under enemy guns. *Glorious* already had more than her fair share.

The ship had just celebrated its 26th birthday. Originally designed as a battlecruiser, along with her sister ship *Courageous*, she was laid down on the 1st of May in 1915, built by Harland and Wolff, a company that had recently launched another pair of doomed sister ships, the *Titanic* and *Britannic*. One sunk on her maiden voyage, and the other was soon lost in the Aegean in 1916 after striking a mine. And so the shipwrights in the know had whispered that a curse was on the keels of ships laid down in that yard, and no good would come to any ship built there.

Commissioned in 1917, *Glorious* and *Courageous* both seemed to prove the rumors wrong, leading charmed lives in the beginning.

They both fought at the Battle of Heligoland Bight that same year, when it was discovered that the simple act of firing their guns was sufficient to warp and damage the lightly armored deck structure. So the two ships went into fleet reserve, and for a time *Glorious* served only as a gun turret operations training ship before someone in the Royal Navy decided the two ships might be easily converted to a new role as aircraft carriers.

Just after her conversion in 1930, *Glorious* had another brush with fate when she collided with the French liner SS *Florida* in a heavy fog off Gibraltar. The bow of the carrier plunged right into the liner's port side, and the two ships seemed locked in the grip of death, though both survived. Her bow was crumpled beyond recognition, but only one man lost his life aboard *Glorious* in that collision. *Florida* took the worst of the damage, and lost 32 souls that day.

The accident started the whispered rumors again. Some said the ship had escaped the curse because her conversion to a carrier had introduced so many changes that she was really not the same ship any longer. Others argued that was foolish, she was still HMS *Glorious*, and that keel had still come from Harland and Wolff. When HMS *Courageous* met her sad end on the 17th of November, 1940, at the hands of U-29, they nodded their heads, knowing it was only a matter of time now before *Glorious* followed her sister ship to the grave.

"Uproarious and Outrageous are doomed ships," they said disparaging the vessels in their strange reincarnation as carriers. Yet fingers wagged on the other side when *Glorious* escaped from her dangerous encounter with *Scharnhorst* and *Gneisenau* in the North Sea. Yet, as Captain Wells watched that fire burn forward, he had a sickly feeling inside. The ship's penchant for bad luck had seen her hit in that *Stuka* attack, and now the situation he was in seemed perilous in ways he could not entirely fathom.

There had once been a 15-inch gun battery where that fire now burned. It was now stowed away in a warehouse in England, also destined to live again when Britain launched her last and greatest battleship, HMS *Vanguard*. Now Wells found himself wishing he had that gun battery back. His contingent of aircraft might have been a useful weapon in this situation, but that fire was preventing him from launching, and to do so he would have to turn into the wind in any case, right towards the shadow that now darkened his horizon.

"A bit of a pickle," said Woodfield at his side, looking from the fire to Wells, and then out to sea where the destroyers were making their bold charge in the hopes of fending off this threat. "At least we have a little more company this time." He nodded to the cruiser squadron steaming in close escort, *Coventry* off the port quarter, and *Sheffield* to starboard, with *Gloucester* following in the carrier's wake. Two more destroyers, *Fury* and *Fearless,* were also in attendance, but they gave Wells no real comfort. The cruisers had nothing bigger than 6-inch guns, twelve each on *Gloucester* and *Sheffield*, and five on the *Coventry*. The distant boom and rolling thunder on the horizon told him the Germans were coming with something considerably bigger.

Wells had done everything right this time, remembering the mistakes made by Captain D'Oyly-Hughes in that first harrowing encounter with enemy warships. Hughes had the destroyers in too close, but Wells had posted three on picket, and they were now making a desperate charge at the enemy. Hughes had no air cover up, and no planes ready below decks for a quick spot. Wells had four fighters on overwatch, but they had been brushed aside by hot German pilots off the *Goeben*, and could serve no vital role now. He also had *Swordfish* ready and armed below decks, but that damnable fire forward was preventing their launch, and the German fighters were still up there somewhere, though thankfully the *Stukas* were gone.

"If it comes to a fight, the cruisers will do their best," he said quietly to Woodfield. "But that ship out there looks like it will have a big walking stick. Listen to those guns!"

It was then that a runner came in with the news that *Impulsive* had been lost, which did nothing to raise anyone's hopes or morale at that moment. Wells looked at his watch, noting their speed was just under 30 knots now. He figured the enemy was perhaps 30,000 meters off. His horizon was 22,000 meters, but he was seeing the high conning tower of the enemy well before that. If the Germans had a five or six not speed advantage, this might be a long chase for them if they wanted to close the range. But they were already in range of those heavy guns, or would be very soon.

"Sir, *Icarus* reports damage forward as well. They make their range 10,000 meters, but the Germans are still coming."

Woodfield looked at Wells, his jaw set. "Those destroyers will all go down," he said flatly. "They'll have to get to 5,000 meters to launch torpedoes."

"Signal Lieutenant Commander Maud," said Wells. "Tell him the Germans seem to be calling our bluff. He is to make smoke and break off at once. We've lost one destroyer. No use losing two more. It will just have to be a foot race now, and at least we have our speed."

"For the moment," said Woodfield.

"What's on your mind, Woody?"

"Well sir, that German carrier is still out there. Those *Stukas* may be back. I think we should try to get more *Fulmars* up instead of the *Swordfish*."

"We'll need both aloft soon," said Wells. "Fire or no fire, I want planes spotted for takeoff at once. Alright, Woody, get me six fighters up first. Then we go with the torpedo bombers."

"Very good sir." Woodfield was off to the voice tube to call down the orders.

Wells looked at the fire again, gritting his teeth. We're running fast, he thought, and that will be all the headwind I can give them. And they're going to have to go right through that business forward. I'm launching whether that fire is out or not. We'll try, by god, and if necessary we'll do just what Lt. Commander Stevens did the last time—turn the damn planes around and launch off the aft quarter!

It was then that he saw what he feared, big, heavy rounds coming in wide off his starboard side, but with a good fix on his range. "Come five points to port, and all ships to follow," he said, the order echoed by the helmsmen and relayed to the flag bridge. No sense giving them an easy target. It was time to squirm a bit, and he would put the ship in a zig-zag until he had his planes on deck and ready to go. He looked for his executive officer, Lovell.

"Mister Lovell, kindly sent to the W/T room and advise Admiral Somerville and the Admiralty of our present predicament. They were sending us help, but we've heard no word. Then send to *Fury* and *Fearless*. Have them fall back on our wake, zig-zag, and make smoke."

It was going to be a very hard morning.

* * *

When Lieutenant Commander Maud got the order to break off he thumped his briarwood walking stick hard on the deck of the bridge.

"Damnation!" he swore. "We've run up under that monster's guns for the last fifteen minutes, and now we're to break off? What's the bloody range?"

"Sir, I make it 7500 yards,"

"Then steady as she goes. Make ready to fire torpedoes! We'll not turn tail without sticking it to those bastards out there."

He waited, the tension on the bridge obvious, and then gave a final order. "Hard to port and fire when we turn!"

Icarus launched her torpedoes as the destroyer turned, getting only five in the water as the destroyer wheeled about in a wide arc. The range was still about 7200 yards, but the enemy was coming at them fast, and they would have to run full out just to keep the range from closing further now. They were going to be in the soup for a good long while, and Maud immediately gave the order to make smoke and continue evasive maneuvers.

* * *

"That's done it," said Schirmer. "Those destroyers have finally had enough. They're breaking off."

"Good," said Kapitan Heinrich. "Now re-train your guns on that smoke on the horizon. Can you get me another long shot, Schirmer?"

"We will certainly try, sir."

A minute later the *Kaiser Wilhelm* rotated its forward turrets, the guns elevating and booming out a challenge to the distant enemy. Heinrich knew his guns could already hurt the British carrier, if they could find it. He could range out over 36,000 meters with his guns at maximum elevation, but chances of hitting anything at that range were very slim. The hit that had sent *Impulsive* to the bottom had been a lucky shot, one in a hundred chance at 28,000 meters, and would stand as one of the longest hits ever achieved by a gun in this caliber firing at sea. *Warspite* hit the Italian battleship *Guilio Cesare* in July 1940 at a range of about 26,000 yards, but *Scharnhorst* had bettered that when it first set its teeth into *Glorious.*

"Torpedoes off the starboard side!" The watchman's voice was loud as he called from above, prompting Heinrich to rush to the weather deck and look for himself. There they were, three, then five white trails in the water, and he knew he had to turn quickly.

"Come hard to port!"

The ship lurched with the sudden turn as the helm answered smartly, and the Kapitan's hands were heavy on the gunwale to steady himself, but even at high speed like this, *Kaiser Wilhelm* maneuvered like a much smaller ship, turning easily, her long sleek bow cutting through the sea. They were going to avoid the main spread, but one torpedo would make it very near the ship, fuming by and finding the wake where the big battlecruiser had once been, but nothing else to strike there. The hard turn bought *Icarus* and *Intrepid* just a little time to make smoke and race off on a new heading.

"Shall we pursue those destroyers?" asked Schirmer.

"Let them go. The secondary batteries can busy themselves firing at their smoke. Today we have bigger fish to fry. That carrier looks to be burning badly. Signalman! Get a message to Fleet Admiral. Tell them we have engaged as ordered and sunk an enemy destroyer. The carrier is on our horizon, and easy prey. How soon before *Goeben* will have more planes up?"

He rubbed his hands together, eager for the kill. Kriegsmarine intelligence indicated that this was the carrier *Glorious*, the same ship that Hoffman hit last year. It slipped away back then, but not this time. With a little help from the *Goeben*, we may catch this ship in short order. Then Schirmer will have something big enough to justify using the main guns like this.

Kaiser Wilhelm is changing everything out here. The British once had the game there way, with aircraft carriers to find our ships, and fast cruisers to shadow them until the battleship advantage they have allowed them to pile on more and more heavy guns. The outcome was inevitable. They hunted down the *Graf Spee*, and stopped our first major breakout attempt with those amazing new naval rockets. But apparently those weapons are not in the equation here. They must only be carried by their battleships, and perhaps only a very few. We've seen nothing of them since HMS *Invincible* re-deployed to the Mediterranean. So now we raise hell.

With the *Goeben* we have just enough fighter support to neutralize a single aircraft carrier like this. They will now have to change their tactics and fight their carriers in pairs to have any chance of enjoying air superiority again. And we have several more surprises in the works, in spite of that latest blow with the cancellation of the *Oldenburg*. *Peter Strasser* is more than 85% ready, and Raeder will stop at nothing to meet that January deadline the Führer has set for ship completion. Beyond that, we have those captured French ships converting to carriers as well, and the *Europa* is nearly ready. Things are about to get very interesting in the Atlantic, but much will depend on the success of the *Hindenburg* this time out. We must prove to the Führer that we can fight and win, and I can start right here, finishing the business Hoffmann started with this carrier.

* * *

Miles to the northwest, the W/T room on HMS *Repulse* picked up the plaintive call from *Glorious*, the fated ship crewed by walking ghosts. The message went quickly to Captain Tennant, who read it with some concern. His thoughts seemed to mirror those of Heinrich now.

As he scanned the typewritten lines, he could read more there than he liked. *Glorious* had suffered a hit from German *Stukas*, and well beyond the range of land based German planes of that type. That meant a carrier was about, and he knew the Admiralty had sent him south to look for Lütjens task force. Now he had found it. The enemy was somewhere to the southeast, already engaging Force H under Captain Wells.

A pity Somerville lost all his teeth when the last of his battleships were sent to the Med. Now the baton falls to me. *Renown* and *Repulse* are good ships, but that last engagement with the Germans up north proved one thing, we can't stand long against their big ships with our thin armor, and we bloody well need air cover if the Germans have another carrier here. So my job may not be what it seems. Under other circumstances, I would be fixing to engage the enemy, and at least get hold of his ankle until Home Fleet came up with the battleships. Now the prospect of trying to engage the *Hindenburg* is completely out of the question.

All we have is a two knot advantage over that monster, and we'll need it. My job is to find and shadow this beast, and the game is on. This message indicates they've been engaged by the *Kaiser Wilhelm*, a ship faster than any cruiser we have, and one able to sink any cruiser that gets lucky enough to intercept it. Yes, things have changed, but not for the better. And with all this talk of those naval rockets we have, my request to Admiralty for more information about them has been met with complete silence, a silence that speaks volumes, so I'd best let the matter go. For now, the hunt is on. But god help *Glorious* until I can get there!

Chapter 6

It was once said that god is on the side of the heavy cavalry. In this case he was siding with the heavy artillery. *Kaiser Wilhelm* had been running full out, with "Wagner's Girls" singing as the four high pressure boilers fed steam to the turbines. The ship had been gaining on its prey for the last twenty minutes, and had now slowly closed the range to about 26,000 meters. The two British destroyers had been thickening up their smoke screen in an effort to mask the carrier's retreat, but the German optics still had enough of a glimpse of the carrier to judge the range accurately. *Kaiser* fired, and four 15-inch shells soon bracketed the carrier, sending tall geysers of angry white seawater up on all sides.

At this point, the situation becoming grave, Captain Charles Arthur Larcom, on *Sheffield,* requested permission from Wells to break formation and attack, even though his cruisers would be outgunned by the enemy. Reluctantly, Wells agreed, and at 16:40 hrs on the 3rd of May, the second surface engagement with *Kaiser* began at just under 26,000 meters. *Sheffield* and *Gloucester* turned, with the AA cruiser *Coventry* remaining with *Glorious.* The British cruisers each had twelve Mark XIII 6-inch guns mounted on four triple turrets, but needed to close the range to under 22,000 meters to open the action. With the two sides closing on one another at a combined speed of 65 knots, or about 2000 meters per minute. So it was no more than a few minutes before the gunfire started.

Aboard the *Kaiser Wilhelm,* Kapitan Heinrich saw the cruisers turn to challenge, smiling. He had expected this action, knowing the British could do nothing less with a primary fleet asset at risk like this. In his mind, it would only pose a brief delay here, and he ordered Schirmer to shift main guns to the cruisers. The long barrels lowered, re-trained, and then boomed their challenge as the first British rounds began to sprout up in the sea ahead of his ship.

The British guns were only throwing shells weighing 112 pounds at the enemy, but the two forward turrets on each ship opened with a twelve round salvo against *Kaiser's* four 15-inch guns. Schirmer ordered his two secondary turrets, one mounted on each side of the ship, to join the action as well. His third turret was super-mounted above the aft main guns and could not join in just yet.

Neither side scored hits in that first exchange, and the British gunners enjoyed a speed advantage in reloading their guns, firing again 8 seconds later. This time they drew first blood, with a round from *Sheffield* striking *Kaiser* on the long deck, forward of Anton turret. But the ship's armor had been designed to counter the bigger 8-inch guns of the British heavy cruisers. The deck armor there was just under three inches, which was enough to absorb most of the punishment without serious damage below deck, yet a small column of smoke now trailed from *Kaiser's* nose. The ship was hit, but not hurt, and it would shrug off the 6-inch rounds easily enough.

At 18,000 meters the British cruisers turned hard to port to get all their guns into play, and it was then that disaster struck when *Kaiser* scored a direct hit on *Gloucester*, right on her forward turret, which put it completely out of action, its guns elevated and twisted like broken fingers. The fire below decks spread quickly to B turret, which had to flood its magazines to avoid further explosions. In one swift blow, the odds had shifted considerably, and now *Kaiser* turned to starboard, coming around to bring her aft guns into action.

Aboard *Gloucester,* Captain Henry Rowley had just lowered his field glasses to note the damage forward. He turned his head, looking for his executive officer and started to give an order, but his words were cut short with a tremendous crash when a second German round blasted right into the bridge and conning tower. Not a man there would survive. The explosion was seen by everyone on *Sheffield*, being about 500 meters behind *Gloucester* when the turn was made.

There was a moment of shock, stunned silence as eyes widened with the broiling fire and smoke that engulfed the cruiser's conning tower. Then, as though dazed and drunk, *Gloucester* wallowed to starboard, her bow coming round in a turn toward the German ship. It was soon clear to both sides that the cruiser was no longer under control, though her aft turrets let off one more salvo as the ship turned.

Sheffield dashed behind the chaotic scene, her gunfire temporarily blocked by the intervening hulk of *Gloucester*. Captain Larcom could see his brave challenge was not going to do anything more to dissuade the enemy than the destroyer rush had accomplished, and the sea around him soon erupted again with wild spray from the big 15-inch guns. His own batteries scored yet another hit, flush against *Kaiser's* conning tower, and another very near the aft turret, which was flayed with shrapnel from the deck where the round struck. The heavy turret, with over 8 inches of armor, was not harmed, and it soon boomed out a reprisal, the rounds straddling *Sheffield* and rocking the cruiser as it turned away, making smoke.

Meanwhile, the men aboard *Gloucester* realized their ship was describing a wide, uncontrolled circle, with no one alive on the bridge to issue commands. Both her forward turrets were out of action, and the Germans shifted fire to finish off the ship, scoring two more heavy hits with those fearsome 15-inch guns. The hit amidships was the worst, penetrating all the way to the boiler room and ending the ship's mad dance as it lost all steam, her guts ripped apart by the explosion of the heavy round.

Kaiser Wilhelm slowed to 28 knots and continued her turn to starboard to swing around and resume her course in pursuit of the carrier. It was then that Kapitan Heinrich was handed a message from Admiral Lütjens. He was ordered to break off and assume a course to the northwest.

Break off? He was not happy with the order, folding the message and slipping it into his pocket, eyes narrowed with thought. He raised his field glasses, looking to find the British carrier, but it was lost in a heavy roll of black smoke. The cruiser action had done one thing in buying Wells a little time, and now, to his surprise, Kapitan Heinrich saw an aircraft rise above the distant smoke, then another.

That damn carrier is launching planes! Where are our own fighters? He could send a message and ask about that, but it would reveal his situation plainly to Lütjens, who would realize his Kapitan was not in compliance with his last order. Heinrich considered the consequences of that, and what might be gained if he maintained his turn and came around to continue the pursuit. With Schirmer still dueling with that last British cruiser, it would be some minutes before he could get around and fix his attention on the carrier again, and the action had seen his prey slip away over the horizon. But it was there. He had the speed to get after the damn thing, and clearly had the guns to sink it in due course. There was *Gloucester*, her speed down to no more than ten knots, and yet still afloat. He decided to claim his kill, report, and see if he could obtain permission to continue.

"Torpedoes!" he said loudly. "Finish that cruiser!"

Kaiser Wilhelm also had six 21-inch torpedo tubes, in two triple mounts to either side of the ship. He had come a full 180 degrees, and was lined up well for a good shot on *Gloucester* now. The three fish fired, and two would find their target.

The resulting explosions would be enough to seal the fate of the light cruiser, battered by four heavy rounds, and now two good torpedo hits. Of the 807 men aboard, only 85 would get into the sea and survive in the wreckage.

"Send to Lütjens. Sunk enemy cruiser and requesting permission to proceed against carrier on my horizon." He folded his arms, looking at Schirmer now, who was beaming jubilantly with the performance of his guns.

"We cannot spot the carrier through that smoke," he said. Then the first of the *Fulmars* launched by *Glorious* came in low like an angry hornet from the hive, its guns blazing as *Kaiser's* twenty 2cm AA guns got their chance to get into the action. They were joined by eight 3.7cm guns, and eight more bigger 10.5cm guns, a considerable flak defense for a single ship. The first *Fulmar* made its strafing run, but the second was blown out of the sky. Yet Heinrich knew the carrier would soon be launching everything it had, and the lumbering *Swordfish* torpedo bombers would be his next foe.

For him the choice was simple. He could either obey his orders, break off, and find himself swatting at these British planes and dodging torpedoes for the next two hours, or he could go right to the source, here and now, and end this with *Kaiser's* guns. He looked at the ships chronometer, seeing the time at 17:20 hours. Then he decided. He would obey his order, but ever so slowly.

"Helm, come five points to starboard and ahead full."

He would come five points to starboard again in another five minutes, and make a slow turn while he continued to run for the enemy on the horizon. By his calculation, the greatest part of that slow arc would still see his guns in range of the enemy, and he would have his cake and hopefully eat it too. He had one last message to send—*Coming round on 300. Enemy launching planes. Request fighter support.* He knew he needed those Messerschmitts up there now, or his day would get very tiresome, very soon.

* * *

Aboard HMS *Glorious*, the news that *Gloucester* had been badly hit was not unexpected. Desperate times required desperate actions, and the first six *Fulmars* spotted on the aft deck roared right through the smoke and fire forward as they took off. They were going to be too late to help *Gloucester*, and could only make one angry pass at the enemy ship before climbing up to take station on overwatch. Now the torpedo planes of 823 Squadron were coming up on the elevator, and they would soon run the same gauntlet of fire and smoke, with the only headwind for takeoff being that provided by the carrier's headlong rush at her top speed of nearly 30 knots.

Wells could feel his pulse rising, and the heat of the action had sent that surge of adrenaline through his system. He wanted to move, get his limbs in motion in response, and remembered that hectic moment when he was an intern on Admiral Tovey's staff aboard HMS *Invincible*. No need to run, Tovey had cautioned him. A brisk gait will do. He looked for that well of calm that Tovey seemed to draw from, but could not find it within himself. It was all he could do to keep himself in one place, hands clasped behind his back as he watched the *Swordfish* come on the flying off deck. It was only later, when the urgency of the moment had ratcheted up yet another notch, that the Admiral had given him a wry look, and the words he spoke still echoed in Wells' mind. *"Mister Wells, now you may run."*

It was that time now, time for every expedient measure against the hour, and the enemy that continued to bear down on him like the shadow of death. It was his hour again, as the first *Swordfish* sputtered to life and went careening down the long deck to wallow aloft through the smoke. There he stood, icy heat on him, commander of Force H. There went the second plane, up through the licking flames and aloft. Now they will do the running, he thought.

Thunder rolled on the far horizon, and he knew his enemy was reaching for him again. The cold steel was in the air, rising up, plunging down, and soon it would find the sea, very wide and long, but a clear warning that *Glorious* was still in the gravest danger here.

* * *

Aboard *Hindenburg*, Admiral Lütjens received the message and frowned. Heinrich has the bit between his teeth, he thought, but he smells a kill here, and he wants to attack. That engagement was forced. The British reacted only to his own advance, that much is clear, and they've been hurt. So *Kaiser Wilhelm* has sunk a destroyer, and now a cruiser! Clearly there is nothing wrong with her guns, but now we have a carrier launching planes, the last thing I wanted here.

"Some news, Admiral?" Adler was at his side, a curious light in his eyes. He could smell a battle as well, and the man was already quite perturbed that *Hindenburg* was nowhere near the action.

"*Kaiser Wilhelm* has engaged as ordered, but they have not broken off. It looks like Heinrich has sunk an enemy cruiser to go with that destroyer."

"Great news, Admiral! Heinrich is pouring the brandy today. I knew that ship would do the job."

"Yes? Well unfortunately, it is not doing the job I asked of it. *Kaiser* was to break off if challenged strongly by the British. Now they are launching aircraft."

"Sir, we have the *Goeben* right off our starboard beam. Let me get word to them at once."

"That won't be necessary, Adler. I can count. We have had three Messerschmitts up over us for the last three hours. She should have three more aboard, and the *Stukas*. Those six planes are there to prevent the British from using their air units to spot and shadow us. Now *Kaiser Wilhelm* has stuck its finger in the bee hive. Very well, signal *Goeben*. Tell them to send half their fighters to cover *Kaiser*, and then tell Heinrich to get his ship out of there at once. He says he is turning on 300 now, but I have a feeling he may be seeing stars with the success of his gunnery officers."

"But if he can get to that carrier, sir… It's just the victory we're needing now."

"And if those planes put a torpedo or two into his ship? What then, Adler? Then we are forced to turn about and go to his aid. We lose this perfect chance to slip by the British and get out into the Atlantic. Instead we could be tied up here for hours, and if *Kaiser Wilhelm* is seriously damaged…" The look on the Admiral's face indicated his concern, and his displeasure over the zealotry of his subordinate officers.

* * *

Marco Ritter was just off his ME-109T when he saw a flurry of activity on the flight deck of the *Goeben*. The news reached him quickly enough. He was going back up to relieve the pilots flying top cover. Those planes were now heading south to cover the *Kaiser Wilhelm*, where a battle was said to be underway and rumors were flying as high as the planes.

"Have you heard, Marco? *Kaiser* has sunk two British cruisers, and now he's after that carrier!"

"Well don't just stand there gawking at me," said Ritter. "Is my plane refueled?"

"Give me ten minutes. The crews are reloading your guns."

Just enough time to grab some hot tea, thought Ritter. Then there is still plenty of daylight for hunting. I'm supposed to fly top cover, but I think I'll ease over to see what *Kaiser* is up to. Heilich and Ehrler landed earlier, and they are already top side waiting for their planes. I won't keep them long.

The crews were working feverishly on the three Messerschmitts, but it was all of twenty minutes before they finally got Marco's plane on the elevator. He took the ladder up. Wanting to get the blood flowing in his legs before he strapped into the cockpit again. Already a legend over Poland and France, his term as a carrier fighter pilot had only served to further enhance his reputation. But the work crews had been a little too hasty turning his plane around, and that was going to be another of those small little things in the stream of events that would have a subtle effect on the flow.

Marco Ritter would find that out very soon.

Part III

Keeper of the Keys

"Who goes there?"
"The Keys." answers The Chief Warder
"Whose Keys?" the sentry demands.
"King George's Keys."
"Pass King George's Keys. All's well."

— 21:53 Hours, Bloody Tower Archway, London

Chapter 7

Fedorov could sense the veiled animosity from Miss Fairchild in the beginning, but as the meeting ensued, she came to regard him differently. Their mutual frankness, and the revelations they shared, had done much to ease the tension, and he soon came to feel she was now regarding him as an ally after all.

Yet that last statement had shaken him, deepening the feeling of guilt he carried within. Calamity… that was quite a word for all they had seen. Was that what they had glimpsed in the empty, cinder black world the ship had visited when they first displaced forward in time? The shock of seeing that world certainly fit the description she had first shared—Grand Finality.

The thought that Admiral Tovey had established this group he called the Watch was damning enough. A select group of people in the know, all nested within the Royal Navy, had kept a long vigil waiting and watching for the return of *Kirov* at some future point in their time line. They had given the ship a special code name— *Geronimo*, the name of a renegade Indian Chief in the American West. It was a bit disturbing to think of his ship and crew as a renegade, something to be chased after, hunted down, destroyed. But that is what the Watch was established for, and now this odd new circumstance that saw *Kirov* steaming side by side with the *Argos Fire*, a ship of the Watch, was an unexpected twist. Was it the first step in possibly healing and mending the damage they had done to the history? He could not know, though he hoped as much.

Fairchild had told him many things that only deepened the sense of mystery and doom he felt. The revelation of how those messages and signals had come to members of the Watch from the future was most alarming. Yet now that he thought on it, he realized it was only his own sense of self-important arrogance that made him think time went no further than the era of his own life.

We all know and believe in the past, he thought, because it is still alive in our memories. The future was another matter, always a great unknown, never seen but always predicted, and hidden with a shroud of darkness and uncertainty. We have the feeling that we are riding the crest of time, he thought, perhaps like a man or woman surfing on the shore. Our lives are carried inexorably forward by the wave of time, until we reach that final breakwater and the surf crashes to the distant shore. But at least a surfer has the eyes to see that shoreline ahead of him. In our case, we ride the waves blind, never really knowing what lies ahead, though we can hear the churning chaos of the wind and water.

Yes, it never occurs to us that the future is out there somewhere, where billions of souls, unborn at this hour, are destined to walk the world, each wrapped up in their own lives, and creating events that others after them will regard as "history." *Kirov* had already shown it could move forward in time. They had safely returned to their own time in the Pacific, with the foreknowledge of how the war would begin.

It was then that I took it upon myself to try and fix everything we broke with this ship, and it started with fetching Orlov. Yet what else could we do? It was clear that the war was ramping up, even if we did spare the life of the *Key West*. There had to be something else that was acting as the seed of doom, and I foolishly thought that might be Orlov, the only thing from our world we left behind.

No… He was not the only thing. We also left behind downed aircraft, battered ships, thousands of dead men, and the lethal haze of radiation over the sea. And we left behind a history that was perhaps fractured beyond hope of repair, even before I took that daring journey along the Trans-Siberian Rail to find Orlov. I did that as much to try and preserve that unseen future as to mend the broken past.

That chance encounter at Ilanskiy was the great unexpected wrinkle in all of this. So now I learn there are other places like that, rifts in time, cracks and fissures in causality, so deep that a man can slip right through to another point on the continuum. They may have all been caused by that initial impact at Tunguska, and one by one, they were discovered, sealed off, and put under lock and key.

Strangely, the Watch was knighted with the task of minding those rift zones, and each one had a key that could open the doors and allow access. The men and women of the Watch became the Keyholders, or so Elena Fairchild had told him. Yet they were not the ones who built the doors and set the locks. They were not the makers of those keys. They had come from the future, just as those strange signals had come to ships at sea during their long, lonesome patrols. And with those keys there had come a warning—beware another ship, beware a phantom intruder on the high seas of time and tide, beware *Kirov*.

That was enough of a shock to him, to realize that his ship and crew were regarded as pariahs, outlaws, brigands. Now the revelation that those future voices were finally stilled was chilling to the bone. It meant that they would fail here, in spite of every effort. This time they had tried to make amends, first with Admiral Tovey and the Royal Navy, siding with Great Britain as an ally instead of allowing themselves to be drawn into confrontation. It seemed the only reasonable thing they could do, to try and preserve the Grand Alliance that had been forged here to defeat Nazi Germany and the other Axis powers, and by so doing, to preserve the future world that would be born of that alliance.

But if it all fails, he thought, if those future voices fade into silence, then what do we do wrong here? What do we overlook? Elena Fairchild seemed to think it had something to do with that missing key, and by extension, that hidden rift in time that the key might reveal. The keys were important, crucial, and they must all be found. Yet she was as shocked to learn about Ilanskiy as I was to hear all of this. That must be the answer! Ilanskiy! Yes, she said the Watch knew nothing of that place, or its perfect alignment along a rift in time. If that was true, then perhaps those unseen men and women of the future knew nothing of it as well. That could be the one rogue element that results in the chaos she was trying to describe—calamity.

A sudden heat was on him when he realized that he was the one who had discovered that rift. No one in the future knew about it—there was no key for that door. It was not locked away and guarded. But how was that possible? I have just told Elena Fairchild about it, and others know of it here. Certainly Sergei Kirov knows about it, as he walked those stairs to see the world Josef Stalin built, and made an end of that monster. And that was all my fault…

Again the sense of shame and guilt was on him. He wanted to save the life of one good man, and that took the life of one of the greatest demons ever to live on this earth. Stalin killed and tortured more souls than any man who had ever lived. Some say Mao Zedong's policies killed more, but for pure deliberate murder, Stalin claimed the laurels. It was Stalin who said that death was the solution to all problems—no man, no problem, and he went about solving his difficulties by simply eliminating any man he perceived as a threat. Wasn't it a good thing to rid the world of a man like that? How could it lead to this Grand Finality?

He realized that there was no way he could learn the answer to that, yet at the same time he felt compelled to try. What are we here for, he thought, if not to try and find a solution to this mess we've created? But did we cause it? Is all this my doing, or simply the inevitable result of Stalin's death? Did it take a man as ruthless as Josef Stalin to hold the Soviet Union together through the revolution and long civil war?

That thought led him nowhere, because he had to believe that his efforts here had some hope of saving those future lives, and preventing the calamity that Fairchild spoke of. What was this Grand Finality? How could it be avoided? Did that possibility rest on the finding of these strange keys? Where were these other rift zones in time? Were they all caused by the Tunguska Event? Where did they lead? How deep were the fractures? How far back into the history did these rifts go? Did the fractures also extend into the future? Was it possible, for example, to get to that inn at Ilanskiy in 2021 and go *up* the stairs to another future time?

His mind was flooded by a hundred questions like this, and the feeling that the sheer magnitude of this problem was beyond him. I tried to seal off that breach in time at Ilanskiy with that raid staged by Sergeant Troyak. Yes, I've led Troyak and his Marines about these last months thinking I could find some moment in the history that would make a difference. I suppose I did some good with that, and the presence of Brigadier Kinlan here was the great unexpected dividend—or curse. The consequences of his intervention here remain to be seen. Yet that all has something to do with Orlov, doesn't it?

He thought about that, realizing it was Orlov that sent him west on the rail to Ilanskiy, and Orlov who found that strange object in Siberia, the Devil's Teardrop. Somehow his fate has had a great deal to do with all of this.

Now he felt restless, anxious, like a man watching a candle burn away, and when that light went out, there would be nothing left but darkness. Darkness, a Grand Finality, calamity... Call it by any other name, that black rose was seeded now, and growing here in the Devil's Garden of this war. Its thorny stalk was lengthening, the dark buds opening to a bloom of death.

That was how Director Kamenski had described it, and that thought made Fedorov remember his first discussion with the Director over the question that still plagued him—what was going to happen to them if they remained here on July 28th of this year? That was the day *Kirov* first arrived in the past, and clearly there could not be two ships occupying the same moment in time. Kamenski had suggested something quite different might be going on...

"What you say is very interesting, Mister Fedorov, assuming this is the same meridian of time we were on before... much has happened to the world, and most of it our doing... If something happened in 1908 to change the history, then the 1940s we find ourselves in now may not be the same as those you visited earlier."

Fedorov had heard such theories before. Some call this notion the "Many Worlds" theory, saying that a world existed for each and every possible outcome of events, which would mean there might be an infinite number of worlds, an infinite number of Anton Fedorov's out there somewhere, each one living out the infinite number of possible choices he might make in life. He remembered his objection to that, the fact that he was standing right there on the deck of the battlecruiser *Kirov*.

"*I do not see how that is possible at the moment,*" he had said. "*Wouldn't the history have to remain cohesive enough to give rise to the building of this ship? That would have to occur for us to even be here at this moment. It's maddening, sir.*"

"*Yes it is,*" Kamenski said in return. "*Other men have gone mad over it—the Siren's Song of time—yet we dare to sit here and listen, and it seems we have been bold enough to hum along as well! Remember that we remain loose variables at large in history until all these events reach some definite conclusion. We undertook the dangerous mission to try and reach the ship in 1908 and remove it from that time, and that we have done. But the job is not yet complete. We are still a needle in Mother Time's finger as she darns her dress, and as long as we are here, the possibility of changing everything that follows this moment still exists. That said, we must not be surprised to find that all the days between 1908 and this moment may have already changed, and that the world we sail in now is not the same one we left. I do not know if we can untangle that knot just yet, but at least we have a year before we would ever have to face that paradox you raise, which is plenty of time to shift elsewhere.*"

That time was now running thin, thought Fedorov. *The year has burned away, like that candle, and it is already May.* That was one fear, but another arose from what Kamenski had asserted—*the possibility of changing everything that follows this moment still exists.*

There was hope in that, or why would they remain here in this struggle, but there was also fear. He had already seen the terrible consequences of his blundering. What if these changes give rise to a future where his objection could not stand? What if the history never leads to the design and building of a ship like *Kirov*? After all, it was the enmity of the long cold war that saw this ship built in the first place. Suppose this Grand Alliance here does succeed, and we avoid that cold war. Would the Soviet Union have built *Kirov* anyway? Would we have built *Kazan*? Would the ship have ever left Severomorsk like that, packed with missiles and bombs to conduct those live fire exercises?

He realized now that his very existence here rested on a tall stack of plates and cups that was teetering on a very shaky table. And everything they did here was like trying to remove a chipped plate from that stack, and replace it. One slip and the whole thing could come tumbling down and break into a thousand pieces. The life of this ship, its very existence, and his own life and fate was all there in that stack of plates, and behind that thought was that persistent thrum of anxiety again.

We *are* outlaws, he thought. *Geronimo* was a very good name for this ship. We've caused nothing but trouble on this long sojourn in time. Yes, we've been a needle in time's thumb, and she must be very upset about our meddling here. So this time we shifted to a place where we must finally account for our actions, an hour where our very existence rides in the tightening knot of paradox, an hour when we face the prospect of our own Grand Finality, our own personal calamity—*annihilation.*

Now he remembered how he had tried to explain his fear to Kamenski: *"Paradox is not simply some thorny problem—I think it is the force that rearranges things when time is confronted with an insoluble contradiction. It is a real and dangerous force."*

Fedorov had hit on a great truth. Paradox was time's black hooded executioner, the slayer of impossibility, a sharp sword that cut through the Gordian knots they had twisted with their meddling.

Kamenski had given him a solemn nod. *"This is the first time our own necks have been on the chopping block,"* he had said. *"Yes, the edge of paradox is a very dangerous precipice to hike along. We must be very careful here. I cannot say how that problem might resolve itself, Mister Fedorov, but something tells me that time would find a way. Yes. Mother Time does not wish to have her skirts ruffled any more than necessary. She would find a way."*

Fedorov wondered if that were true. They were putting Time in a very difficult position here. Suppose Kamenski was wrong, and the Many Worlds theory was only that, a theory, but not a reality. Suppose there was only one world, one ship, one Anton Fedorov. I am more than matter and material, he thought.

I also persist through time. Now I find that because of this impossible journey in time, my own future self may be coming to judge me here. But I am that self! How could this happen? That future Fedorov cannot exist until I go there in time, either by living out my life, day by day, or in one great leap through time as we have done with *Kirov*. And what if our actions here change that future, and this ship is never built? What if we change things and some of the crew are never even born? What if I am never born? One question tumbled after another…

His dilemma was the very essence of the word paradox, and that was the heart of his fear—Paradox Hour.

If there was only one world, then these changes we have made in the history might be permanent. We've been chipping away at the decades, like a sculptor chiseling fine marble. One false tap; one slip of the hand, and we could chip away a piece that can never be recovered. This is what we have been doing here, what I've been doing. I presume to have the skill and knowhow to chisel time. It's like a man trifling with one of Da Vinci's greatest works, and thinking he can fix the weathering of time by altering the sculpture or painting! Time took the careful progression of countless moments to create this history, and now along comes Anton Fedorov…. Isn't that what those voices from the future were trying to warn the Watch about? Beware a ship, *Geronimo, Kirov*…

This was what he realized when he called off Troyak's mission to try and use the stairway at Ilanskiy to go back in time and fetch Ivan Volkov. He realized that Troyak could not bring the man back to this era from 1908, because he already existed here. A person cannot go to a time or place where he already exists, and if he tries to do so he puts

Time in a most uncomfortable position.

It was that same basic paradox that had led him to the more desperate decision to simply demolish the stairway, to close the breach in time, if only for a while. But now he had learned another startling truth. There were other breaches in time, other rifts, hidden passages under lock and key.

And one of those keys had gone missing…

Chapter 8

Yes, one of those keys had gone missing, but they knew where it was—or at least where it once was. And they also knew the approximate time and circumstance of its disappearance. The key was embedded in the base of the Selene Horse, a precious artifact that was about to be shipped to Boston for safekeeping. When he learned that, he urged Admiral Tovey to simply send a message to Scapa Flow and prevent that shipment from being loaded, which he did as soon as the meeting concluded. As fate would have it, they soon learned that they were too late. Due to the secrecy involved, *Rodney* had been loaded three days earlier than the Admiralty originally planned. The battleship was now well out to sea.

"Most unfortunate," said Fedorov. "We know that key must be there, and yet it turned up missing when the ship finally reached Boston. It must have happened during the battle *Rodney* fought with *Bismarck*, but I can't see how that could happen now."

Even as he said that, Fedorov had a sinking feeling. *Bismarck* was out there this very minute, part of Lütjens' task force attempting to break out into the Atlantic. They were rushing west for the Straits of Gibraltar in hot pursuit, but they were not the only ships maneuvering in this chase. Home Fleet, now being handled by Admiral Holland, was already counting battleships and nervously watching other movements of the German High Seas Fleet. Fedorov learned this when he suggested that Admiral Tovey order *Rodney* back to a safe harbor.

"The moment I heard this news," said Tovey, "that was the first thing that entered my mind. Yet as simple as it may sound, getting it done may not be so easy. Yes, I may be commander of Home Fleet, and that charge will immediately revert to me from Holland the instant this ship enters the Atlantic, but *Rodney* is about the King's business at the moment, and suggesting we turn it around will have the Admiralty asking a lot of questions, not to mention the King himself."

"I can see how that may be uncomfortable," said Fedorov through Nikolin as always, "but surely the stakes here are too high to risk the ship at sea until we have that artifact in our possession."

"True, but I may not be able to offer an acceptable reason why the ship should be taken off active duty. In fact, if I suggest this, the Admiralty will say that is exactly what *Rodney* is about. Her decks are loaded with equipment and new boiler tubes for her refit in Boston, and I don't think the government wants this other business delayed. *Rodney* is the goose with the golden gullet now. She's carrying a good amount of gold bullion in addition to the Elgin Marbles."

"What about Mister Churchill?" said Fedorov. "Now that we've let him in on the secret, he should be a powerful advocate on our behalf in this matter."

"Yes, I suppose Winston can throw his weight in gold around when he sets his mind to it. But such a request will need some explanation before he can grasp the urgency as we have here. Churchill is in London. Would you advise that I attempt to relate all this to him over Admiralty signals channels? That could be very risky."

"I understand," said Fedorov. "Yet there must be something we can do."

Tovey nodded. "I am thinking we might be able to solve this problem another way," he said. "quietly, at sea. When things heat up in the Atlantic, I take command, and I can come up with any good reason to pull *Rodney* off by the collar. Then we can arrange a rendezvous at sea. We can go aboard and see about this business— why, you could do so personally if you wish, Mister Fedorov."

Fedorov still seemed troubled, but relented. Yes, it would be too risky to try and explain all this through coded signals to Churchill. And that would likely take a good deal of time in any case. What Tovey was suggesting seemed workable, though he still had reservations.

"What if the ship gets involved with the Germans. I have listened in on German Enigma traffic, and there is a lot of movement in the north now."

"Unfortunately so," said Tovey. "Admiralty believes they will make another run at us with a second powerful task force. They still have *Tirpitz* up there, along with the Twins, and that aircraft carrier that bedeviled us before, the *Graf Zeppelin*. Put those ships together and it spells a lot of trouble for Home Fleet and Admiral Holland. We can match them. Home Fleet has four good battleships standing to arms right now, and the battlecruiser squadron is coming south to reinforce Force H."

"Any word on that battle?"

"Not yet, but we should hear soon. That young man I put at the helm on *Glorious* has a head on his shoulders, but if he's tangling with Lütjens, things could get out of hand. This business in the Mediterranean forced me to weaken Somerville considerably. Thank god the French moved all their heavy units from Casablanca to Toulon, otherwise things could get very ugly in the Atlantic."

"We won't get through the straits until the night of May 4th," said Fedorov. "I plan to run the straits after midnight on the 5th. We're a full day behind the action."

"Yes, we can't offer Somerville any assistance just yet," said Tovey, "and remember we still have to win through at Gibraltar."

"Don't worry about that," said Fedorov. "We'll get through. *Kazan* will clear the channel of enemy U-boat activity. They'll know we are coming, but we'll run the straits in the dark, making enemy air strikes very difficult, particularly with our potent missile air defenses. As for the shore batteries, I'll handle them. We'll get through."

"I like your confidence, Captain." Tovey smiled. "Then once we do get through, the pickle will be this—how to arrange this meeting at sea with *Rodney*, while still staying in the hunt for *Hindenburg*. There are hundreds of ships at sea just now in the convoys. This is a maneuver the Admiralty did not expect. They'll be burning the lamp oil late tonight trying to see how they can re-route convoys to avoid the worst. My job is to protect those convoys."

"Do you think Force H can delay the German battlegroup?" asked Fedorov.

"Possibly. We'll know the answer to that shortly. I'm headed straight for the W/T room to get at the latest signals traffic. My Mister Wells hasn't got much to work with, a few cruisers and destroyers along with *Glorious*, but he's a determined young man. Reminds me of you in many ways."

"Can we count on any help from Admiral Holland?"

"He's already dispatched the two battlecruisers, *Renown* and *Repulse*. I suggested *Hood* might go along as well. That ship has the speed we need in a chase like this, but Holland has his flag there, and wants this dance. I suppose it's a wise decision. With *Hood* up north he can sail with *Duke of York* and cover the Faeroes passage, and then send *King George V* and *Prince of Wales* to the Iceland channel. It's that same old game again. The Germans always have the edge at the outset, as they can pool all their major fleet assets together, and then pick one channel or another, while we have to cover everything, and we never seem to have enough ships for the job. So you can see how my suggestion that we retire *Rodney* in the middle of all of this would raise eyebrows in the Admiralty."

"I understand," said Fedorov. "Well, let us hope we can arrange this meeting at sea somewhere safely away from the action. What is your plan, Admiral?"

"That remains to be seen. Circumstances will dictate, as they always do at sea. We have to be ready for every contingency."

"Well," said Fedorov, "we have four ships here, counting *Kazan*. Any ship could make this rendezvous, though I would think we might want to keep our strongest assets in the hunt for the *Hindenburg*. Both my ship, and *Argos Fire*, have radar sets and our helicopter assets. We should have no trouble finding Lütjens at sea. And we have the speed to get after him, if he's not too far ahead of us. Remember, our missiles have considerable range."

"Indeed," said Tovey. "Perhaps we could send the *Argos Fire*. After all, Miss Fairchild claims to be the keeper of these keys. I would think she would want to get to *Rodney* herself, and from her warnings in that meeting, she'll want to find that key as soon as possible."

"Agreed," said Fedorov.

Tovey perceived some slight reservation in the Russian Captain now. "Ah," he said, "I'm thinking you are very curious about this key, and what it might open, Mister Fedorov."

"That I am, sir. But I can see that it's not mine to meddle here. Our task is to get to *Rodney*, and keep the ship from harm until we do recover that key."

"And after that?"

"I think you said it best earlier, sir. Circumstances will dictate, in all of this. I have faith that we'll determine what needs to be done."

"As do I," said Tovey. "After all, I'm supposed to be the one who arranged this whole party, yes?"

He smiled, but Fedorov could see that Tovey was wrestling with demons of his own over all of this. He has to be wondering about that, he thought. How could he have written that note? What circumstance is waiting for us out there that sees that possibility made a reality? It would certainly keep me up at night, and Tovey must be at his wits end. Yet the man is a well of calm and reserve. I must give that some thought myself, if I can manage any time. Perhaps I had better enlist some help in all of this. Admiral Volsky suggested I go talk with Director Kamenski about it. Perhaps that would be wise when I get back to the ship.

"Very good, Admiral," said Fedorov. "Please let me know the moment you hear news of Force H. If they are in difficulty, we might be able to offer support with our helicopters."

"I'm off to the wireless room," said Tovey. "But something tells me we may have some bad news waiting. I've a sixth sense at sea, and there's something on the wind, Mister Fedorov. It doesn't smell good."

Fedorov nodded, saluted, and was on his way.

* * *

After making his report to Admiral Volsky, he excused himself, saying he would like to speak with Director Kamenski concerning the revelations made by Miss Fairchild at their meeting.

"Yes, do go and see Kamenski about all of this," said Volsky. "And while you are there, ask him how his garden is doing. It seems he's been having problems with gophers. We all have."

"Sir?" Fedorov did not know what to make of that.

"Just mention it, Fedorov. You will be surprised by his answer, I assure you."

Fedorov found the Director in the officer's stateroom, quietly reading a book from the ship's library, and smoking a pipe.

"There you are, Director," he said with a smile.

"Ah, Mister Fedorov. I trust your meeting went well."

"It did, sir, but I have learned something I need to discuss with you, if I am not intruding."

"Not at all. Have a seat here if you can tolerate my tobacco. A pity it is one bad habit that I never really could shake. Then again, at my age, you do not fret over such things."

Fedorov was seated, wondering how to begin. He decided to come right to the point. "Director, in our earlier discussions you revealed that our government, the Soviet government at that time, had made the alarming discovery that nuclear detonations disturbed time. Would it be a breach of security for me to ask what was done about that?"

"Oh, it probably would, but I do not think that matters, given the fact that we have all been sailing through the decades here together. You know, I am beginning to settle into this year, 1941, as odd as that may seem. As to your question, yes, once we confirmed these secondary effects after Tsar Bomba went off, a program was developed to test this further. In fact, that was the real reason there were so many tests in those years. We wanted to know how pronounced these effects were, what amount of force was required, and what might be moved."

"And the Americans?"

"They were also involved, and even before we were! We do not know the full extent of what they learned, but we knew they had discovered the effect as well. There were all sorts of tests in those days, atmospheric and high altitude exoatmospheric tests in space revealed the EMP effect. Underground tests in tunnels and bore holes were also common. Then there were salvo tests to see what might happen if we ever did use multiple weapons on each other. I suppose the idea was to see how much abuse the world could take when we start tearing apart and destroying the fundamental particles of the universe. No one dreamed it might disturb the fourth dimension, as well as the other three that shape the contours of this world. But we learned. Things happened. Things disappeared, then reappeared weeks later, sometimes years later. That was when we realized they had moved in time. So how much mass might fall prey to these effects, we wondered? Then we recalled those underwater tests conducted by the Americans, and became very curious. It occurred to us that some of those nice little shows they put on in the Pacific were all intended to test one very interesting thing."

"What was that, sir?"

"We believe they were trying to see if they could move something as massive as a warship."

"Through time?"

"Precisely. Gives one a chill, doesn't it? It's a trick your ship manages quite easily, but that was not supposed to occur until 2021. Yet the Americans were testing this prospect with their Castle Bravo test off Namu Island, in the Bikini Atoll, and that was in 1954. Some say they were testing as early as 1946 in their Operation Crossroads detonations."

"Yes," said Fedorov, aware of that test. "That was where the carrier *Saratoga* died. It was anchored there, and was swamped by a 100 foot wave. A *Fuso* class Japanese battleship was also anchored for that test, the *Nagato*, and the American battleship *Arkansas*."

"You are certainly very knowledgeable when it comes to naval history," said Kamenski.

"But I don't understand," said Fedorov. "Are you suggesting they had foreknowledge of what would happen to *Kirov?*"

Kamenski smiled. "It certainly seems that way. Don't forget that the Americans witnessed a detonation like that first hand in the north Atlantic, and a ship they had been pursuing with the British suddenly vanished, along with a flotilla of their own destroyers. Things like that can get people very curious, particularly when the destroyers show up twelve days later with quite a tale to tell."

"I had not heard about this," said Fedorov excitedly. "You are referring to *Desron 7*, but I never knew what had happened to those ships."

"They vanished," said Kamenski, "then sailed into Argentia Bay twelve days later. Oh, the Americans tried to cover that up. They renumbered the ships, dispersed the crews, and buried the matter, because they had already told the public those brave sailors had sunk the raider they were pursuing—your ship, Mister Fedorov. So yes, they must have been very alarmed to hear what those destroyer Captains told them. Perhaps, after they finally developed their atomic bomb, they were testing to see if ships might vanish like that. Then again, it might have been a simple test to see how a fleet would fare at sea if attacked by nuclear weapons. Who can really know? Well, that was my business throughout most of my life. I was one of the men who were supposed to know these things." He gave Fedorov a penetrating look with that, almost as though he were trying to size the man up, gauge him in some way. Then Fedorov said something that surprised him, and brought a knowing smile to his lips.

"Director Kamenski... The Americans did not witness that nuclear explosion in the North Atlantic in our history, yet they clearly conducted these tests. So how could they know anything might happen to *Kirov?* Unless... let me ask you this. Did *we* have foreknowledge that one of our ships would go missing in this way?"

Chapter 9

"A most interesting question," said Kamenski. "If by 'we' you mean the Soviet government, then I think not. But there are many things the intelligence services find out that never come to the awareness of the central government. This is true in most countries, yes? Don't the Americans refer to a kind of Shadow Government that lurks behind the facade of their so called democracy over there? We had such shadows as well. I was one of those shadows, and so let me rephrase your question. Did *I* have foreknowledge that one of our ships would go missing in time? Well, I certainly had my suspicions, Mister Fedorov. In fact, I have been watching this ship of yours for some time, and you already know through your discussion with Admiral Tovey, that other men were watching for *Kirov* as well."

"You mean the organization that Tovey founded, the Watch?"

"Exactly. Well, it may not surprise you to learn that we found out about that as well. Secrets are very difficult to keep over the years. We didn't know exactly what the British and Americans were up to, but we realized that it had something to do with time. You see, their own testing of these strange effects preceded ours. Ivy Mike took place in 1952, and Castle Bravo in 1954, but we did not learn definitively that time displacement was possible until our big Tsar Bomba test of 1961. It was only then that we realized the full implications of what the British and Americans had been doing. But that only confirmed a suspicion I have held about your ship for a very long time."

"You mean you suspected *Kirov* had moved in time?"

"I did, and I was sleuthing the history for hard evidence of that."

"But why, Director? Why did you suspect this?"

"Because that magic wand of yours, Rod-25, changed things, Mister Fedorov. But I remember how they once used to be. Yes... I remember it all very well."

Kamenski's assertion was most alarming. Fedorov did not know what to make of it at first, until he thought deeply for a moment, realizing that this Director Kamenski was a man they had encountered after their return from their sojourn in the Pacific. He had been enmeshed in the mystery of *Kirov* by Inspector General Kapustin, who had used him as a sounding board for the evidence he was digging up concerning *Kirov*. Yet that world was subtly altered. Men aboard the ship found that out the hard way, when they went ashore to see expected loved ones, and found strangers living in their homes! One crewman was so distraught over what he had discovered, that he committed suicide… Just like so many in the crew of the cruiser *Tone*.

Was Kamenski altered with the changing of that world? Was he the same Director Kamenski that might have existed before *Kirov* ever left Severomorsk? He seemed to be saying that he had been able to perceive the subtle changes introduced in the course of events. Yet how was this possible? Wouldn't he have changed right along with everything else. He asked Kamenski about this.

"Sir, how could you know anything changed?"

"Because I could still remember the world as it once was," said Kamenski flatly. "I went over this with Admiral Volsky once. You can remember Pearl Harbor, yes?"

"Of course," said Fedorov.

"But yet you realize that your intervention after that first displacement, the use of an atomic weapon in the North Atlantic, caused the United States to enter the war early. You know both entry dates. In the same way, I know several versions of the history, and I have watched it change in my history books for some time. Yes! The books change, Mister Fedorov. But this old head seems immune."

So Kamenski remembered things from other time meridians, thought Fedorov. Just like Admiral Tovey seems to be haunted by memories of his interaction with *Kirov* in 1942. I wonder how this is possible? Yet I remember things from the world we first came from easily enough. I remember having that last breakfast on shore leave at Severomorsk before we left for those live fire exercises—something that may never happen now that we have twisted these events so badly.

"Yes," said Kamenski. "I thought retirement would be a nice quiet time with my books, good wine and tea, and a little gardening—but look at me now!"

Fedorov suddenly remembered what Admiral Volsky had asked him to mention. "Director," he said. "The Admiral asked me to enquire as to how your garden was doing... Something about gophers?"

At that Kamenski smiled. "Ah, that was a metaphor I used to try and describe this business with Karpov to the Admiral. Gophers can be very persistent little devils. You see their effects on the surface of your lawn or garden, then dig down to try and expose their tunnel and set your traps. Unfortunately, by that time they have most likely riddled your lawn with even deeper tunnel networks, and your traps will fail."

"I see," said Fedorov. "Then Karpov was the gopher?"

"You might think of him that way. We thought he was up to his mischief in 1945, in fact, I read about it in my history books! Then it turns out that he had dug himself an even deeper tunnel, all the way to 1908. That took a good bit of digging to root him out. Now we look and see he is still here."

"Yes," said Fedorov, "and still up to no good, if I know the man. But what has this to do with our discussion?"

"The tunnels, the little gopher holes in time," Kamenski explained. "Karpov is not the only little devil in the garden."

"I suppose not," said Fedorov. "I've been rooting around in the history myself."

"And with every good intention," Kamenski wagged a finger at him. "So don't go moping about how all of this is your fault again."

"But it is, sir. I'm responsible. I was the one who warned Sergei Kirov about his own assassination."

"Yes, we've had this discussion," said Kamenski quickly. "Don't forget that it was Kirov's finger on the trigger that killed Josef Stalin, not yours. He was a willful agent, a Prime Mover. He might have decided otherwise, but he didn't. You see? If he had allowed Stalin to live, then you could not shoulder the blame, could you? So don't try to carry it now. It was Kirov's choice. Never forget that. Now, as to those gopher holes I mentioned, you have found one at Ilanskiy. Yes? Well Mister Fedorov, there are others. This is the sum of what Miss Fairchild revealed to you. Correct?"

"Apparently so, sir."

"Yes, there are others, all possibly created from that event the world endured at Tunguska. This is the theory we came to in some very select circles within the intelligence community."

"She revealed something very strange, sir—a key that opened the heavy machined doorway in the passage hidden beneath Delphi, and then activated the device she found there. That was how *Argos Fire* moved in time, or so I finally learned."

"I understand," said Kamenski. "A key you say? Would it look anything like this?" Now Kamenski reached into his pocket and produced a key, and Fedorov's eyes widened when he saw it looked identical to the one Fairchild had shown them.

"Yes, Miss Fairchild is a Keyholder," said Kamenski, "and now you will learn that I am a Keyholder as well. Seeing is believing."

Fedorov was flabbergasted. "You sir? A Keyholder? Miss Fairchild said nothing about this! How is it possible?"

"She said nothing about it because she simply didn't know. The Keyholders are a very select group, yet they do not even know who else may hold a key, or how many there may be. You are the only other person on this earth who now knows that I possess this key. I was about to tell Admiral Volsky once, when the two of us were huddled in the command bunkers beneath Naval Headquarters at Fokino. We were discussing a good many things, and waiting on the outcome of your mission to the Caspian."

"How did you find it, sir?"

"A very long story, Mister Fedorov. Suffice it to say we acquired it. Intelligence services collect more than information, you know."

"I see…" As the shock subsided, Fedorov suddenly realized something about this revelation. "But sir," he said. "I was under the impression that these Keyholders were all members of the group Admiral Tovey founded—the Watch."

"Interesting. Miss Fairchild told you that?"

"She implied it—or perhaps I jumped to that conclusion. I was about to tell you one other thing she revealed sir. She said that she had been designated as Keyholder Alpha, the keeper of the keys, as she described it. She was very keen on the fact that these keys are crucial, as they all seem to be related to another rift in time that has been carefully secured. One was obviously there at the Shrine of Delphi, and she said there were others, just as you have confirmed. Each key has information machined on the shaft that can reveal the locations of these time rifts, and they must all be found. She was very insistent about that. In fact, that's what I came to discuss with you. We are out chasing after Admiral Lütjens on the *Hindenburg*, but Miss Fairchild has interjected something that may have a big impact on our mission."

"Indeed? What is that, Mister Fedorov?"

"One of the other known keys was found embedded in the base of the Selene Horse—an artifact that was part of the Elgin Marbles. It was being shipped to Boston for safekeeping aboard the battleship *Rodney*, and that ship is at sea, with that cargo in her hold, at this very moment!"

"Yes, that is very interesting," said Kamenski. "Here it is, May of 1941, the very month that key went missing."

That struck Fedorov again, and he gave the Director a perplexed look. "Then you knew about this sir? You knew the key was aboard *Rodney*, and that it disappeared during her engagement with the *Bismarck?*"

Kamenski took a long puff on his pipe, exhaling as he thought for a moment. "The short answer is yes. I knew the British had possession of another key, and that it went missing. We eventually narrowed it down to this incident with *Bismarck*. Others knew about it as well, and it has been sought, very ardently, for decades, but never found."

"Well it's right here, sir! Admiral Tovey is going to arrange a meeting with HMS *Rodney* at sea. We can go and inspect that cargo ourselves—or perhaps Miss Fairchild will. I suppose this is more her business than mine, though I'm very curious about all of this."

"Stay curious, Fedorov. That's what I like about you. Never be afraid to ask the big questions. I could see you had a keen mind for this time displacement business long ago. That is why I teased you with that bit about the assassination date of Sergei Kirov changing. Did you ever give that further thought?"

Fedorov remembered that now. One telling of those events held the date was December 1st, and yet others swore it was on the 30th of that month. It all came tumbling back in his mind now, an avalanche of realization. He could hear Kamenski's voice in his recollection, when the man had first challenged him with this oddity. *"It may interest you to know that he was assassinated on December 1st, and not on the 30th. That was the way it happened the first time. Then things changed....*

"Just a moment, Director." Fedorov could hear his own voice raising an obvious objection. *"It's clear to me that we caused the Americans to enter the war early, yet I would have told anyone that Kirov was assassinated on the 30th even before we left Severomorsk."*

Admiral Volsky had remembered that same date, and the two of them had just stared at Kamenski, waiting.

"Yes, and many others will have that date in their heads," Kamenski had said. *"But this old head remembers it on the 1st of December. A few of the Party elite would celebrate it quietly, behind closed doors. I have drunk many a toast to Sergei Kirov on that day. But the people I can raise a glass with are now few and far between."*

Fedorov remembered the astounding conclusion that provoked. *"But that would mean ... Well that would mean something happened to change the history even before Kirov left Severomorsk!"*

"You are very astute, my young man. Yes. That is exactly what it would mean. There may be only a small handful of people who know what you have just concluded—and know it to be a fact and not mere speculation. I happen to be one of them, and I have lived with that knowledge for a very long time..."

"Simply because of the slight difference between those two assassination dates?" asked Fedorov.

"It seems a small thing, but small things lead to big things, Mister Fedorov. If you have ever worked in a garden, you know this to be true. So if you and I recall different dates for that event, it is either evidence one of us is mistaken, or else it is equally clear evidence that the history has changed. This, I can now confirm. The world has been changing quite a bit, and for a good long time. I've been reading about it in my books. You thought it all began with the sailing of your ship from Severomorsk, and that accident with *Orel*, but that is not the case. And you correctly concluded this earlier, that the world you were born to was an altered state of affairs. It was not the Prime Meridian. No. There you were, living your life, not knowing any of this, but now you learn the truth, now you *do* remember things have changed. I was once in your shoes, Fedorov. I once had to solve the mystery of why my history books kept being edited, and then I became very interested in what may have happened to your ship. Now I know to a certainty."

"If this is so, Director, who is behind it all? Could these changes have been initiated by the same people who made the keys?"

"That would be a sound conclusion," said Kamenski. "In fact, the keys, and the time rifts they expose, may have been the means of initiating these changes."

That struck Fedorov a hard blow. Someone has been tampering with the history.... And not just by blundering about in a warship. Someone has been deliberately changing things. But who? Was it the sender of those signals from the future?

"Well, Miss Fairchild revealed something else, sir." Now he told the Director about those voices from the future, and how they had suddenly gone silent. He used the very word Fairchild had given him—Grand Finality—calamity.

Kamenski listened quietly, thoughtfully smoking his pipe. "Very dramatic," he said. "I think I will need to have a nice quiet talk with this Fairchild lady. She calls herself the keeper of the keys? Well, I think she will be quite surprised to learn I've had this one in my pocket for decades."

"Sir," said Fedorov, a question hot in the wake of the Director's statement. "Miss Fairchild told me that the keys are all connected with one of these known time rifts, is that true of yours?"

"An obvious question. Keys are supposed to open something. Yes? Well, you say these keys all have numbers machined into the shaft. That may be so, except for this key." He dangled it again at the end of a chain."

"Are you certain, sir?"

"Oh yes, quite certain. I've had it examined very closely, even with an electron microscope. The shaft is completely smooth—absolutely unblemished."

"I see..." That set Fedorov back a moment, an unaccountable wrinkle in this mystery that was already folded inward on itself so deeply that it seemed he might never get it sorted out. "I wonder why, sir. If all the other keys are associated with rifts, then why not this one?"

Kamenski smiled. "Because Miss Fairchild is mistaken, Mister Fedorov. In spite of what she chooses to call herself, she does not hold the master key. Nor is she the keeper of these keys as she might believe, because I am. I believe the master key is here, right in the palm of my hand!"

Part IV

Turnabout

"Turnabout is fair play."

— Ravi Gomatam

Chapter 10

The first of the *Swordfish* came lumbering in towards *Kaiser Wilhelm*, low and slow. 823 Squadron was not supposed to be flying that day. After the loss of *Glorious* in Fedorov's history, it was disbanded at RAF Watson, and not reformed until November of 1941. But that had never happened. Now Lieutenant Commander Elles was leading out the first subflight of four planes, with eight more racing to get airborne as *Glorious* ran south. Falkson, Jacobsen and McNamara were up with him, and they would be quick to the target looming on the horizon.

Expecting the attack, and actually seeing the planes taking off, the German AA gunners were ready. They soon began filling the skies with the dark puffs of their flak guns, knowing each plane out there had a torpedo on its belly that could wreak havoc if it found their ship. Of this first subflight, only three planes would get close enough to launch, with McNamara going into the sea after being hit by a 3.7cm round.

On the bridge of *Kaiser Wilhelm*, Captain Heinrich saw them coming. Two were going to be wide off the mark, but the third required him to come fifteen points to starboard, and fall off briefly to 30 knots, the ship turning just in time to avoid the lance. This is what we'll be doing until sunset if I don't get at that carrier, he thought. It would be dangerous work, but if the bear wants the honey, he must risk getting stung by the bees. Heinrich wanted that honey, for the sinking of a carrier would be a prize to rival any other obtained by the Kriegsmarine to date in the war.

Ede, Purdy, Vickery and Williams were next on deck, rumbling forward through the diminishing smoke on the bow, as the damage control teams slowly put out the fires. This time the German flak was even better aimed, as they had adjusted to the slower moving targets. Purdy would not get a chance to launch his torpedo, and Ede's plane was riddled with shrapnel, his left arm nicked with the near miss explosion, and bleeding. He requested permission to jettison his torpedo and fly for home, but Lieutenant Commander Elles was still up in his plane, circling and spotting, and he would hear nothing of that.

"Get your fish in the sea alright," he said on the radio. "But be bloody well sure you aim it at the Germans! Otherwise none of us may get home."

It was a point well made, and Ede relied on his good arm to make do, pulling his *Swordfish* around again and coming in very low. The German gunners were on to him again, soon pocking up the sky, with some rounds hitting the wave tops as Ede came in. He got lined up, pulled right a bit to lead his target, and let loose. Yet the British pilots were making a mistake. They were accustomed to judging the speed of a large ship like this at no more than 28 knots. Most of their target practice runs had been on ships steaming at even slower speeds. They were not leading the target enough for *Kaiser's* speedy 36 knots, and both Ede and Vickery saw the ship slip by, leaving their torpedoes in its wake.

Williams saw what was happening and changed the angle of his attack at the last minute, and he would force Captain Heinrich to dance again, this time with a turn hard to port to literally run ahead of the oncoming torpedo, which had no more than a four knot speed advantage on *Kaiser*. Williams saw the ship turn to run parallel to his torpedo, nearly as fast, and the British would be frustrated again.

Yet all these maneuvers did one key thing, they bought valuable time for Captain Wells aboard *Glorious*, still running south at his best speed behind as much smoke as his destroyers could give him. *Sheffield* was maneuvering to join him, and *Coventry* was still providing close support in case any more German *Stukas* showed up. The German pilots were now very close, but this time they were ME-109Ts.

* * *

Marco Ritter was smiling when he saw the second flight of

Swordfish fluttering well below him like cumbersome moths. He wanted to get down there immediately, but first things first. There were four *Fulmar* fighters up on top cover, and he needed to deal with them. He was high enough to challenge them, but tipped his nose up to get more elevation as he signaled Heilich and Ehuler to follow him.

"Only four this time," he said. "They are making it too easy!"

His Messerschmitt climbed steadily, a faster and more maneuverable plane then the British Fighter. It was well armed with two 20mm canons on the wings and a pair of 7.92mm MG-17 machineguns on the fuselage above the engine. Ritter was quick to get on the tail of the first *Fulmar*, and had it ready for his 20mm cannons. He pulled the trigger and got off a short burst, but then something unexpected happened, a result of the feverish turnaround performed by the aircrews back on the *Goeben*. The ammo feeder jammed on his right cannon, causing his attack to fail. If that were not enough, the left cannon was not even reloaded! He pressed his trigger again, and realized his wing guns were dead.

The delay and distraction was just enough for his prey to wheel away, and try to swing up in a wide loop to come around and attack. The Fairy *Fulmar* had been built thinking its principle adversary might be twin engine bombers. As such, the design sacrificed traditional fighter assets like speed and maneuverability for longer range and better armament. Though the *Fulmar* was not as agile as the German plane, it now enjoyed a considerable advantage in firepower, with four 7.7mm Browning "303s" in each wing, or eight machineguns to the two remaining on the nose of Ritter's Messerschmitt. There was also a rear cockpit gunner in the *Fulmar* with a Vickers K firing from the cabin, so winning the air dance and getting on an adversaries tail was no guarantee you would not be hit. In spite of its liabilities against other single seat fighters, the *Fulmar* would produce nine aces in Fedorov's history books, and get 112 kills, more than any other F.A.A. fighter in the war.

It was going to come down to guts and flying skill now, and

Marco Ritter had both in abundance. He was able to evade the attacking pass, breaking right as the dogfight was on. Heilich and Euhler were up after the other three fighters, leaving Ritter alone with this single plane. He had reasoned out that his best bet with this new British plane was to try and make his attack run above and perpendicular to the enemy plane, raking the fuselage and wings instead of trying his luck against that rear gunner, and holding on to the enemy's tail while he was being fired upon.

Yet today Ritter was up against a fairly skilled pilot, a man who had come over to *Glorious* from the *Illustrious*, Lieutenant Commander Alfred 'Jack' Sewell. Known as "Jackie" to his mates, he had flown *Fulmars* in the Med, and had logged twelve kills thus far, seven against the Italian SM-79 tri-engine bomber, and the other five against seaplanes. He had yet to face a good fighter like the 109T, or a pilot like Ritter, but the two men put on quite a show in the skies above the naval chase, with Ritter using his speed and maneuverability to dodge the heavy firepower of those eight Browning 303s, while trying to get into position to put his two machineguns to good use.

The duel resulted in a draw, with Ritter's wing nipped by the flashing rounds of the other planes fire on one occasion, and the *Fulmar* taking a bite that nearly hit the rear gunner on the fuselage. But Ritter was soon out of ammunition, sorely missing the hard hitting 20mm wing cannons now.

Damn, he thought, I've no more teeth. It's all wings and tail for me now. All I can do is wheel about this fellow and hope to scare him off. So that is what I'll have to do, stay in the fight until I can see what Heilich and Euhler can do. One enemy plane was already down, making the odds three to three now, and Ritter came around in a wide turn before pulling a maneuver on his pursuer that surprised the other pilot. He swung up and over, finding himself in a perfect position to fire, and could only curse as he squeezed his guns to no avail. That would have been a kill, he knew. Then the duel became a game for him, to see how many times he could get what he knew would be a sure kill on his adversary, and he counted three before Euhler came flashing down from above and rattled off a quick burst.

"What's the matter Marco?" came a voice in Ritter's ear. "Why don't you shoot?"

"Nothing left!" said Ritter in return, and he knew that he should stop this nonsense now and get back to the *Goeben* to chew on the necks of the air crews.

The British lost two *Fulmars* in the engagement, and the other two were driven off, one with damage, though Jackie Sewell had managed to come away unscathed. In a better plane, he might have given Ritter a run for his money, but for now, with two mates down and a third in trouble, discretion was the better part of valor. He kept looking for enemy *Stukas*, saw none, and decided to vanish into a cloud to see if he could evade the German fighters and stay aloft to lend a hand if the dive bombers appeared.

* * *

Back on the *Kaiser*, Kapitan Heinrich watched the air duel with a smile, knowing he was out of the woods now. At the same time, the fighter cover advantage he now had, meant that he was pressing the line by persisting here in his chase. His main battery had been silent for some time, with the gun directors unable to pick out the target through the heavy smoke. All these engagements, beginning with the pluck and determination of Colin Maud on the *Icarus*, and right on through to those *Swordfish* crews, had cost him precious time. His many maneuvers in dodging torpedoes had enabled the British to slip over the horizon again, and now he knew that he was only going to close that range at a speed advantage of five or six knots. It might take him an hour to shave 10,000 meters off that range, and he was still clearly in defiance of a direct order by the fleet Admiral to break off this engagement.

He sighed, giving his Chief Gunnery officer Schirmer, a wan look. "We're going to have to turn on 300," he said.

"But we have them, Kapitan. Another twenty or thirty minutes and we'll be back in good range."

"Yes? Well I have orders. Look at that smoke, Schirmer. Another twenty minute run will get us closer, but you still might not be able to see anything. In the meantime, the British will still try to launch everything they have left at us, and I will have a good deal to explain to Admiral Lütjens if I stay on this heading. So it can't be helped."

He turned to a signalman. "Inform Admiral Lütjens we are back on our designated heading, and have the navigator estimate our arrival time. Helm, come about to three-zero-zero at once. Maintain speed. A cruiser and a destroyer are not bad pickings for our first engagement. As for the carrier, perhaps another time." There would be no honey for the bear this day.

But there would be a sting…

Even as *Kaiser* turned, the alarm was raised again when another British plane was reported approaching off the port bow, a lone *Swordfish* that had been lost in the smoke of the battle, and not seen until it emerged from a low cloud. The gunners were quick to react, re-training to engage this new target, and Heinrich watched coolly as the skies began to blossom with dark fire.

The plane came on, low and slow, steady at first, until the flak began to rake the sea around it, and the pilot jogged to one side in an evasive maneuver. The gun directors were shouting, the 2.0cm guns rattling with an awful racket, and the 3.7cm batteries were cracking with their steady fire. One round was very close, but the plane continued to bore in on them, dogged to the last.

This pilot is either very stupid, or very brave, thought Heinrich. Then he looked up, and saw a Messerschmitt diving from above and well behind the enemy plane, swooping down in a long arc towards the sea. The excitement of the engagement had the crew out on the decks in spite of the danger. They were hooping and shouting, whistling as the gunners poured on the fire. When they saw that Messerschmitt swooping down, a loud cheer went through the ranks, and Heinrich smiled.

Yet the smile seemed to hang on his cheeks for a time, slackening, until his eyes registered growing alarm. He should have launched by now, he thought. What's he doing? Come on! Get that plane! It was driving in, right over the wave tops, closer and closer. Now he saw the Messerschmitt pulling out of its dive, roaring in pursuit as it streaked over the water.

The German fighter was close enough to fire, but the *Swordfish* fired first. Heinrich saw the dark lance fall from its belly, and he knew that they were in trouble. The plane had come in through fire and hell to make that attack, and the pilot would not survive. The *Swordfish* was riddled by machinegun fire, then finally hit by the flak. It went cartwheeling into the sea as the crew cheered the kill, but it had delivered its barb before it died. Now Heinrich turned quickly, shouting an order to the helm.

"Belay that last order! Come hard to port!" The ship was turning right into the path of the torpedo, and now it was down to these last desperate seconds as the helmsman pulled the wheel hard over and *Kaiser Wilhelm* lurched in response.

Kapitan Heinrich was out through the hatch to the weather deck, his hands gripping the gunwale as he leaned over to look for the oncoming torpedo. It was going to be close…. Very close….

Kaiser turned, its sleek bow coming around in a boiling swell, and then Heinrich's eyes widened as he saw they would not evade. The torpedo came in and struck the ship on its starboard side. The explosion sent up a fountain of seawater, and the ship rolled with the hit.

Pilot Michael Bently was dead in the sea, but he had braved the fire and guns to even the score. Heinrich rushed back onto the main bridge, quickly giving the order 'All Stop' to slow the ship and assess the damage. It was soon learned that the torpedo had struck the bulwark, but still managed to penetrate and blow a good hole in the starboard side hull. The flood doors were down in that sector, and the engineers were on the scene.

Fifteen minutes later the news came that they would have to

slow speed to no more than 10 knots while the damage control crews fought to get the situation in hand. Heinrich cursed under his breath. So much for chasing carriers, he thought. Now he would have to send yet another message to Lütjens to explain this fiasco. His neck reddened as he thought about that, realizing there would be a good many questions concerning his actions here. If this damage was heavy, it could mean he would be forced to return to Gibraltar, or a French port.

In one brave act, a single man had traded his life to get this hit, but it was to impact the entire mission. Heinrich looked at Schirmer, then turned and walked off the bridge, heading below to meet with the engineers. You wanted that damn carrier, he thought as he went. Be careful what you wish for…

Chapter 11

Aboard *Hindenburg*, Lütjens was pacing, and waiting for news of what was happening with *Kaiser Wilhelm*. At last a messenger came up, handing him a decrypt from the fleet cypher unit: "NOW ON DESIGNATED COURSE – EXPECT CONTACT IN 40 MINUTES."

At last, he thought. I will have all my sheep in the flock again, though this one has proven to be quite the wolf. "*Kaiser* is now moving to rejoin us," he said casually to Adler, extending the professional courtesy of informing him of the message contents.

"Don't look so glum, Adler. Kapitan Heinrich has already acquitted himself well in sinking those two British ships. Now we get out into the Atlantic to look for our real prey, the convoys."

"We will have to get well to the west," said Adler. "The British certainly know we are here, and I am told the U-Boats have had slim pickings on routes from the UK to Freetown."

"When the sharks are in the water," said Lütjens, "the little fish do not feed so well," but Adler simply proffered a thin smile. The two men were on the weather deck now, away from other ears on the bridge. The Admiral could perceive the cold in Adler, a chill that was almost disdainful. He decided to sound out his Kapitan and end this nonsense once and for all.

"You do not agree with my recent decisions, Kapitan?"

"What difference would it make," said Adler quickly. "The Admiral clearly has plans that do not involve the sinking of British capital ships."

"Speak your mind, Adler. Do you not understand my reasoning here? I could not afford to risk the *Kaiser Wilhelm*. We need that ship."

"For what, sir? If you are unwilling to pursue a wounded carrier in a situation like this, then what good are those 15-inch guns on the *Kaiser?*"

Lütjens smiled. "You may think it a glamorous thing to hunt

down that carrier. Yes, I could turn now with everything we have and do exactly that, but have you forgotten what you just said a moment ago? The British know we are here. They will be maneuvering this very moment to bring ships with guns of their own into this little adventure. A fleet attack on that carrier would take time, more than I am willing to spend just now. Instead I will use that time to maneuver to evade the enemy, while pursuing our primary objective—the sinking of British merchant shipping. Believe it or not, Adler, that is what will either win or lose this war for us."

"Yet now you will leave this aircraft carrier in our wake, sir. Do not be surprised if they follow that wake. They will be able to match our speed, and shadow us with planes."

Lütjens smiled. "So now you are not so enthusiastic about our pilots off the *Goeben?*"

"They will do their job, Admiral, but you and I both know that if the British persist, they will be able to maintain a good general fix on our location. So the advantage will be theirs, as they will now maneuver heavy ships to intercept us, just as you say."

"Perhaps," said Lütjens. "And then you fight your battle, Adler. Until then, we move west for the convoys out of Halifax. And don't forget that we may soon be joined there by the *Tirpitz* battlegroup and *Graf Zeppelin*. Then we will truly have a fleet at sea."

At that point a runner came onto the weather bridge, saluting as he handed Lütjens yet another message. It was a fleet intercept concerning a planned rendezvous at sea, and Lütjens stared at it for some time, not quite knowing what to make of it.

"This is from Wilhelmshaven," he said at last. "It is signed by Admiral Raeder, but it makes no sense."

Adler raised an eyebrow, leaning to glance at the message. "What do you mean, Admiral?"

"Apparently the British have an important shipment at sea just now—so important that they chose to utilize the hold of a battleship instead of sending it in normal convoy traffic. Look here, this message details presumed course, speed, and destination for a British man-o-war, the HMS *Rodney*. Raeder is ordering us to intercept! What's gotten into that man? What could be so important that it had to be shipped on a battleship?"

"It could be that they have an important high level delegation at sea, Admiral. Perhaps even Churchill himself."

"Yet it says nothing of the kind here in this message. If this were so, why wouldn't Raeder advise me properly? Here we are, set to make our breakout, and now we get orders to find this battleship! This is ridiculous!"

Now it was Adler's turn to give Lütjens an admonishing look. "A moment ago you were bemoaning your overzealous subordinates, Admiral. Now who is chafing at the bit when orders come from senior authorities?"

Lütjens did not appreciate the remark, but he said nothing more. He was considering what this cryptic message could be about. He wasn't here to chase after high level officials. This was not like Raeder to make such a dramatic change to the operational plan in mid stream like this. Something was going on here that he could not yet fathom, and he wanted to get to the bottom of this at once.

"I will be in the wireless room," he said to Adler. "You have the bridge, Kapitan."

Adler watched him go, glad to look about him and realize that he was now the man in charge here. He shook his head, still inwardly bemoaning the lost opportunity here. In a few hours they would lose the light, making pursuit very difficult. They should have turned long ago, and by now they should be pounding that British carrier with the guns of *Bismarck* and *Hindenburg*. This business concerning the British battleship was very strange, and the orders to adjust course to look for it even stranger. Yet it may do one thing, he thought. Lütjens won't be able to find a way to squirm off after the convoys this time. Those orders come directly from Admiral Raeder. If we do find that ship, then I finally get my battle.

This ship wasn't built to chase steamers and oilers. No. It was built to face down the Royal Navy, and beat them. And that is exactly what I intend to do.

* * *

When Lütjens reached the wireless room, the news he had been dreading was waiting for him. *Kaiser Wilhelm* had been hit by a torpedo! He gritted his teeth, his hand stroking his chin as he took the message and read it with growing anger.

It was just as I feared, he thought. Adler had only one thing in mind, and Heinrich was too damn eager for a fight. I will have to sit the both of them down and knock their heads together! So now what? He kept looking at the message, hoping to find his answer there, but the words were stark and cold… TORPEDO HIT TO STARBOARD SIDE… The ship was still underway. Perhaps the damage was not all that serious, but *Kaiser* did not have the armor of the bigger ships, and he had grave misgivings about this now.

One message came after another, and he read them with growing concern. The Italians reported that a flotilla of three enemy ships were maneuvering to run the Sicilian narrows. They had launched an air strike, but encountered rocket air defense fire! That sent a chill down his spine, as it could mean only one thing. I'll bet my grandchildren that this is HMS *Invincible*. Bold of them to try and move west through the Med like that, but very much like the Royal Navy I know. Desperate circumstances call for desperate acts. How do they think they will get through our defenses at Gibraltar?

Yet even as he thought that, the situation they now faced with *Kaiser Wilhelm* weighed heavily on him. They would have to slow and effect a rendezvous with *Kaiser*. Darkness was just a few hours off, but tonight they should be able to assess the damage and determine whether the ship was still able to operate effectively.

Yet this will cost me eight hours or more, he thought. I could be well out to sea in that time, and in a good position to plan my convoy actions. Now this strange order to alter course and deliberately seek battle with a British battleship! What was Raeder thinking?

Soon we will have those battlecruisers sniffing about, and I must still consider that carrier to the south. *Kaiser* gave this Force H a bloody nose, but not without a cost. Everything is a trade off. There is always risk in any engagement, and we must never think we are invulnerable here. Yes, we have the best ship in the fleet, but I can already feel the air thickening around us. The British are following with the best they have, and there will be threats ahead if we alter course as Raeder orders. Damn! I need more information!

"Send a message to Wilhelmshaven," he said. "Request clarification on last order. Indicate *Kaiser Wilhelm* struck by torpedo, and say we are loitering on these coordinates to make a full damage assessment. Ask for an immediate reply."

* * *

Just after midnight, in the early hours of May 5th, *Kirov* was in position to run the Straits of Gibraltar. They had been monitoring signals traffic, on both sides, and Nikolin had a great deal to report to Admiral Volsky. They finally had news that the Germans had engaged Force H off Cape Saint Vincent, and inflicted some harm, but not without taking a scratch themselves. The Germans had reported one of their ships had taken a torpedo hit, and some hours later, as *Kirov* approached Gibraltar, they learned that *Kaiser Wilhelm* had detached from the main body and was now heading north.

"They are probably making for Brest," said Fedorov.

"Most likely, said Volsky. "Which means that torpedo hit was significant enough to hamper that ship's speed, and one more thing. It also means they are well aware of our presence here. Gibraltar was much closer, yet they do not turn about for that port, or Casablanca further south. So they are not all that confident about stopping us here after all."

"Agreed, sir," said Fedorov, "though we do not yet know what they are planning. This engagement with Force H left the enemy about 400 kilometers west of Lisbon. That puts us about 900 kilometers behind them now. That is sixteen hours at full speed, and twenty hours ahead two thirds."

"Something tells me they will not be waiting for us all that time, Mister Fedorov."

"It's this latest enigma intercept that I'm most concerned about," said Fedorov. "We may not have such a long chase ahead of us. Wilhelmshaven has ordered Lütjens to alter course to the northeast. I was thinking he would head due west at this point, but these orders to intercept *Rodney* are most alarming. I can see no reason for such an order. Why would they deliberately seek an engagement with a British heavy warship, just when they are in the perfect position to run west for the convoys?"

"The Germans obviously learned of this King's business you told me about," said Volsky. "So the *Rodney* is carrying a belly full of gold bullion, and these artifacts from the British Museum. What were they called?"

"The Elgin Marbles, sir. Parts of a carved relief taken from the Parthenon. Thomas Bruce, the 7th Earl of Elgin, excavated and transported them to England over a period of years, between 1801 and 1812. They are very valuable in and of themselves, but the fact that this key is possibly still embedded in the Selene Horse makes them priceless."

"Could the Germans know about this key?"

"I do not see how, yet we know very little about all of this. Miss Fairchild said the Watch knew of these keys. They were very secret, but imagine my surprise to learn that Director Kamenski had such a key in his possession, and for many decades!"

"That is very strange," said Volsky. "There is more to that man than meets the eye, Fedorov. He's like an onion, layer after layer. At first I thought he was merely working with the Inspector General, then he produced that letter you deposited in the Naval Logistics building, and those photographs. Yes! He had photos taken by the British when we last sailed through these straits. Remember?"

"Only too well, sir. That seems like a lifetime ago now. Back then we had just made our peace with Admiral Tovey, and we were en-route to Saint Helena. Now here he is, steaming in our wake as an ally, and on a ship that was never supposed to have been built!"

"This has been a most remarkable journey," Volsky agreed. "Yet what you say about these keys is very alarming. What are they for, Fedorov?"

"I've spent some time piecing it all together, sir. Both Kamenski and I now agree that it all dates back to 1908, the Tunguska Event. That impact did more than level trees in Siberia and provide fodder for the fire of many stories and legends thereafter. It also fractured the fourth dimension, time. It seems that several fissures resulted, like cracks in that mirror, as I tried to explain it before. Some were discovered, and because of the obvious danger should anyone move through them to another time, they were well secured and guarded."

"By who?" Volsky scratched his head.

"This we do not really know, but we now believe it was done by the same people who made these keys—the same who sent those signals back through time to the ships of the Watch."

"Then men from the future did all this?"

"I know it sounds fantastic, sir, but considering the fact that we are men from the future meddling about here makes it easier to believe."

"How did these keys appear here, in the past? You say Director Kamenski has had one for decades?"

"They must have been brought here," said Fedorov, "possibly by using the very same time rifts they secured. I'm not sure how long the Watch knew about them, or how they came into their possession. Kamenski didn't say how he came by his key, though he alluded that it was probably obtained by the KGB. Who knows when?"

"The British have keys too?"

"Miss Fairchild certainly has one. She used it to activate one of the rift sites, at Delphi."

"How many keys are there, Fedorov? Did you learn that?"

"Fairchild says they knew of at least two others. One was in the possession of another member of the Watch, though she did not name that person, and she said nothing about any time rift associated with that key. The second was in the Selene Horse, aboard *Rodney*."

"What about Ilanskiy?" Volsky asked the obvious question. "Is there a key for that rift?"

"The British knew nothing of that," said Fedorov. "In fact, I may have been the one to first discover it. Even these men in the future did not know about it, which leads me to think that our mission, the ship, my actions, are deeply implicated in all of this. We're a wild card in the deck, sir."

"But you say those stairs took you back to 1908, Fedorov. That means anyone could have used them. It's a long way between 1908 and the 1940s where you stumbled upon it. We know Sergei Kirov used them, and Volkov. Look what resulted!"

"True, sir. That's very worrisome. All the other rift zones were well guarded, but not Ilanskiy. I think this is what unhinged the key makers plan—Ilanskiy."

"What plan do you speak of?"

"I'm not sure, sir, but I've been thinking about all this for some time. If men in the future discovered these time rifts and secured them, then they were obviously trying to prevent this Grand Finality Miss Fairchild told us about. But they failed—at least that is what Fairchild believes. She tells me the voices went silent. The watch stopped receiving instructions, and their last message urged them to gather and secure all the keys to the rift zones, and one thing more. It was a warning."

"About this calamity you mention?"

"In one sense, but it was much more specific. It was about us."

"About us? You mean the ship?"

"Yes sir. That is why Tovey founded the Watch, to keep vigil for our next possible appearance."

"Yes, and understandably so," said Volsky. "But this sounds a little more sinister, Fedorov. You say they were told to secure all these keys, but then they are warned about us? What do these men from the future think we are going to do?"

"I don't know, sir…" Fedorov had a frustrated look on his face now. "When I first heard about these keys, these other rifts, I thought I could finally set down the burden I have been carrying, thinking all this was on my shoulders."

"On *our* shoulders, Fedorov, the ship and every man aboard. Do not be so greedy and try to take all the blame yourself."

"I have tried, sir, but learning about this warning leads me to suspect our part in this tale has not yet run its course. We're going to *do* something. This is how I see things now. We're going to do something that could make it impossible to prevent this calamity Fairchild talks about—this Grand Finality."

"And it has something to do with these keys?"

"Apparently so, sir. The thing is this…. We don't know what we may do, or fail to do. Here we are trying to help Fairchild secure this key. Our whole mission to get after the Germans has suddenly become a race to find and protect the battleship *Rodney.* And this latest message Nikolin decrypted indicates that the German operation has also been re-focused on that as well. It's as if the lines of fate are setting course for some distant rendezvous point, a nexus point, and I'm not sure what is supposed to happen there. We are living all this through moment by moment, and groping like blind men."

"You want certainty, Fedorov, but you know that is impossible. There is no way we could know this."

"But there is, sir. We've seen the results of our actions. We can look ahead in time and know what we have done. These men from the future might also know. To them this would all be history, but they have gone silent. The only thing we have is that last warning. Beware a ship… beware *Kirov*…"

Admiral Volsky frowned. "I'm not sure I like the sound of that."

Chapter 12

Aboard *Kazan*, Gromyko was the first element of the allied task force to open the action. The keen ears and sensitive sonar equipment on the sub had detected a pair of German U-boats creeping silently in the narrow straits. There were six stationed at the new German base, but four of them were out in the sea lanes off Casablanca lying in wait for British convoy traffic to Freetown. Aside from the two remaining, there were only a few captured trawlers, oilers and merchant ships in the harbor. The only surface assets the Germans had in the region were with Lütjens. Though the French had superb destroyer assets, they were still operating from Casablanca.

This basic lack of a sound cooperative effort had hindered the Axis fleets earlier, and it was also going to severely weaken their defense of Gibraltar. The Germans relied on these two U-boats, thinking they would be more than enough to fill the narrow channel with torpedoes against any surface group attempting to pass. Beyond that, there were six *Stukas* and six fighters staged at the small airport, along with a number of seaplanes and a few JU-88s.

It was clear that the Germans had yet to fully appreciate the strategic value of the prize they had taken. They had not placed anti-submarine defenses, thinking their U-Boat defense was sufficient. The mines they had sewn were largely in fields designed to protect the entrance to the harbor, and the only anti-submarine nets were there as well. As for shore batteries, the British had destroyed all their guns before the Rock fell into enemy hands, and the Germans had simply thought to rely on regular artillery. They had not yet installed radar sets, and relied on aerial reconnaissance to detect any approaching threat. Fedorov had chosen the darkness of early May 5 to make this run, conditions that would make German air attacks very chancy. The moon set at 02:53 that morning, so it was completely black, and all the ships were running dark.

Though the British task force had been spotted at sunset well to the east, approaching Algiers the previous day, the British continued in an attempt to deceive the enemy as to their real intentions. They sent signals in a code known to be compromised, and indicating that their planned mission to attack Algiers was well in hand. The messages indicated they would bombard the port and return to Alexandria this very day, striking Tunis on the return trip. When no attack occurred after sunset on the 4th of May, the Germans sent alerts to Gibraltar to be wary.

As a precaution, the Germans had two sea planes up just after sunset, to look for enemy shipping. They loitered for some time, patrolling east, and saw the oncoming British task force off Oran. Fedorov considered whether or not to shoot the planes down, but he realized the missile fire would announce their presence there in the Alboran Sea in any case. So the Germans knew trouble was coming, and the six *Stukas* were ready on the small airfield just after midnight as the U-boats moved into their defensive positions.

Viktor Schultze in *U-103* and Heinrich Liebe in *U-38* had the duty that day, lurking in the waters off Gibraltar. A hovering diesel boat would be very difficult for the enemy sonars to hear, or so they reasoned, but they had not counted on the advanced capabilities of *Kazan,* the skill of sonar operator Chernov, or even the presence of an enemy submarine at all. Their own U-boat fleet could have never kept pace with the fast moving surface ships, but for *Kazan,* this was no problem. They heard the U-boats easily enough, and Gromyko put two 533mm torpedoes in the water at 03:00. Seconds later the thump of two underwater explosions had laid bare the sea lanes from underwater threat.

The *Stukas* scrambled, launched, and soon met a similar fate as the *Argos Fire* easily put six Aster-15 missiles into the air. Not a single plane or pilot survived. Now the only remaining threat was from shore batteries, and Fedorov had planned to use the helicopter assets they had to easily spot the guns with their high powered optics and sensors. It was then a simple matter to use the deck guns, which outranged the enemy batteries and was able to strike them with accurate 152mm fire.

It all came down to the superior sensory capability of the modern ships. They could find and target the enemy defenses long before they had any chance to fire their weapons. So the Rock of Gibraltar did not prove to be very much of a barrier that night. By 04:00, the three surface ships had swept through the channel and were already in the Western Approaches, heading into the Atlantic.

* * *

"**Well** done, Captain," said Volsky, congratulating Fedorov on his successful operation to run the straits.

"That was easier than we thought it would be," said Fedorov. "I expected mines and much more air defense, and yet this make some sense after all. Gibraltar is really a backwaters base for the Axis. They don't need it for their operations in the Med, and the Germans haven't been able to move very many assets there beyond these U-Boats we encountered."

"Having *Kazan* with us makes up for the loss of the bow sonar dome," said Volsky.

"Yes sir, but even so, I think Tasarov would have been able to find those subs with our towed array and the KA-40."

"So what is our situation now?"

"Admiral Tovey has indicated that Force H has moved south, away from the threat of surface interception. Their carrier *Glorious* took a single bomb hit, but is still operational, and it seems they managed to get a hit on one German ship."

"The *Hindenburg?*"

"No sir, on the fast escort battlecruiser *Kaiser Wilhelm*. This is a new ship, one designed but never built in our history. I think the British got very lucky. That hit saw Lütjens linger here at slow speed for some time. Otherwise the lead they have would be much greater. At present, the last British sighting had them here, sir."

He tapped the clear Plexiglas vertical panel, where a digital map was displayed in phosphorescent green. "That's about 450 nautical miles to our northwest—twenty hours ahead two thirds, and fifteen hours ahead full at 30 knots. This blue dot here represents a pair of fast British battlecruisers. They are now about 250 nautical miles northwest of the Germans, and in a very good position to intercept, even if the Germans head due west now. They would not be wise to do so, however."

"Oh? The odds are not in their favor?"

"No sir, they are fast at 32 knots, but carry only six 15-inch guns each. The Germans will have eighteen big guns between their two battleships, and they are much better armored. The British will most likely use those two ships to shadow the Germans, so we should have a much better fix on their position after they make first contact."

"So now we rest a little easier in these waters, Fedorov. The Royal Navy is on our side this time, and for that, I am thankful."

"True sir. They are a very professional force, and have good ships in the game now. There will probably be another aircraft carrier and cruiser force out there coming from Home Fleet. Between the two carriers they will have a good chance to saturate the airspace and neutralize the advantage the Germans have enjoyed with their light carrier. With *Kaiser Wilhelm* hit, and now returning to Brest, it then comes down to the battleships."

"Could they win this duel, even without our help?" asked Volsky.

"They would have a good shot at that, sir. Their plan would have to be to get at least two more good battleships in front of Lütjens. Then, between those ships and HMS *Invincible*, they would have enough to force an engagement, but it would be quite a battle. Their *Bismarck* took on two British battleships and prevailed this very month in our history. It sunk the *Hood*, and probably would have made it safely to a French port if not for a very lucky hit by a British *Swordfish* that damaged the rudder and prevented the ship from maneuvering. That isn't likely to happen again, and don't forget that the *Hindenburg* is out there with *Bismarck* this time, a much more formidable ship."

"We can ease their pain, Fedorov. Yes?"

"At the moment our longest range missiles are the ten remaining P-900s we got from *Kazan*. They can range out 660 kilometers, but the Germans are another 200 kilometers beyond that at the moment. We will have to get closer, and get a better fix on their exact position."

"We could use the KA-40," said Volsky.

"Possibly, sir, but it can only carry a single anti-ship missile, or torpedo. That isn't much punch."

"And the helicopters on the *Argos Fire?*"

"Again, they are not designed to carry the heavier anti-ship missiles. Miss Fairchild spoke briefly, and she indicated they mostly use shorter range rocket pods. Those helos were excellent in providing us fire support in Syria, but they won't do much harm to a ship like the *Hindenburg.*"

"Then we will have to close that range."

"Agreed, sir. That said, our speed advantage is very slim. We would have to run all out at our full battle speed of 32 knots to close at all. *Hindenburg* and *Bismarck* can both make 30 knots. To run that fast for an extended period could stress that damaged hull."

"Yes," said Volsky. "The ship still bears the scars of all our past battles. They did more work on that hull patch while we were at Alexandria, but I understand your concern. What do you think the Germans will do now, Fedorov—particularly given this odd message ordering them to find and engage the *Rodney?*"

"Very odd, sir. I still cannot see how they decided to make that their top priority. It is very alarming."

"Can they know about this business with the keys?"

"I doubt that. But Admiral Tovey sent several messages concerning his plan to effect a rendezvous at sea with the *Rodney*. The Germans may have intercepted those, and that alone could be reason for them to target that ship. Then again, we do not really know the extent of their intelligence. Lütjens stayed with *Kaiser Wilhelm* for a time to see that ship safely off to Brest. I think they will now turn and get into a position to intercept *Rodney.*"

"Where might that occur?"

"I suppose that depends on *Rodney.* That ship's course will determine the location."

"So the Germans may not continue running west," said Volsky. "They've already lost time tending to their wounded ship, and now these orders complicate their operation considerably. Perhaps we can get into good missile range sooner than we expected. Until then, it will be up to the Royal Navy. Where do they have ships capable of challenging the Germans?"

"I was briefed by Tovey after that conference," said Fedorov. "Admiral Holland has more than Lütjens to worry about now. There is another strong German force in the Norwegian Sea, and so the four British battleships available have been sent to guard the breakout channels on either side of Iceland."

"If they attempt the passage west of Iceland in the Denmark Strait, we should know soon enough," said Volsky. "Remember, we have that *Oko* Panel team there. They must be getting a bit lonely by now."

"I had almost forgotten about them sir. Yes, that radar set gives us good coverage. But if the Germans move east of Iceland we could be looking at a different battle."

"Oh? How so?"

"It would place them much closer to the *Hindenburg* group, and if the two German battlegroups join, then we have real trouble."

"I can see that we shall have to coordinate closely with Holland and Tovey," said Volsky. "Let us put our heads together and come up with a plan."

"Sir," said Fedorov. "How fast is *Kazan?*"

"It can match our speed underwater, but even so, it would have difficulty catching up to the *Hindenburg* now. As for missiles, Gromyko tells me he has only a few P-800s left. We've pilfered all his P-900s, and remember he fired a strong salvo in the Med, and another to interdict the Turkish Straits. What missiles he has left can only range out 300 kilometers, so he must get even closer than we do, if a missile attack is contemplated. No Mister Fedorov, it's a foot race now, a great naval chase for the new history books we are writing here. Only I wonder how they will account for our presence, two ships the world knew nothing whatsoever about. That will take some explaining, yes?"

It was then that the first odd incident occurred, though it would not be the last. A man came up the ladder to enter the main bridge through the hatch, his face ashen, in spite of the exertion of the climb, and his eyes held fear when Fedorov and Volsky turned to see what he needed.

"Sir…" the man was clearly frazzled about something.

"Yes, what is it Mister Kornalev? A problem in the mess hall? Are the *Mishman* fighting over mashed potatoes again, or are we running out of beef?" Kornalev was a cook's assistant from the galley.

"No sir… It's Lenkov, sir. In the galley…"

"What is wrong with Lenkov? If he is sick, have him go to see Doctor Zolkin. If he is angry again, then that is a matter for the Galley Chief to settle. It should not be brought here, to the command bridge."

"But sir… I don't know how to describe this. He's dead, Admiral. Lenkov is dead, stuck in the galley!"

Volsky gave Fedorov a quick glance. "He is dead?"

"Please sir. You must come and see! No one will go near him, so I ran here as fast as I could."

"Very well. Calm down now. I will leave the bridge to Mister Fedorov here and have a look. Have you informed Doctor Zolkin?"

"No sir, I came straight here."

The Admiral reached for the overhead intercom and flipped the send switch on. "Doctor Zolkin, Please meet me in the galley at once. This is the Admiral." He set the microphone back in its housing and gave Kornalev a smile. "Lead on, Mister Kornalev. Let us see what the problem is."

"Admiral off the bridge," said Rodenko as the two men left

through the main hatch. He gave Fedorov a look, wondering what he thought of the matter.

"Any problems of late with Lenkov?" Fedorov asked.

"No sir, at least nothing that has come to my attention."

"Has Orlov been minding his temper?"

"He's been in good spirits, sir. No, I don't think this has anything to do with Orlov."

"Anything else? I've been away from the ship for some time. How is the crew?"

"Holding up well, sir. But now that you ask, there have been a few minor incidents."

"Of what sort?"

"As the Admiral said, there was a brawl in the galley last week when the potatoes ran out before the last crew shift came in."

"They were fighting over mashed potatoes?"

"So it seems. But I have noticed that things have been... well wound up a little too tight of late."

"Explain."

"It's nothing I can put my finger on sir, but you can feel it. The men have been at sea for many months now, and through a good deal of combat, not to mention the fact that here we are still in the 1940s."

"I understand," said Fedorov.

"It's odd, sir. Troyak had a strange report yesterday. He says one of the *mishman* came in and asked if he could be issued a rifle."

"A rifle? What did he want that for?"

"He wouldn't say. Troyak refused the request, of course. We can't have men holed up in their quarters with weapons. But that did little to calm the man down."

"What was wrong with him?"

"Nothing he could really explain to us, Captain. But if I had to describe it, I'd say the man was afraid. Yes, he seemed frightened of something, and it was a natural reflex to want a weapon at hand to protect himself. I had him go see Zolkin."

Fedorov nodded. "Very well. Keep me informed, Rodenko."

That was a bit disturbing. Here they were, on the most powerful fighting ship in the world, and a junior *mishman* felt compelled to ask Troyak for a rifle! Perhaps Rodenko is correct, he thought. Maybe it is the long duration at sea, and combat fatigue setting in. I must be more attentive to the crew.

A few minutes later the intercom sounded and the voice of Admiral Volsky was on the line. Fedorov could hear something in his tone that was upsetting. Even Rodenko noticed it.

"Mister Fedorov, please come to the galley at once." It seemed simple enough, but it was going to be something much more than any of them expected. And it was only just beginning.

Part V

Lenkov's Legs

"I would rather have questions that can't be answered than answers that can't be questioned."

— Source Unknown

Chapter 13

Fedorov had never seen anything like this before. It was shocking, horrifying, the stuff of science fiction made real before his eyes. Lenkov was stuck in the galley... literally. His body was embedded in the deck, with head, shoulders and half his torso above the level of the floor, and all the rest embedded in the structure of the ship itself. One arm extended looked as though he had tried to reach for the table or chair to prevent himself from being swallowed, and an agonized look was frozen on his face, blotched with eerie blue-pink bruises. The eyes bulged from their sockets, wild with fear. The mouth gaped open, as if the man had died while screaming with terror and panic.

After the shock of seeing that face subsided, Fedorov's mind reasoned the deck must have collapsed beneath him, but upon closer inspection, he saw that was not correct. There was nothing wrong with the deck at all. It was as if the man and ship had simply merged, the deck losing its integrity for a moment, just long enough for Lenkov to fall, before solidifying again, like a man falling into water that suddenly froze all around him.

Admiral Volsky and Doctor Zolkin were there, with two Marines keeping the other crewmen away from the scene. The rumors were already racing through the ship—that Lenkov had fallen right through the deck!

One image now immediately came to mind for Fedorov, that horrifying moment in the Pacific as they raced away from the burning hulk of the *Yamato*, and the cruiser *Tone* suddenly appeared on a direct collision course with *Kirov*. The ship had been pulsing, as Fedorov described it, fading in and out of that moment in time, like a radio signal that could not be fine tuned, quavering on the airwaves of infinity. Volsky was looking to his Captain, his eyes carrying the obvious expectation that Fedorov would know what had happened here, and that was the only thing he could think of.

"So it begins," he said darkly.

"Fedorov?"

"We must be pulsing again," said Fedorov. "The ship… Like we did before in the Pacific."

"Pulsing?"

"Our position in time is becoming unstable. Remember, Admiral, we no longer have Rod-25 aboard, and the other two control rods have been stowed in Rad-safe containers. In the Pacific, we began to shift in and out of that timeframe. I first noticed this during that surprise strafing run that wounded you, sir. Some of those rounds went right through the command citadel, and through the deck, but left absolutely no mark. They could not have penetrated the citadel armor in any case, but several men on the bridge saw them. It was just as we were shifting to another time in the Mediterranean. We were there, but yet not there, still not completely manifested in that moment. And then do you recall how that Japanese cruiser seemed to go right through us?"

"Who could forget that little experience," said Zolkin. "The men had nightmares about it for weeks after. I nearly ran out of sedatives."

"Well, it's happened again," said Fedorov. "The ship must have faded, pulsed, I don't know what to call it, but we wavered in this time briefly, and became insubstantial."

"But not Lenkov?"

"Apparently not."

"How could this be, Fedorov?" asked Volsky.

"I wish I knew, sir. Does his body extend through to the space below this deck?"

"That is the strangest thing," said Volsky. "No, there is nothing there. It is as if he was ripped in two, with half his body somewhere else."

"Very strange… He must have fallen out of phase with the rest of us… with the ship itself."

"Out of phase?"

"It's as if he lingered in this time when the ship began to move. His link in time with us became broken somehow, and he fell through…"

"Right through the deck?"

"Right through time itself," said Fedorov, not quite understanding what he was saying, but doing his best to put some rational explanation to the horrific scene before them.

"Wonderful," said Zolkin facetiously. "Now each time I roll over in bed I must worry that I might fall right off the edge of infinity? What is going on here?"

"Believe me, Doctor," Volsky placated him. "We've all been wondering that ever since that first accident in the Norwegian Sea. Can you shed any more light on this, Mister Fedorov?"

"That's the only way I can understand it sir. Either Lenkov, or the ship and everyone else, pulsed in time, and Lenkov was not in sync."

"This pulsing you speak of. Will it continue?"

"It might, Admiral, but I cannot know that for sure."

"Why is it happening? Any ideas?"

Fedorov took a deep breath. "This may sound stupid, sir, but the simple fact is that we do not belong here. This is not our time. We are intruders, and we have already seen that our position in time is often not stable."

"Yet wasn't that because Dobrynin was dipping that control rod every twelve days?"

"We thought that was the reason," said Fedorov, "but these odd pulsing effects lead me to suspect that time is having difficulty with our presence in the past."

"Difficulty? No argument there, Fedorov. We've been giving her fits! Look here, is this part of that paradox business you keep bringing up? Did this happen because we are getting close to the time of our first displacement to the past?"

"I must suspect that, even if I cannot say anything for certain."

"What paradox business?" Zolkin gave them a questioning look.

"It's a long story, Dmitri," Volsky explained. "We first shifted to the past on July 28th, and appeared in this very year, 1941, on that same date. Rod-25 was very meticulous in the beginning, though we did not know that at the time. Then, as Dobrynin performed that maintenance procedure, we began shifting all over the place. We would lose hours, days even, and skip about—how did you describe it Fedorov?"

"Like a rock skipping over water, sir."

"That's it. We hopped from one time to another, causing a good deal of mayhem every time we appeared. We got Tovey and the Royal Navy up in arms, and if that wasn't enough, then we took on the Japanese in that trip to the Pacific!"

"Not to mention Karpov's sortie to 1908!" Zolkin folded his arms, his eyes still riveted on Lenkov. "Now how in god's name am I going to get that man out of the deck? It looks like he has been welded in place! And where did the rest of him go? Headaches, I can handle. Broken bones? No problem. I have pills and splints for that. But we never discussed anything like *this* in medical school."

"Alright, alright…" Volsky raised a hand, as if trying to impose some sense and order on the scene by virtue of his rank and authority in the navy. But Mother Time was not a member of his crew. He knew that, yet his instincts led him to look for a solution in any case. He was the Admiral. It was his to give the orders and keep the ship on an even keel. Yet now, as he stared at Lenkov, his mind was completely lost, aghast, nonplussed by this bizarre twist of fate. Was a similar doom awaiting them all? Were they all going to be devoured by time, fall through the deck into oblivion like poor Lenkov?

"First things first," he said. "Doctor, I will leave it to you as to how the body is removed. If you need the engineers, just call them, but I would like to keep this incident quiet, if possible. Did anyone witness this happen?"

"Three other men were here in the Galley," said Zolkin. "Two came to the sick bay, Shorokin and Gorich. They say they were cleaning the pots and pans when they heard a scream, then they ran in here and saw this mess. I sent them on leave to their quarters and I'll check on each man soon. As for Mister Kornalev, he went straight to the bridge. I haven't spoken with him."

"I'm not sure you will have anything in your Doctor's bag for this, Dmitri," said the Admiral. "But do your best to keep things calm. I will walk the decks for a while and see to the crew. We've been plotting grand strategy up on the bridge, and in all these meetings with Admiral Tovey, and I have neglected my boys here on the ship. That ends now. Let's get this cleaned up, a fresh crew assigned here, and a good meal ready for this evening mess. As for you, Mister Fedorov, I think you might wish to go and discuss this with Director Kamenski. Perhaps he knows something more. I wonder if that key of his has something to do with this?"

"Key?" Zolkin gave the Admiral another clueless look.

"Never mind that, Dmitri. See what you can do about Lenkov."

Volsky crossed himself, then started for the hatch.

* * *

"Yes, Mister Fedorov, I hear what you are saying," said Kamenski, "but consider this. Everything on this ship existed in some other form in this time when we arrived here. Some of the metals and materials used to build *Kirov* were fabricated, but we didn't really create anything new, just re-arranged the particles, if that makes any sense. The hull was in the ground somewhere, as raw ore, I suppose."

"I never thought of that," said Fedorov. "I thought it would be impossible for us to shift to a time when we already existed, but I never gave a thought to the metal in the ship itself. Yes, what you say is true, but if that is the case, how could the ship shift here?"

"Quite the mystery," said Kamenski. "Perhaps that material simply vanished when the ship manifested in the past, and gave up its seat at the theater to us, though I doubt that. As for the men, none of them existed in this year, so every molecule in their bodies was... new to this time."

Fedorov frowned, trying to comprehend what Kamenski was telling him. The Director had explained that things had vanished during their nuclear testing, a consequence of time being fractured by the intense shock of the detonations. Yet the odd thing was that these items later reappeared, and they had never discovered where they had gone in the time they were missing.

Things tumbled over and over in Fedorov's mind, then he suddenly remembered what he had learned about those American destroyers.

"Desron 7," he said. "You told me those ships reappeared like that, all on their own."

"Yes, at the time I described them as little fish time threw out of her nets. They must have shifted forward in time with *Kirov,* perhaps because they were within the sphere of influence of Rod-25 when this ship moved in time."

"But we saw nothing, Director. There was no sign of them. If they did shift—"

"Yes, they did not quite reach the same moment *Kirov* did." Kamenski completed his thought for him. "Perhaps they were ahead or well behind you in time. In that case, you would have never seen them. They were obviously in that same bleak future you sailed through for a time, but their position in that timeframe was not ever stable. They did not belong there any more than *Kirov* belongs here. So time cast them back to their own era, and they reappeared in 1941. The story they told has been a mystery ever since, but one we may have solved. Yes?"

"Then do you believe that the same thing is happening to us," asked Fedorov. "Are we being pulled back to our own era? Is that why the ship lost its solidity in this time for a moment?"

"Possibly. This pulsing effect usually occurs just before or after you were about to displace in time, correct?"

"Yes sir, but that was because we had Rod-25 in play. Yet it isn't even on the ship now, Gromyko has it in *Kazan.* How could we be shifting or pulsing in time without it?"

"How did those destroyers get back to the Argentia Bay of 1941? I hate to answer your question with another, but that is what happened, so it must be possible. What we have seen, Fedorov, is that once a thing first displaces in time, it is never really stable again, in any timeframe. It's as if it has come unglued from the fabric of reality—a slippery fish, as I like to say. And when it moves, slips away, it often disturbs things, as we have seen. If my theory is correct, then all the material that makes up this ship had to pay a very heavy price for our admission to this time."

"You say it may have simply vanished?"

"Just like Lenkov's legs."

"Where did they go, sir?"

"Where does the flame go when you blow out a candle, Mister Fedorov? That's an old Zen Koan, is it not? The Zen Master wants his answer, just as you do."

Kamenski was lighting his pipe now. "I am blowing out this match," he said calmly. "Tell me, where has the flame gone?"

Fedorov looked around, realizing the question was a deliberate trap, designed to challenge and frustrate the reasoning mind, and bring it to a crisis point where no answer it could give would make any rational sense. Then his mind seemed to slip, like Lenkov falling through the deck, and he realized what the trap was.

"The flame isn't a thing," he said suddenly, prompting a smile from Kamenski.

"Ah, yes, the solution is in the grammar, is it not? This isn't a word puzzle, Mister Fedorov, but a literal truth. The flame is not a thing, not a noun as we choose to label it. What is a noun? A person, place or thing, as the teachers would drill us over and over. But there are no nouns in this universe. Everything is a process, a relationship. That flame is a result of the interaction between chemicals, the match stick, and the oxygen in this room. All three must be present, and then we get that flame, leaping into existence as if manifesting here from nothingness! It is a process, an activity, a verb. Yes, my friend, everything in the universe is like that. Everything is a verb. There are no nouns, if you really think about it. That is just a pleasant and useful convention. Everything is a process. When I blow on this match, I disturb that process, and also disturb the delicate relationship that has conspired to bring us that flame. But where does it go?"

"Out of existence," said Fedorov.

"Correct. The process we call 'flame' simply stops. The oxygen is here, the match stick still has substance to be burned, but my breath has forced the heat away from that one vital element of the process, and so it stops, taking that flame to the void from whence it came."

Silence. A ship's bell rang, timing out the change of crew shifts, the sound emerging from that same void, lingering for the briefest moment, and then vanishing. Where did it go?

"And now the reason for the Zen Master's question." Kamenski took a draw on his pipe, blowing the smoke and watching it for a moment. "You see, we are all candle flames, are we not? We aren't nouns either, Mister Fedorov. We are just a process, something the universe is doing right there where you stand in your uniform, and right here where I sit trying to keep warm in this old wool sweater. If you had the eyes to see, then you would know that all these so called things in the world are mere conventions of thought, just like that flame. If you could see it all, right down on the level of quantum particles, it would just be this undifferentiated soup, a quantum haze where everything was happening—every thing, and I separate those two words deliberately. Understand?"

Fedorov blinked.

"Understand that, my friend," said Kamenski, "and you will know what happened to Lenkov's legs."

Chapter 14

Tasarov had heard the rumors circulating below decks. He had collected more than an earful on his way to his shift on the bridge. Now he sat at his station, settling into his chair and initializing his surveillance panel. One screen remained dark, the feed from the forward sonar in the bow that had been shattered when *Kirov* struck an old mine—in 1908! He still had difficulty getting his mind around all that had happened to the ship, and everything they had seen and done.

"Hey Samsonov," he said to the big man at the CIC station near him. "Have you heard about Lenkov?"

"Who's Lenkov?" said Samsonov.

"The galley server. You know, the one who gives out extra portions for cigarettes."

"So what of him?"

"He's dead! They found him on the floor of the galley—or rather *in* the floor of the galley. He was stuck there, right in the deck!"

Samsonov gave Tasarov a look that said he was listening to some bad *vranyo* now, the exaggerated stories one Russian would tell another. The rules of *vranyo* were well established. The teller spins out the tall tale, and the listener was supposed to take it all in, without objection, simply nodding his head until the story was concluded. Only then could he make any complaint. But Samsonov was not a stickler for convention. He frowned at Tasarov, waving his story away.

"Someone is chasing the wind," he said.

"But it's true," Tasarov insisted. "Doctor Zolkin was there with the Admiral and Fedorov, and Marines had the whole place sealed off. The engineers are doing something now—they say they are trying to get the body out of the deck."

"Yes? Well I am trying to get the missile crews to respond to my maintenance cycle checks. Forget these stories, Tasarov. Just mind your sonar."

Tasarov could see he would find no sympathy with the weapons chief, so he slipped on his headphones and sighed. Time to take an initial sounding of the sea space around them. He would listen, with eyes closed, getting a baseline feel for the acoustics. His information wasn't as good as it used to be without that forward sonar dome, but he still had his side hull sensors, and the towed array trailed behind the ship on a long steel cable.

He found it difficult to get settled into his shift. Normally he would chat with Nikolin for a while, but he was on leave for another hour, and probably eating. *I hope he's not anywhere near the galley,* he thought. *Better in the officer's mess hall now. He'll probably have more news about Lenkov when he gets here.*

Tasarov wasn't just missing a sympathetic friend to talk to now. It was more than that. He had been listless and fatigued of late, and had trouble sleeping. They said he was the man with the best ears in the fleet, so when he slept he always put in earplugs to filter out the sounds of the ship. But even so, he had been hearing something, though he did not quite know what it was. It was more a feeling than a sound in the beginning, a strange sense that something was amiss. He knew that even a hushed silence could carry that feeling. People would often say they felt ill at ease when things were too quiet.

That's how he had been feeling—ill at ease. It was too quiet when he put the ear plugs in, and out of that silence there came a growing sense of dread. So he had taken to listening to music on his earbuds instead, and hoping that would lull him to sleep. He always started with an old favorite band, the song "Good Night" by the Beatles. *"Now it's time to say goodnight, good night, sleep tight."* But he had been unable to do so for the last several days.

It was probably the fatigue setting in from the long journey. He had seen an attempted mutiny right here on the bridge, defended the ship against numerous undersea threats, and even launched Vodopad torpedoes against enemy battleships. He had watched enemy planes blown from the sky; seen the awful carnage inflicted by the ships missiles, and the terrible fire of a nuclear warhead. Closer to home, he had seen Captain Karpov shoot the Doctor with a pistol, right in front of him, and that had been a very difficult moment. The stress had been building up for some time, and his good friend Nikolin had been away too often in his role as a translator for Volsky and Fedorov.

Maybe I'm losing my edge, he thought. At least now, with *Kazan* along, my job in being vigilant against enemy submarines was a little easier. It was always a relief to know that Gromyko was out there somewhere on patrol ahead of the ship, clearing the sea lanes of enemy U-boats. So why do I still feel so uneasy?

He settled in, headphones on, thinking he might go into that deep listening mode he was famous for, like a man sitting in meditation, eyes closed, ears sensitive to every nuance in the data stream. One of his favorite games was to try and hear *Kazan*, the fleet's most stealthy sub. If he could do that, then he thought he was still sharp enough to find anything else in the sea. So he closed his eyes and listened, and it wasn't long before he heard it again.

Not the submarine. Not *Kazan*. It was the sound again, the same deep, threatening sound that had been disturbing his sleep. It emerged from the unseen depths of the sea, like sound emerged from nothingness. What was it, a whale song the like of which he had never heard before? Was there some great behemoth down there plying the depths and moaning in this deep vibrato?

Yet it wasn't that kind of sound…. It wasn't a vibration, though he reacted to it as if it was exactly that—a thrumming sensation, deep, powerful, threatening. Something was growling from the depths of the ocean, and this time it was not the distant subterranean rumble of a volcano. He switched on his seismic processor, to see if he could find any known correlation to the sound in that database, but no match was found. It wasn't an undersea landslide, or an earthquake. It wasn't the gurgling of a hot spot on the mid-Atlantic ridge. It wasn't *Kazan*…

He opened his eyes, taking off his headset for a moment to chase the strange chill the sound instilled in him, a feeling of dread and fear. To his great surprise, the feeling remained heavy on him, like a shroud. He closed his eyes, and even without his headset on, he could hear it, feel it, sense that dread.

"Samsonov…"

"What now, Tasarov. More Vranyo?"

"Not that… I'm hearing something."

"Contact? Something on your board? Report it to Rodenko!"

The ship's *Starpom* heard that exchange and Rodenko drifted over, curious. "Something to report, Mister Tasarov?"

"No sir. No formal contact. It's just that… Well, I'm hearing something, but I can't make out what it might be."

"Nothing in the database?" asked Rodenko. "No there probably wouldn't be any correlations here in 1941. Describe it."

"Very deep. I'd say it is below the threshold of human hearing, but I can pick it up, sir. I can feel it."

"And what does it feel like?"

Tasarov hesitated, not wanting to sound like a fool, but then he spoke his mind, just one word that seemed to sum the feeling up well enough. "Fear."

Rodenko had been the ship's radar operator before being promoted to his new post as Executive Officer under Fedorov. "Mister Kalinichev," he said. "Anything on your screens?"

"No sir, all is clear."

"Switch to phased array."

"Aye sir. Initiating phased array feed now…. No contacts. My board is clear, except for the *Invincible*."

So there was nothing in the sky, or on the surface of the sea within the range of their radars, but Rodenko knew Tasarov too well to dismiss what he was saying here lightly.

"When did you first pick this up, Tasarov?"

"Three days ago, sir."

"And you didn't report it?"

"Well sir, I was off duty at the time, trying to get some sleep in my quarters."

"You heard this in your quarters?"

"And I heard the same thing again here, sir. Just now. I know it sounds silly, but I feel something is wrong."

Rodenko crossed his arms. He had heard the rumors about Lenkov as well, though he had not been fully briefed on the incident. Whatever had happened to the man, it seemed to have a good many crewmen upset. But Tasarov was telling him he heard this three days ago. He might have a case of the jitters, he thought. Lord knows they all had frazzled nerves these days. But something in what Tasarov was saying touched one of those nerves in him as well. He could not quite put his finger on it himself, but it was an odd feeling of discontent, a strange, unaccountable disquiet that had come over him of late, and he could sense that others in the crew also felt this way. Now, for the first time, he had Tasarov telling him he was hearing something—a sound—something deeper than sound at the moment—and it was raising the sonar man's hackles. He looked across the bridge to the weather deck where Orlov was taking in some air. Then he remembered something.

"Very well. Mister Tasarov, I want you to listen for this as you would any potential undersea contact. Let us classify it as Alpha One for the moment—One being an unclassified sound that cannot yet be reported as a contact. Report suspected contact on Alpha Three. Alpha Five is your threshold for confidence high, and Alpha Seven is your threshold of absolute certainty. Listen to this sound, whatever it is, and treat it like any other potential undersea threat. You are the best in the fleet, but I'll get a message off to *Kazan* as well and tell them we may have hold of something. Their man Chernov can lend a hand, and he can send us data from beneath the thermocline."

"Very good sir." Tasarov felt better now that he had at least reported the matter. He always liked Rodenko. The *Starpom* was a sensor man at heart, and knew what it was like to ferret out certainty from the data cloud that was at times very fuzzy. He felt relieved, the situation was heard and handled as any ship's business, and now he also had an ally out there on *Kazan*. He knew Chernov, and together they made perhaps the best sonar team in the world. In this world, that went without question, but even the Americans of 2021 would have a tough time standing up two men as skilled at the art of sonar as Tasarov and Chernov.

Now Rodenko was out through the hatch to the weather deck where Orlov was just finishing a smoke. The moon was finally rising, a thin crescent low over the sea, as they were now some hours west of Gibraltar after their successful run through the straits.

"Looks like nobody is getting any sleep tonight, Chief," said Rodenko. "Aren't you scheduled to go on leave soon?"

"Ten minutes," said Orlov. "I always have a smoke on the weather deck just before I go below."

"Tasarov is on to something."

"Oh? Enemy U-boat?"

"He doesn't think so. The signal is too undefined at the moment. Funny thing is this. He says he heard it three days ago in his quarters."

"Off duty? I know he listens to his music on those head sets down there, but how could he hear anything unless he was processing it through our sonars?"

"Best ears in the fleet, Chief. You know that as well as I."

"So what did he hear?"

"He wasn't sure—just a feeling, but it has him a bit rattled. He says it's some kind of deep sound, and maybe below the threshold of hearing at this point. But he can feel it. Didn't you report something like that on the mission to Ilanskiy?"

Orlov had been trying to live that down for some time. "So I got spooked down there on the taiga, what of it? Better men than me have gone mad down there. You know where we were?"

"The Stony Tunguska. Yes, I heard the story. Look Chief, I'm not riding you here. I just want to see if Tasarov might be hearing something like that sound you reported."

"I see… well I wasn't the only one. Ask Troyak, he heard it. The other Marines heard it too."

"What was it like?"

The Chief took one last drag on his cigarette, and blew the smoke away, flicking the butt over the gunwale into the sea far below them. "It was just like that," he said. "Like something was breathing you in, and out again, real slow, and then they threw your burned out soul off into oblivion. It was feeling like you were a doomed man, damned, and hell was finally right there beneath your feet. Oh, you couldn't see anything, just the trees, the sky, and that weird cauldron in the clearing where we landed. You couldn't really hear anything either. It was so still you could barely breathe. In fact, your breath was the one thing you could actually hear, that and your heart beating fast. You wanted to run, but could see no reason why. Ask Troyak, He has a name for it. Deep sound. That's what he called it. He says they trained the Marines to listen up to that shit and take it like a man. Well, I never got the training. Whatever it was, it made me feel like I wanted to crap in my pants. Seriously!"

"Ever hear anything like that again?"

"Nope. Not since we got away from that damn place…. Wait a second. Now that you mention it, I found that object there, the thing I gave Fedorov. Troyak called it the Devil's Teardrop. Well, I still had it in my pocket when we went out to the Libyan Desert with that Popski fellow. I was playing with it, just tossing it about from one hand to another, when I started to get that same odd feeling again, just like before. Next thing I knew the damn thing got hot as hell, and I dropped it right in the sand. It was glowing like those radar screens of yours, and the sky was all lit up. After that we ran into the Brits, and Fedorov says he thinks that Devil's Teardrop had something to do with that. Who knows Rodenko? That thing is still on the ship here. Fedorov says he's locked it away, but its right here on the ship. Maybe its acting up again. Tasarov feels upset? So do a lot of other people on this ship."

Orlov looked at his watch, seeing his last ten minutes were up and he was now scheduled for leave. "That's my shift, Rodenko. I'm off for a good meal and a good sleep, and I better not hear any of this Tasarov crap, or this Lenkov shit either. Can you believe that?"

"I heard the rumors. Sounds pretty strange. You going to check in on the galley? I hear Zolkin is still down there with the engineers."

"No thanks. I eat in the officer's mess again, like always. Have a good shift, Mister Starpom." Orlov nodded as he left, leaving Rodenko alone on the weather deck..

Deep sound, he thought. Orlov is no pushover. If he was rattled by something like that, then maybe it does have something to do with that thing he found on the taiga. After all, Tasarov says he heard this sound in his quarters. He first heard it right here in the ship, not by listening to something in the sea. Yet now he hears it on his headset, if I understood his report. I'd better keep an ear on this one as well. Fedorov may want to know about it, and the next time I go below, I'll run it by Troyak and see what he says. If he gave that thing a name, maybe the Sergeant knows more than he's said about it.

As for this business with Lenkov... What in god's name happened to that man? Stuck in the galley deck? Fedorov should be back soon. He'll know something about it. But why do I have the feeling that something is starting to slip here. The ship seems fine. Engines are running smooth. Dobrynin has not reported anything unusual. Yet Tasarov had it right. Something is wrong.

I can feel it...

Chapter 15

"**You** mean to say that Lenkov's legs simply ceased to exist?" said Fedorov. "Why not the rest of him?"

"Who knows?" said Kamenski. "He was out of phase with the rest of things. Why? Who can say? It could have been mere happenstance, a local event that was confined to the space he inhabited at that moment."

"Why did this happen to him and not anyone else?"

"Now you question the choices Death makes," said Kamenski. "Yes, why not you; why not me? I'm an old man, with far fewer days ahead of me than those I left behind. Lenkov was young, with his whole life before him. Yet it was his process that fell out of sync with the rest of us, and through no failing of his own. Why do leaves fall in autumn, Fedorov? Who decides which ones go first?"

Fedorov knew the questions he was asking were those asked by millions before him. Why my son, my daughter, mother, father? One day we all realize the truth of what Kamenski was saying, that the solidity and apparent permanence of our lives, our minds, was a fragile and transitory thing. Yes, one day we realize we are verbs, and not nouns after all. But none of this was going to help him with the problem he struggled with now.

"But the galley table and chairs are all there," he said. "Nothing seems disturbed or out of place. If this was a local event, wouldn't it effect the table, or the chair he was sitting on?"

"Everything has a vibration, Fedorov. Those things may not have phased."

"Phased?"

"Yes, we had a name for it, or at least the technicians and scientists did. They called it quantum phasing. It happens in the thermodynamic universe as temperatures change, like water changing to ice. In this case, it is something more. The phase change causes the object to fall out of sync with time. It falls behind, or moves ahead, and if the ship itself was also phasing, then when

Lenkov settled down, he found himself in the wrong place at the wrong time, quite literally. I have seen this before. We put an apple in a lead box during one test, and watched it disappear. Where they went, nobody knows, but the box reappeared some hours later. The apple, however, was gone."

Fedorov did not like the sound of that. Thus far all their time displacements had left the ship and crew remarkably intact—until Lenkov. These phase changes, as Kamenski described it, were only transitory effects on the edges of a shift. But here they were, with no Rod-25, no nuclear detonations, and yet the ship was phasing, pulsing, as he liked to think of it. And now Lenkov's fate endowed that behavior with a peril he had not considered before.

"Do you think this will happen again?"

"You might ask Chief Dobrynin how the ship is doing," said Kamenski. "You say this pulsing has happened before, then yes, it seems likely it will happen again. Lenkov's fate was a new twist in that rope, a new consequence."

"I have wondered if it is an effect we experienced because we are approaching Paradox Hour," said Fedorov. "I have come to believe that Paradox can exert the force of annihilation. That's what I thought was happening when I first saw Lenkov. In fact, I was thinking we would be forcing time to do something about us if we lingered here, and Lenkov's fate sends chills up my spine. Yet now you bring up this point about the ship itself. It shifted here safely, yet surely the metal in this hull was in the ground here somewhere, just as you say."

"But in another form," said Kamenski. "Down on the atomic level, yes, the atoms were here. They have very long lives. Do you realize the atoms that make up your body this moment are ancient, perhaps billions of years old, all forged in the heart of stars eons ago? Yet there they are, all neatly arranged to give us the pleasure of your company. The same is true of me, though they might have worked in a few more for the hair on the top of my head."

Kamenski smiled, tamping down his pipe a bit. "All this talk, sounding like philosophy, is actually the reality of things. A billion years is a very long time, Mister Fedorov. Who knows what those atoms in your body were once part of, and what they have been doing in all that time? Might they have been a dinosaur once? Now they are a ship's Captain, with a lot on his shoulders at the moment. Just remember, you are not responsible for the way fate and time chooses to play with all the particles of this universe. We won't be here long, you and I. My flame is already guttering, though yours may have a while to burn before it is blown out. Yet all the time that remains to us both here is but the wink of an eye in this universe. It's a pity that we will never know what time chooses to do with the stuff of these old bones down the road. Forgive me for running on like this. I realize this does little to console you or solve your immediate problem."

"I think of these things myself," said Fedorov. "Yet now, facing the prospect of this Paradox, I reach for the answers with a little more urgency. Your point about the metal in the ship's hull caught me off guard. How could the ship be here if the atoms that make it up were also here, no matter what form they were in? You just said they have a very long life span. They were here! Yet so is *Kirov*. I don't understand."

"Quantum entanglement," said Kamenski. "Do you know down on that level just about everything is a real slippery fish. Particles wink in and out of existence, like Lenkov's legs. They are here, then not here, which is also true of particles that make up our bodies at this very moment. You see, we are really very insubstantial, speaking in quantum terms. Everything is inherently uncertain, according to a fellow named Heisenberg. You can't even specify exactly where any of these little particles are. Particles arise in pairs where one partner seems to know what is going on or happening to its mate, even though that other partner may be millions of miles away… or millions of years. Einstein called it 'spooky action at a distance.' He didn't like it, but the theory put forward by Niels Bohr has subsequently been proven correct. Yes, things act that way. It's as if you had an identical twin back in Vladivostok, and still living in the year 2021. Yet he seems to know what you had for breakfast this morning. Interesting, yes?"

"Are you suggesting the atoms in the ship's hull were paired with those in the ground? Entangled?"

"That's one possibility. If so, they would get on quite well together, like a pair of dance partners, no matter how far away they were from one another, or how close. Here's another idea. In making this ship, we interacted with that material to a very significant degree. Interacting with quantum particles, even something as simple as observing them, can change them. We altered temperatures, blended the metals into alloys and with other synthetic materials, moved electrons around. Frankly, I think that interaction was sufficient to alter the state of the material on a quantum level, so when the ship displaced here, there was no conflict with the atoms that were already in the ground. They simply were not sharing the same quantum state any longer."

"Altered states," said Fedorov slowly. "What you said a moment ago is very intriguing... quantum entanglement... Like Tovey!" Fedorov exclaimed. "Yes... A quantum pairing. Admiral Tovey seems to be able to recall experiences he had with us when we first met him in 1942, yet here he is in 1941, before any of that ever happened, and in a life line that will probably preclude those events from ever occurring here. Yet he knows about that other John Tovey. The word *Geronimo* struck through him like a bolt when he first heard it. He instinctively knew it referred to *Kirov*. How is this possible, Director? How could he know things he experienced in the future?"

"Yes, it is very surprising, But it has been demonstrated that quantum particles can do some amazing things. Another physicist, Yakir Aharonov, was looking at entangled particles, and trying to gain information about them without disturbing them or altering their state—taking a little peek at them without really looking. I suppose we've all done that when a pair of pretty legs goes by. Yes? It was determined that these little peeks, which he called weak measurements, might be added up to provide enough information about the particles to predict the state of one or another. Then it was shown that this activity also caused the particles to alter in the past! They were changing to make the information he was obtaining possible! Consider that for a moment. We easily grasp that things we do in the here and now might affect our future, but never our past. In this case, Aharonov showed that activity in the future can indeed affect the same particle in the past, because entangled particles seem to possess information or qualities from both temporal localities, past and future. This all gets very confusing, Fedorov. But there is your Admiral Tovey, here in 1941, and he is being obviously affected by experiences he had in 1942! I do not know if this theory is correct, but it at least gives us some way of trying to understand it. Think of it as backward causality."

"But how, sir? Are you saying that the future Tovey was in another world, another universe, yet remains entangled with the man sailing off our port side in this moment?"

"Some people think of time like a tree, Mister Fedorov. Think of the trunk as the present. It grew from the roots of many possibilities in the past, which all joined to create this reality, and here we sit like a pair of squirrels clinging to the bark. Above us the tree again branches out into many possibilities—the future. As we climb, we have to choose which branch to jump on next. Maybe we choose a branch that eventually leads us to fruit, but suppose we end up on a dead branch instead, with withered foliage. That's life at times, eh? Sadly, we never get to back-track, as the squirrel might, and choose another branch—until now... You were here *before*, Fedorov. You have seen that withered branch and returned to the 1940s, and now you make choices and decisions that continue to prune that tree and shape how it grows in the future."

"Is information from that other world being communicated to this one? Like a squirrel finding an acorn on one branch, and bringing it with him when he jumps to another?"

"That may be a good way to understand it," said Kamenski. "It's a trick entangled particles pull off quite easily, in spite of Einstein's objection. No one knows how they do it yet, but it happens. It's been proven in physical experiments. Lagrangian mechanics says that if the past affects the future, the opposite relation is also true—the future can affect the past. That said, neither you or I are going to solve this by discussing quantum mechanics. The fact remains that Admiral Tovey has been influenced by those future events, even if the new state he finds himself in now precludes those events from ever taking place. Information is coming to him from another branch, and you may be the squirrel that brought it here."

"Me?"

"I should say we, the ship, our presence. These things started with Tovey only after *Kirov* manifested here. He was not remembering things from your earlier encounters before our arrival. Correct?"

Could this be so? Fedorov had been doing a good deal of reading in the ship's library, trying to find any information he could that might help him sort through this situation. Could this be so? Could our very presence here be catalyzing these entanglements? Then he suddenly remembered the other anomalies Tovey had revealed.

"It was more than information that passed from that world to this one," he said. "There were physical objects, photographs, reports."

"Those may have been brought here, like this ship we are sitting on, Mister Fedorov."

"Agreed, though we have yet to put our finger on who may have done that. Alan Turing suggested something else, and it had something to do with his watch. Yes, Turing's watch!"

"Refresh me on that, Mister Fedorov. Things go in and out of my head too easily these days."

"Alan Turing, sir. Surely you know who he is, the famous British cryptographer."

"Of course," said Kamenski. "We owe a lot to that man. What would the KGB have done without him?" He smiled.

"Well sir, I was told something by Admiral Tovey that was quite startling. He said Turing had a favorite watch that went missing one day, and it was later discovered in that file box I told you about."

"You mean the one with all that material dated to 1942?"

"Yes sir. Now the odd thing is this… Turing claims that the watch appeared the very same day we arrived here, in June of 1940."

"I suppose he had some evidence for that?" said Kamenski.

"Apparently so. Yet the point is that he correctly deduced that the file box was a remnant of our first encounters—from that other time. He suggested it may have been dragged into this time when we appeared here last June, like a bit of seaweed trailing behind the ship. The problem was that he found his watch in that file box. Who knows how it got there, but this is what Tovey told me. Now then… when that file box appeared, Turing says Time would have been faced with a little problem. His watch was already here! Yet it went missing in this world, until he found it in that file box."

"Interesting," said Kamenski, taking a long draw on his pipe. "Very interesting…" He leaned forward, and Fedorov could sense something was of some concern to him now.

"I was not sure what to make of that file box being discovered here," he said. "In fact, I hoped my first assessment of that was correct—that it was brought here by someone. That alone is enough of a mystery to keep one up a good many nights, because it would mean we have another agent at large in the history here."

"Another agent? You mean someone else capable of moving in time? That would mean they deliberately brought that material here."

"Indeed it would," said Kamenski. "Yet this business with Mister Turing's watch is another unexpected wrinkle. You are correct in thinking it was a nice little bit of work for Paradox. The way it resolved itself was rather clever, don't you think? It simply moved the watch, but moving it may have meant that when it first disappeared, it literally winked out of existence for a time until manifesting again in that file box."

"Like that apple that disappeared from the box you mentioned," said Fedorov. "So now you see what has been weighing on me so heavily, Director. In my mind, *Kirov* is like that box, and everyone else on board is just like that apple. Time will soon be faced with the arrival of this ship here on July 28th, and I would hate to think my fate, and yours, would be resolved in the same way Turing's watch was handled. Winking out of existence may be very uncomfortable. Thinking about that, and seeing what happened to Lenkov… Well that will keep me up a good many nights. My great fear is that this is only just beginning."

Now Kamenski was silent for a time, thinking… thinking.

"Do you play chess, Mister Fedorov? Most people think of time like that—a good game of chess. It has a clear opening, development, and then the end game—beginning, middle, end. The pieces dance around the board until one King or another, light or dark, becomes frozen, unable to make any move without exposing itself to fatal capture—checkmate. People think of their lives that way, piece by piece, move by move. They play the white pieces, always stalked and pursued by the dark side—fate. Each new move creates a new position or circumstance, and the players sit there, thinking through each position and trying to analyze all possible outcomes in the future. Those chess positions, the placement of pieces on the board after any given move, are like the moments of our lives. We decide something, push a piece to another square, then swipe the start button on the chess clock, while the other side, dark fate, acts in consequence to what we have done. As the game progresses, the board changes from one position to another, like the days of our lives. And so people think it goes, move by move, day by day, moment by moment…"

Kamenski smiled, taking a moment to savor his pipe. "But time isn't like that at all," he asserted, "because there are no moments in life, only moves. Yes, that is the reality of things! The pieces always keep moving, and there is never ever any instant when they are frozen in place for us to contemplate what we might do next. A good chess player must think on the move, because that clock is always ticking. Consider that, Mister Fedorov."

Kamenski shifted quietly in his chair, scratching his chin as he continued. "There are no 'moments,' only a constant expression of motion. That realization alone upsets Zeno's applecart full of paradoxes. He was another fellow a bit obsessed by the notion of paradox. Take his assertion about the arrow, for example. He said that if every object occupying a point in space is at rest, and a moving arrow must past through a series of points in space, then it must be at rest in each and every one, and therefore could not be moving."

"Very clever," said Fedorov.

"But very wrong," said Kamenski. "Old Zeno tried to prove motion was an illusion, that life was like a series of frames in a movie—or a series of positions in a chess game, but he actually had it backwards. This notion of fixed moments in time—that is the illusion, a mere convention of thought. To put it simply, things don't stay put. They are never here, never in any frozen moment we may choose to call this present, because *there are no such moments*, only constant change and motion—constant uncertainty. And if they are never here, then they are never anywhere else either. In that light, time takes on a whole new meaning. 1941? 2021? These are not places, Fedorov, they are activities, movement in a dance. To go to one or the other you simply have to change your behavior—step lively, and learn the dance of infinity. You see, anything can be expressed in that dance—anything—but the opposite is also true. Nothing is just as satisfactory a state of affairs as everything, as far as the universe is concerned, and one may become the other in the wink of an eye…"

Kamenski set down his pipe with a sigh, watching the last curling wisps of smoke rise from the bowl, thin and insubstantial. When he finally spoke, his voice had a grave tone, and the usual glib confidence of the man was gone. Instead he was darkly serious, eyeing Fedorov with his unwavering gaze as he spoke.

"Your fear is that Lenkov's fate is a foreshock of what is to come for the rest of us—for the ship. That may be so, Mister Fedorov. Soon it won't be just the watch we quibble about, or those file boxes, or even the fate of this ship and crew. You see, time is not what you think it is. Nothing ever stays put, and things seem to be shaking loose in some rather alarming ways these days. If this continues, that word Miss Fairchild used to describe the situation we may be facing here was quite accurate—Grand Finality."

Part VI

The King's Business

""Is there not here under thine hand spear or sword, for I have neither brought sword nor my weapons with me, because the king's business requires haste"

— 1 Sam. 21:8

Chapter 16

Air defense officer Lieutenant Don Campbell did not expect to be very busy that week. HMS *Rodney* left the Clyde some days ago, steaming with the troop ship *Britannic*, the third ship in the ill-fated White Star line to bear that name, and four destroyers, *Eskimo*, *Mashona*, *Somali* and *Tartar*. A bright faced young man, Campbell was glad he was not yet on duty in the gun director Octopodial behind and above the bridge. It was a lonesome, windswept eyrie high above the conning tower, and very lightly armored. While the men there had a splendid view of everything around them, they also suffered from numb hands, red noses, and cold faces, with too little to keep them warm. Instead, Campbell was on the bridge, seeing to some crew re-assignments with a staff officer.

"I'll be one man short today," he said. "Lennox is down with a gut buster. Anyone free for duty on my station?"

"I can give you Mister Byers when he's finished ferrying Captain Coppinger back over to *Britannic*."

"Good Enough. Shall we say zero nine-hundred hours?"

"I'll have him there."

Rodney was well out to sea on her secret mission, the King's business beneath a cover of old crates and boiler tubes all over the decks. A message had come in from the fleet flagship, and it was something Captain Dalrymple-Hamiltion wanted to discuss with Coppinger, Captain of the White Star liner *Britannic*. The two men were meeting in the plot room, their voices low and hushed, which was enough to arouse Campbell's curiosity. Campbell was just about to leave when they emerged on the bridge again, and the ship's Captain caught his eye.

"Ah, Mister Campbell, I'll want you and your people sharp today, and I'll have to ask you to take your watch station a bit early."

"Of course, sir," said Campbell, realizing that there went breakfast, and he would be lucky if he could even get down a cup of tea now before he went aloft to his assigned perch on the Octopodial. "I was just seeing to crew assignments."

"Very good," said Hamilton. "Because it seems we're going to be paid a visit soon. You'll probably be one of the first to make the sighting, so be on the lookout for a ship coming up from the south. We're to make a rendezvous, and will have visitors aboard soon after."

The staff officer heard that, realizing the man he had just re-assigned might be needed at his regular post. "Excuse me, Captain," he said. "Will we be needing the cutter?"

"No, they'll come to us when they get here."

It was not the only thing coming at that moment. A watchman suddenly shouted out a warning: "Torpedo off the starboard bow!" Yet it was too late. Seconds later the was a dull thump, and then a shuddering explosion. Far beneath the sea, a man with a very peculiar fate had just struck a blow that would change the whole complexion of the mission.

* * *

Days earlier, *U-556* under her young captain Herbert Wohlfarth had left the submarine base at Kiel for his first patrol in this new boat. It was the third U-boat he had commanded, after logging nine kills in U-14 in the first eight months of the war, and then almost equaling that when he was re-assigned to U-137 in September of 1940, with eight more kills. The biggest feather in his cap to date had been the armed merchant steamer HMS *Cheshire*, at over 10,000 tons, and now he was hoping to better that on his maiden patrol in U-556.

Strangely, his personal fate seemed to be entangled with that of one of the ships now operating in these waters, and the connection persisted, like that of two entangled particles, even though this was an altered state of affairs. Newly built, U-556 had the distinction to berth right next to the mighty *Bismarck* while she was also fitting out, and came to think of her as an elder sibling.

Wohlfarth had developed a strange connection between his boat with *Bismarck*, perhaps like a pair of entangled quantum particles, as Director Kamenski might have explained it. He had pledged he would defend the mighty *Bismarck* in any sea, and do his utmost to keep the ship from harm. And now he was to get his chance in a way he could not yet truly fathom.

His big brother had been gone for some time, sailing in the Mediterranean with the fleet flagship, and Wohlfarth had been appalled when he heard the news that both ships had been hit by a strange new British weapon at sea—a rocket. It worked just like a torpedo, or so the rumors had it, only it flew through the sky instead of hiding beneath the sea, and like an aircraft, it had a very long range.

Wohlfarth went so far as to request his next mission might end in a French port instead of seeing him return to Kiel, thinking he might slowly work his way into a berthing at the new German base at Gibraltar, and a Mediterranean patrol to be closer to *Bismarck*. He learned that both Bismarck and *Hindenburg* would be laid up in the French port of Toulon for some time, getting refitted with fresh armor plating and a few innovations designed to give them better protection against these rocket weapons. Then news came that *Hindenburg* was returning to the Atlantic, and *Bismarck* would be coming along with the flagship to prey on the convoys Wohlfarth had been feasting on in his earlier patrols. What could be better!

He set out from Kiel ten days earlier than he did in the history Fedorov knew, and soon got his first chance at action when he encountered a small 160 ton steam trawler off the Faeroes Islands. He had been ordered there to observe and report on operations at the new British airfield, but when he encountered the *Emanuel*, he could not resist. Not wanting to waste a torpedo on a small vessel like that, Wohlfarth surfaced and sunk it quickly with his deck gun. It was a small kill, and nothing much to boast about, but he would take it, and sail on with the hope of getting many more.

Fleet rumors had been circulating at Kiel, saying that the whole navy was out to sea now, and something very big was in the works. The truth of that was soon made apparent to him when he was ordered to scout the channel between the Faeroes and Iceland. *Tirpitz*, the sister ship of *Bismarck*, was leading another powerful German task force there, intending to break out and join the *Hindenburg* group in the Atlantic.

It was a grand operation, and he was proud to be a part of it. Then came the coded orders from Group West that befuddled him. He was ordered to alter his course immediately, turn south, and be on the lookout for any British convoys escorted by battleships.

"A pity," said Wohlfarth. "We're going to miss seeing the *Tirpitz* in action. All the fun will be further west."

"Perhaps," said his navigator, Sub-Lieutenant Souvad. "A convoy to the south sounds like good prey."

"Escorted by a battleship? You know they only assign the older ships to that duty," said Wohlfarth. "They are too fat and slow to run with the action out west. And where those ships sail, there will be destroyers."

"Still, we might find better fare there," Souvad suggested. "Destroyers are always a problem, but this new boat is very quiet. And remember, *Bismarck* is coming out of the Med. You may get a chance to make good on your pledge, Kapitan."

"*Bismarck* has good company now," said Wohlfarth. "But orders are orders. Come to one-eight-zero. We will see what has Group West all in a tither."

A few days later he had his answer. There, right in the center of his periscope, was one of those old battleships he had been talking about, and a nice fat steamship liner right in her wake! Wohlfarth had come upon a small, heavily guarded convoy, and he knew immediately what he was looking at.

"Good lord," he said. "That's the *Rodney!*"

HMS *Rodney*, an interwar build, had an unmistakable silhouette because all of her big guns were on the forward segment of the ship, with her armored superstructure and bridge con well back of the huge turrets, like a solitary iron tower. Slow and heavily armored, the *Rodney* was often used in convoy escort roles, as her best practical speed was in the range of eighteen to twenty-one knots, though she normally cruised at fifteen to eighteen knots. From the size of her bow wash, Wohlfarth estimated the ship was moving with some urgency, and he could see a pack of fast destroyers steaming in escort, four in all, with two well ahead, one behind and one closer to *Rodney*, yet on the far side of the ship.

Four destroyers… There must be some reason these two ships are given such an escort. He wondered what it was, having no idea of what *Rodney* carried in her hold, or the fact that there were 550 precious pilot trainees embarked aboard *Britannic* at that moment, bound for training in the US under a secret agreement with the Americans. It was the business of war, made even more vital by adding in the King's business. And yet no one back in London, or Buckingham Palace, knew the most precious thing at stake at that moment—the key embedded in the base of the Selene Horse, crated away in *Rodney's* hold.

He had been lucky enough to get this sighting in a perfect position to fire, and perhaps he could get both these big ships before those destroyers forced him to run for his life. The temptation was overwhelming.

Sink an oiler or merchant ship, and they say well done when you get back home, he thought. But if I were to hit that battleship… That's a knights cross sitting out there, right in front of me, and right behind it is my oak leave cluster. This is too good to be true!

He turned to his Executive Officer Schaefer with a gleam in his eye. "Pass the word for battle stations, but make it very quiet. No alarm. There are four destroyers up there!" His blood was up and he was eager for a fight.

"You're going to take a shot at that battleship?"

"What do you think they give us torpedoes for, Herr Schaefer? I think this is the ship we were told to look for."

"Are you certain?" asked his navigator Souvad. The thought of those four destroyers was none too comforting.

"Look out for convoys escorted by battleships," said Wohlfarth. "Well, that is exactly what we have in front of us."

"Shouldn't we report it first?"

"And let it slip away? The damn ship is probably zig-zagging. It could turn at any moment, and right now, we have perfect alignment, and plenty of torpedoes. Ready forward tubes!"

And so he fired his underwater version of a naval rocket. The torpedoes had a very short range, but they were very deadly, and soon struck home with a big water splash and booming sound that they could all hear. U-556 had put its hands on HMS *Rodney*, interfering with the King's business, and it was going to complicate things more than anyone realized just then.

* * *

"**Well** Gentlemen," said Tovey. "We have a problem." The Admiral had signaled *Kirov* that he wished to convene a private conference using the special equipment the Russian engineers had given him. They had rigged out a small radio set, with special encryption module, that would allow *Kirov* and *Invincible* to communicate by voice without the need to worry their conversations might be intercepted. Using the computing power available to them, they were rapidly rotating the encryption stream on the data, and unscrambling it as the signal was received on each unit. Anyone listening in would just hear a wash of static that would sound like jamming, but the communication was crystal clear on both the friendly ships, and it was something no power on this earth of 1941 could ever decipher or unscramble. A similar unit was given to the *Argos Fire* to allow Miss Fairchild to listen in from her executive office.

Tovey had more to discuss than simple wireless message traffic could easily carry. He opened the conference with the news he had just received from Captain Dalrymple-Hamilton on *Rodney*.

"In spite of our best effort, it appears we're already too late. *Rodney* has happened across a German U-boat, and she's been hit by a torpedo, right amidships. There's flooding below decks, very near the cargo hold, and a small list has started. They will counter-flood, but the outcome is uncertain. Seas are rising, and things could get… difficult."

Elena Fairchild cringed at that. She was listening with her own Captain Gordon MacRae, and Mack Morgan. She fingered the send button, unable to contain herself. "Is the ship in danger of sinking?" she asked, the worry evident in her voice.

"Not at the moment," came Tovey's reply. "But that could change. There were four destroyers in escort, and they went off like mad hounds after that U-boat. There was no confirmed kill, but the enemy appears to have been beaten off. *Rodney* has had to cut speed to ten knots, and now it appears unlikely that she'll be able to make the transit to Boston. Her Captain has convened a meeting of his own, and he's asking me for orders now. Admiralty will hear about this in due course and weigh in. It's very likely the ship may be recalled to a British port. In that event, sailing in and announcing you have a cargo inspection to make will be somewhat complicated. In fact, it may be out of the question. Any suggestions?"

"We need to get to that ship while she is still at sea," said Elena. "I can break off and make the rendezvous directly if you still wish to stay in pursuit of the *Hindenburg*."

"Yes," said Tovey. "I had thought I might be of some use in that meeting, but we've other news that bears on all of this. The *Tirpitz* group is making a good run on the Faeroes-Iceland Gap. *King George V* and *Prince of Wales* are on that watch, but we must plan for every contingency. If those ship's break through, I'm afraid *Invincible*, and the Fleet Admiral commanding her, will have to continue west."

"Then we must divide our forces," Admiral Volsky suggested. "I might recommend that we send our own submarine, *Kazan*, along with Miss Fairchild. That would secure the undersea threat to *Rodney*. As for your business west, Admiral Tovey, I do not think it wise that you sail alone. *Kirov* will accompany you, and we will stay in the chase. Does anyone object?"

"That is well and good, Admiral," came Tovey's voice. "Captain Hamilton has asked about transferring his cargo to *Britannic*. In fact, if it is determined that his ship is seriously compromised by this damage, I believe that is exactly what the Admiralty will order."

"They'll attempt to move all that cargo?" said Fairchild. "Won't that be dangerous. Gold bullion and these Elgin marbles are quite heavy."

"Indeed," said Tovey. "It would mean that Britannic will have to moor alongside Rodney, and the two ships will be one big target if there are any more U-Boats in the region."

"All the more reason to get *Kazan* moving as soon as possible," said Volsky. "Gromyko may have more work than he expected out here."

The Admiral's comment was prophetic, and it was a matter of some discussion far to the north, where another conference of Naval hat bands was being convened aboard the Battleship *Rodney*.

Chapter 17

HMS Rodney, 00:10 hours, 6 May, 1941

"Well Gentlemen, that's our present situation," said Captain Hamilton. "We've no further instructions from the Admiralty, but that could change. Your thoughts are, of course, welcome."

The Captain had pulled his senior officers together, the Commander John Grindle, RN, the navigator Lt. Cdr. George Gatacre, RAN, the Torpedo Officer Lt. Cdr. Roger Lewis, RN, Captain Coppinger from *Britannic*, and an American, one Lieutenant Commander Joseph H. Wellings, USN. He looked at the American as if he knew the man would be the first to speak, and he was not disappointed.

Wellings had come aboard as a liaison officer, and was now returning home to the United States. He seemed to want Dalrymple-Hamilton's ear the moment he arrived, and had pressed him on details concerning the ship's course, and other events underway that might affect operations here.

"If I may, sir," said Wellings. "What's to be gained by holding this heading? With that torpedo damage, we'll be lucky to make ten knots, and the danger from U-boats remains very real. Beyond that, I have learned there is a strong German battlegroup to our northeast. A lame duck makes for easy prey. If they get wind of us here, our situation could become even more perilous."

He was a tall, thin man, dark eyed, clean, and dressed out in proper US Navy whites. The stripes on his cuff and shoulder insignia made him to be a Lieutenant Commander.

But Wellings was more than he seemed.

He had first come on the scene in Bristol, England, near the Clyde anchorage where HMS *Rodney* had been waiting to escort Convoy WS-8B on her initial outward leg, before breaking off with *Britannic* and heading west to Halifax and Boston. It was the second half of the 'Winston Special' series that was bound to reinforce the British position in Egypt. The first half had been designated WS-8A, dubbed the Tiger Convoy by Sir Winston himself, as he wanted it to sail boldly across the Med instead of going round the Cape of Good Hope. Thankfully, he had been persuaded that would be suicidal, and the presence of unexpected reinforcements in Egypt mitigated the urgency.

So Tiger Convoy had become a domestic cat instead, passing safely round the cape, and making a much needed delivery of precious Matilda and Crusader tanks, and Hurricane fighters, to General Wavell. Those tanks would soon help Wavell and O'Connor hold off Rommel's new offensive aimed at Tobruk.

That night in Bristol the real Lieutenant Commander Wellings, USN, was having dinner at a hotel when a tall man in crisp navy whites came drifting into the dining room, his eyes searching and immediately falling on his fellow naval officer. He came right over, removing his cap as he spoke.

"Lieutenant Wellings?"

"Yes?"

"May I join you, sir?"

Wellings was accustomed to receiving odd messages at any hour, for he had been an American Assistant Naval Attaché in London for the last year. Now he was heading home, scheduled to board the British battleship *Rodney* for the trans-Atlantic cruise. The battleship would escort Convoy WS-8B out of the Clyde, and then eventually steam for New York and Boston for a refit.

The man seated himself opposite Wellings and smiled. "Forgive the interruption, sir, but I have new orders for you."

"New orders?"

"Yes, sir." The man handed him an envelope. "It seems Washington would like you home just a bit sooner. You're now scheduled to fly out of Bristol on DC-3 number 171, sir. Your flight will leave at 20:30 hours. One stop at Reykjavik, Iceland for a 24 hour layover."

"Damn," said Wellings. "That's only just enough time to get to the air field."

"Oh, don't worry, sir, I've arranged a cab for you. It should be waiting outside in about twenty minutes. They'll hold the plane." The man looked at a wrist watch, too loose on his thin wrist, and smiled again. "I'm terribly sorry, sir. Somewhat of an inconvenience, but at least you'll get straight home in a couple of days."

"Better than idling aboard *Rodney* for a week," said Wellings, finally warming to the idea. The man saluted, excused himself, and slipped away. He didn't even recall his name, though he did note the man was of equal rank. Funny he should not have met him sooner, but he assumed he was one of many new officers arriving in theater as the war began to heat up to a low boil.

We'll be in it soon enough, he thought, but for the moment I'm happy to be out of it. Wellings finished his steak, quaffing down the glass of wine he had hoped to linger over, then opened the envelope and briefly noted his new assignment. Everything seemed in order—a bit hastily typed, but in order. He sighed, looking at his watch, then got up and went to look for the cab.

Hours later a man boarded HMS *Rodney* with a crisp salute as he was piped on, one Lieutenant Commander Wellings, American Liaison to the Admiralty, at least according to the guest manifest. Yet he was not who he seemed.

Sometime later Wellings sat contentedly in his navy whites, and comfortably in his assumed identity, one of seven men around a table in the Captain's quarters on HMS *Rodney*. They had been detached ten hours ago, and Convoy WS-8B was now steaming due south, diverted away from the area where the Royal Navy was trying to find and engage a German raiding task force led by the much feared battleship *Tirpitz*. Captain Hamilton was looking for support for a decision he was already leaning heavily on, and Wellings was just the man to give it to him.

"I've got some information I've been ordered to share, sir."

"Information?"

"Yes, sir," Wellings leaned in, lowering his voice slightly as if to convey the notion that he was now speaking confidentially. The others were clearly interested.

"We have a Coast Guard cutter at sea in the vicinity of the operations out west," he began. "Her regular duty is ice watch patrol, but it seems one of your convoys out of Halifax took it on the chin recently. She was therefore detailed to assist in survivor recovery for convoy HX-126."

"Yes," said Hamilton. "Bloody business that. The poor lot ran afoul of a wolf pack. Lost quite a few ships, I'm afraid."

"Right," said Wellings, "*Cockaponset*, and *British Security* went down in the final attack. *Darlington Court* had a near miss. Well, the *Modoc*, that's our cutter, reported in yesterday, sir, and I am now at liberty to disclose this message to you here. She sighted battleship *Tirpitz* at these coordinates and times." He handed the Captain a paper, and Hamilton squinted at it briefly before handing it off to his navigator.

"If you chart that," Wellings continued, "You'll see that this present heading is all wrong, sir. Your Admiralty may believe the *Tirpitz* group was still on a heading to the southwest, but from this sighting, it's clear they have turned southeast. We believe they are now attempting to rendezvous with another German task force emerging from the Med."

"Bad dinner guests," said Captain Hamilton, "the lot of them."

"I'm afraid so sir," said Wellings. "Remember, *Tirpitz* is not alone. We had seaplanes up from Iceland to see if we could spot this battlegroup, and one had a good look… before it was shot down."

"Nasty flak guns on the *Tirpitz*," said the Captain. "Or so I've heard."

"Oh, it wasn't shot down by flak, it ran into a German fighter patrol. Gentlemen, the German carrier *Graf Zeppelin* is also a part of this enemy battlegroup, along with the battlecruisers *Scharnhorst*, *Gneisenau*, a heavy cruiser and two destroyers. If this is so, our position here, and any further movement west on this course, is extremely hazardous. You'll have to turn due south at once to have any chance in the world of evading the *Tirpitz* battlegroup. In fact, returning to England would be the better course."

"I see," said Hamilton. "Excepting the fact that I have orders to the contrary, Mister Wellings. I assume this report of yours was also forwarded to the Admiralty? We've heard nothing from them at all on this."

"As you might imagine, sir, Western Approaches Command is all astir with this business. The message was sent, but whether it received prompt attention or not is anybody's guess. They may not have picked up this heading change yet. I've been there, and I can say the situation gets a bit chaotic at times, if you don't mind my saying so, sir."

"Not at all," said Hamilton. "Get enough Admirals in any one room and no one ends up knowing what to do." He considered for a moment. "And what course would you say we adopt, Mister Wellings?"

"If you intend to stay at sea, then 180 degrees due south, sir. It's really your only option, and you will have to make your best speed even then, in spite of the damage. Wellings folded his arms. He had made his pitch, and knew enough not to say anything further until someone else spoke first.

"Gentlemen?" Captain Hamilton regarded the other men present, but no one seemed to have any objection to the idea. The navigator knew his business well, and even without having to look at a chart he confirmed what Wellings was saying. "We'll definitely be in the stew here if we don't turn, sir," he said.

"Very well, gentlemen," Captain Hamilton decided. "It may also interest you that I am in receipt of a message from Admiral Tovey that pertains to this decision. In fact, I was just discussing it with Captain Coppinger of the *Britannic* when this damn U-boat stuck it to us. This isn't just any mission we're on here. This is the King's business, and my charge is to get this ship, and its cargo, safely to Boston. However, Admiral Tovey is of a mind with Mister Wellings here. He suggests that given the German operation now underway, to proceed west as planned would be very perilous. In fact, he has asked me to move south to effect a rendezvous at sea with a ship being detached from his task force, an air defense cruiser, though he did not mention what ship. Considering his opinion on this matter as the commander of Home Fleet, and in the absence of any response to my request for instructions from the Admiralty, I think we have a consensus here. I must agree with everything that Mister Wellings has said."

To his navigator and senior staff officer he said: "Come round to course 180 degrees south at once, and give me all the speed we can manage. The faster the better, should there be any more U-boats about. I know the damage control teams will have fits, but it can't be helped. That's a good bit of timely intelligence, Wellings. I appreciate your candor. Now then, let's get another signal off to the Admiralty notifying them of our intentions. I daresay Admiral Pound may have other ideas about it, but I believe Admiral Tovey on *Invincible* will be more than gratified to learn of the action we're taking here."

"Very good, sir," said Captain Coppinger. "Then you won't be transferring your cargo to *Britannic?*"

"That may become necessary at some point," said Hamilton. "But for the moment, we'll keep things as they are."

"Of course," said Coppinger. "And as I would be a fool to continue west under these circumstances, *Britannic* will stay right in your wake."

"That would be wise," said Hamilton. "At least there's nothing wrong with those guns on my forward deck. If things heat up, you'll be glad we're here. Then again, we may be grateful to have a ship at hand capable of taking on our cargo and crew if that damage below cannot be controlled."

"If I may, sir," said Wellings. "I'd like to have a look down below at the damage situation. I heard it was very near the torpedo magazine."

"Close," said Torpedo Officer Lewis, "but no cigar, as you Yanks like to say. We've managed to seal off the water tight doors, and the magazine is not in danger at the moment."

"Might I have a look?" said Wellings again.

"I don't see any harm in that, Wellings. Suit yourself, but some of the engineers can get a bit surly with officers underfoot. Just a warning."

"I understand, sir."

So it was that Wellings had given the situation a brief nudge in the right direction, insofar as he saw things. His intelligence concerning the German movements had been most alarming, and enough to move Dalrymple-Hamilton off his perch of uncertainty. Tovey's request had made that a little easier, in spite of what the Admiralty might say when they got his message informing them of the decision to head south.

All of this had been an unknowing conspiracy of sorts, for Director Kamenski's assessment of one possible reason how those mysterious file boxes might find their way into this world had been very telling. There were, indeed, other agents moving in time, and not only Karpov, driven as he was by his own quest for revenge and personal aggrandizement. They were not the key makers, as Miss Fairchild came to call those mysterious voices and signals from the future that had suddenly gone silent, but one man had once been a key holder himself, the same enigmatic figure who had stopped off at that hotel on a cool night in Bristol, the man who now posed as one Lieutenant Commander Joseph H. Wellings, USN.

Wellings was off at once, soon making his way into the bowels of the lumbering battleship *Rodney*. He knew the way well enough, for he had been there once before, in another time, another evolution of the history of these events. This time, things were different, for he now had foreknowledge of what he would find hidden away in *Rodney's* hold, or at least he believed as much.

Thank God the Captain was as amenable this time as he was before, he thought to himself. Now to get down to that cargo hold and find that key. Will it still be there? Last time the crate it was in took a hard jolt to enable my discovery. Will that have happened again this time? It was only by chance that I went that way, and made my little discovery. I heard the call of that seaman in distress, and my impulse was to answer it. That too was a part of all of this, that one moment of compassion in the heat of all that was happening. Yet something tells me there was more than chance or luck at work in that damn torpedo hit this time around.

Wellings knew much more about all that was now transpiring than he could ever reveal to Captain Hamilton. He knew more than the names of the ships that had suddenly turned in his direction, with new orders—find the *Rodney*, sink her, at any cost... Yes, he knew so very much more... He knew the number on the U-Boat he believed responsible for this recent attack, and who was out there commanding it, caught between a moment of both jubilation and fear as he struggled to evade those four British destroyers.

Wohlfarth! I'm on to you again, you rascal! Something tells me you have much more mischief in mind here, but first things first. Let's hope that torpedo hit was enough to shake things loose here in this Meridian, but not enough to sink this ship before I get my hands on that key!

Chapter 18

There were four of them, and they had been hot on the case for some time now, about much more than the secretive business of the King. One was a Keyholder, or at least he was for a while, until the fitful warning of the machine that had started this whole intervention again, a mindless bank of computer circuits that seemed to have an uncanny ability to ferret out the ripples and aberrant eddies in the quantum fog of time.

There were four of them, each with a peculiar skill to make them the perfect team, a synthesis of four determined minds, involved in a project that would decide the fate of untold generations yet to be born. They had names, Dorland, Nordhausen, Ramer, Lindford, and one of them was now dressed in the naval uniform of a Lieutenant Commander, a costume that had been dredged up for a mission very much like this one, pressed into service again in a desperate gamble to set a situation right, where it now threatened to career into utter chaos. This would be the last mission, or so they hoped, though it had not been the first.

They were children in the beginning, he realized. They thought they would use their amazing new technology to go see a Shakespeare play. They made enormous errors, landing in the late Cretaceous at one point, and bouncing all over the history until they managed to get their methods understood and well honed. Once they had dallied in time for personal fetishes, to find and retrieve things they had always been curious about, until they discovered what was really happening—they were not alone. Others were moving in the unseen meridians of time, agents from a unknown future, locked in a bitter struggle with one another. A Time war was underway, and it was causing more damage than the alterations to the history these agents conspired to bring about. It was causing damage to the fabric of time itself!

Their chief research consultant, Robert Nordhausen, was finally convinced of the serious nature of any further breach of the continuum. Considering what they had seen in recent events, the many interventions were now becoming very dangerous. Their last operation had tried to be careful, sending information back through time to try and catalyze the actions of Prime Movers instead of directly intervening themselves. In the end, it had taken considerably more effort, and Wellings had intervened like this on *Rodney* once before, giving this whole affair a strange feeling of Déjà vu for him.

The effect of information sent back through Time, particularly to Prime Movers, was also very unpredictable, particularly in the deeply fractured Meridians of World War II where their last mission had been run. There were so many Pushpoints there, lurking in the Nexus Points of battles, campaigns, and roiling sagas at sea, that even the slightest nudge could set the whole mountain of events tumbling. A tiny drop of information could cause an immediate and significant change, like a sudden chemical reaction in a lab beaker, and the changes were no longer predictable with any degree of certainty. It might fall like a saving antidote, or fester like a lethal poison, and there was no way to predict all possible outcomes, or to safely restore the time meridian to its former state.

Realizing all this, the presence of this key hidden in the Elgin Marbles was baffling and surprising to the man who had posed as Lieutenant Commander Wellings. He knew to a certainty what Kamenski had come to suspect, that there were other agents at large in the history, and many had very dark agendas. Why was this key embedded in the base of the Selene Horse? Was it evidence of a failed operation by one of these hidden agents, or was it placed there deliberately? If so, what did that operation entail, and why was it mounted? Or worse, why was it called off in such a way that this object would have been so carelessly left behind? Was it meant to be left behind, and if so, why? And why did they have no inkling of it in the Golem alerts?

Yes, the Golem system bad been a life saver. That was the name of the intrepid computer module that was ceaselessly scanning the history over the vast web of the Internet, and making lightning fast comparisons to information about that same history stored in a secured RAM Bank. Whenever a major deviation was found, an alert was sounded, analysis run, and the moment of deviation from the norm could be isolated, the very Pushpoint of divergence, where history that had once been codified in the stillness of the past was now spinning off in a wild new direction. One module in particular had been very enterprising, Golem bank number seven. It produced the warning that had led to the discovery of that key, and that changed everything.

Yet as Wellings descended into the lower levels of the ship, every question in his mind led him on to another, a long corridor of unopened doors that perhaps would be breached with this very key if he chose the correct one. First off, how was it that the object itself could have moved forward with him in time when he returned from his last wild ride aboard HMS *Rodney* in the Atlantic ocean? Never mind that, he thought. It did come forward, and he once had it well in hand.

He remembered how he had placed the key on a chain and wore it around his neck, under his shirt at all times, from that moment on. He also made an entry in Kelly's protected RAM Bank, describing the key, how and where he found it, and including a set of images. It was well encrypted, so he had no fear of that data ever being discovered. If something did slip, he wanted to know it immediately—at least insofar as this key was concerned. He had the RAM Bank programmed to notify him once a week about the hidden file, and ask him a question only he would ever know the answer to before allowing him to view the contents. If the key ever vanished, he wanted to know it immediately—know that it had existed, where he had found it, and what he had discovered about it since.

Yet how would any of them ever know again what was real, or what was the contorted product of another Time intervention? They were the first, or so they thought, to ever open Time. They had created the device, the Arch, their gateway to a thousand yesterdays, or a thousand tomorrows. Yet now they would have to keep the Arch spinning on low standby mode at all times, an enormously expensive proposition, and one that also presented challenges involving maintenance and engineering.

Even so, he worried that one day, by some means, his machine would falter and fail when it was most needed. Yes, there were others operating on the Meridians of Time now. They were not alone. They had discovered that two sides in a distant future were at war with one another, one known as the Order, the other labeled Assassins, each side attempting to bend the lines of fate and time to their liking—Time War.

They had met some of these nefarious agents in time, and eventually forced the two sides to agree to a truce and end their Time War. Now he wondered if the Golem alert system would be efficient enough to pick up any potential violation of the truce they had negotiated. What if the warring parties used some unknown technology, or even a principle of physics unknown to his day, to spoof their system and conduct another stealthy operation? Was this key evidence of exactly that?

He said nothing of his discovery during those negotiations, but kept that thought in the back of his mind. What were these future agents really up to, he wondered? Was it *Rodney* they had been gunning for all along? Old lumbering *Rodney*, with a secret cargo, in more than one way—the King's business, the gold bullion, the Elgin Marbles, the hidden key… and me!

We had to threaten them, both sides at war in the future, before they would listen, for they knew we had power. We were the first, the Founders, and from our unique position on the continuum, we had the ability to frustrate any move they made. What if the Assassins took our threats to heart, and decided that their next and only mission must be to eliminate the meddling Founders from the continuum in a way that still permitted Time travel to occur in the future?

Physicists were still taking pokes at Einstein. The CERN research institute near Geneva recently announced they had measured particles that had to be exceeding the speed of light. It was only a matter of getting somewhere 60 nanoseconds sooner than expected, but it was enough to raise a lot of eyebrows in the physics community. It meant, in one possible application, that it would be possible to send information back through Time, something Wellings could clearly confirm now if ever asked around the water cooler conversations at the Berkeley Lab facilities, though he could never speak a word of this to anyone outside the four core members of the project. Even the interns and lower level staff had been banned from the main facilities after that first mission. The team could take no chance that the true purpose and utility of the Arch would ever become generally known. If the government ever discovered what they were doing here, it would be confiscated and shut down in a heartbeat. In that event he had little doubt that a new Time War would soon begin.

It was a very slippery slope, he knew. Others would reason that if information could be sent back in Time, matter and people would come into the discussion shortly thereafter. He smiled inwardly when he learned that Steven Hawking had remarked: "It is premature to comment on this. Further experiments and clarifications are needed."

He could write them all a book, but the more he considered things, the more questions piled up, one on top of another. Be careful what you wish for, went the old maxim… You may get it. And what did he have hanging round his neck that day when he first revealed the existence of the key to his good friend Kelly Ramer. The key… a strange relic that should never have been found, or left, where it was discovered—the very same key he was laboring to find again now as he reached the lower decks of *Rodney*, and began to make his way forward towards the main cargo hold.

A curious man, he had immediately applied a little forensic investigation to the key, regretting that he had twiddled with it in his pocket and largely extinguished any finger prints he might have found on it. Yet a little non-invasive scan revealed something very interesting, for this key was not what it seemed at all. There was something machined on the side, a series of numbers that could only be read under intense magnification. Beyond that, it was hollow! There was something inside it, and he would spend a good bit of time thinking about that before he went any further, or even whispered the fact to his closest associates.

There was something inside it! The metal end, machined to engage lock tumblers, had clearly been designed for some other purpose as well, and this turned the cylinders of his mind, opening a universe of possibilities. What was it, he wondered? Surely the contents would tell him where it had come from, and what its purpose was, he thought.

Now all he had to do was find out how to open the damn thing. Yet, being inventive and resourceful, he soon answered that challenge. He found that the head of the key could be turned with sufficient torque, and slowly unscrewed. He still remembered that moment of breathless opening, when everything he ever knew and believed turned at the head of that key, and its slow untwisting became the great unraveling of all that ever was. When he finally had it open, and tilted the shaft ever so gently to urge the hidden contents out onto a lab dish, he stared with amazement and perplexity at what he had found.

Days later, he knew the answer to many of his questions, and he also knew why there had been no answer from the distant future when others had called out to their successive generations. From that day forward his life, and his entire understanding of the world he lived in, was never the same. But who to tell?

He spent a long time thinking about that before he ever spoke a word of this key again. Yet it was something too big for him to carry alone. Like Frodo's ring, it began to weigh upon him, seeming heavier and heavier with each day that passed. But unlike Frodo, there was no place he could take it and cast it away, and there was no way he could simply forget about it either... not this... not this...

Then one sunny afternoon at his cottage in Carmel, he was sitting with his good friend Kelly, down on a getaway visit while the other team members stood watch back in their Berkeley Lab facility, the Arch complex as they called it now. They had been walking on the coastline of Asilomar that day, and later dined at a favorite restaurant, the *Sardine Factory* in Monterey. Afterwards, they were drinking wine in the cottage, looking at some of Kelly's photo albums, and listening to the music they loved and shared together, talking over things in a way only two very old friends could. The music played on in the background and Kelly came in with a good bottle of Pinot Noir from the wine rack.

The man who would be Wellings knew that he had to finally unburden himself concerning his discovery of that key. Yet he knew the moment he opened his mouth, he would pass this hidden knowledge on to his friend, germ like, and Kelly's life, and his awareness of life itself, would change forever. He, too, would never be the same. He hesitated briefly, thinking to leave his friend in the relative innocence and simplicity of his life, to leave him unbothered, unburdened, unaware. But if this would eventually lead them all to renewed Time missions, the whole project team would have to be informed. He could bear it no longer. The sheer loneliness of carrying the key, and all he knew about it now, was like a great weight crushing down on his soul.

He reached into his shirt and slowly drew out the key on its chain, feeling like Gandalf visiting Frodo in the Shire, there to tell him what the quaint little magic ring was really all about.

For one last moment he waited. Then he spoke. "It's about this key," he said…

* * *

Later that night, the Arch was still slowly spinning on low power mode back in the Berkeley Hills, just enough to keep the systems energized and ready for quick startup if needed. The project team was taking no chances. They wanted to be able to monitor the newly enforced cease fire closely. The Golem Module was to be in use 24/7, now strongly reinforced with the addition of many new data banks and much more processing power.

At around four A.M. that evening, the Golem Module suddenly came to life again. The threat warning filters had been jarred awake by a lone sentry, while the world slept, blissfully unaware of the impending danger. Normally it would take an assessment from at least three Golem Banks to trigger a warning like this, a call to arms as it were. This time, however, the system had been reconfigured to move into alert mode if just one Golem Bank reported sufficient evidence of a variation. They were taking no further chances. So the alarm went out again, the threat module responded and sent start signals to the main turbines, and the low thrum of the Arch immediately revved up from 20% to 40% power, just enough to open and sustain a small Nexus Point around the facility. Signals were sent out to each of the four project team members, and they were all bound to come to the facility as soon as possible. Within that Nexus, they would be immune to any changes resulting from a Heisenberg Wave that may have been generated by the variation.

One of the Golem banks had found something oddly incongruous while it performed its routine scans of data available on the Internet. It was out of alignment with at least fifteen data points in the RAM bank, and so the digital "stand to" had been sounded again by the vigilance of this single search cluster. It was Golem 7, the same dogged module that had first set them on the trail of German warships on the seas of WWII.

The alarm came in, and that was the night everything again took a most unexpected turn. The man who now called himself Wellings had another name, Paul Dorland, Chief Physicist in the time travel project in Berkeley, one of the four "Founding Fathers" that had first opened the continuum and discovered the Time War. Something had happened. The Golem module was returning red flags concerning an incident in the Norwegian Sea. A Russian battlecruiser had been involved, and then suddenly went missing... as did something else.

That night, as he reflexively reached for the key that had been hanging around his neck since that last harrowing mission, he found that, like Alan Turing's watch, it was gone...

Part VII

Choices

"In any moment of decision, the best thing you can do is the right thing. The worst thing you can do is nothing."

— Theodore Roosevelt

Chapter 19

Lieutenant Commander Wellings' advice on that new heading was very timely, because the Germans were coming. Kapitan Friedrich Karl Topp, a stalwart Prussian who had joined the Kriegsmarine in 1914, was leading Group North aboard the *Tirpitz*. He had served in the U-boat force during WWI as a first officer, and then assisted Raeder with the administration of the new ship building program he was now trying to save from oblivion. He had his eye on the *Tirpitz* for some time, and was elated when they gave him the ship. He sat on the bridge, feeling the surging power of the warship beneath him, all of 53,500 tons when fully loaded for battle, as it was now. In spite of that weight, the ship could run easily at 30 knots, and had even bettered that speed once in trials.

The ship was a marvel of refined engineering, raw power and sheer beauty in design. When launched, Frau von Hassel, the daughter of the famous Admiral the ship was named for, attended the ceremony, along with Adolf Hitler. Dubbed the King of the North, the ship had been based in Norway rather than the Baltic, and now it was the centerpiece of a strong battlegroup that had no difficulty breaking out into the Atlantic.

The British dilemma was obvious. Their fast warships had to be divided to cover every possible exit the Germans might use, and with both *Scharnhorst* and *Gneisenau* along, not to mention *Graf Zeppelin*, the Germans again had a real fleet task force at sea, not a lone raider that could be easily harried and hunted down by cruisers.

There had been a brief air action in the Faeroes-Iceland Gap, where the *Stukas* off the *Graf Zeppelin* had succeeded in posing a considerable threat to the two British battleships that had tried to challenge the Germans. *King George V* and *Prince of Wales* had fought a sharp duel, where their lavish suite of anti-aircraft guns had proven to be life savers, until fighters off the *Ark Royal* and *Illustrious* had arrived on the scene. There were two near misses as the *Stukas* came in, and *King George V* bore a few scratches from the bomb shrapnel, but the thirty *Fulmars* of 806 and 807 Squadrons had been enough to drive the Germans off.

It looked as though the British battle squadron, under Captain Patterson aboard *King George V*, was going to intercept the Germans, but the enemy suddenly turned after sunset on the 6th of May. The last of the British fighters had picked up the maneuver, and radioed Patterson, who quickly ordered his ships, and the carriers supporting him, onto a parallel course. The maneuver had surprised him, for it had been the British belief that the *Tirpitz* group was intending to effect a rendezvous with the *Hindenburg*, now well out to sea after emerging from the Med.

Kapitan Topp was equally befuddled when he got the orders to turn from Wilhelmshaven. He was to assume a new course of 135 degrees southeast, and directed to seek and engage any British forces encountered, with specific orders to find and sink HMS *Rodney*, if at all possible. It was the same order that had so puzzled Lütjens. The reluctant Admiral had steered north, then northwest, then north again, jogging up to get into a perfect position to effect a rendezvous with *Tirpitz*, but now he finally turned to the east, still muttering under his breath when he gave the order, much to the delight of his Kapitan Adler. Soon every warship within a thousand miles was angled on a new heading, with their bows all pointing *Rodney's* way.

"What do we have ahead of us," Topp said to his staff aide, Muller.

"Everything that was once behind us," said Muller, with a shrug. "Those two British battlecruisers will be out there now. Spotters off the *Graf Zeppelin* have them maneuvering to head off our approach to this British convoy we are supposed to find. It seems we have just had a little help. One of our U-boats found that ship we're after, and put a torpedo into it!"

"The *Rodney?* Excellent. It was slow enough before, but now we should have no difficulty running it down. Has Lütjens been informed?"

"Most likely, sir."

"This turn leaves that British battleship squadron in our wake now. They are also most likely pulling their ships down from the Denmark Strait, but they won't catch us before we get to this wounded British battleship. I wonder why Wilhelmshaven is so obsessed with this single ship?"

"Who can say, sir? The signal indicated it was escorting a big troopship liner. Maybe that is our real quarry."

"You read the signal as well as I did, Muller. It specifically instructs us to engage and sink the *Rodney*. Yet I can see no reason why. We had two perfectly good British battleships we could have sunk on our old heading. What's so important about this one?"

"I did a little digging, sir," said Muller. "It seems this ship was scheduled for a refit in Boston. In fact, our operatives in the UK reported she took on a considerable store of cargo, including many crated boiler tubes."

"That old ship is a relic from the interwar period," said Topp. "It has bad lungs and bad legs, and probably a nice little belly ache now that one of our U-Boats got that torpedo hit. Very well, we will sink it, and then we turn to deal with the rest."

"There is one other squadron we might be wary of, sir." Muller was looking at the plotting board now."

"Show me." Topp came over, eyeing the charts as his staffer pointed out a thinly drawn course plotting.

"Here sir," said Muller. "This is that British squadron that had the audacity to run the Straits of Gibraltar. Neither the Italians nor the French lifted a finger to stop them, and now they are in the western approaches to Gibraltar."

"Astounding," said Topp. "What about the Luftwaffe? Didn't we have planes at Gibraltar?"

"Six *Stukas*," said Muller. "All shot down in the attack. And we lost two U-boats in the straits."

"How big is this squadron? Were there destroyers along?"

"Three ships were spotted, the battleship *Invincible*, another battlecruiser, and a heavy cruiser—at least this is what was reported."

"Another battlecruiser? You say that like the British have been growing ships on trees. The only three battlecruisers they have are out here looking for us. What do you mean?"

"That's all the report indicated, sir. It was a large ship, the size of *Hood*, but not well armed. We are waiting for conformation on what it might be. The other ship was smaller, but it engaged our planes with rocketry."

Topp shook his head slowly, his eyes registering some inner conclusion. That was exactly the way Hoffmann had described it to Lindemann. He recalled the meeting of fleet Kapitans they had nearly a year ago, when they had first encountered a strange ship in the Denmark Strait. They were all there, Hoffmann of *Scharnhorst*, Lindemann from *Bismarck*, Fein from *Gneisenau*…

"*To be honest, Kapitan,*" Hoffmann had said. "*I thought it was the size of HMS Hood. In fact at first blush we thought it might actually be Hood, but the silhouette was all wrong.*"

"*It had no stacks as Hood should have,*" Fein put in.

"*That was another thing,*" Hoffmann held out his cigar, letting the thin trails of smoke curl their way up from the ashen tip. "*No smoke either. The ship was cruising at probably fifteen knots, but making no visible smoke.*"

"*You engaged this ship?*" asked Lindemann.

"*We did. I fired a warning shot across the bow thinking this might be an American ship. That is the last time I act as a gentleman in these waters,*" said Hoffmann. "*But I wasn't quite sure what I had in front of me. It's what came back that we must now discuss.*" Topp still remembered the grim expression on Hoffmann's face.

"*Your dispatch said something about a rocket,*" Lindemann pressed. "*I assumed you were writing poetry, Hoffmann. You say this ship had no big guns but it obviously returned enough fire to blast that hole in Gneisenau.*"

"*Oh it returned fire, Kapitan Lindemann, but not with its guns. We were hit by something else, something quite extraordinary, and every man here would be wise to heed my words on this, because if the rest of the British fleet has this weaponry, the entire nature of warfare at sea has just sailed into new waters, and we have missed the boat."*

Topp looked at Muller, a glint in his eye. "These are the ships the British rushed to the Mediterranean. They gave the Italians and French fits, not to mention the damage that was put on *Hindenburg* and *Bismarck*. Kurt Hofmann says he was almost certain the British had another large warship in that last big engagement we fought north of Iceland. He's seen this rocketry first hand, and so have I. The damn things claw through the sky like shooting stars, high up, and then descend like meteors. They come in right on the water, and never miss. If this is the same ship we encountered before, the same ship that struck *Bismarck* again in the Med, then it is nothing to be trifled with."

"True, sir, but we hurt the Royal Navy badly in that first engagement."

"Yes, and it has taken both sides a year to repair all the damage. Now we're out for round two. Let us hope we do a little better this time, or we may find that the Führer will order our ships scrapped as well!"

Muller nodded, knowing that Topp was referring to the order to cancel all further work on the *Oldenburg*. "Yet we have seen no sign of those rocket weapons thus far, sir."

"Be glad for that, Muller. But I think you may be correct. Those weapons are on the *Invincible*, this is what the Abwehr now believes. They may have one or two other ships with these new anti-aircraft rockets, and this is most likely what we are looking at in that squadron you point out here. *Invincible* is their fleet flagship. I have little doubt that we may soon make its acquaintance."

"Excellent sir," said Muller. "Sinking the *Invincible* will teach the British to name their ships more carefully."

"That may be more easily said than done," said Topp. "For the moment, let us keep our eyes on this *Rodney*. With any luck we can get to that ship before the British flagship does."

"Two for the price of one if they get there first, sir."

Topp smiled. "I appreciate your confidence, but don't underestimate the British. They've been out here for generations—professionals to a man. They will fight, and give a damn good account of themselves, and this is the first time the bow of this ship has tasted the salt of the Atlantic. This may not be as easy as you think."

"Well sir, Admiral Lütjens and *Hindenburg* have turned as well."

"Have they? Well don't forget the British will still have another four battleships and two aircraft carriers behind us. Contact Kapitan Böhmer on *Graf Zeppelin*. I want to know how their air wing looks after that last engagement."

"Right away sir."

Muller was off to the wireless room, leaving Topp to mull over the navigation plots. He could see the course tracks twisted on to new headings, and the predictive plots all pointing to what might be a massive engagement off to the east. It was as if some strange gravity was pulling on all these ships now, the lines of fate bending under its influence. What was so damn important about this single British battleship that Raeder orders the entire fleet to reverse course and go hunting? Well, we probably would have had our battle with those battleships behind us tomorrow. Now that will have to wait. *Rodney* is limping south, and we will visit her soon enough. She'll have no speed, but still has heavy arms with those 16-inch guns...

I'll have to be careful here.

* * *

Wellings made his way forward, past squads of sailors, and gritty damage control teams that were none too happy to see him there, as Captain Hamilton had warned. One spied his dress whites and officer's cap, without even realizing he was an American.

"No worries, sir," he said gruffly. "You can attend to your business topside. We've the situation well in hand here."

"Glad to hear it," said Wellings. "Where was the hit taken man?"

"Right ahead, sir. In the cargo hold. We were lucky with that, as the torpedo tube and magazines were missed by a whisker."

"Can I get in there?"

"Not on your life," said the Chief. "We've had to shut watertight doors in those compartments. It's all sealed off until the lads get here with the hull plates and welding torches. Then we'll have to rig the pumps. The worst of it is in hold B. A lot of that cargo will be well submerged. But a few of the other holds may only have minor flooding."

"I see," said Wellings, cursing his bad luck. Was it his luck? Something told him more was at work here than that. He could feel the heavy hand of fate on the bulkheads around him, and knew that key must have something to do with it.

"Any chance we may go down?" he asked. "Is the ship in danger?"

"No sir, like I say, we'll manage well enough. You'd be better up topside. It's tight enough down here as it stands with the hoses coming forward now."

"Very good. Carry on, Chief."

Wellings shrugged and turned about, casting one last glance at that sealed hatch on the near bulkhead behind him. No way to get in there now, at least not from this deck.

"Chief," he said, one hand on a hand rail to steady himself as the ship rolled. "Are there any ladders down into those holds?"

"Sir? Well, I suppose there are. But you'd have to get up to number four deck. That's where the survey teams are working now to see what's what. You don't want to be anywhere near there now sir. The lads are probably knee deep in water and grease if any managed to get in there."

"Thank you Chief. Good advice."

Wellings turned and was on his way, looking for the nearest ladder up. He was going to number four deck strait away, but now he realized that the sight of his dress white officer's uniform would likely be greeted with the same unwelcome reaction as he had here. The man was polite, deferring to his obvious rank, but it was clear he wasn't happy to see an officer here now.

I might do better looking more like a grease monkey down here. In fact, if I shed this officer's coat and get myself into some dungarees… Yes, he thought. It was very likely he'd be swept up in anything that was going on, and if there was any way he could get into that cargo hold, he had to try.

He started off, thinking to find the nearest crew's quarters. The men would be at their stations. He might find what he needed easily enough. Then again, the ship's laundry would have everything he needed. Another work party appeared in the corridor, and he hailed one man.

"Dirty business down here," he said lightly. "Which way to the ship's laundry, seaman? I've gone and soiled my jacket."

"Oh? Right that way, sir, another deck up and amidships."

Wellings was on his way with a grateful smile, but the man just shook his head.

Chapter 20

Volkov stormed down the long hallway, his footfalls hard on the marble as he went. Before him the great doors of the grand gallery loomed, the lacquered mahogany easily ten feet tall. Two guards waited like stolid statues, their boots clicking sharply at the heels as the General Secretary approached, hands taut on their rifles, elbows jutting at perfect angles, chins up. They moved, robot like, opening the doors and then standing stiffly at attention as Volkov blew past them like bad weather, oblivious. The instant the doors closed behind him it began.

There was a moment of breathless silence, then the guards herd the harsh clatter of a chair being thrown across the gallery floor. There came a shattering noise of a chandelier being smashed, then the smoking urn, table lamps, more chairs, and the mirror on the far wall all fell before the wrath of Ivan Volkov. Not knowing what was happening, a steward came rushing in, to see the General Secretary at the height of his rage. Volkov turned, his eyes white with anger, then simply reached into his grey jacket pocket, pulled out a revolver, and shot the man dead.

Outside the doors the two guards knew better than to move a single muscle in response. This was the inner sanctum, the heart of Volkov's secure command center in Orenburg. Layer after layer of security cordoned off these chambers, and it would be impossible for any person to have entered with a weapon here. They immediately knew who had fired that pistol, and only the cautious sideward glance of one to another marked their response. Then, as quickly as the tumult had started, a heavy silence fell. Moments later they heard the hard footfalls recede deeper into the complex. Apparently things had not gone well in the operation recently mounted against the Siberians.

After his jousting duel of words with Karpov, Volkov had pointed *Pavlodar* west and ran at the highest speed he could achieve at that elevation, his eyes warily scanning the underbelly of the rolling storm clouds above, like a submarine Captain might fearfully regard the imminent attack of a hunting destroyer. He knew that if Karpov pursued, there was every chance that he might out run his ship. *Tunguska* was a massive adversary, with six powerful engines, and at higher elevation he might catch a jet stream and race ahead.

But not this time. The weather system he had emerged from would not allow that, with the winds swinging round, and now blowing from the west. *Pavlodar* raced away, and for a moment Volkov thought a rain of bombs might soon fall from above like depth charges, but nothing came. It was long hours in his cabin alone before they finally reached the city his fleet flagship had been named for. Officers of every stripe saw the formation come in, shocked and surprised when *Pavlodar* finally tethered to the main mooring tower near the complex, and the rattle of the elevator slowly descended. Where was the *Orenburg?*

Volkov had moved like a grey shadow, in through the concentric layers of security, layer after layer, onion like about the center of his command bunker. He had not spoken a word, and no man had been bold enough or foolish enough to approach him. As he passed, men stiffened to a stony silence, for they knew what was coming at the end.

Now the silence again. Sometimes long days would pass before Volkov emerged from his hidden chambers. Then, one by one, the warden of the gate would call out names, Generals, Admirals, Captains and Colonels, each one summoned to answer for the holes they had left in the planning. There would be questions, interrogations, the hard whip of Volkov's voice as he shouted his displeasure. And sometimes there came again the harsh crack of that pistol, and a gilded body would be carried out by two stretcher bearers, their faces white with fear. The fallen Captains, usually cogs in Volkov's vast security apparatus, were simply carried to a deep trench outside the main complex walls, and summarily dumped, like so much unwanted trash.

Then the orders would come, new orders that would begin moving divisions on the land, airships in the heavy skies. The long front with Soviet Russia was now teeming with men and machines as the hour drew near for the real war to begin. Volkov's forces stretched from the city of Ufa well north of his capitol near the lower Urals, then west along the winding Belaya River until it joined the Kama, that soon merged into the mighty flows of the upper Volga. Troops from either side manned outposts along that river, reaching down to the great knobby bend of Samara, which was a hard fortified city controlled by Volkov's 2nd Army. From there it flowed down through Balakovo and Saratov, eventually reaching the vast Soviet stronghold of Volgograd, the city that had been called Stalingrad in another telling of these events.

Divisions of his 3rd Army faced off against the bristling gun forts of the Soviet forces there, with each side routinely shelling the other across the wide expanse of the river. The Volga dog-legged east, then splayed through the thick marshlands as it made its way down to Volkov's main base on the Caspian at Astrakhan. He had tried for a decade to take Volgograd and secure the lower Volga region, but the city was now an impregnable stronghold, where Kirov posted some of his best divisions.

So a new strategy would have to be devised, one that would soon see Volkov's armies strike across the Volga to the north, between Saratov and Volgograd. There were only a few suitable crossing points in that region, and it was difficult to achieve surprise. The Soviet controlled west bank of that mighty river had higher ground, and steep ridges in places, while the east bank lay on open, exposed flat ground. But years ago, the Grey Legions had fought for a bridgehead near Samara, which they stubbornly defended, and now they would use it to make a daring attack timed with the great onslaught the German Army was about to unleash.

When he learned trains had come, taking some second echelon Soviet divisions west to the main European front, Volkov had smiled, knowing he would not have to face the full strength of the Red Army any longer. With vast manpower resources, and most of the heavy industry, Sergei Kirov could have rolled east into the Orenburg Federation if he had been willing to pay the price in blood. Volkov's armies had been strong enough to pose a credible defense, but not strong enough to mount a real offensive against Soviet territory. But now, with most of the better divisions moving west to man the main front against the Germans, the Grey Legions could again contemplate the prospect of a successful attack.

2nd and 3rd Armies would make the push from Samara. Their intention was to make a bold thrust aimed at the long, sweeping bend of the Don. The previous year, just after Volkov signed his accord with Adolf Hitler, the Soviets had begun an offensive into the Caucasus. They crossed the lower Don from Soviet controlled Rostov, overran the Krasnodar District, cutting off the Taman peninsula in thirty days. Then Volkov's defense had stiffened near Novorossiysk, and in the tumbling foothills near the rich oil production center at Maykop. This had been Sergei Kirov's real objective, for all the ground he had taken between that place and Rostov was little more than useless steppe land.

There was now fighting along the wide bend of the Kuban River, near Kropotkin, and Volkov was slowly marshalling his reserve divisions from the vast hinterland provinces he controlled. From Kazakhstan came the heavy rifle brigades and swarthy cavalry. From Turkmenistan, the hard mountain troops that would be perfect defenders in the highlands if Kirov's troops tried to push further. Volkov had also called up his Georgian reserve, and when the German attack began, it was his intention to begin a long planned counteroffensive.

After he had been back in his inner offices for some days, the livid anger over what had happened with his second raid on Ilanskiy slowly subsided. He had bigger operations to plan now, men to move, armies to command. In the vast scheme of things now about to unfold, Vladimir Karpov and his Siberian Free State was a small concern. It would have been that way in his mind all along, if not for one thing—Ilanskiy.

He could still hear Karpov's last taunting argument… *"You're forgetting one thing,"* Karpov came at him. *"You're forgetting the very reason you tried to pull this little maneuver here again—Ilanskiy. I beat you here, Volkov, and decisively, no matter how many airships we traded. I control Ilanskiy, and that's the end of it. Do you realize what I can do when I complete the reconstruction of that back stairway? Yes, I've got all the original plans now."* He let an interval of silence play on the airwaves before he finished, then spoke only one word. *"Checkmate!"*

That sent the rising bile of anger loose in Volkov's gut again. Yes, Ilanskiy. It's clear what Karpov was doing there now. He said as much. He's trying to rebuild that stairway, just as it was before. Will he succeed? What if he does? Can he really use those stairs to reach our own time again, in 2021? Could he find me there, and prevent me from ever discovering that damn railway inn?

That thought returned him to the threat he had made as the two men parted. He said he would summon his entire fleet, return and crush the last of Karpov's little Airship navy. He's lost *Yakutsk, Tomsk, Krasnoyarsk.* And we put damage on a few other ships there as well, though we paid a very heavy price for that. I lost six damn airships in that operation, with damage on three more, not to mention Colonel Levkin's troops. After we repair the damage, I still have sixteen more airships, and if Karpov can patch up the ships we hurt, then the Siberian fleet is now reduced to six, I outnumber that bastard by nearly three to one, but that would mean I would have to pull in every airship on the front.

He thought about that. He could carry another sixteen battalions, actually companies, as his Generals kept reminding him. That's just one light brigade, and Karpov was correct. He could post three divisions around Ilanskiy, and all I would do is throw my troops away again. So he has that railway inn, and if he can ever rebuild those stairs and use them …

He did not want to contemplate that. The thought that in spite of the power he wielded, there was really nothing he could do now about Ilanskiy, was infuriating. Karpov was infuriating. That impudent ship's Captain had been a foil ever since the two men first met. What was it he said about that lunch he served us aboard Kirov? Like revenge, it was a dish best served cold. Should I muster enough muscle on the Ob river line to really push through and take that place? It's 750 kilometers, through some of the most murderous country in Asia. I would need twenty divisions, and those troops will be required for Operation Don. I've made promises to another little devil here, Adolf Hitler, and I must not disappoint.

So I must make the west front my primary operations now, an deploy just enough troops in the Caucasus to fend off Kirov's offensive there. Then, after the Germans break through, and the smoke has settled, I'll deal with the Siberians and this piss pot of a man with his big fat airship. I've half a mind to carry out my threat and go back there right now, just to smash what remains of Karpov's fleet. How enjoyable it would be to see that monstrosity of his surrounded by six or eight of my ships, and to pound the damn thing to a flaming wreck.

All things in time. Until then, I have chosen to smash furniture here instead, and a few heads in the process as well. It's very good theater. I wonder if Kymchek got off that damn airship alive? He was supposed to go in with the troops to take care of things, but I wonder if I'll ever hear anything from him again? A pity… In the meantime, I shall have to appoint a replacement as head of security and intelligence soon, and then make sure Karpov hears about it. I need him to believe that Kymchek was no more important to me than an overcoat I might leave in a cloak room. Grechenko is competent, if uninspired, and thankfully he had nothing to do with the intelligence work on this last operation, so he can't be blamed for anything. Yes, time is on my side now, as much as Karpov believes he can master it. His days here, are numbered.

* * *

The hard fist came in answer to Volkov's inner query, smashing right into Kymchek's already bloodied face. He was tied in a chair, beneath a single bare light bulb under a conical metal shade hanging from the ceiling. A burly Sergeant was standing in front of him, sleeves rolled back over well muscled arms, the bare dome of his head gleaming with the effort of his work—a good beating for Kymchek, head of Volkov's Internal Security, and Intelligence Master. He had been rounded up by Karpov's men on the ground just south of Ilanskiy, not far from the burning hulks of Big Red and *Orenburg*. One arm was already broken, as was his nose now after a few hard blows from the Sergeant's meaty fist. His eyes were bruised, and a dark weal scarred his right cheek. Blood trickled from his lower lip after that last blow, and his head lolled.

"That will do, Sergeant." Karpov strode in, wearing well polished knee high black boots, and a dark overcoat covering his service jacket, and the precious computer embedded in its lining. It held the history of all the days to come, whispered in his ear just as it had been with Orlov after he jumped ship.

Yet Orlov was an idiot, thought Karpov. He would never have known what to do with the knowledge he took with him. And here is another little intelligence windfall, Volkov's number one man in that sprawling network of thieves, villains, and saboteurs he's created. It was said in many circles that Volkov's intelligence was the best in the world, though they missed this little maneuver I just pulled. He smiled.

"So… you thought I was dead and long gone, eh Kymchek? You thought I was fish food in the English Channel. I can imagine the look on your face when Volkov asked you what I was doing here with *Tunguska*. That must have been priceless!"

Kymchek knew he would likely endure hours of this, so he cut to the quick. "Get on with it, Karpov. I'd rather let the Sergeant finish than sit here and listen to you gloat for another few hours."

"The Sergeant? Yes, Grilikov is very good, though he's hardly broken a sweat. But enough is enough." He nodded to the Sergeant, dismissing him so he could be alone with his newly caught fish.

"I have no intention of calling him back, Kymchek, that is unless you get stupid here and prefer death. Yes, that beating was necessary, a little thank you for helping to plan this ridiculous operation against Ilanskiy. That said, I can find you very useful. Yes?"

Kymchek raised his head, trying to force a grin onto his wounded face. "You expect me to sing like a morning dove here? You think I'll do any less than what I expect of my men should they ever be captured?"

"Quite frankly, I do. Look, Kymchek, you are not an ignorant man, even if you did plan a very stupid operation here. That said, were it not for my timely arrival, you might have succeeded! You just factored me out of your equations a little too soon, that's all. So Now I will give you a chance to redeem yourself—a chance to make a few choices on the kind of life you want to lead in the years remaining to you. Those years can be long, productive, rich, and full of comfort. You can take a position here with authority, become part of the inner circle of the Free Siberian State, enjoy the luxuries of power and privilege, good food, better women, and a little respect."

"You want me to turn?"

"Of course! You're a very valuable man. You can think, and I need men who know how to use their heads in a crisis. Face it... Suppose I send you back to Volkov tomorrow. What do you think he has waiting for you after this little debacle here? A firing squad may be the best you find back in Orenburg. Your General Secretary just got his fleet flagship blown up right beneath his ass, and went falling from the sky in his little metal escape pod. Well, some snakes can be very hard to kill. He's alive. He made it to *Pavlodar* and scurried off west instead of facing my ship in a good honest fight. I don't blame him. Once burned, twice shy."

He stepped forward, the cone of light on the soiled floor gleaming off his dark boots now. "Yet in your case Kymchek, he's been burned twice. Didn't you also help plan the first raid on Ilanskiy? Of course you did. Volkov threw two airships away in that raid, and all his men, This time the price was three times higher—including you! Yes, you've probably been written off by now, along with your Colonel Levkin and all his men. You want to be a write off? I can arrange that. My Sergeant Grilikov is very good at taking out unwanted trash. So now it's time you did some hard thinking about that, and made your choice."

Chapter 21

It was a long, cold night in the room where they left Kymchek to think about his fate. A pack of Siberian Huskies was tethered just outside the small shack in Ilanskiy where he was being interrogated. A train rolled in with a low rumble just after midnight, sent there by Karpov to haul off all the prisoners from Levkin's forsaken 22nd Air Mobile Brigade. They would be taken east, to a "rehabilitation camp" where some would die, while others would eventually be offered the chance to fight with the Free Siberian Army. Those that refused would be sentenced to 20 years hard labor, as enemies of the state.

Kymchek knew that he would surely suffer a similar fate. The pain in his broken arm was very bad that night, and he shivered with the cold. He knew he had the stamina to endure many days like this, a beating from Grilikov in the morning, and a long, empty day on that chair beneath the light bulb, listening to the snarling of the Huskies and Malamutes outside. Yet how many days before his body would just give out, and then how long to die after that?

These thoughts pulsed in his brain like the throbbing pain, and behind it all was the livid visage of Ivan Volkov. He had served Volkov for the last five years as his intelligence chief, an inner circle confidant that saw him come to know a great deal about the man. Volkov was a pig at heart, or so he thought. He was devious, ruthless, determined, yet mindless at times. The objections Kymchek had raised to this latest operation had not been heard, but the blame would surely be waiting for him in wheel barrows if he were ever so lucky to escape his fate here and get back to Orenburg.

The demands of his position had left Kymchek no time for family. He was an only son, and at the age of 40 both parents were already gone. He had taken up with women at times, but never allowed any real attachment to form, and was unmarried. So who will miss me, he wondered, or mourn me when they get the news I was executed here, or died in a prison cell?

And yes, they would certainly get the news, wouldn't they? He could already name at least three other men in this very town that were operatives in his vast spy network. He had labored to recruit the men, infiltrate them, and now he sat at the center of the web, a lost spider, feeding on the flies that he would catch, day by day. He knew that his capture was an amazing windfall for Karpov.

I know Volkov's operation chapter and verse, he thought, every division, every brigade, the officers, equipment, men. I know what Volkov knows, because I was the man responsible for telling it to him. I know what offensives he's planned, and where, and the orders of battle right down to battalion level. I can tell you what weapons he has in development, their progress, all his new construction programs, how many divisions he can raise in Kazakhstan and Turkmenistan, when they can arrive, all of it. And that is just a thimble full of what I know. My principle activity was in sounding out all that same information about the Soviets, the Germans, the British and all the rest—even the Siberians.

That's a lot of chips on my side of the table if it comes to bargaining with Karpov here. Yet, amazingly, he hasn't asked me a single question about any of that. I was given three days to think about things, and this is day three. Who comes through that door this morning? Will Karpov be back again? Will the real interrogation finally begin now? Yes, after Grilikov has had a little time to soften up the ground, the real digging will begin, and with each shovel full of information they extract, the hole will grow bigger—my own grave.

He shook his head, inwardly, because it would take too much effort and hurt too much to shake it outwardly. So I die here, painfully, in another week or two at best. In the meantime, Volkov will have already appointed someone to fill my shoes, probably that fat fool Grechenko. He was an accountant, good with numbers, but with no real intuition. He can tell Volkov how much and how many, but never why. His reports will be well drafted, yet starchy and dry. He'll never take a risk, and always play things safe. That's Grechenko, the clerk become too fat for his own britches, and now he will try to squeeze himself into my job. Yes, that was all part of the plan, but it doesn't make this any easier at the moment. It's not his fat ass in this chair—it's mine.

He could think of that no longer. The door opening brought relief with the thought that Sergeant Grilikov was back again this morning, but the footfalls on the floor behind him were not heavy. He could feel someone there, a shadow darkening his shoulder, then he started with a sudden touch, thinking Grilikov was going to position his head and box his ears again for his morning greeting.

To his great surprise, the touch was soft, lingering, comforting. He slowly turned his head, wincing with the pain and squinting at the garish light. There stood a tall, slim woman, with long curls of brunette hair, almond eyes, and a face any man would call beautiful. The woman moved, with silky softness, coming round to stand before him. She was dressed in a plain brown dress, and tan blouse, with an army blazer over it, and the rank and insignia of a Major. In her hand she held a brown leather bag, and now she stooped down, her eyes always on his as she opened the bag. They were eyes a man could drown himself in, and she gave him a warm smile.

It was a medical bag, and the woman was a nurse. For the next half hour she cleaned his face, and then tended to his painful right arm. It took several swigs of good vodka, but Kymchek knew this pain was a vital prerequisite to his healing, if he ever could. At times, when she leaned close, her scent was captivating, like violets in summer, and her blouse was conveniently loose on her ample chest to allow him a glimpse of what lay beneath that plain brown uniform.

When she had bandaged his face and secured his arm in a splint, she just walked slowly across the room, sitting quietly in a plain wood chair, her skirt riding a little above the knee, when she crossed her legs, ever so invitingly. Then the door opened, and this time it was Karpov.

"Good morning, Kymchek. I trust you were able to get some sleep, in spite of the dogs and that light bulb there." He tapped the hanging bulb, setting it to move, pendulum like, and creating a strange effect as the light fled from the woman, then returned. She seemed to recede into shadows, appearing again, angel-like, her dark eyes always on his, her face always pleasant, smiling, promising.

"I see you have met Major Yana, as we call her. Grilikov is still having his breakfast, and none too happy that we were out of sausages until the next train. He'll be here shortly, and probably in a very bad mood. But before that, I thought I would check on you and see if you have given any thought to our previous discussion."

Kymchek blinked as the light slowly settled, leaving most of the Major wreathed in shadow, except those long, long, legs. He knew what was happening now, first the gruel, then the honey. It was nothing unexpected.

"Well then," said Karpov. "What shall it be, Kymchek? You can have it either way, Grilikov with his bad temper, big fists in your face again, and then more long nights with the dogs. We'll feed you, because you know too damn much to simply let you die here. Then we'll have to let Grilikov get serious to get the answers to a lot of the questions you know will be coming your way. He has a fetish for very sharp knives, and I'm told he starts with fingers and toes, just for openers. It won't be pleasant, you know that, and it won't be brief. Eventually you will tell us what we want to know, but that will be a long, painful process, and the questions may never end. Understand?"

Now Karpov stepped into the light again, his uniform immaculate, boots shined, hand resting on a the pistol in his side holster. The door opened and another man came in, stepping to Karpov's side, hands folded behind him, his uniform equally smart and dressed out. He was holding a small bundle, and a pair of military boots. Kymchek recognized him through bleary, bandaged eyes. It was Tyrenkov, Karpov's own master of intelligence and security. The two men had been rivals for some years now, each one trying to out-maneuver the other to get the best information. They were as different as yin and yang, Kymchek fair skinned, with short cropped grey hair and pale blue eyes, Tyrenkov dark haired, steely lean, the light of his quick mind seeming to glow his eyes. They were fire and ice, yet both grimly calculating in their own way, and with devious intelligence.

"You know this man?" asked Karpov. "Of course you do. Well he is here to welcome you to our side of the game, if you so choose. You will be working directly with Tyrenkov, and together you will make an unbeatable intelligence team. See those boots he is holding? The bundle there is a uniform—with the rank of Major General in the Free Siberian Army. It's yours. Step into those boots and stand with us. This war is only beginning, and there is much you have to learn about what will soon happen to our dear Mother Russia. Yes, even you, the man who knows everything. Well, you will soon learn that is not the case."

Karpov was pacing now. "I need you, Kymchek. I need your mind, your skills, your competence. I would embrace you as a friend here, if you so choose. As I have said, you will have rank, the power and privilege that comes with it, and the pleasures. Yes, Major Yana there will gladly tend to more than that broken arm, whenever you desire, and there are a hundred others just like her. So face the reality here, the information you have will come to us one way or another. I would prefer to sit with you over a good meal and discuss things like a gentlemen. We have plans to make, and battles to fight. Join us."

The logic of Karpov's appeal was hard. "Together with Tyrenkov, we can settle the matter of Ivan Volkov once and for all, " he said. "He's an aberration, a blight in history, and an insult. Curse that man for shaking hands with Hitler, and curse him for raising his hand against his brothers, and shedding Russian blood so wantonly in this hour of our greatest need. I'm going to destroy him, just like I destroyed his damn flagship out there, one way or another. That is inevitable. So the choice before you now is very simple. Do you hold with him, Kymchek? Is that the kind of man you will sit there and endure this shit for? What will it be, Major Yana or Sergeant Grilikov? Don't think you'll be a hero if you see some warped sense of virtue in being loyal to a man like Volkov. But choose otherwise, and you can be a hero—not for me, but for your country. Decide."

The door opened again, the snarl of the dogs louder as Grilikov finally came tramping in, his hard soled boots soiled with mud. He yelled at one of the dogs over his shoulder, slamming the door as he cursed.

"Sorry, sir. Breakfast was late."

"No bother, Sergeant. Stand there, will you?"

"Certainly sir." The big Sergeant took his place at the edge of the light, the shadows rising up his stolid form, legs planted wide, heavy arms crossed over his chest. He was slowly rolling up his sleeves. At a nod from Karpov, Major Yana stood, and walked sinuously to the edge of the light, the same shadows fingering the curved lines of her body. They stood there, two ends of a choice that would now decide Kymchek's future life. Tyrenkov slowly handed the bundled uniform and boots to the woman, and then stepped to Karpov's side.

"Come now, Tyrenkov. We're off to the officer's dining room. I think your breakfast was late, Sergeant, because the chef was too busy preparing our meal. I'll make that up to you."

"Thank you, sir."

"Good enough." Karpov started away, with Tyrenkov in his wake, then he stopped, just short of the door, looking back over his shoulder. "Oh yes, there is a third table setting and a chair for you, Kymchek. Come over dressed in that uniform and join us, and let's put this unfortunate incident behind us and talk about the Rodina. There is more to be healed here than that right arm of yours, and we men must do that work. Our nation stands or falls in the years ahead, and now you get a chance that comes to few—a chance to right the wrongs you have done in this world. Decide, this very hour, and join us. There will be more than Major Yana's smile in that choice for you. History will smile on you as well."

He turned, and stepped through the doorway. The dogs saw the door opening and were up with a snarl, but one look at Karpov and they were immediately stilled.

Kymchek never forgot that.

Across the way, Karpov sat at the breakfast table, the white linen cloth lending a pristine quality to the setting. The silver was laid out next to well folded napkins, the tea hot in the polished samovar, the smell of the blini and porridge enticing. The sausages Grilikov had been missing were here in abundance.

"That was quite a find, Tyrenkov. You are to be congratulated. What do you think Kymchek will do in this situation?"

"That's anyone's guess, sir. You were very persuasive. A punch in the nose and a kiss on the cheek is old hat when it comes to interrogation. Kymchek knows that, but your other arguments were very convincing."

"He would be a fool to die here out of some misplaced and foolish loyalty to Volkov," said Karpov. "I might expect you to do this for me, so believe me, it was not easy asking Kymchek to throw away those years he stood by Volkov. Why should he? Only to save his skin, and perhaps do what I suggested, right some wrongs, and salvage what remains of his life, his pride, his sense of being a useful man. We all want to be useful, don't we? The information he has will be vital in the campaign ahead, but the man is also a great asset. You can use him, a very able addition to your team."

"No question about that, sir."

"And Tyrenkov, I also want you to know that your position as head of security and intelligence is completely secure. Don't entertain the slightest thought that Kymchek might ever replace you. You've proven yourself to me many times, and I will never do what Volkov has just done here to Kymchek. The man was simply thrown to the wolves. This is why I had those dogs tethered right outside his door—a little subliminal message to that effect. Well… I wonder if the blini is getting cold. Perhaps we should begin."

At that moment there came a quiet knock on the door. Karpov had given both the Sergeant and Major Yana very specific orders. Should Kymchek remain obstinate, or fail to choose within one half hour, the Sergeant was to come over and report this, and get Karpov's approval to begin more intensive interrogations. Should Kymchek choose to side with the Siberian State, then Major Yana was to accompany him to the Officer's Dining room.

"Come…" Karpov turned, wondering who he would see when that door opened, and hoping he would not have to grind Kymchek like so much meat in the days ahead. He was not disappointed.

There stood Kymchek, dressed out in the uniform and boots that had been tailored for him, his General's cap under his good left arm, where Major Yana guided him with a smile. As much as he wanted to smile himself, Karpov maintained a well practiced decorum. He stood up, gesturing to the third place at the table, his hand extended graciously.

"General Kymchek," said Karpov politely. "I am very glad you have chosen to dine with us this morning, very glad indeed. Every choice makes a difference in this world, and I know that in a way that few men understand. This next choice will be a little easier for you… Do you prefer honey with your tea? And will it be boiled eggs, sausage, or black bread and cold cuts?"

It was only then that Karpov allowed himself a smile, not to taunt the man, but to welcome him. Kymchek never forgot that either. There was another side of this man, though he knew Karpov had good reason to be accommodating here.

I hope I didn't make this look too easy, thought Kymchek. *Volkov was very insistent about that, and I told him that two or three days, and a good beating, would be the norm. But Karpov was certainly eager to get me here to his table. So here I am, you conniving little bastard. Did you really think I would turn so easily? Yes, the walk over here with Major Yana cradling that wounded arm of mine was much to be preferred over Grilikov breaking the other one. But that had little to do with anything. As you said yourself, Volkov is an aberration, but so are you—a little weed that needs plucking out, and I've been sent to till the garden. So I'll play your game now, and tell you anything you might care to know. Then, one day, when the time is right, I'll find a way to do what we came here to* do in the first place, and make an end of your little theater on the taiga.

Tonight he would consider how best to contact his operatives in Ilanskiy, and discretely have them get a message to Volkov, telling him all was well, and everything was going exactly as they had planned it.

Part VIII

Peake's Deep

"Cast your bread upon the waters, for after many days you will find it again. Give portions to seven, yes to eight, for you do not know what disaster may come upon the land... Sow your seed in the morning, and at evening let not your hands be idle, for you do not know which will succeed, whether this or that, or whether both will do equally well."

— **Ecclesiastes 11:1-6**

Chapter 22

Engineering Chief Dobrynin was the next man to hear it, the same deep disturbance in the sound field that Tasarov had heard earlier. The Chief's ears were fine tuned to the nuances of the ship, every squeak and rumble and grind of the turbines and engines, the hum of the reactors, the symphony of the entire machine itself as *Kirov* cut its way into the Atlantic. He had been reviewing service readouts from the main propulsion system, pleased that the reactors had been holding up very well, in spite of long hours at high speed. As he folded the file closed, he heard something that prompted him to incline his head, listening…

"Mister Garin," he said to his reactor Technician, Ilya Garin. "Any disturbance on your monitors?"

"Sir?" Garin looked over his panels, noting nothing out of order, and reported as much.

"Very well… " Dobrynin should have been satisfied with that situation, but he was still not content. He set the sheaf of files down, sat in his swivel chair and put his feet up on the low stool he often used like a makeshift ottoman. Then he closed his eyes, listening… Listening…

There it was, something barely perceptible. Was it a vibration, or a sound? It seemed to reside on some undefined grey zone between those two sensations, and it was as if the Chief had a sixth sense that could perceive the medley. A sound… a tremor… a warning… There was nothing in his file readouts, and nothing on Garin's monitors, but he could feel it, sense it, and it gave him a deep sense of misgiving. He listened for a time, and the longer he did, the more foreboding the feeling became. After a while it began to create a slowly rising anxiety in him, as if his body could feel the vibration, and interpret it as danger. He could feel that thrum of adrenaline in his torso, and could no longer sit still.

"Mister Garin, I believe we should initiate a diagnostic routine of the reactor system."

"Again sir? We only just completed compiling the data from that diagnostic we ran two days ago."

"So we will have new data to compile. Yes? Let's begin with the thermodynamics. We will use the primary monitor, and the backup system as well."

Garin shrugged, but knew there was really only one response that was acceptable. "Aye sir. I'll get started right away."

* * *

Fedorov could feel the tension on the ship. It had been a very long journey, perhaps one of the longest deployments at sea ever endured by any modern ship or crew. After those first harrowing encounters in the North Atlantic, Mediterranean and finally in the Pacific, the crew had some brief relief off the coast of Australia, and on that island Admiral Volsky had been longing for. The time they had in Vladivostok was brief, and provided no real sense of homecoming for them. There were odd incidents there, resulting from the subtle changes in the time line caused by *Kirov's* intervention. The city was different, yet in places oddly familiar. There had been restaurants that were apparently meant to be, in any time line, and other familiar businesses. Yet some crew members had gone home to find total strangers living where their house once was, or worse, to find their home, or even street, was entirely missing!

So we left a different world from the one where we started, he thought. I was lost along the Siberian Rail line when Karpov took the ship out, so all I know of that period was what I have learned from the others here. There was more combat against the American navy, in two different time periods. And then that unfortunate situation that saw the ship blasted deeper into the past must have been very hard. When that happened, I think the crew abandoned any hope of ever seeing home again as they once knew it. Even Admiral Volsky took to a little relief in a bottle of Vodka in his quarters. I certainly don't blame him.

Doctor Zolkin has been a life saver, and in more ways than one. It was his character and opposition to Karpov at that critical moment that eventually enabled us to complete our mission and remove *Kirov* from the early 20th Century. Yet we remain stuck here in WWII, the great catharsis of the modern world, the most devastating war mankind has ever inflicted upon itself—save that last one, the war we were trying so hard to prevent.

We arrived here last June. Now here it is May of 1941! In all that time the crew has been faithful at their posts. They got some relief when we sailed north to Murmansk, yet I think all that did was give them a taste of what they had lost. The brief shore leave we arranged in Alexandria was hardly enough. They must be wound up tighter than a spring, and this incident with Lenkov was most unsettling.

Everywhere Fedorov went as he walked the ship, he got the same questions. The crew wanted to know what was happening, and he had no real explanation for them. "We experienced a moment where our position in time was not stable," he said in one compartment near the missile bays. "You remember what happened to us when that Japanese ship seemed to move right through us."

"Who can forget that sir?" said a *mishman* of the watch.

"Well it was something like that, only a very minor incident. Lenkov was just unlucky, that is all I can say. I know you men have had a hard time here, We have asked more of you than any man should have to give in the service of their country. I thank you for being the strong bone and muscle of this ship, and I am sorry I have put you through all of this."

The men were silent for a time. Then the *mishman* spoke up, going so far as to even put his hand on Fedorov's shoulder. "We stand with you, Captain. Where you lead us, we will follow. Don't worry sir. We are all fine."

That was a hard moment for Fedorov. He felt the emotion clench his throat, nodded his acknowledgement, and moved on. Here the men were trying to comfort me, he thought. This is a good crew, loyal to a man, and god go with us now. God help me lead them, and if there is anyplace out there that we can ever call home again, show me the way…

He finished his silent prayer, ducked into a hatch, and found the ladder down to the next deck. That was when he ran into Chief Dobrynin.

"Good day, Chief. How are the engines holding up?"

"Well enough, sir, but there was something else I wanted to speak with you about."

"Oh? Shall we go to your office?"

The two men walked down one more ladder, and found the Chief's working hideaway. Fedorov took note of the books he kept there, a mix of technical manuals, physics, thermodynamics, engineering, and strangely, music. He had several books on the great Russian composers, and even a few musical scores of symphonies by Shostakovich, Stravinsky, and Tchaikovsky.

"When do you ever get time to listen to good music?" said Fedorov.

"Not often enough," said Dobrynin. "In fact, it is something else I've been listening to that I wanted to discuss with you. You know I have good ears. That's how I was able to try and control those flux events when we used Rod-25. Well… I've been hearing something of late—something strange."

"A problem in the engines?"

"I'm not sure yet, though I have Mister Garin running the second diagnostic this week."

"Have there been any unusual readings."

"Not lately. Not even with this Lenkov incident. I went over the charts very carefully, but I could not see anything in the data that would lead me to believe that the ship had any kind of problem."

"That is some relief, I suppose."

"Perhaps," said Dobrynin. "But if the ship did lose its integrity in this time, even for a brief moment, I should have noticed it. There should have been some readings in the reactor flux."

"But why, Chief? We are not using Rod-25, so the reactors were not exposed to anything it may have contained. Why would we begin to pulse again? Have you given that any thought?"

"I don't know sir, but remember we do have those other control rods aboard, and that thing Orlov found in Siberia."

"Yes, the Devil's Teardrop. Is it still in a secure location?"

"As far from the reactors as I can get it," said Dobrynin. "I have it down in the empty weapons storage bay for special warheads. That area has extra radiation shielding, which should be some protection, assuming this thing emits that kind of energy."

"Explain."

"Well sir, this whole business of the ship moving in time… It must be happening on a quantum level. I can't say that I can give you any real explanation, but whatever is in that thing may be in a concentration great enough to have an effect, even far from the reactors. It certainly sent us right into a flux event any time it came within ten feet of the reactor room."

"I see… Then what have you been hearing, Chief?"

"A sound of some kind. A vibration. Both."

"A vibration in the propulsion system?" asked Fedorov.

"I don't think so, Captain. In fact, I have listened very carefully of late, and I don't think its mechanical at all. But I can sense it."

"Yet it is coming from somewhere on the ship? Have you localized it?"

"Not exactly, sir. That was the first thing that came to my mind as well. So I walked the ship from stem to stern, thinking I would hear it more in one place, less in another, but that was not the case. It seems to be resonating from all directions. I could not get any sense that it was emanating from a specific place on the ship."

"What does it sound like?"

"Very deep, sir. A very low sound, so low that it becomes something felt as much as anything heard. It may be well below the threshold of human hearing. But I can pick it up with these dog's ears of mine."

Now Fedorov remembered a report that Rodenko had given him concerning Tasarov. He had reported hearing something, first in his quarters, then at his post while listening on sonar. Rodenko had him prosecuting it up on the bridge as if it were an undersea contact, yet there was no data trace in the electronics, not on radar or sonar. Now Dobrynin was hearing something odd, and it was clear that it was bothering him, if only because he could not isolate it and determine the cause.

"Now here is the strange thing," said Dobrynin. "I have tried for some time to locate the source of this sound, but with no results. In fact, I have come to think I might get out in a launch, away from the ship, and then see if I can still hear it."

"I'm afraid we haven't time to stop for a boat launch operation, Chief. There's trouble ahead."

"I understand, sir. And that is a good way of describing this sound—trouble ahead. It's what it feels like, Captain—trouble."

Fedorov looked at him for a moment, then scratched his ear. "Keep listening, Chief. Let me know if you think this is having any effect on the engines or reactors. I'll go down to the missile bays, and see if any of the men there report this, and I'll make sure Admiral Volsky is informed."

"Thank you, sir."

A sound that could not be heard, but it could be clearly felt. Every good ghost story has seen the dogs and cats become aware of something long before it came on the scene. Dobrynin's comment about his dog's ears was very telling. Tasarov hears it too. In fact, didn't Orlov report something like this on that mission to Siberia? Perhaps Sergeant Troyak can shed some light on this. I'm told he heard what Orlov reported, along with several of the Marines.

Now he found himself heading for the Helo Bay and the Marines. He thought he would find them involved with routine operations, cleaning rifles, tending to the KA-40, but when he got there he could see that Troyak had a problem on his hands. There was some commotion, swearing, and the sound of obvious alarm. He could hear Troyak's deep voice interrogating a Marine as he came on the scene.

"Then nobody knows about this? No one saw a thing?"

"No Sergeant. It was just there! I was stowing this equipment from the desert mission, and when I opened that locker—"

"Captain on deck!"

The Sergeant turned, saluting as Fedorov came up. The other Marines were at attention, and Fedorov could see they were in some distress.

"I'd like to say as you were, but is there a problem, Sergeant?"

"You had better have a look in that storage locker, sir."

Fedorov was surprised for a moment, wondering what this was about. He stepped over to the half closed locker, and eased the metal door open, his eyes widening as he did so. Several of the other Marines leaned in to peer into the shadows of the locker once again, as if to convince themselves they were actually seeing what they had reported to Troyak.

"My god..."

"Litchko found it a moment ago," said Troyak.

"Yes sir," said Litchko. "Like I was telling the Sergeant. I was just going to stow away those mortars after cleaning and inspection. When I opened the locker..."

"I had a closer look," said Troyak. "I found this."

He handed Fedorov a piece of crumpled paper. It was a list of supplies, cooking oil, flour, potatoes, starch, salt, and then below a line at the bottom of the note that read: *"One pack of cigarettes for one extra serving. No exceptions."*

"I don't understand," said Fedorov. "Who is that?" He pointed to the shadows of the locker."

"I think it is Lenkov, sir... or at least a part of him. That note was in the trouser pocket. He had a game going taking cigarettes in trade for extra servings at the mess."

"Lenkov? But we found him dead in the galley?"

"We found a part of him there," said Troyak. "Those are Lenkov's legs. Just that, nothing more. They're stuck right in the back side of that locker at the waist. The rest of him was left in the galley."

Trouble ahead, thought Fedorov. Too many questions, and not enough answers. Here were Lenkov's missing legs! They did not simply wink out of existence as Kamenski suggested, like Turing's watch, because the damn watch never winked out of existence either—*it simply moved!*

And so did Lenkov's legs.

Chapter 23

Fedorov gave orders that this latest incident should be kept quiet, as far as possible. "No need to let this get out among the crew," he said. "The first incident was bad enough."

He wondered if this had happened at the same moment that the other half of poor Lenkov had turned up in the galley, and why his body would have been split in two like that. But with no answers, all he could do was try to minimize the psychological damage, and carry on. He pulled Troyak aside, asking him about that sound he had been discussing with Chief Dobrynin.

"Yes," said Troyak. "I heard it when we found that cauldron in the clearing. Devil's Cauldron, Devil's Teardrop, *glubokiy zvuk*. It is not the first time I have heard it. Very deep sound. Bone deep."

"Tell me more."

"I come from the Chukchi Peninsula, and as a boy I would often hike the highlands and taiga. Yes, I have heard such a sound before. But you do not hear it, unless you have very good ears. You feel it, sense it, and it is very strange."

"You say you heard or felt this on that mission to Ilanskiy... Have you heard anything lately, here on the ship?"

"No sir, just my men complaining more than they should."

"Complaining? About what?"

"Little things. Nothing in particular. They're just edgy."

"Give them some rest, Sergeant. They were away on combat tour for several months. Getting back into the routines of the ship may take a while. Give them some rest."

"I will sir, but it would be better if we don't find any more body parts in the lockers." Troyak smiled. "Sir... There was one other time when I heard this sound. It was in the desert, just before that incident—the lights in the sky."

"I see... And did it continue?"

"No sir. It settled down when the sky did the same."

And that was when Kinlan's Brigade came right through a breach in time at the Sultan Apache facility, thought Fedorov. Orlov had that object with him, and he reported it changed temperatures at that same time. The dots were slowly connecting in Fedorov's mind, and he was slowly convincing himself that this sound being reported by Tasarov and Dobrynin had something to do with the Devil's Teardrop.

"Very well, Sergeant. If you hear this sound again—any sign of it at all—please report it to me at once. Keep that locker sealed off for the moment. I'll have Doctor Zolkin and the Engineers take care of everything."

"Good enough, sir."

Fedorov was off, returning Troyak's salute and heading forward and up, bound for the bridge. He stopped several times along the way, and made a point of visiting Doctor Zolkin, where there were several men waiting in a line outside his sick bay. Zolkin saw the Captain and stuck his head out.

"Privilege of rank, gentlemen," he said with a smile. "Let me have a moment to see what the Captain needs."

"I hope you are alright sir," a man said, as Fedorov stepped in through the hatch.

"I am fine, Mister Yakov. I just need to see to the doctor's supply needs."

The men smiled, somewhat relieved to know that Fedorov might not be coming here for the same reasons they were. Once inside, with the hatch closed, Fedorov folded his arms.

"We found the other half of Lenkov," he said starkly, getting right to the point.

Zolkin raised his cinder grey brows. "Where?"

"In a locker near the Helo Bay. Can you summon those same Engineers and see to it?"

"Of course, Mister Fedorov." Zolkin shook his head. "Now I have the whole body, and we can arrange a proper burial at sea. Should it be a ceremony with the men standing by?"

Fedorov thought for a moment. He wanted to keep the discovery of Lenkov's legs quiet, to still the rumor mill that was already troubling the ship. But the thought of just summarily dumping Lenkov overboard like so much trash was distasteful. The man deserved more than that.

"Yes, Doctor," he said. "Arrange it and inform the bridge ten minutes before you begin. Either I or the Admiral will have some words for the crew over the P.A. system. Lenkov sailed with us, fought with us, and endured everything we have been through. He will be given his due respect."

"Agreed," said Zolkin. "And let us hope we have no further incidents like this. What could have caused it?"

"I'm still not certain, but it may have something to do with that thing Orlov found. We have it stowed in a radiation safe area, but its effects may not work that way."

"Quite a little bag of wizards tools we're collecting here, Fedorov. First the control rods, now this!"

Fedorov nodded. "That line out there is a little troubling," he said, thumbing the hatch. "What's going on with the men?"

"Nothing serious. Oh, there were a few bruised shins from the engineering section, a cut thumb, and the rest just seem to be complaining they can't sleep well. And several have complained about hearing something. I asked what it was, but they had no real answer for me."

"Who were these men?"

"Tomilov for one…. And Sorokin."

"They're both assigned to the missile bays, yes?"

"Ask Orlov. I just pass out the aspirin and sedatives, and take care of men who end up in two places at once when the world can't decide where they belong. This is very strange, Fedorov. I hope you get to the bottom of it. But do be careful."

"I will, Doctor, carry on, and thank you. I know this must be hard on you as well."

"I can't say it's all in a day's work, but I'll manage." Zolkin smiled.

Fedorov was out past the line of waiting crewmen, talking briefly with the men there, and then on the way to the bridge to report to Volsky.

"Things are adding up now, sir," he said. "But I haven't decided what we should do about it. If this sound is associated with a time breach, as Troyak's report seems to suggest, then its emergence here is most alarming. I'm beginning to suspect that object may be responsible for destabilizing the ship's position in time. The fact that several men are now reporting they hear or feel this deep sound, as Troyak calls it, is not something we can ignore."

"What do you suggest we do, Fedorov?"

"We're well out to sea," he started, thinking. "I once considered dropping that thing from the KA-40 into the Qatarra Depression, but held on to it to see what we could learn. Dobrynin gave it a good inspection. He does not think it is a natural object. He thinks it was machined, which made me all the more curious about it."

"Machined? By who?"

"We don't know, but the level of technology required to achieve the properties he observed was very high. It could not be from this era."

"Then you believe this thing came from the future? Our Future?"

"Dobrynin says we might create something like this in 2021, so it must be from some future time, possibly even beyond those years. Remember, time goes both directions. We arrogantly believe there is nothing after our own time until we live it, but the future is as real as this past, or at least I think it is."

"You don't sound all that convinced," said Volsky. "And what we may have seen of the time beyond our own was not very pleasant."

"Miss Fairchild strongly indicated they believed that future time was attempting to contact them."

"Yes," said Volsky, "and sending them warnings about this ship! What do they know that we don't know, Fedorov. This is what I wonder now. I think you were going to suggest that we throw that object Orlov found over the side. Yes?"

"Well, these strange effects associated with it are putting us all in grave danger," said Fedorov. "Lenkov got the worst of it, and I must think now to the safety of this ship and crew. If that object is affecting our stability in time, then we might continue to phase, and that could happen on a quiet night at sea, or right in the middle of a battle. Suppose it gets worse? Suppose the entire ship moves again?"

"We'd be leaving Tovey high and dry here," said Volsky, "and then this history would take its course as it might have without our meddling. Didn't you say yourself that it may be something we do here that causes this great doom the Fairchild lady was speaking of?"

"Or something we fail to do…" Fedorov was deep in thought. "That's the dilemma, sir. We could throw that thing overboard, and it would most likely sink to the bottom of the sea. Unless we get to an abyssal trench, it might be discovered again one day, and who knows how long it would still remain active, and cause these strange time aberrations?"

"A little like contemplating throwing radioactive waste into the ocean," said Volsky. "Well, the Japanese didn't worry much about that after the Fukushima disaster. Out of sight, out of mind, Fedorov. Nobody knows what that contamination really did to the sea, or the coastlines all around it."

"This is why I hesitate to simply throw it over the side, but then I think that decision may be wrong as well. It's maddening."

"But yet we must choose," said Volsky. "Few men have the privilege of knowing what the consequences of their actions may be when they must make a choice. We at least had a peek at that when we shifted to the future, and the world we see here now is also the result of our choices in the past. I do not think we can sit on the fence here. We must decide. I could make this decision now on my own, but I ask your opinion. What should we do?"

Fedorov hesitated, but he knew there was nothing to do but choose one course or another. He could think of no reason to keep that object aboard the ship. What good would it do them? He already suspected it had caused grievous harm here… then he remembered what Dobrynin had said about his attempt to localize the sound.

"One more thing, Admiral. Chief Dobrynin said he tried to find the source of this sound, but could not localize it. He wanted to get out into a boat and listen—away from the ship. I wonder if we could try that?"

"You mean put that thing in a launch and tow it—get it off the ship while still keeping it under our control? I see what you are thinking now."

"That may not work, Admiral. Its effects could have a very wide radius. Remember, it may have helped open that breach that brought Brigadier Kinlan's troops here to this time, and that force was spread over many kilometers."

"So what then? You propose to just send someone out in a launch with it?"

Fedorov shook his head, realizing he was being foolish. "No sir, you are correct. I've been stubbornly holding on to that thing, though I don't really know why. Now I think we must put the ship and crew first. Let us dispose of it, in the deepest water we can find out here, and soon. We should be approaching the Peake Deep. That is a small trough or depression on our present heading. The water there is the deepest in this region, over 4000 fathoms."

"Deep enough," said Volsky. "Very well. Then it is decided. I will rely on you to take care of this matter. Please let me know when it is done. Then, once the ship has sailed on, we will see if Tasarov and Dobrynin can still hear this thing."

"Agreed, sir. I will handle it, and I think now is as good a time as any." He reported what the Marines had found in the helo bay locker. Volsky nodded gravely, and agreed that the man should be given a decent commemoration.

"I will make a statement to the crew," he said. "In the meantime, I suggest you steer for this deep water."

Fedorov consulted a few navigation charts, then had the navigator plot an appropriate course adjustment, and told Nikolin to inform Admiral Tovey that they would need to steer a little to port for a time. So here we are, he thought, caught between the Devil and the Deep Blue Sea. He smiled, glad to have finally made a choice in this matter, and started aft again to go and retrieve the object.

Sometime later he had the small radiation safe box in his hand. It is probably not necessary, he thought. Orlov had the damn thing in his pocket for days on end, and with no ill effects. I wonder why he never heard anything—this sound the others are reporting. I hope I'm not wrong about this. What if I toss it overboard, and Tasarov and Dobrynin still report this sound? Then what?

Still, he could think of no good reason to keep the object on the ship, though if it was responsible for catalyzing the shift of Kinlan's brigade, it was an object of considerable power. Yet it did not seem to act on its own, unless Lenkov's fate is evidence of that. It needed a nuclear detonation in the future, and then served like some beacon or magnet, opening the breach here in this era. Very strange.

From what we already know, there will be no shortage of nuclear detonations in the future. Thus far we've been lucky not to sail through a place where one went off. Gibraltar would have been a most likely candidate for an early ICBM strike, yet we sailed on through the Pillars of Hercules with nothing else following in our wake. At least nothing we know of…

Thank god for that.

He removed the object from the box, staring at it as he felt the cool smoothness of the metal surface, and seeing his own distorted features reflected on its gleaming shape. He suddenly felt a strange sense of dread, and quickly slipped the object into his pocket and started on his way.

Doctor Zolkin had arranged the sea burial for Lenkov off the starboard side, and while the crew focused its attention there, Fedorov made his way to the opposite side of the ship. He consulted his watch, seeing the time was right now. For the next ten minutes they would be over the Peake Deep, and so as the sound of Admiral Volsky's voice came over the intercom, speaking of Lenkov, and how he served the ship, shared their many days at sea, the good times, and the bad, Fedorov took a deep breath. He took the object out of the box, then hurled the Devil's Teardrop as far as he could, watching it vanish into the choppy green sea. He did not know if he had chosen rightly, or if he had just secured the doom of the world, or even if this strange object had anything to do with that at all, but he had made his choice.

As he went to rub his hands together to warm them, he was startled to see that his right hand seem to be wrapped in a strange luminescent aura. Then, for the briefest moment, he was aghast to see his hand phase and vanish! Thankfully it reappeared immediately, and he blinked, his heart racing as he flexed his hand to see that it would still work. There was no pain, the light was gone, and all seemed well, but the incident weighed heavily on him, and he did not put that hand into his pocket all that day, in spite of the cold. He wanted to keep an eye on it at all times, afraid he would look and find it missing, and then discover it in a drawer somewhere... Like Lenkov's legs.

At the same moment Fedorov threw the Teardrop overboard, Lenkov's body, its two parts finally together again, slipped silently down the ramp and joined the object that had taken his life. Now they would both take the long journey down into the deep trough beneath the ship. Lenkov fell like a grim shadow, descending slowly with the weighted body bag dragging him inexorably down, down, down...

Not far away, the Devil's Teardrop fell with him, still glittering with eerie light. Then something happened that no one saw, and that no one could ever imagine. Fedorov would never know about it, nor would any other man aboard the ship. The only witness was poor Lenkov, but the old maxim that 'dead men tell no tales' was very true, and he would never speak a word of what he had seen.

Chapter 24

Darkness had put an end to the fitful air attacks mounted by HMS *Glorious*, and the guns were finally silent on *Hindenburg*. Six enemy planes had been blown from the sky, one small reason for Lütjens to be confident. Yet he was not happy. The fact remained that his task force was now one ship light, with *Kaiser Wilhelm* forced to detach and return to a French port.

After lingering to see *Kaiser Wilhelm* off to France, Lütjens had turned northwest. The enemy carrier he had driven off was still in the game, however, and was running on a parallel course. Both sides had planes up sparring with one another, but neither was able to mount a serious threat. *Goeben* had only three *Stukas*, and the pilots aboard *Glorious* were licking their wounds until late on the 5th of May when they came again, just before sunset.

The action had been hot, the AA gunners doing an excellent job against the low flying *Swordfish*. Two enemy fighters fell to the *Goeben* air defense screen, and the flak gunners got four *Swordfish* before it was over. Three enemy torpedoes posed a threat, but all were easily evaded. Yet the incident had Lütjens thinking now, and he was feeling a rising sense of discontent. *Goeben* had only six fighters. Thus far they had been enough to fend off this single enemy carrier, but he knew the British had several more at sea, at least according to the latest reports out of Group West.

We thought that carriers might be good for little more than scouting operations, thought Lütjens, that and onshore support in the Norwegian operations. Now they have proven to be a principle offensive weapon here! We spend years designing and building these ships, and untold numbers of Deutschmarks. When finished they are the most marvelous warships in the world, yet all it took was a single old plane, obsolete before it was even put in service, and the fastest battlecruiser in the world was hobbled. The fighters off *Goeben* did a fine job, and the gunners here as well, but fill the sky with enough of those flying fruit crates, and something just may get through.

He shook his head, feeling a strange sense of presentiment, almost as if the fate of *Kaiser Wilhelm* was predictive, a prelude to what may come. It was May of 1941, a dangerous month for the Kriegsmarine as history might have it, though only the likes of Fedorov would know that.

By now I should be well to the west, joining up with Topp to plan the destruction of the entire British convoy system. This order to turn east again, and seek out this small British force makes no sense.

He had waited for some time for confirmation on that order, and when it finally came it was stark and to the point. REPEAT: ALL UNITS TO LOCATE AND SINK BATTLESHIP RODNEY. NO EXCEPTIONS – THIS ACTION IS OF UTMOST IMPORTANCE. PRESUMED POSITION AND HEADING TO FOLLOW.

Some U-boat Kapitan must have found that ship, thought Lütjens. But what was so important about a single old battleship? Why that ship and not the others that were now surely maneuvering to engage us? Is Raeder so sent on achieving some victory here that he wants us to gang tackle this ship to assure success? Thus far we have killed a couple destroyers and an enemy cruiser, but it cost us *Kaiser Wilhelm* in the bargain. That ship will live to fight another day, the damage can be easily repaired, but the fact remains that I am one ship light. Perhaps Adler was correct about this enemy aircraft carrier. Am I failing to see something here?

He paced slowly on the bridge, his eyes scanning the dreary horizon. In the Mediterranean, it was those damnable rockets that put the damage on us, and not shells from the enemy guns. And when we struck back, it was the land based planes the enemy feared most. Am I witnessing a sea change in naval tactics and strategy here? Look what the presence of *Graf Zeppelin* did for us in the Norwegian Sea last year. It was that ship that so bedeviled the British. Yes, our battleships were a real threat, but first blood went to those hot *Stuka* pilots off the *Graf Zeppelin*, and that will likely be the case here. Even though *Goeben* has only nine planes, it has been very useful. Again, it was a *Stuka* that put that hit on the enemy carrier, not *Kaiser*

Wilhelm. Things are changing. It is no longer the big ships like *Hindenburg* that will rule the sea, but the aircraft over those waters, and these long range rockets. How long before we have them ourselves?

Lütjens had turned north around midnight, stubbornly thinking he might still meet up with Topp on that course and then continue west. When this last signal came from Group West, firming up his orders to seek out this British battleship, he also learned that Topp had been given the same order. *Tirpitz* had turned southeast, and if he did not turn as well, he could not rendezvous with the northern task force.

And so, reluctantly, Lütjens turned east on a heading of 080 degrees. As the light faded on the 6th of May, the alarm was sounded again and the gunners ran to man their stations. This time, however, the planes in the sky were friendly. It was a flight of three fighters off *Graff Zeppelin*, and they were soon dancing in the sky with Marco Ritter above the task force. Topp was getting close.

"Admiral," said Adler, coming in with the latest status report. "*U-556* is still shadowing that British battleship. We have a good fix on its location, heading south. Even if we make only 24 knots they are only about ten hours east of us now. If they continue south, we could possibly intercept them mid-day on the 8th."

"Where will Topp be if we keep to this heading until dawn?"

"Very close, sir. About sixty miles to our northeast tomorrow morning."

"And the British?"

"Over a hundred and twenty miles behind us to the west—at least the two battleships that were trying to catch up with Topp."

"What about that enemy carrier that has been bothering us?"

You mean the ship you failed to order *Kaiser Wilhelm* to sink, thought Adler, but he was wise enough not to speak his mind.

"Our turn to the east seems to have shaken them off. I don't think we have anything more to worry about from them, particularly now that we are coming in range of our planes off *Graf Zeppelin*."

"And the *Invincible?*"

"The last information we have is that they have detached a cruiser north, probably to lend additional support to the *Rodney* group. Two ships were seen by a *Kondor* out of Spain, and their last known heading was 330."

Lütjens was plotting out that course on the map room in his mind. Still on an intercept course with us now. Could they know we have turned? Then again, we were steering that course earlier, and they could still be following our presumed track. In any case, it appears we may meet them soon, sometime tomorrow. The only question is whether we should effect a linkup with Topp first. I think this wise.

"Very well," he said. "Yes, Adler, I have been thinking about that British aircraft carrier. Perhaps you were correct. If I had ordered *Kaiser Wilhelm* to go in for the kill, we might not be worrying about it now. Then again, we both saw what happened. Where is the *Kaiser*? Back in a French port, and with a good stomach ache. So my caution was not without merit either."

"Of course, sir," said Adler. "Yet now the situation has changed. *Graf Zeppelin* has a full complement of aircraft—twelve more fighters to go with the six we have on *Goeben*, and another thirty *Stukas!* Nothing can stop us now. Nothing."

"Are you forgetting what happened in the Mediterranean?" Lütjens wagged a finger. "We had plenty of land based air cover, but they could do nothing against those naval rockets. This is why we must keep an eye out for this British flagship. You say those two heavy ships are still steering 330? We must confirm that. Send a message to *Goeben* and see if they can locate that ship. If we can strike it with those *Stukas*, and eliminate it early on, then we can take these rockets out of the equation here. After that, I will share your confidence and enthusiasm, Adler, but not before."

"Agreed, sir. That would be best. But how many rockets can the British have on a single warship? Once we join with Topp, we will have ten ships, the most powerful task force to sail these waters in decades."

"Suppose they have twenty missiles," said Lütjens. "You saw what they can do, Kapitan. It took us hours to put out those fires, and months to repair the damage. It was uncanny how they seemed to leap at us, just before they struck the ship, and avoided our main belt armor."

"This time things may be different, sir, if Koenig's hydraulics actually work."

The time in the docks at Toulon had been put to good use aboard *Hindenburg*. Chief Engineer Viktor Koenig had been shaking his head at the damage to the superstructure, and wondering how he could increase protection there. They were lucky that there had been fresh secondary batteries available, waiting on the trains for delivery to the *Oldenburg*, but diverted south to Toulon for *Hindenburg* instead. And he had also managed to pilfer a good deal of excess armor in storage for that ship, and had several tons left over when the repairs were complete. He came up with an ingenious idea that he could mount these armor plates on sections of the deck, raising them with hydraulics when needed to provide several inches of armor protection to the main superstructure that had been so severely damaged earlier. When not in use, *Hindenburg* would also have a much thicker hide against plunging shell hits in those sections.

The extra weight shaved off just a little speed, but with her great beam, *Hindenburg* still handled well, and rode easily, even in very heavy seas.

Armor, thought Lütjens, we certainly have that in abundance now. But it was not merely the structural damage that compelled me to break off that last engagement, it was those terrible fires. If we are hit like that again… And we never once set eyes on the ship that fired at us. That was the most frightening part of that battle. How do you kill something that is not even on your horizon? What good are these massive gun turrets if they have no targets? He looked up again, hearing the drone of the fighters swirling in the skies over his task force.

Graf Zeppelin... The carrier.... That ship was now the most important vessel in the entire navy, and it was humbling to realize this. With the carrier he had much greater situational awareness, and the same long range over the horizon striking power that his adversary had. The *Stukas* had proven to be most able threats, particularly against more lightly armored ships. We very nearly destroyed the entire British battlecruiser squadron in that engagement up north. Then again, if we had stayed in the fight in the Med, this ship might not even be here now... another humbling thought.

Things have changed. Hoffmann was correct. The entire character of naval warfare at sea has taken a pivot, and we failed to see it coming. Koenig is rigging out makeshift steel plates to try and compensate for our short sightedness. The carriers will mean everything now, and any surface warship without these naval rockets will be at a decided disadvantage. Everything has changed, yet in the meantime, we must fight with the ships we have...

He thought of that fluttering old *Swordfish* torpedo bomber again, obsolete before it was even introduced, and realized that may very well apply to his own ship now, the pride of the fleet. He looked at his Kapitan, a haunted look in his eyes as he spoke.

"So you will soon get your battle, Adler. This is all or nothing now. It is time to fight. I intend to find this British battleship, sink it, and then turn to do the same to anything following us. We will fight to the last shell here if need be. See that Eisenberg is ready on the guns!"

"That is what I have been waiting for you to say all along, Admiral. Have no fear! We will win through. I promise you this."

Lütjens smiled as Adler saluted and rushed off to see to the ship. He was like a steed that had been given free rein, and now he wanted to gallop into battle as soon as possible. The smile faded on Lütjens' face as he watched his Kapitan go, and his eyes darkened with that odd feeling that had plagued him all morning. He could feel the rising adrenaline in his chest, though all about him the sea was clear and calm, and nothing threatened his ships.

But he could feel something was very wrong here, a strange sensation that was almost a tangible thing, something he might hear on the wind, or in the depths of the ocean, something moaning, lost, dangerous. What was it? He listened, but could hear nothing beyond the normal sounds of the ship, running smoothly at 24 knots now, the sturdy bow cutting the sea with little effort. He could hear nothing amiss, but he could *feel* it, sense it, a persistent sensation of rising danger.

I must be getting old, he thought. Am I getting butterflies in the belly now that the ship is heading into combat soon? I am Admiral of the Fleet!

That afternoon two seaplanes off his own ship set off to look for the British flagship. They searched down a heading of 120 southeast, and neither one would return. The radio man came running onto the bridge an hour later saying the planes had seen the one thing that was haunting Lütjens now.

"Rockets in the sky, Admiral! That was the last report we have from the Arados. Both our seaplanes are gone!"

So they were out there, he thought. 120 southeast. "How far out were those planes when they last reported?"

"About 280 miles, sir. They were just about to turn back."

So there is your confirmation, thought Lütjens. They are still steering 330, coming at us as if they know exactly where we are. That was another odd thing about these engagements. The British seemed to have eyes everywhere. Well, if my seaplanes have spotted them at this range, then they could do the same. But there have been no reports of any further enemy planes, and we still have six fighters overhead. How are they seeing us? Could they have submarines out here too, or is this just good British seamanship? Probably the latter, he thought.

He looked at his watch. If they are coming fast, then Adler will be busy sooner than we think. He walked to the plotting table, looking at the lines drawn to indicate the converging courses. The task force was at 24 knots, and the enemy was easily making at least that speed. This meant the two sides might be converging at nearly 50 nautical miles per hour. Those 280 miles would diminish rapidly. In just under six hours he might have the enemy on his horizon, right near dawn. Then we will see what the sky holds for us, a good sunrise, or the tails of those cursed naval rockets. He did not have long to wait, and it would be a fitful night's sleep before he got his answer.

Part IX

Maxim 17

"The longer everything goes according to plan, the bigger the impending disaster."

— Maxim 17: The Seventy Maxims of Maximally Effective Mercenaries

Chapter 25

Admiral Volsky was on the bridge when Fedorov came up, his heart heavy as he had just lain yet another man to rest, where he would stand his watch for eternity in the deep sea. How many had died? The fact that he did not know the number was equally disturbing. When you start losing count, then you know the bill is too high, he thought. And how many more will die before this is over, if it will ever be over?

Fedorov came onto the bridge, announced by Rodenko, and he saluted with that hand, giving it a sidelong glance as he did so, and flexing his fingers after Volsky returned his salute.

"Welcome Fedorov, something wrong with that hand?"

"Not at the moment," said Fedorov, "as long as the damn thing stays put."

"I don't understand," said Volsky, and Fedorov stepped closer, lowering his voice as he told the Admiral what had happened after he threw the Devil's Teardrop overboard.

"That is most disturbing," said Volsky. "And this is why you do not have on your leather gloves. Yes? Have you seen Doctor Zolkin?"

"I doubt there is any pill he can give me for that, sir. But this reinforces my belief that the object may have been responsible for destabilizing the ship's position in time."

"I am glad that thing is off the ship. Will you be alright now?"

"I hope as much," said Fedorov. "It may be just a temporary effect from handling the object those few moments. It happened so quickly that I thought I might be seeing things."

"Let me know if you have any further trouble."

"I will, sir."

"Now then," Volsky adjusted his officer's coat. "Mister Rodenko has our situation report." He looked over his shoulder for Rodenko, and the *Starpom* was ready at hand.

"The KA-40 was up just after sunset," he said. "We could fly any time, but why waste the air defense missiles if those German fighters are about. In any case, we've had a good look forward, and can now report the locations of both German battlegroups. One is here, about 280 miles northwest, and the other due north of that position, about here. They have turned on these new headings to effect a rendezvous. This contact here is a British battlegroup composed of two ships, and there are another two here, due east of the predicted German rendezvous point."

"The first group will be *King George V* and *Prince of Wales,*" said Fedorov. "The second group are the battlecruisers *Renown* and *Repulse.*"

"A lot of power there," said Volsky.

"Perhaps," said Fedorov, "but this single German group to the north could match all those ships. My enigma decrypts show the *Tirpitz,* with two battlecruisers, another heavy cruiser, two destroyers and the wild card, *Graf Zeppelin.* The situation is not favorable. As the Germans come east for *Rodney,* the two British battlecruisers will not be able to stop them, and the remainder of the British heavy ships will arrive piecemeal, behind the action from the west. Admiral Tovey tells me that they are also bringing *Duke of York* and *Hood* down from the Denmark Strait, and they would be the last to arrive."

"Then we must give the Germans something to think about if they continue to move east." Volsky tapped the enemy contacts on the Plexiglas screen. "We are in missile range now with the weapons we received from *Kazan.* They range out over 600 kilometers. Unfortunately, they are not our heaviest warheads, only 200 kilograms, and firing at this range will also expend most of their fuel, so the fires will not be as much of a factor. You know these enemy ships, Fedorov. How do you suggest we proceed?"

Fedorov took a deep breath, realizing he was now about to plan their battle action, and sign the death warrants of many men with each word he spoke. Yet it could not be helped. They had committed themselves to this course, to this battle, and now it had to be fought. It was either that or they would surely see the British take heavy losses. The *Rodney* alone, even with the two battlecruisers in support, could not stand against the German fleet. They had to act.

"Given the situation," he began, "I see the main threat at the outset to be the German aircraft carrier, *Graf Zeppelin*. I believe they will be launching *Stukas* at dawn, and so we must strike them tonight, and attempt to either sink that ship or take it out of the action. The *Stukas* are a grave threat."

"And the battleships?"

"They won't reach the scene until later tomorrow, and as they approach, they will come within range of our heavier Moskit-II and MOS III missiles, so we have plenty of time to plan for them."

"Agreed," said Volsky. "Always get the carrier first. That is a rule that will stand even to our time in 2021. But there are seven ships in that German battlegroup, can we identify that target?"

"They will come into range of the Fregat system radar in three or four hours," said Rodenko. "With that I think I can select out the carrier. We will see the radar returns of any planes it launches or recovers, and I can designate it as the primary target for any salvo you fire."

Volsky looked at his watch. "They are not likely to fly off much tonight. Let us wait until the pre-dawn hours. Then, when you identify your target, we'll give them a rude awakening with the Onyx missiles we stole from *Kazan*. They will do the job, yes, Fedorov?"

"*Graf Zeppelin* has armor, but not anywhere near the protection of the battleships. Yes sir, they will do the job." Fedorov rubbed his forehead, a worried look on his face.

"I know what you are feeling, Fedorov," said the Admiral. "Legendary ships out there, commanded by men you have read about, and perhaps idolized in your mind these many years. But you must kill them."

"Correct, sir. Once, after *Yamato*, Karpov told me it would get easier in time, but I have not found this to be the case."

"That is because your conscience is still intact. Killing is never an easy thing to do for a man of conscience. Karpov sees things otherwise, because his soul is darkened. He is an efficient and deadly man at the helm of any ship he commands, but he kills wantonly, and without regret. So be thankful that you feel some of the pain our missiles may inflict on these men and ships out there. Yes, I say ships as well, for we live with them, bond with them, whenever we take to the sea. They are the raft of life itself for us here. Without them we are like Lenkov, sinking into the depths of oblivion. So when we sink one, we know what it is to put men into the cold sea, and know we cannot save them. Never forget that, but also never let it prevent you from doing what is necessary to win the day."

"I understand sir, but this does not make it any easier."

Volsky nodded. "Once I relied on you to do what we should do in these situations, and on Karpov to do what we must. Now I'm afraid that you must wear both hats, Fedorov. You are Captain of this ship, and I may not always be standing at your side here."

"I will do my best, Admiral."

"Then we attack near dawn. They will see the missiles fire, and know we are here. It will be another red day, Fedorov, and when we are done, Lenkov will have more than a few friends, but it must be done."

"I will see that Admiral Tovey is informed, sir," said Fedorov. "Nikolin will be here soon. And sir, why don't you get some rest now. I can relieve you for the night shift."

"As long as you are fresh for the morning, my young man. Very well, I will see if I can get some sleep." He lowered his voice. "But let me know if you have any further problems with that hand…"

Carrier Graf Zeppelin ~ Norwegian Sea ~ 7 May, 1941, 04:00

The flight deck of the carrier *Graf Zeppelin* was still and calm, with the first of the morning fighter contingent still below decks being armed. Six fighters were scheduled for launch at 06:00, to be followed soon after by the first squadron of *Stukas*. The carrier had sortied *streikschwere,* with a strike-heavy compliment primarily composed of modified *Stuka* dive bombers. There were two *Stuka* squadrons aboard, a baker's dozen in each, for a total of 26 strike aircraft, and another six BF-109Ts in reserve, with four *Arado* seaplanes to make 42 planes in all.

The former first officer of the *Admiral Scheer*, Kapitan zur See Kurt Böhmer, was still in command of the carrier, arriving on the bridge early that day to oversee the morning launch.

We are missing Marco Ritter these days, he thought. I was thinking to see him down on the flight deck with that red scarf flapping in the wind. But he'll be out there. Word is that the *Goeben* did very well in the Med as a scout ship, and Ritter cherry picked the best *Stuka* pilots from my flight crews here to look after *Hindenburg*. That said, they could not stop those rocket attacks. Nothing we have can stop them. So the only thing we can do when the sky lights up with those missile trails is put up a good shieldwall.

Brinkmann is in *Prinz Eugen* out in front, and I have the new destroyers *Loki* and *Thor* to either side. After what happened to *Sigfrid*, we must have a destroyer abreast of us at all times, and that failing, one of the heavier ships must stand in for that duty. We can take no chances that those rockets will find us again. Yet for now, the sea is empty, and we will pluck out the eyes of any aircraft that come looking for us. The British carriers are well to the south and west in any case, so we should rule the day here. Now to get our boys up and after the British. If I can sink that old battleship we're looking for, I can save Lütjens and Topp the trouble. Then they can turn and slug it out with the battleships.

The *Schweregruppe* of the task force was out ahead of *Prinz Eugen*. He could not see the tall main masts and superstructure of *Tirpitz* in the darkness, but he could feel the ship's presence, the cold hard Wotan Hart steel plying through the waters like a great shark. *Scharnhorst* and *Gneisenau* were cruising to either side, guarding the battleship as the destroyers stood watch over his carrier. Once bitten, twice shy. Now that the Germans had faced the British rocket weapons, they sailed in shieldwall formation, with one ship protecting another from the deadly sea skimming missiles.

Kurt Böhmer looked at his watch, seeing the elevator bringing up another two fighters, wings still folded as they rose to the main flight deck. It was then that he saw what he had feared since that first astounding attack near Iceland. There were lights in the sky, high up, rising like shooting stars fleeing the earth and seeking the darkness of the night again. But they would not stay high for long. The watchmen had seen them as well, and alarms were ringing all over the ship. He looked to see men running to battle stations, and reached for his field glasses, his heart beating faster.

One… three… four rockets were in the sky now, climbing, then appearing to hang in the darkness like a line of cold steel stars. Then they fell, one by one, as if they were a formation of precision fighters peeling off to attack a target at lower altitude. Down they came, as the men shouted and footsteps rattled the decks. Guns were turning and training, barrels elevating, and then he heard a gunnery officer shouting at his men.

"Not there!" he pointed with a baton. "Lower your guns. They will come in right over the wave tops!"

It was something his men had been oblivious of in that first attack, but forewarned was now fore armed. The Germans knew what to expect. According to plan, they tightened up their sailing order, like a school of fish seeking safety in a group of closely packed ships— like a group of Viking warriors crouching behind their shields. *Graf Zeppelin* held *Loki* on the right arm, *Thor* on the left. Now the guns began firing, for the director had been correct, and the missiles were diving for the sea.

Böhmer knew what to expect, that dizzying dance over the wave tops, as if the rockets were deliberately taunting the gunners to try to hit them. The roar of the AA guns now became deafening, the bright fire of the exploding rounds lighting of the sable sky and glowing on the dark waters below. He watched, spellbound again, thinking they must surely miss. How could the British even know where his ships were to target them? Did they have a U-boat nearby to give away his position? They could never find him with a random shot like this. He was thinking of them as a spread of torpedoes, dangerous, but something that might be avoided by maneuver. Yet nothing would stay these lethal weapons from their appointed round…

On they came, low on the sea, the bright fire from their tails now suddenly visible. They were so fast that it was impossible for the gunners to adjust for the oncoming range. Böhmer would see them come right at his ships again, unerringly, as if they had night eyes, bat like things, creatures of the night that flew with senses unknown to man, vampires. To his utter amazement, the first of five came boring in right towards his formation.

"Hard to port! All ahead full! All ships to match speed and turn!"

He scarcely had time to shout out the order when the first lance struck his shield on the starboard side. *Loki* was hit just forward of the bridge, smashing right into a 4.7-inch dual purpose gun turret as it fired in futile reprisal. The turret exploded, completely obliterated by the 200kg warhead, and bright orange fire lit up the scene with its angry light.

Then the second missile pummeled *Loki* amidships, the small 6800 ton destroyer rolling with the heavy punch. It was just the size and type of ship the missile had been designed to kill, and it would do exactly that, just as *Sigfrid* had died in this same way a year earlier.

Then, to Böhmer's amazement, he watched the next two missiles alter their course. They were not simply well aimed lances thrown from beyond the horizon, a feat that was astounding enough. They maneuvered, making lightning quick turns that not even the most agile fighter could have achieved. They maneuvered—right into the gap between *Prinz Eugen* and his own ship, but it was not the veteran Prince they were after that morning.

Graf Zeppelin was struck on her starboard side, about 200 meters forward of the main elevators. There were two 15cm guns there in twin-gun *Dopp MPL C/36* casemate mountings, with 1.2 inches of armor. It was not enough to stop those 200kg warheads, and the turrets fared little better than the smaller guns on *Loki*. The fury of the fireball glowed orange and red on the grey hull of the ship, and then the second missile smashed right behind the heavy anchors suspended on the bow, piercing the thin armor and blowing clean through the ship and out the port side.

The last thing to strike the bow of the ship had been a bottle of champagne during the launch, but now it was a blackened wreck, with heavy fire and smoke coiling up from the wound.

Böhmer soon learned that neither rocket had penetrated to the arming deck, where the *Stukas* were sitting like a flock of densely packed black crows, with heavy bombs mounted beneath the stubby, folded wings. How in god's name could they move like that, he thought? These are precision guided weapons! Nothing on earth could fly so fast, and turn so smartly to find his ship in the middle of the formation like this. It was almost like magic!

And it was only the beginning.

Chapter 26

Aboard *Kirov*, Volsky was standing by the Captain's chair, where he had insisted Fedorov take his seat to lead the opening action against the German fleet. He was watching his young Captain closely, as if he thought Fedorov might wince when Rodenko reported that all five missiles launched had found targets. That was no surprise. Karpov had said it many times before—*what we target, we hit, and what we hit we can destroy.*

Yet Fedorov did not feel like Karpov that day. Yes, he was bothered by the thought that each order he gave here was sending men to their death, and burning their ships, still unseen over the far horizon. At least it was not as bad as that day when they had faced off against the great battleship *Yamato*, its mighty guns flinging massive shells at *Kirov*, coming within a hair's breadth of striking the ship at one point, and sweeping away the top radar mast as it passed overhead like a merciless hammer of doom, striking the sea with a thunderous roar.

Thankfully, they had replaced that system when they returned to Vladivostok, and now it spun rapidly on that same mast overhead, its electronic fingers seeking out the German task force in the early predawn hours.

"They had another ship in tight on the primary," said Rodenko. "It looks like it absorbed two hits, and I think we will sink that ship. Two more missiles struck the primary. They have made a hard turn to port and are coming around 180 degrees."

Fedorov looked at Volsky. "Two hit's sir."

"What is your assessment, Fedorov?" said the Admiral. "Will they be enough to put that ship out of action?"

"We will not know that unless we get the KA-40 back up for battle damage assessment, or unless they begin launching planes. In that instance, I believe we must fire again."

"Agreed," said Volsky. "This is an armored ship?"

"No more than 100mm on the belt," said Fedorov. "45 to 60mm

on the flight deck."

"Then it is vulnerable to plunging fire as well." The Admiral folded his arms. "We might do more damage that way if it becomes necessary."

They had decided to strike in the early pre-dawn hours, thinking to pre-empt any air strike that may be launched by the German carrier. Now they sat like a dark spider at the center of an electronic web spun out by the ship's powerful radar systems. All about them, their adversaries were creeping into that web, unaware of the danger that lurked over their horizon… until those first missiles broke the stillness of the dawn, and the battle began.

Fedorov knew it was to be a one sided affair. Their enemy could not even see them, let alone strike at them in reprisal. With their speed, they could stay well beyond the range of the massive guns on the German battleships, so it would be a simple and merciless equation as he saw things. It would be a contest of fire and shock against German steel. How much of a pounding could their ships take before the steel broke in the wills of the Admirals and Captains who commanded them.

Before the action he had discussed the situation with Admiral Volsky, and came down to a grim conclusion. Fedorov had pointed out that they had only 28 anti-ship missiles, still more than a normal combat load, due to the fact that they had pirated missiles from the submarine *Kazan*.

"This is the heart of the German fleet, is it not, Fedorov?"

"It appears so," said Fedorov. "We've identified all three battleships, the two battlecruisers, the carrier *Graf Zeppelin* and the light escort carrier that was with *Hindenburg*."

"Then if we use the power we now have, we can literally take the German fleet out of the war. Yes? I am not speaking of a nuclear option here. Yet my question to you is this—can we cripple the German navy for good here by using the conventional warheads we still have?"

"Very likely," said Fedorov. "That will depend on how we hit them."

"Hard, Fedorov. We must hit them very hard. A carrier must be saturated to achieve a certain kill. I know this is our tactic in modern times, but will it apply here?"

"The *Graf Zeppelin* has only a third the displacement of a typical *Nimitz* Class carrier, sir. And the *Nimitz* could sustain three times the damage of even the best built carrier in WWII. We may be able to mission kill this German carrier with two or three hits."

"Yet that would allow it to survive, would it not? Now I begin to sound like Karpov, but would that mean we must fight this same battle all over again, and without the missiles we fire here today? No. I think we must take a hard line here. If we engage, then we must do so with the intent of killing these ships, not just putting damage on them to discourage them. Do you agree, Fedorov?"

After a deep breath, Fedorov nodded his assent.

"But you still have reservations," said Volsky. "I can see it in your eyes."

"It's not that, sir," said Fedorov.

"That hand again? Is all well there?"

"Yes sir, my hand seems to be fit and staying put now. I think that was a temporary effect, or at least I hope as much."

"Then what? Tell me why you hesitate?"

"It isn't the tactics, Admiral. I agree. If we fight here now, and with a limited missile inventory, then we should seek a decisive engagement. Yes, I know I also sound like Karpov now, but we both admit that in many ways he was correct when it came to battle. I was thinking about something else—how the Germans could have learned about *Rodney*."

"Volkov? Might he have tipped them off?"

"I've wondered about that, but cannot see how he would be privy to that information Miss Fairchild disclosed. Yes, he might be able to look up the service record and see that *Rodney* did have that gold bullion aboard, and the Elgin Marbles, but that would be of little consequence. It would not be anything that would compel the

Germans to maneuver as they have here, and seek out that single ship."

"Could we be reading more into their maneuvers than they really know, Fedorov? After all, both task groups now appear on a course to rendezvous by mid-day, and they are merely heading away from the British battleships behind them."

"Yes, and directly towards us. I think they must know we have followed them through the straits of Gibraltar, sir. Yet that northern group is not bearing on our position. It is on a course to intercept *Rodney*. So is the *Hindenburg* group."

"Mere coincidence," Volsky suggested.

"No sir, they know the position of *Rodney* well enough. The U-boat that torpedoed it will have reported this information."

"Then they are obviously out to pick off the wounded water buffalo, and thin out the herd," said Volsky.

"Possibly, but I would think they would not perceive *Rodney* as a threat here, given the speed advantage they have over that ship. The *Invincible* is a real threat to them, and yet they are not maneuvering to intercept us at this time, even though they had a fix on our position yesterday with that seaplane."

"It does seem odd," Volsky agreed.

"And don't forget that we have that previous message intercept. It appeared Lütjens was ordered to take this course—ordered to seek out *Rodney*."

It was then that Nikolin turned with a report that deepened the mystery. He had picked up another signal using the German naval code, and was translating it with the application Fedorov had in his pad device. When he finished, it soon appeared that there was now some confusion on the German side. Wilhelmshaven was asking what orders needed confirmation.

"Repeat order needing confirmation. Objective is as per original orders in *Fall Rheinübung* ..." Fedorov's eyes narrowed. That was the first time they had picked up the actual name of the operation now underway, and it was identical to the one put forward by the

Germans at this same time in the history he knew. It was an oddity, as the history here was vastly altered. And now it also seemed that the intent of the German battle strategy was no longer clear. Fedorov did not have the original orders, as they must have been given by other means than coded signals, possibly transmitted to Lütjens before he left Toulon. The sudden turnabout made by the *Hindenburg* group appeared to be in response to a direct order from Wilhelmshaven, but now this directive seemed to contradict that and re-affirm the original plan. What was going on here?

"Confusion in battle is commonplace," said Volsky.

"Yet we have the decoded message received earlier, Admiral. It was a clear order to find and sink *Rodney*. Lütjens requested confirmation, and now we have this? Wilhelmshaven seems to know nothing about that earlier order."

"Very strange," Volsky agreed. "Yet I do not see how this impacts our decision here on how to proceed. I believe we must eliminate the German carrier as our opening move in this chess game. Correct Fedorov?"

The Captain nodded, again with some sense of misgiving obvious on his face. Minutes later they began their attack, and now the next move was plotted in this uneven chess game, where the Russian ship could move to develop all its pieces before the enemy could lay a finger on a single pawn.

"Twenty four missiles remaining," said Volsky. "Two must have struck a smaller escort ship."

"They are learning, Admiral," said Fedorov. "They are trying to steam in tight formations around the carrier to protect it."

"Correct," said Rodenko. "I can now read two ships in close proximity to the primary. They must have redeployed the cruiser escort to replace the ship we hit with those first two missiles."

"All the more reason to change our angle of attack," said Volsky. "I was told we still have several *Moskit-IIs* programmed for vertical strike profiles—is this so, Mister Samsonov?"

"Correct Admiral. I have three of nine missiles in that system programmed for vertical strike."

"Then I think this is the next move, Fedorov," said Volsky. "A knight leaping from above, and not the slashing, sea-skimming attack of the Bishop."

"I'm seeing air activity over the primary," said Rodenko. "I think they're launching."

"So out first strike was not enough," said Volsky.

Fedorov hesitated, just long enough for Volsky to turn his head from Nikolin to regard him more closely. Then the young Captain swallowed, nodded, and turned to Samsonov.

"How many *Moskit-II* missiles remain?"

"Nine missiles loaded and ready—one in the number ten bay." Samsonov was reminding Fedorov that one of the nine was mounted in the special weapons bay, where a nuclear warhead could be loaded onto the missile if so ordered. That was not to be the case today, but Fedorov took note of that. They still had three special warheads, and if they ever had to use them, they would need missiles. So instead of 24 missiles available, he really had no more than 21 now if he wished to retain three for those special warheads. It was time to do some heavier hitting.

"Ready one *Moskit-II* for immediate launch," he said. "Vertical attack profile. Target the primary, carrier *Graf Zeppelin*."

With over twice the warhead weight of the missiles they had received from *Kazan*, this was the ship's premier ship killer. It was normally programmed to be a fast supersonic sea-skimmer, but they had found that the heavy side armor of the battleships of this era had been able to survive hits at the water line. So it was decided to reprogram missiles to pop up and hit the superstructure, or simply strike from high above, where the thinner deck armor could easily be penetrated by the big 450kg warhead moving at the blistering speed of Mach three.

"Very well," said Fedorov. "Mark your target and fire."

* * *

Two of three fighters on deck had been damaged by shrapnel hits from the missile strike that struck *Graf Zeppelin* near the bow. This had prompted Kapitan Böhmer to urge his flight engineers to get as many *Stukas* up on the deck as possible. He was determined to launch, even if it meant his planes would have to storm right through the smoke forward, blinded by the dark smoke now rolling right down the flight deck when he turned into the wind, and licked by flames as they took off over the bow. The British had done the very same thing with those fluttering moths of theirs. So he urged his crews and pilots on.

While Fedorov and Volsky had discussed how to proceed, sorting through the contradiction in German orders, the Germans got up a flight of six *Stukas* and had them all airborne.

And then it came…

It was the same as before when Böhmer saw it, a bright light ascending from the purple edge of the coming dawn, climbing, climbing. Then it arced over and began to fall, a fiery comet that seemed to grow larger and brighter with each passing second. Down it came, swift and silent, as it was moving three times faster than the roar of its own engines. The eerie silence of its coming was deceptive, and then it thundered down on his ship, plunging right through the armored deck amidships with a shattering explosion.

Graf Zeppelin rocked with the blow, the orange fire erupting from the guts of the ship in a broiling mass. It was as if the carrier had been struck by a swift kamikaze, but one weighing over 4500 kilograms, and with a 450kg warhead. The rest was the great fuel laden mass of the rocket itself, which penetrated the deck, exploded with torrential fire and shock below, and plunged right through the maintenance deck where another twenty *Stukas* were still being armed. The explosion erupted from the machinery spaces below, and set off 500 pound bombs, one after another, in a terrible sequence of death and destruction. Planes and flight crews were immolated, bulkheads blown apart, fuel set fire in a raging inferno. The damage extended all the way down to one of the two propulsion shafts, severing it, and then the shock of the attack blew completely through the hull.

Graf Zeppelin keeled over to one side as the hull was breached below the water line. But it was the raging inferno within that would consume the ship, the fires reaching one plane after another, the ordnance and aviation fuel feeding the conflagration. The ship was doomed. Germany's first aircraft carrier, famous even though it never steamed on the high seas or saw combat in the war Fedorov knew, would not survive the hour.

High above, the six lucky *Stuka* pilots who bravely took off through the deck smoke, now saw the volcanic eruption below, and gasped at the fireball that now consumed the ship. The destroyer *Thor*, steaming off the port side, had to make an emergency turn away from the carrier to avoid the holocaust. Even so, the sides and superstructure of the smaller ship were lacerated with shrapnel. *Prinz Eugen* had fallen off to take up a position to the starboard side of the carrier when it turned after the initial missile strike. Now the men aboard the heavy cruiser gaped in awe at the scene unfolding.

The carrier was soon in a heavy list, still burning fiercely when it began to keel over, the hot fires hissing into the sea. All the remaining fighters and *Stukas*, and the elite pilots that had trained to fly them off the carrier, would die in those desperate, violent minutes, along with nearly 1,700 officers and crew of every rank.

There would be twenty two survivors.

Chapter 27

Numbers…. Facts that Fedorov could call up from the library of his mind, or look up if he ever forgot them. Carrier *Graf Zeppelin*, 33,550 tons displacement, 262 meters in length, four geared turbines producing 200,000 shaft horsepower. Aircraft carried: 42. Ship's Compliment: 1,720.

It had taken just one missile, angled at the right attack, and falling into what amounted to a readymade explosive mass of 500 pound bombs and volatile aviation fuel. The damage was violent, catastrophic and final, and this was a ship they would never have to face or fight again, thought Fedorov. The legend was gone—killed by me. All those lives… I'm responsible…

Admiral Volsky was watching him closely again, understanding what he was feeling. He knew that he could never reason away the emotion, and the heavy burden of having to kill. It was not even as if the ship itself were in any danger. They struck down their enemy before they even knew they were in harm's way.

"It had to be done, Mister Fedorov," said the Admiral.

"I understand, sir."

"Yes," said Volsky. "I know it was a hard blow to those men out there. Yet we must be prepared to do more here. This was a ship that was never even supposed to be at sea in this war."

"Another interloper," said Fedorov, "as we are, sir."

"Very well," Volsky nodded. "Now we must consider the battleships. There will be time enough later to think about what we have done here. At the moment, the enemy is approaching our horizon. One missile—one ship." Volsky shook his head with as much amazement as he had regret.

"I'm afraid that the battleships may not die so easily," said Fedorov. "When Tovey caught the *Bismarck* in our history with three British battleships, *Rodney* included, they put 2,878 rounds of all calibers into that ship, and *Bismarck* was still afloat. It took three more torpedoes, and some say deliberate scuttling, before the great ship went down."

"Nothing is unsinkable," said Volsky.

"Yes sir, that we know all too well. Oh, we'll hurt what we fire at, but it will take a good deal to sink these ships."

"Then our intention will be to disable them, mission kill them, and leave the rest to the Royal Navy."

"In that case, we may wish to program more of these high angle attack profiles. And I would also suggest we use the Vodopads"

"Torpedoes?" said Volsky. "I see. That was how we bested that big Japanese battleship."

"Yes sir. Our missiles hurt the enemy, but have not really killed any battleship we engaged. Yet a torpedo hit, particularly one designed to break a ship's back, or follow its wake to the rudder, is a very dangerous weapon, for any ship."

"Agreed. We are in range of this same task group now. The Vodopads rocket assisted approach can take it out 120 kilometers. How many rounds do we have remaining on that system?" Admiral Volsky looked to Tasarov, who seemed lost beneath his headset, his eyes closed, listening very intently to something.

"Mister Tasarov?"

"I'm sorry sir…"

"An undersea contact?" Volsky moved to the young Lieutenant's station now.

"No sir… I do not think so…"

Volsky took one look at Tasarov, and he could see that something was very wrong. The man looked like he had not slept in days, with dark circles under his eyes, and a haggard expression on his face.

"Mister Tasarov, when was the last time you took leave?"

"I was off during the night shift, sir. But I could not sleep."

"Oh? Have you seen the Doctor?"

"No sir…. I'm not sick. It is just that I cannot shake off that sound."

"Sound?"

Now Rodenko looked at Fedorov, and the two men shared a knowing glance. "He's been trying to process a sound, Admiral," he explained. "Tasarov reported it some time ago."

"The same sound Dobrynin reported," said Fedorov. "They both still hear something, but cannot seem to localize it, even though I disposed of that object Orlov found some hours ago."

"You still hear this sound, Tasarov? You can hear it now?"

"Yes sir, very deep sound. I hear it with or without my system acoustics. I hear it even in my sleep."

"I see…" Volsky could see the man needed some help. "Go and see the Doctor, whether you are sick or not. Tell him what you have told us here, and see if he can give you something to help you rest. Then after that, go to the officer's mess and eat well. This is an order. Tell the Chef this comes directly from me, and he is to prepare any meal you request. Understood?"

"Yes sir… Thank you sir…" Tasarov saluted, and started to stand up, but his legs would simply not hold him. He collapsed.

Rodenko and Fedorov were quick to his side, and Fedorov told Nikolin to send for a stretcher team. "And get Velichko up here to take the sonar station."

"Now I find myself hoping his ears are not as good as Tasarov's," said Volsky. "Yet that would do us very little good on sonar."

"Velichko is competent, sir. We'll be alright."

"This is getting serious, Fedorov," said Volsky. "It would be my guess that many others are in the same shape as Tasarov, or they may be soon if we do not solve this riddle. So this sound, whatever it may be, was not being caused by that thing Orlov had?"

"Apparently not. We are hours and miles away from the Peake Deep now. There is no way Tasarov could be hearing that sound if the object caused it."

"Get Dobrynin on the intercom. See if he can still hear this noise."

Nikolin put in the call, but soon reported that the Engineering Chief had also reported to sick bay that morning, and so they got

Doctor Zolkin on the line.

"*He's sleeping now,*" said Zolkin. "*I had to give him a sedative. The same problem many others have reported. Some kind of sound that nobody seems to be able to describe. I cannot hear it, but they certainly perceive something.*"

"Very well, Doctor. Carry on."

Volsky folded his arms, clearly not happy to have these officers disabled and unfit for duty in the midst of combat. He realized again what a temperamental thing a ship could be at sea. At the moment, everything seemed in order, at least mechanically, and they had no reports of flux in the reactors, but these events, particularly Lenkov, had caused a great deal of alarm. He could feel it in himself, a rising sense of dread, as if some great danger was upon them, though he could not see what it was.

"Fedorov? Any thoughts?

"We can proceed with the torpedo launch as soon as Velichko arrives."

"Not that—this sound. What is going on?"

Fedorov pinched the bridge of his nose. "I do not know sir, but it may be as I have explained it earlier—we simply do not belong here, and these effects may be related to the strange phasing events we've seen. I can speak of that with firsthand experience." He smiled, looking at his right hand to be certain it was still there, then became serious again.

"Admiral," he continued. "Up until now we have assumed that these effects were directed at us, coming to us like bad weather. Yet now I suggest another alternative—that *we* are the source. The ship itself may be causing these effects."

"How so?"

"I can give you no technical explanation," said Fedorov, "but we do have those two control rods aboard, and we know they contain material mined near Tunguska. They were also stored very near that thing Orlov found, and so one may have affected the other. This is all speculation, but if I am correct, then we could be having an effect on the space-time continuum. We are an entity capable of displacing in time, a slippery fish, as Director Kamenski might describe it. Everything else around us is native to this time, but we are not, and we are capable of moving… elsewhere."

"That doesn't sound very comforting," said Volsky. "They may not make good Vodka elsewhere."

Again the edge of a smile tugged at Fedorov's lips, but the situation was too grave to take any solace from humor.

"Yet we are not the only slippery fish here," said Volsky. "What about Gromyko on *Kazan*? What about the *Argos Fire*? We should contact them to see if they also report any odd effects."

"Yes," said Fedorov. "Why didn't I think of that earlier? I'm sorry sir… This situation with Lenkov…"

"We'll have Nikolin put in the call," said the Admiral. "But what does this mean, Fedorov? We are affecting space and time? Could this be why men in the future gave warning of our ship?"

"I have considered that, sir. We thought all this was accidental in the beginning, until we discovered what Rod-25 was doing. Then our own experience confirmed that we could initiate a time shift at will. Rod-25 was very consistent in selecting out this era when we moved. It did so even when we used it in the test reactor at Vladivostok, and aboard the floating reactor we used to find Orlov."

"And with *Kazan*," said Volsky. "Yet Dobrynin's skill was required to manage that. Those ears of his were needed to control everything. With our Chief Engineer disabled, and now Tasarov, this situation is becoming serious. I have considered what you fear may happen come July. Could these be foreshocks to that event?"

"Possibly," said Fedorov. "Time knows we cannot remain here if that other ship must arrive. Yet I suppose that all depends on what is really happening, on what time really is."

"I don't understand."

"Neither do I, Admiral. Kamenski said time may not be what we think it is, and that got me wondering in light of all these odd occurrences."

"Well, did the man explain himself? If he knows something more, then we should hear it. And this business concerning these keys is very shady. You say he has such a key, and we also have those two other control rods aboard. So we have not taken out all the trash, Fedorov. These things may be responsible for what we have been experiencing."

"Or the ship itself may be responsible," said Fedorov. "*Kirov* has been unstable in any time we sailed."

"Yet we stayed put for nearly a year here."

"Correct, sir. But I am thinking along these lines. Certain metals can take on magnetic properties. When exposed to magnetic fields, even something as simple as a paperclip can become magnetic. What if that applies to our movement through time. I was thinking we may take on some kind of quantum temporal energy, and if that is so, then the ship might be affecting space-time as it moves, perhaps like an ice skater leaving a mark on the ice as they go along. We could be doing that—creating marks and scratches in space-time. We could be causing damage here by our very presence."

"That much is certain," said Volsky. "The men on *Graf Zeppelin* know it well enough. Here we were plotting how to sink these German battleships, and now this time business again! Then if I follow your logic, you are suggesting that we are making this sound, because of some strange energy the ship acquired while displacing in time?"

"Yes sir. Think of it like the ship's hull acquiring a magnetic field as we sail. We have degaussed the hull before to mitigate that. Suppose we are picking up some other kind of energy, on a quantum level. It may have built up over our many shifts in time."

"Well, all this is speculation, Fedorov. Degaussing of the ship's hull is something I can order the next time we make port. Degaussing for this other energy you speak of is something else! We may never grasp what is really happening to us. In the meantime, let us not forget that we have a battle to fight here."

Kalinichev interrupted with a sudden report.

"System malfunction," he said, and Rodenko was soon at his side at the radar station.

"What is the problem?"

"I get no returns on the Fregat system, sir. All contact tracks are void. I can't even read *Invincible* on our wake, yet I have no red light. My system still reads green."

"Switch to phased array and reboot the Fregat system."

"Aye sir. Initializing phased array now."

There was no difference. Both systems now reported no contacts around them at all, which immediately drew Volsky and Fedorov to the radar station to see what was happening.

"Is this a local ship's problem?" said Volsky. "Is it confined to the electronics?"

"Mister Nikolin," said Fedorov. "Activate the aft Tin Man and feed the camera optics to the main viewing screen."

"Aye sir. Tin Man active."

They all looked up at the screen, expecting to see the tall mainmast and superstructure of *Invincible* in their wake, half a kilometer behind them. The weather was good, and there was nothing that should have been able to fool the optics of that hi-res camera system.

But the sea was clear and calm. They had been calmly planning the destruction of the entire German fleet, a feat they might have easily accomplished, until Maxim 17 exerted its unseen hand.

Fedorov looked at Volsky, and then moved immediately to the weather bridge hatch, intending to have a look with his own eyes. He knew it was a foolish thing to do, as the Tin Man signal was clearly showing the empty sea, but something in him just wanted the confirmation of his own senses, with no digital interface.

HMS *Invincible* was gone, and all around the ship, a thick grey haze began to fall like a shroud.

Part X

The Uninvited Guest

"If history starts as a guest list, it has a tendency to end like the memory of a drunken party: misheard, blurred, fragmentary."

— **Sarah Churchwell**

Chapter 28

Admiral Tovey was on the bridge, watching the recent missile fires off *Kirov* with the same sense of awe and amazement that he had felt when he saw it before. He had seen the ship defend the Suez Canal from incoming bombers on its arrival in the Med, and seen how it fought later against Iachino's fleet. He still remembered those first moments when he stepped aboard that vessel, like a man setting foot on a phantom ship, a ghost ship, something that should not exist, yet something that was clearly there, as hard and substantial as the cold steel under his feet now.

The missiles had fired, streaking off in the pre-dawn, and soon after the last, he could see a disquieting orange glow on the far horizon. He knew those rockets had found their targets, found ships out there somewhere with their cold precision violence. That's what the waging of war will become, he thought. It will be no less violent than this war, only more precise, and by extension, more deadly. Here was a single ship, capable of just sitting here in the shadows and destroying each and every German ship that might oppose them.

In some ways, he felt as though his own fleet flagship was an afterthought in this small task force. *Kirov* was the king of the sea here, unmatched by anything this era could ever build and commission. Admiral Volsky had told him they had weapons of even greater power, of unimaginable power, and when he said that, one of those haunting memories had emerged in his mind again, a feeling he had seen what the Admiral was describing, something vast, towering over the cold sea like a massive thunderstorm, with lightning on its flanks, red-orange fire above, and a massive veil of steam that seemed a shroud of doom.

Somewhere out there, his enemy had been found and gored by those rockets. Ships were burning, men were dying, adrift on the sea in the oily blood that was shed by stricken warships in battle. Other Admirals and Captains were staring in shock at the damage inflicted, yet helpless to do anything whatsoever about it. It was a new evolution in naval combat—over the horizon warfare, where a battleship like *Kirov* fought instead like an aircraft carrier. It had the same striking range of ships like *Ark Royal* and *Illustrious*, yet when launched, the missiles never came back. That was the trade off for the precise certainty that every rocket would find its enemy after being fired.

Kirov killed with deadly sureness. There was no wondering how many salvos it might take to straddle or hit the enemy in the distance. Yet with every round the Russian ship fired, its amazing powers diminished, burning like a candle against the surrounding darkness of this war. It was an amazing windfall to have this ship in the vanguard now—to have Brigadier Kinlan fighting side by side with Wavell and O'Connor in the desert. Yet for how long? This war goes on for years, or so I have learned. How long will we have these doughty knights at our disposal, fighting for King and country, just as I am.

His inner question was immediately answered, when it seemed a shadow fell over the ship steaming ahead of him, and a strange mist enfolded the ship.

Tovey perked up, squinting ahead, and reached for the field glasses hanging from the thin leather strap around his neck. He looked, adjusting the lenses, and looked again.

"Mister Boffin."

"Sir." Boffin was standing the watch on the far side of the weather bridge.

"Can you spot the Russian ship off our starboard side?"

"No sir, I thought she had come round to port."

"Kindly call up to the mainmast and see if the lookouts have a fix." Tovey was heading for the hatch to the bridge, even as Fedorov was stepping out a similar hatch on the bridge of *Kirov*, like two men lost in a painting by M.C. Escher. They were in the same place as before, but something in the ground of the reality around them had shifted in perspective.

Tovey asked his own radar station if they had any signal on the

Russian ship, and was dismayed to learn the screen was clear. What had happened? The watch reported all clear ahead, and there had been no sign of anything amiss—no explosions, nor any sign of distress. The Admiral went immediately to the W/T room to see if they had received anything on the new radio equipment the Russians had given them.

"Any word from Admiral Volsky?" he said, stepping through the door. The men saluted stiffly, and then Lieutenant Medford shook his head. "No signals of late, sir. The last we had was this notification that they were about to begin hostilities. Still felt bloody strange, sir. I mean, seeing as though there isn't another ship on any horizon."

On any horizon…. Tovey found himself looking about him for a moment, as if some sign or evidence of *Kirov* would be neatly stacked there in the message trays, a simple explanation for why the ship might be missing. He had learned that something about their propulsion system allowed them to initiate a displacement in time at will. That was, in fact, how they arrived here last June, though the young Captain Fedorov had explained that they were leery of attempting the procedure again.

Tovey did not understand it, but his common sense was telling him that the Russians must have initiated this procedure—that this was deliberate. Yet if that were so, why wouldn't they signal their intentions?

"You are certain there was no message traffic on the Russian radio set?"

"Quiet as a mouse, sir. No signals since 04:00."

"Very well."

He started back for the main bridge, clearly disturbed. If there had been no signal, might they have had some emergency involving their mysterious propulsion system? His watchmen reported nothing unusual, and there was no residual sign of smoke from any explosion. Clearly nothing catastrophic had happened ahead of them. They had been no more than half a mile behind the Russian ship, and would have seen or heard any explosion capable of seriously harming the battlecruiser.

Yet they were gone—gone as though they had never even been there in the first place. That realization fell heavily on him, like a shroud it seemed, and he had a feeling of profound isolation. *Invincible* was alone on the wide Atlantic now. Both *Argos Fire* and the unseen Russian submarine had gone off to see to *Rodney*.

That thought stopped him short, three crewmen in the passage ahead stiff at attention with arms raised in salute. But Tovey simply turned about and headed for that radio set again—the one the Russians had given them to link all the ships of their task force together. He realized he needed to report this event to Miss Fairchild, and the Russian Captain Gromyko.

Perhaps they can shed some light on this magic trick, he thought. Yet even as he did so, he was beset with a deep sense of dread.

No. This was not intentional. It was not something they planned. They would not have deliberately initiated another time displacement without notifying me. This was an accident, perhaps just like that first accident that sent the ship through time. Fedorov had been worried about that, and now something has slipped. Everything had been going off smoothly, right according to plan. They had slipped through the Pillars of Hercules, and into the Atlantic easily enough, and though the Germans still had a big lead on them, they had suddenly turned about to head east again.

We couldn't have planned it better, he thought, realizing that was very unusual when it came to battle at sea. Always expect the unexpected. Things were never certain—except one fact was plainly obvious. At least for this moment, in this here and now, the Russian ship was gone.

* * *

The message came in at a little after 05:00, and Captain MacRae took it in hand, opening it slowly as he continued to study the large ship they were now approaching.

"Signal from *Rodney*?" he asked Mister Dean.

"No sir. It's from Admiral Tovey on *Invincible*."

"Very well." He opened the message and looked at it for some time, his expression deepening to a troubled frown as he did so.

"Any word from that Russian ship earlier?" he said to his intelligence master, Mack Morgan.

"Which one, the submarine or the battlecruiser?"

MacRae folded his arms. "A submarine is a boat, Mister Morgan. A battlecruiser is a ship. So I ask again—any word from the Russians earlier this morning?"

"Now that you mention it, there was one message—half an hour ago. They wanted to know if we were picking up any odd signals on radar or sonar."

"Odd signals? I've had no reports, and this ship's eyes and ears are the best in the world. Oh, Templeton is on sonar this morning, and a bit grumpy as always. But other than that, it's been quiet all night—until that fireworks started. He thumbed at the missile trails in the sky, the early light of dawn slowly illuminating the contrails as the wind dispersed them like ocher mist.

"Then they signaled no planned course change?" MacRae was still looking at the message.

Morgan was drifting to his side, seeing something was amiss. Things gone awry were never welcome, as they stood as evidence that he had missed something he should have been aware of. What good was an intelligence chief if he didn't already know what was on that signals message in the Captain's hand?

"A problem with *Kirov*?" He gave MacRae a serious look.

"Have a look at this. Tovey reports he's lost contact with the Russian ship."

"In this weather? It's clear and calm, with visibility for miles with that sun coming up. Beautiful morning—until those damn German battleships get here. You sure that Russian sub is going to handle things?"

"That's what I was told in the briefing."

"So what's up with the battlecruiser?"

"Read it yourself, Mack. 04:40 – *Kirov* missing off our port bow. Initiating search."

"Missing? Ship's boys and brandy go missing, but not bloody battlecruisers! Then who's out there firing off those missiles? What does Tovey mean by this?"

"Maybe they put on speed and had to maneuver to make that missile attack," said MacRae. "The moon was good all morning, but it set at 03:16, and we had no sun until just a few minutes ago."

"Why would they need an interval of darkness for this attack?" Morgan didn't buy that. "The bloody Germans don't even know they're here."

"Oh, they do now," said MacRae. "Something took a hard hit out there. Look at that smoke."

"Maybe the Russians had a misfire and blew their damn ship to pieces," Morgan suggested glibly. "In any case, that smoke has to be well over the horizon, fifty or sixty nautical miles away. My boys tell me the Russkies are giving that northern German group a hard whack of the Shillelagh. You're suggesting they slipped off on their own for this missile strike?"

MacRae nodded. "Maybe they want to keep their missiles under their hat. Lots of eyes on the *Invincible*. We're supposed to use discretion in the employment of advanced technology—or so we were told."

"True, but they would have informed Tovey if they were breaking off. This message makes it sound like the bloody ship simply vanished!"

MacRae looked at him. "Like we did?" he said with a grin. "I'm sure you noticed that. In fact, I've often wondered if anyone on the tankers saw us go. Poof! One minute we were there—the next minute we were here."

"You're suggesting they moved like we did—in time?" said Morgan.

"From what we've learned that ship has been in and out of this pub more than once—shifting all through this history!"

"Well good riddance." Morgan rubbed his hands. "No offense meant to our new Russian allies, of course, but we ought to finish off this pint, pick up our coat, and be on our way ourselves. I've already had my fill of World War Two."

"You fancy number three?" said MacRae. "I would have given even odds that we'd be at the bottom of the Aegean Sea by now if we were back on our old beat."

"That may be so, Gordie, but this situation is bonkers. It's creepy. Did you know about all this—her ladyship and all? This business with the Watch?"

"Can't say as I did. No, her ladyship had the sheep's wool pulled down over both our eyes on that count. She was running us about on one mission or another. Remember all those quiet nights in the Indian Ocean? I thought we were out there to run deep field surveys for future oil operations. Turns out that was all a ruse, and you, my good man, bought it hook, line and sinker."

"Well it's not like I had any say in the matter," Morgan protested, his hand scratching his thick black beard. "Look here, Gordie. What's this rendezvous all about?"

"*Rodney* ran afoul of a U-Boat and took a torpedo. We're here to provide fleet air defense. That Russian boat is down there with us, somewhere, and they'll handle surface threats. That's all I was told."

"There's more to it than that," said Morgan. "I can smell it. My nose is too damn good, even if I don't have all my intelligence network assets to keep me in the know as before. Something's up. Now this message says the bloomin' Russians have gone missing?"

"We'd better fill in Miss Fairchild," said MacRae.

"I'll handle it," said Morgan, taking the signals message. "But something tells me she may know more about it than either of us."

"Well, when you find out what's up. Let me know." MacRae gave him a wink."

Morgan went down to the Fairchild executive suite, pressing the bell softly, as if it might ring softly on the other side, though he knew that was a foolish thought. Yet the early hour, and Fairchild herself, gave him pause. He waited for some time, wondering whether he should ring again, and realizing he must. Yet before he could thumb the button the door opened, and Miss Fairchild was standing there in a long cotton robe.

"Yes? What is it, Mack?"

"Signals traffic from Admiral Tovey, Mum. It seems the Russian ship has gone missing."

He handed off the note, and as she took it, Elena motioned for him to enter. The smell of freshly brewed coffee was in the air, and Mack eyed the pot enviously. Another cup would do him some good. For days now, he had been bothered by something. That nose he had bragged about to MacRae had been itching again, itching in a way that told him something was up. He could feel it, something impending, looming, and it was a most uncomfortable sensation.

Now that message he had received earlier, asking if they had picked up any odd signals, took on more significance. He shared that with Miss Fairchild, thinking she might know something more, and inwardly still upset that *he* did not know more himself. I'm supposed to be here explaining why all this is happened, he thought, not looking for answers here.

"Can't SAMPSON see them?" She was referring to the state-of-the-art radar system mounted on the tall mainmast of the ship.

"We were outside our surface coverage radius over an our ago."

"I see… Then get one of the X-3s up and have a look. How soon until we can board *Rodney*?"

"Another hour at this speed… Assuming that Russian sub out there does its job and we don't have unexpected visitors for breakfast. Last word was that the German northern group has split in two. We think the Russians hit their carrier and lighter escorts. But those battleships are making a beeline for our friend out there."

"That's why we're here, Mack. You'd better tell Gordon to stand the men up."

Morgan waited after that, a brief interval. He wanted to ask if there was really some other reason they were here. After all, why did they need to board the battleship? Was there something wrong with the radio? He knew there was some hidden reason, perhaps this special mission the battleship was assigned—King's business. He had asked Miss Fairchild if she had an interest in that, but never got much of an answer. One fact remained—his nose. It was itching again, and it told him there was more to all of this than it seemed on the surface.

He would have his answer before his next cup of coffee.

Chapter 29

Some thirty nautical miles up ahead, Gromyko was on the bridge of *Kazan*, considering a strange situation that had just been reported to him by his sonar man. For some time now, Chernov had been ill at ease. Gromyko had seen him fidgeting at his station, hunched over his equipment, switching on different signal processing filters, as though he were looking for some particular pair of shoes in a dark closet. When he asked him what he was doing, the Sonarman told him he had been asked to listen in on certain frequencies to see if he could detect a signal. Apparently the Sonarman aboard *Kirov* had gotten hold of something, and wanted a little help from the undersea ears of *Kazan*.

Chernov worked the problem, until it was decided that the task force would split, and *Kazan* would accompany the *Argos Fire* to rendezvous with *Rodney*. After that Gromyko thought he would forget the matter, but Chernov still seemed to be fussing about with his equipment, almost as if he could simply not let this loose thread go.

"Any problem, Chernov?" he had asked his young Lieutenant.

"No sir. No undersea threats of any note. I was just running some diagnostics."

"Something wrong?"

"Not that I can determine, sir."

"Then you are still chewing on that bone *Kirov's* Sonarman threw over?"

Chernov smiled. "I think I might have hold of the dog's leg it came from," he said. "I picked up an odd signal on the ultralow sonic bands. We get message traffic down there, but this could not be anything coming from our world."

"No," said Gromyko. "I don't suppose it could. Then what is it?"

Gromyko came right to the point. He liked answers, not questions, and the fewer uncertainties he had to deal with, the better.

"I'm not exactly certain yet, Captain. But it has structure. It's an organized signal—a kind of pulsing wave. It isn't random, and it isn't geothermal or of seismic origin. I was just running recordings through some filters to double check that."

"Let me hear it."

"Sir? Oh, that won't work. The signal is below the threshold of our hearing. You might sense it, on one level, but not with your ears—unless they are very good."

"Like the Sonarman on *Kirov?*" said Gromyko. "They say he has the best ears in the fleet, Mister Chernov."

"Tasarov? He's a good man, sir, and I'll vouch for that. I studied with him, and he could hear things no one else in the class was even aware of. He's the best, sir, but our sonar is much better than the equipment he's working with on *Kirov*, particularly after they took that damage up front."

"Very well, Chernov. Carry on, but don't forget that the Germans might have U-boats out here too."

"Don't worry about that, sir. I'll hear anything that comes within 50 nautical miles of us—even a diesel boat."

Gromyko knew that Chernov was not boasting. He was also one of the best in the business, and one day he might put a bet or two on his Sonarman in a runoff with this Tasarov fellow. But now he had other fish to fry.

Three German battleships were on a fast heading to intercept the *Rodney*, and *Kazan* was on point defense. He was considering how to handle the matter, thinking through the cards in his hand. He still had ten *Onyx* missiles, but reports from *Kirov* indicated they were not as effective as hoped against the heavy side armor of these ships, and only three were now programmed for popup attack mode, leaving the rest as sea skimmers. They had good long range, out to 600 kilometers on this variant, but only a 200Kg warhead. The German warships had belt armor exceeding 300mm, and there would be no time to program the missiles for top down approach as Fedorov had advised.

But who needs missiles, thought Gromyko? I'm a sub Captain, and we still have plenty of torpedoes. The Type 65 would be the preferred choice, my 50/50 weapon against large surface ships. It will range out 50 kilometers and give me 50 knots in speed, and I have a few of the big 557Kg warheads, the wake homing model. In fact, I even have those special warheads. One of those would take out the entire German fleet, but I don't think Admiral Volsky would want me to do that here. They're aboard for the hunter killer subs out there that would be stalking me in 2021. This is not their time.

Once in a little closer, I can go to my Type-53 torpedoes, a little slower, and with a smaller 307Kg warhead, but they can also detect the water churn made by a ship, and follow it to find the target. So my attack envelope is from 20 to 50 kilometers, well before they could ever come in range of this British battleship I'm defending.

Yes, he thought. Here come three battleships, but no destroyers. Even if they had six or seven escorts up there, all they would do is make target selection a little more difficult. No ships in these waters, except for that British Type 45 and *Kirov* itself, would have a chance at detecting my boat. So in another couple hours we begin the bullfight. It will be like shooting fish in a barrel—big fish, to be sure, but they will die just the same when those warheads break their keels or wreck their propulsion and steering gear. He looked over at Chernov again, seeing the man was still alert and active at his station.

"Still have a leash on those German battleships?"

"Of course, sir. They're noisy as hell."

"Good. Let me know when they come inside our 50K range radius."

The Matador had made his choice.

* * *

The Germans were coming, shocked and angered by the terrible fate of *Graf Zeppelin*, and bent on getting revenge. *Gneisenau* was out in front, making 30 knots, with *Scharnhorst* following about a kilometer behind, and *Tirpitz* steaming prominently in the rear. The Destroyer *Thor* and cruiser *Prinz Eugen* stood by the dying carrier, trying to pull any man alive out of the water, but now *Graf Zeppelin* had rolled over an slipped beneath the waves, a total loss, and they were slowly following in the wake of the bigger German ships.

Aboard *Hindenburg*, Lütjens got the news an hour after dawn, and he was none too happy to learn what had happened. Damn those British naval rockets, he thought. How in god's name can they hit our ships with such lethal accuracy? This is shaping up to be another disaster at sea, just like the first sortie last year. Ever since we got those orders to turn about and find this old British battleship, the entire plan has come unraveled. We should be well out to sea now, and feasting on the convoys like a pack of sharks. Let the British come to us, and then see what they get. Yet haven't they done exactly that, he thought grimly? And now we lose the best fleet carrier we have.

In one violent attack, those rockets have changed the entire situation here. Now we've lost that powerful air wing, and most of our top fighter cover as well. It means the British carriers will matter here again, and my bet is that there are more than one out there, with spotter planes up this very moment to verify our position. How long before we are under air attack? Only six *Stukas* and three fighters got aloft from *Graf Zeppelin*, and now I must order them to find us here and try to land on the *Goeben*. That will give us eighteen planes, but it will be twice the capacity of that carrier. We can juggle planes for a while, but for how long? We haven't the aviation fuel aboard the *Goeben* to keep that up. So we will have to ditch planes, and that will be very bad for morale.

That is the least of my trouble. Raeder will have fits as well. He's been sitting on those remaining carrier projects like a mother hen ever since *Graf Zeppelin* proved its worth at sea. He has *Peter Strasser* nearly complete, and then there is that French ship we captured at Saint Nazaire. We will likely throw time, steel, and Deutschmarks away to build those out, useful as they might be. What good are they if we cannot protect them? These naval rockets trump every weapon afloat on any ship in the fleet!

What happens when the Führer hears about this? He will make Raeder's fits seem like a poetry recital. The man has already canceled the other two H Class battleships, which means *Hindenburg* is an only child, the first and last of its kind. I stand here upon this Goliath, and yet, out there somewhere, David waits with his sling. These rockets have upset the entire balance of naval warfare. The only thing we have that can escape them are the U-Boats, and something tells me that is where we should have put our entire naval construction effort. It will come down to the U-boats in the years ahead. By the time we get these naval rockets, we may have very little else afloat to use them.

"Adler," he said gruffly. "What is Topp doing now?"

"He has put on speed and is moving to intercept *Rodney*, as ordered."

"Yes, but ordered by who? Have you seen this message from Wilhelmshaven?" He handed off the signal, a restrained fury simmering within him now.

"Repeat order needing confirmation," Adler read aloud. "Objective is as per original orders in *Fall Rheinübung*." He looked at Lütjens, a bemused expression on his face.

"But sir, we had a very clear order to the contrary. You read it yourself."

"Yes? Well who sent it, that is what I would like to know?" said Lütjens. "Alright, the British certainly know we are here, so I see no point in observing radio silence. I want immediate confirmation from Wilhelmshaven. Are we to engage *Rodney* or turn west again for the convoy lanes?"

"That question may be moot," said Adler. "Topp is closing on the battleship now. His task group will be more than enough to finish it off."

"Perhaps, but do not forget that ship has 16-inch guns, and the British know how to use them. And what about *Graf Zeppelin*?"

"Most regrettable," said Adler. "Yet all the more reason to seek our revenge. An eye for an eye."

Lütjens fumed. This could be the final sortie of the Kriegsmarine, he thought, our last hurrah.

"We cannot trade ships with the British and hope to survive this war," he said with a harried look. "Here we have already lost the most important ship in the fleet with the death of *Graf Zeppelin*, and sent *Kaiser Wilhelm* to the docks at Brest for good measure."

"And we have sunk an enemy cruiser and destroyer," Adler reminded him.

"Oh?" Lütjens batted that aside. "Tell me, which side of that apple cart would you buy, Adler?"

The Kapitan had nothing more to say, his eyes shifting out to sea, a tense edge to his movements. He was like a bow pulled tight, an arrow waiting to strike, but held in breathless stillness, the quiver of the Admiral's hand restraining him at every turn. His quest for vengeance was now even more important in his mind. The loss of *Graf Zeppelin* could not go unanswered, and here Lütjens was juggling two contradictory orders, one pulling them east, the other west. He feared the Admiral would take the easy road, and turn about yet again, cowed by the rocket attack that had put *Graf Zeppelin* under the sea. Then the next blow fell, like a cold fist striking his face when the runner came in from the signals room.

* * *

No one saw it coming. The big 650mm torpedo had been coursing through the waters at a shallow depth of just 20 meters, seeking the German battleships. A second torpedo followed in its wake, and their keen senses had detected the churning thrum of the enemy formation long ago. They surged in, about 400 meters off the port bow of *Gneisenau*, and then began a wide arcing turn, sweeping inexorably around and boring in on the ship. The first would strike aft, about ten meters forward of the main propulsion shaft and steering gear, the second would run right under the ship and explode amidships, the fierce upwelling and shock bubble literally lifting the ship's gut above sea level when it exploded. It was to be a very bad day for Kapitan Otto Fein and his crew.

Aboard *Scharnhorst*, cruising behind, Kapitan Kurt Hoffman rushed out onto the weather bridge, his eyes wide with shock when he saw his brother ship stricken. He had seen the rockets come earlier, tearing the pre-dawn sky to shreds, and immolating *Graf Zeppelin*— now this! How could the British have a submarine capable of scoring two hits like that, when we were running at 30 knots? It would take a miracle to line up that shot. He had to be just waiting out there, and we must have run right across his sights. Yet a hit like this was almost unprecedented!

"Fifteen points to starboard!" he shouted back to his helmsman, determined to make sure his own ship did not suffer a similar fate. He would begin a zig-zag course at once, though it would not matter. Gromyko's torpedoes could not be fooled. They were not dumb weapons, running true as aimed. They needed no human eye puckered in the eyecups of a periscope to find their target for them, and no evasive maneuver *Scharnhorst* was capable of could elude them. Hoffmann had just witnessed the fate of the entire German surface fleet. Given time, and as long as he still had torpedoes, Gromyko and *Kazan* could destroy the entire German Navy, just as *Kirov* might have destroyed it, single handedly, with the mailed fist of those plunging *Moskit-IIs*. Hoffmann did not know that, but it was something he secretly feared since the first moment he saw these new British weapons. For now, his eyes were still riveted on *Gneisenau*.

"Get a message to Fein and find out how bad it is. Then signal *Tirpitz* and *Hindenburg* and see that they are informed—*Gneisenau* hit by torpedoes, amidships and aft. Speed falling off and damage appears significant."

* * *

"**Two** hits on lead ship sir," said Chernov. "That had to hurt."

"Two 65s would do the job on most any ship we hit," said Gromyko. "Even a big supercarrier could not shrug off a pair of those lovelies. Very well—load tubes one and three. More of the same. Make your target the number two ship—birds on a wire." He smiled.

But no one's plans were to be left intact that day. The unexpected kernel of chaos at the heart of all battles was again to wreak havoc. Chernov was suddenly very still, his eyes on a module to his left where a red light began to flutter. He inclined his head, flipping a switch there, and listening, eyes closed.

"Con…. Undersea contact. Possible submarine…"

Gromyko turned, a question in his eyes. "An uninvited guest," he said. "German U-boat?"

There was a moment's hesitation as Chernov continued to toggle switches on the module he had been using to process the signal. "Sir… This sounds like a British sub." His voice carried a note of alarm that surprised Gromyko, and he never liked surprises, particularly when he had his bulls lined up one after another, two lances in the first, and was ready to skewer the second.

"British? We were not informed they had anything out here."

"Sir! This is crazy. It's reading as *Astute* Class!" He gave Gromyko a shocked expression. "We got lucky and recorded one boat after learning its deployment date. It's the only profile we've ever managed to get, but my readings are above a 90% match for this signal."

"Impossible," said Gromyko, but then a deeper instinct asserted itself, reptilian, a reflex born of many hours beneath the sea. "All stop!" he said. "Launch noisemaker sled number one. Then right rudder fifteen, down bubble fifteen! Rig for emergency silent running!"

Kazan maneuvered like a shadow, its engines suddenly stilled, a great dark whale rolling over and slowly diving into the depths of the sea. At the same time, a special port on the nose of the ship launched a screw-driven sled, which trundled forward on the sub's original course, leaving a trail of sound behind it designed to imitate *Kazan's* normal operating acoustic signature. The Matador twirled his cape, and now spun deftly away from a threat he presumed was imminent. If Chernov was correct, and he was hearing a British *Astute* Class sub, then they most certainly heard *Kazan* as well. The boat had been very shallow, and Gromyko's instinct was to get down below the thermocline as quickly and quietly as possible. Any adversary stalking him would likely be above it if they had a fix on him, but he needed to move whisper soft... descend... descend... Hoping his noise sled would cover his escape as planned.

Even as he finished his steering order, Chernov's eyes widened again, and he heard the one thing every submariner feared, yet the one thing he might expect if the contact report was solid.

"Torpedos in the water!"

God almighty, thought Gromyko. Which damn war are we fighting here?

Chapter 30

Only one man saw it when it came through—saw it with the dead eyes of a cadaver, bound in the weighted polyurethane of a body bag, and wrapped in the red, white, and blue stripes of the Russian flag. If any part of Lenkov could have seen, he would have borne witness when a hole seemed to open in the sea around him, shimmering green phosphors lighting up the murky depths above Peake's Deep.

It moved like a great whale, silent, sullen, a dark thing in the sea, deathly quiet as it climbed for the wan light above. Its sides were coated with a special series of tiles that muted sound. Two thin fins protruded from either side of its upper body, above the massive, bulbous nose. Behind them the thin metal sail was bristling with strange spikes, the sensory suite of one of the most advanced submarines ever designed.

Chernov had lived up to his reputation as one of the best Sonarmen in the fleet, and the single lucky profile the Russian Navy had obtained on an *Astute* Class British submarine had been just enough of the sound puzzle to let him make the call, and give his incredulous warning. After that Gromyko was all reflex, for there would be time for thought and reason only if he survived to ever think again.

His Sonarman had called it right, and Lenkov would have said as much, for only he had seen it come. And he had also seen one other thing, twinkling with light in spite of the murky gloom as the water deepened—The Devil's Teardrop. It had gone over one gunwale even as Lenkov had gone over the other, and together they slipped silently into the depths, until another moment of pure happenstance came into play, eighty years on…

The sea was no less dangerous there, with the scourge of war imminent as HMS *Ambush* drifted in the vanguard of a small flotilla of ships. The hastily assembled convoy was a motley combination of Royal Fleet Auxiliary ships, and a few civilian transports that had been press-ganged into service. There had been only one surface warship available for escort duty, and Captain James "Sandy" Vann aboard the *Ambush* was tapped to lend a hand. He was commander of S120, boat number two in the class, her keel laid on the 22nd of October, 2003, built out in Britain's premier sub den, the isolated coast near Barrow-in-Furness near Lancaster on Morcambe Bay. The place had been famous for building ships for many generations. Ships for Cunard and the Orient Lines had been built there since 1873, and at one time, Sir Barnes Neville Wallis used it to design and build airships for the British during the First World War. So the people there were long used to strange vessels taking shape in the shipyards, and the sound of engineering and secret works were often underway into the wee hours of the night.

The subs were spawned from within the massive enclosed structure of Devonshire Dock Hall, big enough to house the old airships that had once been built in that place in an earlier time. Now it saw the slow, precision building of the whale-like subs, with technicians creeping over the flukes and flanks of the beast, emerging from its innards on long metal ladders. Using a pressurized water reactor and pump jet propulsor system, the boat was said to be the quietest in the world.

In more modern times, destroyers and even the carrier *Invincible* were built there, and it was also a principle base for the design and secret construction of Britain's most stealthy new submarine, the *Astute* class, which first launched in the year 2010.

Ambush was also strangely entangled with the fate lines of the Russian battlecruiser *Kirov*. The sub had been lurking in the waters of the Norwegian Sea, skulking so stealthily that not even Tasarov had noticed it at first. And it had been witness to a very strange event that day, an undersea explosion that seemed to take both the Russian battlecruiser, and the sub accompanying it, to their doom. It had returned to port, where a change of command took place, and many questions were asked about the mission it had been on, and whether or not it had succeeded or failed.

Now the new commander, Captain Sandy Vann, was out to sea in those dark hours in late 2021. Yet instead of prowling the depths as the hunter-killer the sub actually was, *Ambush* had been posted as a stealthy sheepdog for a most important convoy bound for Mersa Matruh. Seven ships were scheduled to rendezvous there to receive the troops, vehicles, and materiel of the British 7th Armored Brigade, which had been on station in the deep deserts of Egypt ever since the incident at Sultan Apache oil fields.

The little fleet was composed of RoRo units, the 'Roll on—Roll off' ships that could accommodate the heavy vehicles of the Brigade. There sailed *Hurst, Hartland, Anvil Point* and *Eddystone*, and a civilian ferry sailing under an Irish registry was also along, the *Ulysses*. Capable of lifting 2000 personnel and over 1300 vehicles, the multi-deck ferry was the odd-fellow in the group, with three of its twelve decks styled to cater to civilian tourists, and all on a theme dedicated to the author of the great book by T.S. Eliot the ship was named after, *Ulysses*.

But all the curio shops, boutiques and eateries were closed that day, and well shuttered. No children played at Silly Milly's Fun House aboard *Ulysses*, and the seats in the Volta Picture Theatre were empty, the screen dark, as the sky erupted above the flotilla with the explosion of a 15 megaton warhead.

And so, just as the men and machines of Kinlan's had met a similar fate at Sultan Apache, the sailors and ships that had been intended to retrieve them would also be caught between the wild energy of two poles, a nuclear blast above, the strangely shimmering madness of the Devil's Teardrop below—eighty years and long fathoms below, yet right there, in that very same spot where Lenkov drifted in his last, lonesome watch. The object did exactly what it had done before, serving as a beacon that pulled the mass blown through the shattered borders of time that separate one moment from another, one age from another, one arrangement of everything that ever was from some other arrangement. Some strange quantum entanglement had joined these two incidents together in a bizarre twist of fate.

The missile that sought to destroy all these ships had exploded too high, another glitch in a computer that saw the warhead detonate earlier than planned. The resulting shock had been enough to breach the increasingly fragile fabric of space-time in the region, and the Devil's Teardrop had pulled everything within a three mile radius through the hole that opened in time. The entire convoy had been swallowed whole, including *Ambush*, which was cruising beneath them, very shallow. As fate would have it, they had appeared many hours sailing time after Fedorov first threw that object over the side, even as Lenkov and the Devil's Teardrop had both finally settled to their final resting place in Peake's Deep.

Now Captain Vann stood on the bridge of his hunter-killer sub, a perplexed look on his face, his blonde hair and mustache lending him the nickname "Sandy" among his fellow officers.

"You don't look happy, Mister Harland," he said to his Sonarman where he sat before the Thales 2076 system monitors, perhaps the best sonar equipment ever designed. It was said a boat like Sandy's could hover in the English Channel, yet still hear the maritime traffic in and out of New York harbor, and identify specific ships by the acoustic signatures they sent across the wide Atlantic, ripples in the proverbial pond.

The Captain's statement was spot on, for Mister Harland had just seen an odd ripple of another sort pass over his screens, and heard a strange crackle of static in his headphones. He sat there, like a poker player who had been placing bets on a sure hand, suddenly shocked to look down and see all his cards had changed, and he was now holding a whole new hand!

The low suits were still there, the seven convoy ships all in place in their proper steaming order. The clatter of the RFA repair ship *Diligence* was rattling in his ear and scratching the sonic signature lines on his screen with its 10,800 tons. The four *Point*-Class sealift ships were there, all in a row at 23,000 tons each. *Ulysses* and the replenishment oiler *Fort Victoria* brought up the rear, but the Type

45 destroyer *Duncan* assigned for air defense was suddenly missing. It had been well off the starboard side of the flotilla, standing it's vigilant watch.

"I've lost *Duncan*, sir."

"Lost her? Whatever do you mean?"

"Just that, Captain. I have all the convoy ships, clear as a bell, but *Duncan* is gone! I've no reading on the destroyer at all now, and my equipment just experienced an odd glitch."

"System malfunction? Well get it sorted out." Captain Vann turned to his communications officer now. "Send code to *Duncan*. Ask them to report their status and see if they have anything on their Sampson radar that we should know about."

The Com officer had a legendary name, Lieutenant Samuel Morse, named after the man who had helped develop the dot-dash code that once clattered through the airwaves from ship to shore, and was still in use in 2021. Morse got the signal off, but sat at his station, lips pursed, waiting unsatisfied for a reply.

"No signal confirmation, sir," he said.

Vann did not like the sound of that. The system should have immediately returned confirmation, even if no reply was sent by *Duncan*. The electronics on both sides of the transmission would have shaken hands, but nothing came back.

"Send to *Diligence*. They should have *Duncan* on radar. Perhaps something went bonkers up there and the destroyer's communications are down."

Diligence was accustomed to working with the older British *Trafalgar* Class subs as a support ship, mostly east of Suez, but this time she was out in the Atlantic Support Group, assigned to this special run down to the Med. She was the primary at-sea battle damage repair ship of the modern Royal Navy, her holds crowded with material for that job, and equipment like lathes, drills, grinders and welding tools crowding her workshops. She was also a supply and munitions replenishment ship, with a magazine of munitions intended for the 7th Brigade when they reached Mersa Matruh.

If they reached Mersa Matruh… That destination was now a very chancy affair, for the ship now unknowingly led its flotilla thru the uncertain waters of 1941, yet was still bound to make its appointed rounds for the 7th Brigade. It was some time before Lieutenant Morse had his reply.

"The com-channel is very cloudy, sir, but I finally got through. *Diligence* reports odd static on a lot of its equipment. They also report strange effects in the sky and discoloration in the sea."

"Discoloration?"

"That's what they say's sir. In fact, they asked if all was well down here. They say it looks like the Aurora Borealis, but it's on every horizon."

That didn't sound good to Captain Vann, and his mind began to piece the puzzle together, strange as it seemed. "Anything from Whale Island?" he asked, referring to the Maritime Warfare Center HQ there at Portsmouth. He was thinking there may have been a war order, or warning message somewhere in the system.

"Nothing sir."

Now Vann looked at his Executive Officer, Commander Avrey Bell, a thin man with just the wisp of an allowable mustache beneath his nose, and round, brown eyes. "Shall we sneak up to have a look about?" asked the Captain, and Bell nodded, there being no other threats apparent.

"Were running shallow. Make it so."

Vann wanted to send up his photonic mast, replete with sensors, cameras and communications antennae, to get a better picture of what was happening topside. All his ducks were still in a row, except *Duncan*, which remained mysteriously silent. The thought that the strange sky effects reported might have been an attack on the convoy was first to his mind, yet they had no messages from any other ship, and the signals from *Diligence* seemed more perplexing than alarming.

Yet his day was going to get progressively worse from that point forward. Sonarman Harland soon turned his head again, a warning look in his eyes. "Contacts—numerous surface contacts—processing now."

Vann waited, and the news he soon got was most unsettling. His man had some difficulty with the reading, switching from one profile bank to another in an effort to find a signal match, but finding nothing—save one.

"Are you certain?" The Captain gave Mister Harland a hard look. "That ship was reported missing months ago. Why, this very boat was on station when it happened."

"Well, I think we've found it sir. My reading is 90 percent confident, though there's and odd ripple to the signature now."

"Could this be another ship in that class?"

"Possibly sir, but my tonals and resonance factors are all coming up roses for the flagship. It's *Kirov*. I'm almost certain of that now."

"Bloody hell," said Vann, again looking to Bell for his reaction. The XO drifted over, and the three men now huddled over the Sonar station.

"Where have you been, you little bandit," said Bell. "Skulking about, were you?" Submarines like *Ambush* could move about the seas, unseen, unreported for months at a time, but not the big surface ships. He looked at the Captain, waiting to see what he would do.

"It's not alone, sir," said Harland. "There's another big signal here, but I have no profile on it whatsoever."

"A big signal? Another warship?"

"It has to be well over 30,000 tons to be making this much noise, sir. Very strange. Noisy bugger, this one. And now I'm getting data from much farther out. There looks to be something off our port side, perhaps a hundred miles out, also very strong for something at that range. Then here, sir. There are two more groups—one to our west, and one a little southwest. Yet I can't profile a single ship... wait a second... hold on sir..."

"Come on, Harley," said Vann using his Sonarman's nickname. "Get hold of this."

"I've a reading for a Type 45—maybe *Duncan*, sir. But it's over

60 nautical miles out now."

"The damn ship was ten miles off our starboard bow not ten minutes ago," said the Captain. "There's no way on earth that could be *Duncan*."

"It's a Type-45, sir. With the photonics mast up I can pick up a Sampson radar set carrier wave."

Vann put his hands on his hips, like a man about to dress down a group of misbehaving school boys. "What in god's name is going on?"

His mind was racing now. Something swept over their equipment, a subtle glitch, then *Duncan* comes up missing and the Captains up topside report strange effects in the sky and sea. Apparently it took some minutes for his submarine's own electronics to settle down, because Mister Harland reported those additional contacts ten minutes later. Was this an attack? Did it have something to do with the sudden appearance of that Russian battlecruiser? If the damn thing was really out there—*Kirov*—the ship that had started this whole situation unraveling when it went missing in the Norwegian Sea last July, then why didn't old Harley have a leash on the ship sooner? It was only sixty miles off, and all these other odd contacts he was processing now were all within 120 nautical miles. The sea around him was full of ships that simply weren't there fifteen minutes ago, and he found that to be a situation that skirted the impossible. Could this system glitch they experienced have quietly happened some time ago, so subtle that they missed it?

The class had been plagued with problems since the launch of the first boat, HMS *Astute* in late August of the year 2010. The business end of the ship, up front with the missiles and six torpedo tubes for the 21-inch heavyweight *Spearfish*, were all in good working order, but the back of the boat, from the reactor core aft, had many problems. As big as it was, the boat still felt stifling and cramped. They had interior temperature problems, a humid heat that could not be easily dissipated, and even now, five boats into the planned seven, *Ambush* felt like a muggy summer afternoon in North Carolina, where the Captain had relatives living in the states.

They had trouble with the computers, consoles malfunctioned, the reactors were skittish at times, which led him to believe this glitch they experienced might have originated in the reactor room. He made a mental note to give the Chief of Engineers a call, and see what Gibby reported. Lieutenant Daniel Gibbs had managed to hold the boat together in good working order, in spite of the teething troubles she was experiencing, so fresh from the dockyards.

That said, every boat in the class was still using an older reactor plant, one designed for the bigger Vanguard Class SGBN subs. It was supposed to give the *Ambush* speeds up to 35 knots when needed, but seldom achieved anything near that. He was lucky to get 28 knots, even submerged, which made the boat slow on its feet when compared to speedier Russian undersea adversaries. The old Russian K-222 could make over 44 knots submerged, and the *Alphas* were almost as fast at 42 knots. The *Sierras* cruised at a more sedate 32 knot maximum, and the capabilities of the latest Russian models were believed to be in that range.

But teething troubles could not account for the misery that was plaguing him now. These were not things Gibby could fix with a spanner, or some other engineering magic. Where did all these ships come from?

No, he thought, if those other contacts were there, we would have heard them long ago. Mister Harland should have them chapter and verse, no ifs, ands, or buts about it. Bloody ships just don't fall from heaven into the sea, but there they are. Were they friendly? This contact Harland reported with *Kirov* was obviously suspicious. Unless the Russian ship had intercepted another big neutral merchantman, I must presume that contact pair are hostiles. We had no notice that any other merchant traffic would be where these ships are, so their sudden appearance here is also suspicious. And what about that reading we had for a Type-45? One destroyer vanishes, another suddenly appears sixty miles off. This doesn't make any sense. As to the reading on *Kirov*, it soon vanished, just like *Duncan*.

His Sonarman was now completely flummoxed.

Sometime later, with the advantage offered by his photonic mast, he took a 360 degree HD optical and thermal imaging of the whole area. There were his seven ducks in a row, safe and sound, but *Duncan* was nowhere to be seen. Any problem sufficiently grave to sink that ship would have been easily heard by his Sonarman. It was as if someone had just reached down and plucked the ship away, posting it sixty miles off in a heartbeat, like a chess player moving a doughty knight.

"Mister Morse," he said. "Put that finger of yours to work and signal that Type-45. Helm, come about and steer 340 degrees north. Let's find out who's out there?"

It was then that his Sonarman reported another contact, this time an undersea boat, confidence high. Processing soon had a fix on the demon, and it was exactly that.

"Got it, sir," said Harland. "I'm pretty sure it's that new Russian boat—*Kazan*, and I think its engaging a target."

"*Kazan*? That boat was last reported in the bloody Pacific!" That sub should be sailing half a world away, he thought, in another ocean. Perhaps Harly botched the reading, and this is another boat in that class.

Things were really starting to stink, thought Vann. Ships were appearing and disappearing, moving about like chess pieces in a game where he was just a kibitzer. Yet one thing was certain—the Russians were here, on and below the sea he now prowled, and this was his beat. Yet how in the world did they break through the G.I.U.K. gap so easily? That thought, and the silence from Whale Island, were ample cause for alarm, and his instincts told him it was time for action.

"Battle stations, gentlemen," he said quietly. "Get the heavyweights up, if you please, and stand to."

Part XI

Twisted

"In all chaos there is a cosmos, in all disorder a secret order."

— **Carl Jung**

Chapter 31

They appeared in a grey fog, heavy on the sea, so thick that they could not see three feet in front of them. The ship seemed to be suspended in infinity, but soon Fedorov could feel the telltale rise and swell of the sea beneath them. The lights and equipment fluttered on the bridge, and he felt a queasy sense of disorientation, his equilibrium off, and a sensation that he was too light, too insubstantial. Then weight and solidity returned, a heaviness of flesh and bone, yet he found himself stuck in place, looking down to see the soles of his boots seemed to be fused to the deck.

A wiggle of his toes confirmed that his feet were safe and sound, and now he looked to the others on the bridge, seeing the same looks of confused disorientation on their faces. Admiral Volsky seemed to take it the hardest, trying to steady himself with one hand gripping the Captain's chair.

"Are you alright sir?"

Volsky looked at him, his eyes glazed over, and then finally focused. He shook his head, as if trying to revive his dulled senses, and then spoke.

"A bit dizzy, Fedorov. My sea legs are not what they used to be."

"Please sir, take the Captain's chair. Rodenko? Samsonov?"

The other men reported all was well, and Nikolin was secure at the comm station, though he did not look happy or content. The *Starpom* made a quick check of the remaining bridge crew, seeing that all were well, but then noted an odd buckling in the deck near the main hatch.

"Look here, Fedorov," he said, pointing to the obvious depression. It extended two feet out from the hatch, and now they saw that the bulkhead to one side also seemed slightly warped.

"Try that hatch," Rodenko ordered one of the men to check the operation, and they found it wedged tight, as if the ship itself had been greatly stressed, and the metal had simply warped. It was just enough of a distortion to wedge the hatch tightly shut.

Fedorov stooped, untying his boots, and he was soon standing in his heavy woolen socks, noting one small hole where the fabric seemed missing. He had been standing right at the edge of the small depression in the deck plating, and his boots were stuck in place, as if the soles had simply melted into the deck itself. All he could think of was Lenkov's legs when they found them in that storage locker.

"All bridge stations—report!" said Volsky, easing into the Captain's chair and still looking and sounding a bit woozy.

One by one the watch stations sounded off. Radar and sonar both reported all clear with no contacts. CIC and communications indicated no red or yellow lights on their equipment.

"No contacts?" That was a problem. "You cannot read *Invincible* off our stern?"

"No sir," said Kalinichev, "my screen is completely clear on both Fregat and Phased Array systems."

"Sonar?"

Velichko reported all clear again. He had no acoustic reading for the British battleship.

"Well," said Volsky. "That settles it. "Velichko has the best ears in the fleet. If he hears nothing, then either his equipment has completely malfunctioned, or there is simply nothing there."

Fedorov gave the Admiral an odd look when he said that about Velichko, as if something was out of place with the remark, like a shirt buttoned wrong.

"Fedorov, what just happened?" Volsky noted his Captain standing in his stocking feet for the first time.

"We must have shifted just now—phased out of the time we were occupying a moment ago."

"Phased? Where? We had clear skies and dawn just a moment ago, and now this fog is thick as good borscht… And where are your service boots?"

Fedorov pointed, and the Admiral saw the boots stuck in the

deck, noting the strange warp there and the odd distortion near the main hatch.

"What is going on? Time is getting sloppy again, Fedorov. If we moved just now as you suggest, the boat seems to have suffered a few bruises."

"I suggest we get on the P.A., sir. There may be trouble elsewhere. My boots are melded to the deck. Look where I was standing, very near that warped segment near the hatch. Remember Lenkov?"

"Only too well." Said Fedorov. He made a general announcement on the P.A. system, asking all sections to check the status of all ship's bulkheads, cable runs, pipes and equipment. When he finished he looked to Volsky.

"If that happened to my boots, then what if a key cooling pipe in the reactors became misaligned? We need to do a complete sweep of the ship, top to bottom."

"Correct," said Volsky. "You may wish to go below, Fedorov, and check on things yourself. Don't worry about me," he said when he saw his Captain hesitate. "I am quite myself now. It was just a passing dizziness, something I am prone to from time to time. Besides… I think you will want to fetch another pair of boots, yes?"

"Very good, sir." Fedorov found the main hatch could simply not be opened, and so he had to use the hatch off the weather bridge, taking the long ladder down the superstructure, his feet cold on the metal with each step, and a strange, icy chill in the air that was very discomfiting. He felt as though he was descending through a cloud, the fog thick about him, and with each downward step he began to probe with his foot, hoping the ladder rung would still be there. Thankfully, he made it to the deck below, his eyes staring up the ladder, which looked oddly distorted.

He was soon looking for the nearest hatch into the main conning tower, intent on finding Damage Control Chief Byko to see if anything else had been reported amiss. Along the way he stumbled into clumps of crew members in the interior passages, and assured them all was well, setting them to work inspecting cable runs, deck structure and anything else in their sections. By the time he found Byko, initial reports were coming in from Chief Warrant Officers, Midshipmen and Petty Officers, and a list of several odd instances of what the Chief called "metal fatigue" were reported.

Another hatch on a deck serving one of the fire control radar stations seemed slightly off plum, and the gunwale there bulged, as if it had been forced out of alignment by a collision—except the bulge was outward, which eliminated that as the reason for the distortion.

Amazingly, there were absolutely no reports of any equipment malfunction, which impressed Fedorov when he gave that some thought. The ship was packed with electronics and precision machined equipment, yet nothing seemed to have sustained any damage at all. Every wire and cable run was checked, the crew running along the thick bundles with gloved hands to look for any breaks or distortions, but nothing was found amiss. If something as simple as a single microchip had not manifested intact, they would surely notice an immediate system failure, but none were reported. It was as if something about the energy, or perhaps the magnetic field surrounding the equipment, served to shield it from the odd effects being reported elsewhere. The only damage was confined to dead metal—bulkheads, deck plating, and the two hatches that seemed frozen shut.

Fedorov was several hours below decks, getting a feel for the entire ship, and grateful that no further incidents along the lines of Lenkov had been discovered. Every man seemed safe and sound of body, though he could not ascertain how they were holding up mentally. He went past the sick bay to check on Doctor Zolkin and the condition of Chief Dobrynin, and there he did find another line of eight or ten men, all wanting something to offset the same queasy nausea and disorientation that had affected the Bridge crew momentarily.

"He's recovering slowly," said Zolkin. "The rest has done him some good, and he is asking to get back to the reactor room. I think it best to keep him here another eight hours, and get some good food into him."

"Does he report hearing that sound as before?"

"Yes, he can hear it, but the brain compensates for these things, and comes to ignore a disturbance like that in time. Live next to a waterfall, and you don't hear it after a while. I think it was just the early days of the disturbance that he found so intrusive."

"Any other men reporting this?"

"No, but there is a general sense of anxiety among the crew, and I have had to apply first aid to more than the usual number of black eyes and bruised cheeks. There have been a few quarrels below decks. I suggest food, Fedorov. If we have anything the cooks were saving for holidays, roll it out in the galley. There's nothing like a good meal to make a man feel fit and comfortable."

"Thank you, Doctor. That's a very good idea. I'll speak to the galley cooks on my way back to the bridge."

"I do note the Captain is out of uniform," said Zolkin with a smile, looking down at Fedorov's grey wool socks.

"It's a long story, Doctor. Yes, I'm off to fetch a new pair of service boots."

Along the way, Fedorov met one *mishman* who seemed to be bent over a clipboard, pencil in hand, a puzzled expression on his face. He recognized the man, Sub-Lieutenant Gagarin, a workshop and repair technician.

"Something wrong, Mister Gagarin?"

"Sir? I was just checking my shift assignments… very strange."

"Explain please."

"Well sir, I always assign eight men per shift—always. But today, for some reason, I only see seven names on my list. I know them all, because I often pair crewmen who I know work well together. It's this last name, sir, Mister Konalev. He's an OR-4 senior seamen from workshop B, but for some reason I assigned him to the A-shift, and he's not with…" The man's expression deepened, and he scratched his head.

"Not with who?"

"That's just it, Captain. I don't remember. This man, Kornalev... Yes, I always posted him to B shift with a partner, but I simply cannot remember the other man's name now. So here he is, odd man out, and posted over to the A-shift."

"Did you experience any disorientation recently, Mister Gagarin?"

"Me sir? Just a flutter in the belly. Thought we hit a big wave or something, but I have good sea legs. I'm fine, sir."

"Well, we've all been through quite a lot in recent months. Make sure you stay well rested, and spread the word, there is going to be a special meal served in the mess hall tonight. Holiday fare."

After another spooky climb up the long outer ladder, Fedorov was soon back on the bridge, and in shiny new boots, reporting to Admiral Volsky.

"This fog," said Volsky when his Captain was announced, coming in through the side hatch to the weather bridge. "It is very disconcerting. Radar shows nothing around us, not the *Invincible*, nor any of those German ships we were just shooting at a few hours ago. At least they may be having a better day now that the ship has gone and pulled another disappearing act. How are we doing, Fedorov?"

We have another stuck hatch aft, and I'll have engineers on this one in ten minutes. There were two other instances of deck warpage, but both in non-essential areas. Three bulkheads seemed out of alignment, and a gunwale was bulged outward near one of the fire control service decks. Other than that, the ship and crew are fine. We've had no equipment failures. I had the men check every wire and pipe on the ship, particularly in the reactor section."

He related his discussion with Doctor Zolkin, and the decision to get some good food into the men. Volsky was glad to hear that Dobrynin was recovering. "What happened here, Fedorov? Is this just another instance of this pulsing business you have spoken of?"

"Something different, I think," said Fedorov. "When we pulsed before it was a rapid event, and we manifested very close to the moment we occupied when the effect was first noticed. This time we seem to be…"

"Elsewhere?"

"We have no GPS or satellite data, so I do not think we have reached any time in the future when that technology was active. Yet we also have no contact with any of the ships we were able to clearly track on our systems before this happened."

"Admiral Tovey must be wondering what has happened to us," said Volsky.

"I would say so, sir."

"But *how* did this happen, Mister Fedorov? We have not used either of those two spare control rods, and I do not think we were firing any special warheads at the German fleet. The last time this pulsing occurred, it was a result of Dobrynin's attempt to deliberately remove us from that situation in the Coral Sea. Am I correct?"

"That is so, sir, but after Lenkov, it is clear that the ship itself is… unstable."

"That may become a bit of an understatement considering what happened to Lenkov," said Volsky. "What if this continues? We could end up twisted like a pretzel the next time we pulse. And will we stay in this place, or turn up somewhere where the weather is a little better?"

"Chief on the Bridge!" came the boatswain's call, and Orlov huffed through the side hatch in a grumpy mood. "Top to bottom," he said gruffly. "The men are going over the whole damn ship!"

"I trust you are well, Chief," said Volsky.

"Not bad," said Orlov. "But we found another stair missing on the lower engineering level. They had to rig a ladder there. Damn thing was half there, three steps, the rest gone. What's going on around here, Fedorov?" Even Orlov turned to the ex-navigator for answers now, but Fedorov could only speculate.

"We're shifting, yet in an uncontrolled state," said Fedorov. "Remember my example with magnetism? The ship may have acquired some kind of phantom energy throughout its travels. It may be causing these effects. How were the final mast inspections, Chief?"

"Everything seems to be working on the main masts and radar decks. The Tin Man optical units checked out fine too. An Engineering team is on the way to fix that mess." He thumbed the main bridge hatch. "Speaking of magnetism, there's just one other thing gone haywire." He smiled, handing Fedorov his pocket compass.

Fedorov took it, and to his amazement, the needle was completely lost, It spun left and right, then twirled about, unable to find magnetic north, a useless flutter, no matter which way he held it.

"Keep it," said Orlov. "It's no good to me." He tramped over to the coffee station near the plotting table, and looked for a mug. "Who knows," he said. "Maybe the coffee will taste better for a while."

Chapter 32

Lieutenant Commander Wellings had no luck in regular seamen's dungarees and white cap. In fact, every time he tried to get down to the cargo hold on *Rodney*, he found himself press-ganged into some other duty by a burly Chief. What he did discover, is that his pursuit was fruitless. The compartment he needed to get to had been completely flooded, and sealed off. It was going to take a diving suit with oxygen tank to get in there, and he did not think he was going to pull that off any time soon.

He struggled to the upper decks, trying to avoid the scrutiny of any Petty Officer he encountered, and slipped quietly back to the ship's laundry, looking for the bag where he had secreted away his officer's uniform. Once dressed as a Lieutenant Commander again, he felt a little better, though his mission here had been a failure, at least insofar as that key was concerned.

Last time it had been pure happenstance, the shift and roll of the ship under the vibration of those awesome guns above, and the heavy seas. This time, he knew exactly where to go and how to find that damn key, but circumstances had prevented him from getting anywhere near it. He chided himself inwardly.

I should have acted much sooner, but the first order of business was getting cozy with Captain Dalrymple–Hamilton and trying to steer *Rodney* out of harm's way. Now my time here is limited. In another eight hours the pattern signature will begin to erode, and so they'll have to pull me out very soon.

He had been so close to his goal here, and now it was so very far away. Yet a lot could happen in eight hours, and as soon as he was back on deck he could see the fireworks starting on the horizon to the south—missile fire! He watched as the fiery rockets streaked up into the sky, faster than anything he had ever seen. Their white contrails at elevation were already catching the first rays of the sun, and turning to long strands of ocher rope in the sky. The damage they soon caused on the dark western horizon was soon plain to see. Something had been badly hit there, and he found himself wondering if it was the same ship Nordhausen had reported to him in his variation search data—*Graf Zeppelin*. That ship should not even be at sea! Perhaps that problem has already been solved, but that was a grim thought, and he put it aside.

Now what to do? I'd best get up to the bridge to see what the general situation is. Our reading was that the German squadron was forced to turn back when they were struck by British submarines, but we could find nothing in the British service logs about that attack. The information came only from the memoirs of Kapitan Karl Topp. Why do I have the feeling that things are swinging off kilter here? It's that damn battlecruiser again. It's entering the penumbra of that impending paradox, and that will cause considerable phase instability. How much time do we have?

His footsteps were hard on the metal ladder steps, tapping out his haste like the ticking of a harried clock, his breath coming fast as he hurried to the bridge.

* * *

Chernov heard what was coming, and he knew it was trouble. Two heavyweight *Spearfish* Torpedoes, 533mm, built to replace the old *Tigerfish* that had been phased out in 2004. That weapon could run at 35 knots, but only for a very short time, giving it a high speed range of about 7 nautical miles. The *Spearfish* had been conceived as early as 1970, when the speedy *Alpha* Class Soviet subs waited like titanium greyhounds, leashed in port with their lead cooled reactors kept warm at all times, and used as fast interceptor boats that would streak out into the northern seas at speeds exceeding the *Tigerfish* torpedo itself! In fact, if not in close, a British sub of that day would have to be very lucky to get an *Alpha* with a torpedo attack. The enemy sub could simply turn and outrun anything that was fired at it. That, and the fact that only 40% of the *Tigerfish* built met design specs, was a good reason to move them into the dustbin of history.

The *Spearfish* was something quite different, driven not by a battery powered electric motor like its forerunner, but by a new, advanced pump-jet propulsor, coupled with a gas turbine engine using Otto II for fuel. This reddish looking oil developed by Doctor Otto Reitlinger, was an arcane mixture of three chemicals, all synthetic, and they reacted with each other when heated to produce the desired energy. Once underway, the torpedo could catch anything in the sea, with blistering speeds up to 80 knots, and it was smart. It could be fired with wire guidance, but when let off the leash, its microprocessor brain could make autonomous decisions on target runs, using both active and passive sonar to find its mark. If it missed, it had the range at 30 nautical miles, over 50 kilometers, to program itself for a second attack vector. In short, the weapon was fast, intelligent, and very deadly with its Aluminized PBX 300kg warhead.

"How many?" asked Gromyko, quietly, the sweat already high on his brow.

"Two sir, both probably still on wire, running true on our last position before that turn."

"Depth?"

"I make it shallow at 40 meters."

Gromyko looked at his depth reading to see *Kazan* was slowly falling through 60 meters, descending ever so slowly, her engine off and the sheer weight of the boat slowly taking it down. The *Spearfish* didn't even have to hit him, he knew. It could initiate a proximity detonation if its sensed sufficient mass close at hand. These fish would run on their fiber optic wire links back to the firing sub, which had the best ears under the sea ever developed. He knew their Sonarman had probably heard the subtle change in sound on the target he had been tracking.

They were well aware of our position, he thought, and they know we heard those torpedoes fire. So they're listening for our countermeasure, and I don't think the sled will fool them if they heard us when we rolled over for this dive. Everything depended on the range now.

"How far out are they?"

"Quite a ways, sir. Sound Track has them at an estimated 30 klicks."

That was a good long shot, thought Gromyko, but well within that weapon's attack radius. What if I ran now? We've got about ten more minutes until those fish get close. They're moving at 150kph! If I go all ahead full at 65kph now I could run another twenty kilometers. That would put those fish right out near their maximum range, and well beyond their wire guided segment when they catch me...

"Secure silent running!" he said suddenly. "All ahead full battle speed!"

"Ahead full!"

Kazan lurched ahead, her powerful engines straining. If Chernov's read on the firing range was correct, things would be very close. The torpedoes might have anywhere from five to ten kilometers left in them when they hit the red zone. If they had been just a little closer, they would have had us for sure, thought Gromyko, but they were too hasty. Then again, they had to hear us firing at those German ships out there. Perhaps they thought we were hitting British ships. Chernov had also reported more contacts down the firing heading of the incoming torpedoes. Several processed through to known signatures, and it looked like a British fast sealift task force.

Yet the madness of the moment was that Chernov still had all the German ships on his board, churning along to the west and northwest. I look that way and its world War Two—I look behind me and its World War Three! What in hell is going on here?

Think, Gromyko, he shook his head to clear his mind. *Think!* That Type-45 out there came through time, just like *Kirov*. So did we! So someone else has a ticket to this show, that can be the only possible explanation.

"Get a message to the British Destroyer," he said quickly. "Highest priority. Tell them we are under attack by an *Astute* Class submarine and see if they can call their boys off!"

Perhaps he could talk his way out of this mess. Yet the confusion and chaos inherent in this moment led him to believe this would not likely happen, though it was worth a try. The *Argos Fire* would get the message, wonder about it, try to verify the presence of that sub out there, and it would be difficult to find. Oh, they'll hear the torpedoes alright, and hopefully that will convince them, but can they get that sub Captain on the line in time? I don't think so.

He nodded inwardly, his jaw tightening. Then we fight fire with fire, he thought. First we go defensive.

"Load tubes nine and ten—*Shkval!*"

They're coming at me with a pair of fast heavyweights, but I'll damn well show them what speed is under water. How about a pair of supercavitating hyper-torpedoes, running at 370kph? They were lightning quick, designed to kill subs, ships, and for just this tactical purpose as well—other enemy torpedoes. The jig was that they had a very short range, an envelope no more than 15 kilometers. He had to hold them in the tubes until those two *Spearfish* were closing on his tail, and then he would fire, turn his sea rockets around, and give them hell. I'll either get those bastards or not, he thought. If one gets through it won't have much fuel left.

The entire situation had now spun off in a wild twisted gyre of chaos. Two wars were underway at the same time! He was either going to be dead in the next ten minutes, or someone else was. It came down to that single glaring choice.

The best defense was always a good offense, he thought. Those bastards are out there now, grinning at the other end of that fiber optic wire, and as long as that silent devil of a sub is out there, my life will not be worth five rubles. That sub is just too quiet. It's a miracle Chernov heard the damn thing. If they don't get me today, they'll certainly try again tomorrow. He knew what he would do if this were 2021. Time to get serious…

"Load tube number one," he said, his voice hard and low. "Special warhead. Mister Belanov," he turned to his *Starpom*, "stand ready to initiate permissions sequencing."

He was reaching for the Hammer of God.

* * *

Argos Fire was about 30 nautical miles south of *Rodney* when the harried message from Gromyko came in over the secure channel they had arranged. Mack Morgan was in for yet another surprise when he got the message on the bridge, turning to MacRae with a befuddled look on his face. "Russians say they've detected one of our subs— *Astute* Class. They're under attack!"

"Here? In bloody 1941?"

"That's what the message reads," said Morgan, shaking his head incredulously. "They want us to see if we can contact them and calm things down."

They had been quietly advancing on *Rodney*'s position, with *Kazan* well out in front, over 50 nautical miles away on point defense. The submarine had just launched torpedoes at the German battle fleet to the north, and his sonar station had clearly heard two hits. Then, out of the blue…

"Now let me get this straight," said MacRae. "We're sitting here closing on the old British battleship *Rodney*, and out of nowhere we get an *Astute* Class sub here taking a sucker punch at the Russians? What in bloody hell is going on here? They have to be mistaken."

Then another voice spoke, his own Sonarman monitoring the bow-mounted medium-frequency Ultra/EDO MFS-7000 system. It was not good enough to catch the *Ambush* when it arrived, but he could clearly here the donnybrook now underway between the two subs.

"Sir, I have torpedoes in the water, and they sound like *Spearfish*. I'd recognize that pump-jet propulsor anywhere."

Spearfish… MacRae knew that was the premier weapon on the *Astute* Class, and now his temper abated as he moved into battle mode. What was happening here? Did his own ship move again? Were they back in the soup of World War Three?"

"Radar—do we still have a reading on the *Rodney*?"

"Aye sir, I have her at 28 nautical miles, speed ten knots. We should have her on the horizon in about ten minutes."

What kind of salad was he being served at this bloody restaurant? Something slipped here, and he had no idea what it was, but he had to act.

"Put out a warning on standard fleet comm-link channels. See if you can wave off that submarine. Send this: *Astute* class submarine, Stand down! Your attack is blue on blue. Repeat. Stand Down! You are firing on friendly shipping!"

The message went out, but MacRae knew that if torpedoes were already in the water it may be too late to pull the leash on them. Some bloody sub Captain out there was going to be as confused as he was in another minute.

"Sir," came the next report from sonar. "I have a Type 65 in the water now! The Russians are firing back!"

The entire situation had suddenly disintegrated into a Mad Hatter's dance of teacups on the sea. The Russian battlecruiser was suddenly missing from their radar screens, and in its place an undetected *Astute* Class submarine appears, and immediately goes to war with the Russian submarine! All the while, the Germans are still licking their wounds from that missile attack put in by *Kirov*, and by now they will be right on *Rodney's* western horizon, mad as hornets.

"The ship will come to general quarters," said MacRae stolidly. He looked at Mack Morgan. "Is this a private fight? Or can anybody get in on it…. Now then. Get her ladyship up here please. This whole situation is twisted on its head! I'd like to know which bloody side of this bar fight we're on!"

Chapter 33

Kurt Hoffmann was angry, mad as the hornet Gordon MacRae made him out to be. He had seen his brother ship *Gneisenau* stricken by those torpedoes, and now that ship was dead in the water. Though his instinct had been to stop and render assistance, Karl Topp on the *Tirpitz* would hear none of that. He signaled all ahead full, and the formation was to begin an evasive zig-zag approach. The *Gneisenau* would be left to *Prinz Eugen* and *Thor*, their decks already crowded with survivors pulled from the water off *Graf Zeppelin*.

Hoffmann had that same feeling of rising alarm that he had in the North Atlantic the previous year. When he saw the morning sky alight with those golden yellow rocket tails, he knew they had the devil to pay. Somewhere out there, hidden just beyond that glowing horizon, a shadow plied the sea, dangerous, mysterious, and at war. It was here, he thought, the same ship that had bedeviled them in the North Atlantic. Could these rockets be coming off the decks of HMS *Invincible*, as Wilhelmshaven believed? He knew that a small flotilla of at least three ships had been reported running the straits of Gibraltar, and one of those was said to be a battlecruiser.

But we have the positions of all the British known battlecruisers pegged out here in the Atlantic, he thought. So what was that other big ship that blew through the Pillars of Hercules? Yes… it was here. Whatever that ship was, it was firing those rockets again—firing blind from beyond the horizon, unless that submarine that stuck it to *Gneisenau* was reporting our position. It was uncanny how the missiles sought out the carrier, the second time the British had targeted *Graf Zeppelin*. This time the ship did not survive.

And from all reports *Gneisenau* is in very bad shape as well, he thought. So they have a submarine out there calling the shots now, and taking a few for good measure. *Loki* is already gone. *Thor* is busy fishing men out of the sea. Now that we are at full battle speed that sub will not be so lucky again. But in one hot hour, half our battlegroup is simply wiped off the sea! Lütjens must be having fits!

"Ship sighted!" came the call from the high mainmast. "I think it's the *Rodney!*"

"Guns Ready! Now they pay the butcher's bill." Kurt "Caesar" Hoffmann was hopping mad, and the "Praetorian," as he was called, was going to war. The ship's chief gunnery officer, Schubert, was now at the Kapitan's side.

"We're ready, Kapitan. Waiting for orders from *Tirpitz.*"

"To hell with that! Open fire the moment you have the range. This is personal now, Schubert. We're out for our pound of flesh here."

Schubert nodded, Getting the range from Lowisch on the upper gun director. "Target at 22,000 meters."

"Fire!" Hoffman's voice was hard in the cold morning air, and the guns of *Scharnhorst* soon followed, their barrels elevated, and bright orange fire blazoning from the forward turret. Shubert fired Anton to gauge the range, with Bruno loaded and ready to fire after his first rounds were spotted. Nearly a minute later they saw the shellfall through binoculars, leading the British battleship and slightly short. Then Hoffman saw the distant flash of gunfire, hearing the loud boom some seconds later, a low, rumbling thunder on the horizon. *Rodney* was not unarmed.

Under normal circumstances I would never tangle with a ship like this, he thought. That ship may be old and slow, limping from that torpedo hit, but those are 16-inch guns out there…

"Sir, *Tirpitz* signals for a turn to port!"

"Come left fifteen!" Hoffmann knew that Topp was making his turn to get all their gun turrets into action now. It would be the eight 15-inch guns on *Tirpitz*, and the nine 11-inch guns on *Scharnhorst* against those nine 16-inchers on *Rodney*. On paper the Germans had the clear edge, and they also had a considerable speed advantage, making them much harder targets to train on and hit. By contrast, once they found the range on *Rodney*, it would be as if that ship was a sitting duck.

Tirpitz fired, a salvo of four rounds, two from each of the forward turrets. *Scharnhorst* was soon ready for her second salvo, and Schulte decided to fire only his B turret this time, wanting to fine tune his sighting.

"Two degrees down elevation," he called. "Ready… Shoot!"

Even as he shouted, the first big rounds from *Rodney* came arcing in well out in front of the German formation, four tall water splashes marking their fall. The battle might now decide far more than the fate of the three ships engaged had finally begun.

* * *

Marco Ritter was out on the flight deck of *Goeben*, raging at a deck crewman to clear some equipment so he could take off. He had heard the news that shook the fleet. *Graf Zeppelin* had been badly hit, the damage severe, and it looked as though the ship would not survive. Word soon came that their brother carrier had managed to get six *Stukas* into the sky before the ship endured that last fatal hit from the British rocket attack.

Damn those rockets! There goes the bulk of our air defense here, and most of our *Stukas*. Only six made it off, and there are three fighters still up on top cover. That makes nine planes off *Graf Zeppelin* now in the air, and that's all the eggs we can put in this basket. I need to get up there, and with a full tank to loiter as long as possible.

"Rudel!" he had shouted. "Get your *Stukas* up. I'm making you the new Squadron leader—your planes and six more off the *Graf Zeppelin*. Let's get moving!

The chocks were pulled away, and Ritter gunned the powerful engine on his Me-109T, rolling down the short flight deck and into the amber sky. He was on the radio coordinating with the pilots off *Graf Zeppelin* at once, and they were now circling about the *Goeben*, a swarm of angry bees gathering for the attack.

"The target is *Rodney*," he shouted. "All other fighters remain here on fleet defense. The crows follow me!" He put his plane in to a shallow bank, peeled off and led the way, off to the northeast where the action had just been joined by Topp and Hoffmann. They were coming with the six *Stukas* off *Graf Zeppelin,* and Hans Rudel had only just arrived with the three strike planes off the *Goeben*. They all had a bone to pick now, and they put all thoughts of how they might land on the crowded little escort carrier aside.

That would not matter, for the sky was soon to be alight with the hot contrails of Aster 15 rockets. There would be plenty of room on the flight deck of the *Goeben* in due course…

* * *

Now the wild scene in the red-orange dawn would suddenly take yet another unexpected turn. Captains on every ship involved were set on battle, their eyes behind field glasses, faces grim, the boom of the guns loud on the morning air. Thick black smoke erupted from the German battleships, the rolling char of cordite so thick that the men could taste it with each mighty salvo fired. The Germans were finally finding the range on the hapless *Rodney*. There had already been two near misses, when the Anton turret of *Scharnhorst* straddled the British ship, sending shrapnel into the stacked crates of boiler tubes on her decks.

Rodney thundered in reply, her third salvo very nearly scoring a hit on the *Tirpitz*. Now on the bridge, Lieutenant Commander Wellings was in a quandary. He had been unable to retrieve the precious key from *Rodney's* hold, and in spite of every effort to steer the ship away from harm, the tall splash of seawater riddled with shrapnel was now the hard reality at the end of all his plans.

Rodney shuddered with the firing of her own guns, four barrel salvoes that shook loose the deck planks and rattled every loose object on the ship. It was the second time Wellings had heard those monstrous guns fire, and the last time he had found himself flung overboard into a wild sea, witness to one of the greatest naval duels ever fought. This time it was not *Bismarck* out there, but her brother ship, the *Tirpitz*, and this time the odds were different too. That was a *Scharnhorst* class ship out in front!

The history here was still twisted and bent back upon itself, and he could see no way this intervention had any chance of succeeding. The only thing now was to get to his designated retrieval point, a position amidships where the project team would be looking to pull him out.

No sooner had he turned to look for the aft hatch and ladder down, when the first telling blow struck *Rodney,* just forward of her tall coning tower, and right on the number three gun turret there. It was an 11-inch shell flung at them by Kurt Hoffmann, and though the heavy armor at nearly 16 inches was enough to protect the turret from penetration, the shock and concussion was severe. Several packing crates that had been set atop the turret were blown to pieces, and black smoke billowed up, obscuring the bridge with choking cinder.

Wellings heard the drone of aircraft overhead, the scream of the Jericho trumpets, the wild hiss of rockets in the sky. When the smoke cleared he could see the twisting contrails of agile missiles snaking through the thin clouds overhead, seeking out the squadron of German *Stukas.* Then something happened that no one expected, except Gromyko.

He had fired his Type 65 torpedo, back along the axis of the undersea enemy attack. His two supercavitating *Shkvals* had helped clear the way, lancing out in their bubble jet spheres and blistering in to find one of the two *Spearfish* that were slowly closing the range on *Kazan.* The Russian sub had been running at its best speed of nearly 36 knots, heedless of the sound they were making now. Soon, thought Gromyko, the sea will erupt with Neptune's wrath.

It sounded like a great kettle being struck when it happened. Nearly a hundred meters deep, the 20 kiloton warhead went off with a resonant boom, the immense sphere of expanding gas and vaporized seawater creating a tremendous shock wave in all directions. The second *Spearfish* careened wildly off course, its sensitive sonar pummeled with the wrenching sound, dumbstruck.

Gromyko knew his torpedo would take too long to reach the enemy sub, but he only needed to get close. The shock of the warhead would expand out several kilometers, and all he needed was to get some of that awful explosive force close to his enemy to hurt this sub.

And he did.

The *Ambush* shuddered with the blow, emergency signals going off all over the boat, an outer stabilizing fin wrenched by the shock, and the tremendous pressure forcing a hull leak in the sail that sent torrents of seawater down into the compartments below, as men scrambled to seal off the hatches. No one could see what was really happening, the searing green fire at the outer edge of the nuclear bubble in the sea. There came a rending sound, so deep and terrible that every man on the boat covered their ears, their faces taut with pain. It was a sound from another place, the moaning agony of eternity, long and distended, the meridians of infinity being wrenched and twisted until they broke.

The fissure opened, and *Ambush* plowed right into the expanding wave of shimmering phosphorescent plasma. It was as if the edge of that fire was the maw of some great wrathful sea demon, opening to consume the submarine. *Ambush's* rounded nose vanished at the glimmering edge, soon followed by the long, bulbous body of the vessel, which plunged right on through a deep rupture in time, rent open by the violence of the explosion. It was the first instance of atomic fire scorching the lines of fate that shaped these altered states, pre-empting the angry blow that Vladimir Karpov might have flung at his enemies in August of that very year... but it would not be the last.

* * *

The chaos of war swirling above the embattled British battleship was suddenly upstaged by the massive upwelling of seawater on the horizon. All eyes were riveted on the scene, and watchmen on every ship, pilots in their headlong dives, and crewmen at the gunwales of perdition gripped the hard steel there and held on for dear life.

A cold wind swept over the battle, just as Anton turret on the *Tirpitz* sent not one, but two more 15-inch rounds plunging down on *Rodney*. One struck the conning tower, the second smashing into the hull very near the damaged compartment where the battleship hid its secret cargo. The magazine for the forward torpedoes was there and, one by one, the long sleek weapons blew up in a series of shuddering explosions.

Bulkheads burst open and the outer hull itself was wrenched with a great tearing gash. A dark stain of oily blood clouded the sea, and through it, came the glimmering of tiny bars of gold bullion, falling, falling into the depths of the sea. And with them went the great stolen treasures of the Parthenon, a Metope of a Centaur, rearing up and locked in fitful combat with a Lapith warrior, the wild charge of horsemen carved into a marble Frise, and one more thing, the Selene Horse, exhausted by its recent sortie through the heavens, veins bulging, eyes wide, mouth gaping open and gasping for air.

Down they fell, a flutter of debris on the endless swelling currents of the sea. Down and down they went, into the deep depths where only one pair of human eyes could ever hope to see or find them again, the eyes of Lenkov, dark in death, where his body drifted near the silted bottom of Peake's Deep.

No man aboard *Rodney* knew what they had lost, the King's business, made flotsam in the deep green sea, and never to be seen again. No one on *Argos Fire* would learn what really happened, nor any soul on another ship, lost in the grey fog of infinity that now seemed to swirl and eddy about its tall mainmast, where the swirling watch of radar eyes twisted with their ceaseless watch.

Yet in all this chaos, there moved the secret stealthy hand of order, some unseen force, whisper soft, yet bent on its work with mindless logic. All of these various players, like pieces in a great game of chess, were now unknowingly conspiring with one another to reach some unfathomable zero sum in the infinite calculus of time. So while *Rodney* burned, the *Stukas* plunged down through the gauntlet of missile fire, and over it all there rose the massive blight of steam and vapor rising up like a terrible storm, its shadow deep and impending, where the sea itself, sucked up in the torrid gyre of that nuclear fire, stood there like a tower of chaos, slowly collapsing in a roaring wave of destruction.

Part XII

Empty Chairs

"I've crossed some kind of invisible line. I feel as if I've come to a place I never thought I'd have to come to. And I don't know how I got here. It's a strange place. It's a place where a little harmless dreaming and then some sleepy, early-morning talk has led me into considerations of death and annihilation."

— Raymond Carver: *Where I'm Calling From*

Chapter 34

Fedorov had a very odd feeling. It was more than that oddly spinning compass in his pocket. It was more than his boots, a brush with a fate that could have seen him end up like Lenkov. It was more than the unaccountable damage to the ship itself. When he walked the ship, he felt like a man who had left for work that morning and forgotten his lunch box or wallet. Something was off, twisted, rearranged. Something was missing.

He had the distinct feeling that he had misplaced something, but he could not think what it was. As he made his way to the bridge, he found himself peering through one hatch or another, noting the crew at work, the equipment, almost like a mother hen checking her nest to see that all the eggs were still there.

Yes, he thought. That was it. A missing egg... Had something hatched here in this strange displacement the ship was experiencing? Was this the moment he had feared all along, that day of reckoning for all the crimes they had committed in their long, incredible journey through time? What was happening here?

He remembered the many things he had discussed with ... How very odd... with who? The arguments were there in his mind, fresh and clear, but he could not recall the face on the other side of the discussion he had about them. Things had been topsy turvey these last days. He was tired, needing sleep, and it was a miracle he could even still function here. He felt very confused, and he had the distinct feeling that there were others on the ship that felt the very same way, like Mister Gagarin, staring at his work detail clipboard with a bemused and puzzled expression on his face.

These time shifts are beginning to have an effect on me, he thought. This situation is most unusual. Clearly we've shifted somewhere. This is not simply the pulsing instability that we experienced before. The ship seems suspended in time, somewhere, but we are clearly afloat and underway on the high seas. But where? This damn fog is impenetrable.

Volsky and Rodenko were discussing the situation near the Captain's chair where the Admiral sat, tapping his hand on the padded arm rest impatiently. Nikolin, Samsonov and Velichko were at their stations, as always... but there it was again—that feeling that something was off kilter, something wrong, something missing...

"Mister Fedorov," said Volsky. "How is the ship's hull?"

Fedorov put his inner agitation aside and made his report. "Byko put men over the side, sir, and while there is a minor depression on the starboard side, the hull seems intact and sound."

"Very well," said Volsky. "So when does this end? Are we still involved with this pulsing business?"

"The ship seems to have reached some stable state," said Fedorov, "but I have not yet been able to determine just where we are—in space or time."

Volsky nodded. "There's been nothing on our sensors, and I have had Nikolin listening for any radio or short wave transmissions. Nothing. We have tried contacting *Invincible*, *Kazan*, and *Argos Fire*, but get no reply. The equipment does not even handshake, as Nikolin explains it. He sends his signals out, but there seems to be no one listening out there. This is most alarming, Fedorov, and I think he's a bit frustrated."

"Agreed sir," said Fedorov. "Though this situation was not entirely unexpected. I knew we were in for trouble of some kind, and it seems we have found it. This is frustrating for us all, Admiral."

"Then this is that paradox you have warned about? It is only May, and you said that would not occur until late July."

"Frankly sir, we don't know what our position is in time any more than I can determine our position in space. We can't see the stars, so I can get no navigational fix. Radar has no land forms within range. We have nothing on sonar... this fog has us completely socked in. I suggest we send up the KA-40. Maybe it can get up above this sea fog and find the stars. Then we can used the old fashioned methods to at least determine our position. As for where we are in time, we will need some touchstone to ascertain that. Remember, it often took several hours."

"Very well, make it so. In the meantime, we must consider our options. We cannot just sit here in this fog."

"What do you suggest, Admiral?"

"We are capable of making a deliberate time shift," said Volsky, "are we not? We still have those two control rods aboard."

"Yes sir, but I would not recommend using the Alpha rod. We clearly discovered that it can also move us in space. If that were to happen again, we might end up marooned on dry land... or worse."

Volsky shrugged. "You can think of something worse?"

"We could re-materialize inside a landform, just as Lenkov was melded into the deck. And don't forget my boots!"

"Wonderful!" Volsky shook his head, his hand still tapping the arm of the Captain's chair. "Then what about the second control rod, the Beta rod, good old Plan B."

"That remains another unanswered question," said Fedorov. "At the moment we are clearly somewhere in spacetime, and in the physical world, even though it feels like some never-never land with this heavy fog. I suggest we first try an ascertain our position by using the KA-40, and then, if this situation persists, we always have Plan B."

"Assuming Chief Dobrynin is well enough to manage things."

"I checked with Doctor Zolkin earlier," said Fedorov. "The Chief is recovering, and already asking to be returned to duty."

"Well at least we have a little good news," said Volsky. "Strange that he was the only one to hear this odd sound."

That remark struck Fedorov as odd again, strangely provocative of some inner objection on his part, yet he could not see why. The stress of these last hours seemed to weigh on him now, and he thought he had better gets some food and rest himself.

"Sir, if all is well here for the moment, I would like to take a meal break."

"Excellent," said Volsky. "Eat hardy, Fedorov. Let me know what the cook is serving, and I'll add a few more pounds to this belly of mine when you get back."

Fedorov saluted, and was on his way to the officer's dining hall, the hunger feeling like an empty hole in his soul now. He could still not shake that strange feeling of discombobulation. Thankfully, the engineers had worked on the main hatch, and it was now in operation again, so he would not have to take that foggy ladder down.

As he sat at the dining table, he could not shake the feeling that he was overlooking something of great importance. He felt again like a man at a train station or airport, but at the wrong boarding gate, just minutes left before his departure. The food did him some good, but he soon found his mind dwelling on what may be happening to the ship now—to all of them—in this grey fog of uncertainty. The only note of reason in all of this had come to him in his discussions with…

Something was there, something right at the edge of his awareness, yet he could not grasp it… a slippery fish… Something suddenly snapped in his mind with that thought. Yes! *A slippery fish!* Director Kamenski! He took one last sip of wine to chase down the stew he had been eating, stuffed a dinner roll into his jacket pocket, and was up on his feet, suddenly animated with newfound energy.

He made his way to the officer's quarters, to the spare visitor's cabin at the end of the hall opposite the Admiral's room. Stepping up to the door, he quietly knocked, waiting, somewhat breathless with anticipation more than anything else. Perhaps he was sleeping, he thought, but decided the situation was too grave, and he knocked again.

There was no answer.

"Director? Captain Fedorov here. Are you awake sir?"

Silence.

He decided to try the door, finding it locked, and now he became concerned. Reaching into his pocket for the master quarters key that was always on the Captain's keychain, he unlocked the door, knocking again as he inched it open. The room was swathed in deep shadow, and he flicked on the light switch, suddenly afraid he might find Kamenski in a state like Lenkov. The man was always reclusive, keeping mostly to himself aboard the ship, happy and content to stay in his cabin reading and smoking his pipe. He even took his meals there quite often, lost in his deliberations, yet always amiable and willing to receive visitors.

Fedorov eased through the door, a sense of rising anxiety in him now. The light was revealing, and thankfully nothing seemed out of order. Yet that fact alone was still disconcerting. The room was empty. In fact, it appeared as though it had never been occupied, with the bed all made up, the wardrobe area clean and unused, and no dinner tray from the meal Kamenski must have surely ordered tonight. The stack of books on the desk were gone, as was the ash tray, and the Director's pipe. Then he heard an unexpected sound, the meowing of a cat, though faint and far off. Doctor Zolkin's "Gretchko" must be prowling about up here, he thought, but he saw nothing in the room—until he looked over at the nightstand.

There, sitting quietly by the lamp, was the only sign that Kamenski might have been there recently, though it surprised Fedorov to see it there. Why would he go and leave a thing of such importance just lying about like that? He edged around the bunk, stepping over the nightstand, and reached for it, a slight quiver in his hand as he did so. He must be out on deck getting some air, thought Fedorov.

But he was not on deck.

Kamenski had been in his quarters, as always, when *Kirov* vanished from Admiral Tovey's horizon. Then the feeling came, like someone tapping on his shoulder, reminding him of an appointment he had to keep. He looked up, knowingly, a quiet smile on his lips, and slowly set the book he had been reading aside, wondering where it might turn up one day. He put his pipe into his sweater pocket, and when he removed his hand, it held something else.

Quietly, and with little fanfare, he set it on the nightstand, breathing deeply, and taking what might have been thought of as a last look around the quiet room, if anyone had been there to see him.

* * *

Fedorov tramped back to the officer's mess, disappointed that he had not found the Director available to consult with him on the predicament they now found themselves in. Along the way, he stopped off at the ship's Purser to see if other accommodations might have been made for Kamenski. There his evening took another turn for the worse.

"I'm sorry sir, who is the crewman you are enquiring about?"

"Not a crewman, Mister Belov, a special guest—Director Kamenski. He was quartered in the officer's reserve cabin opposite Admiral Volsky, but he doesn't seem to be there. Has he been relocated?"

Belov looked at his clipboard, then went over to his desk and keyed something on a computer. "Sorry Captain, I have no listing under that name. In fact. I'm showing the reserve cabin as presently unoccupied."

"Unoccupied? Well I was just there the other day conferring with the man. He's been quartered there for months!"

"Not according to my records, sir. We had the British Admiral Cunningham there for a night when we were in Alexandria, but no one has been assigned there since."

Fedorov gave the man a stern look, frustrated. We can't even keep the guest roster straight on this ship, he thought, somewhat annoyed. Clearly the Purser must have slipped in making this data entry. Then something occurred to him, and instead of pressing the matter here, he stepped out into the corridor, and found the nearest intercom station.

"This is the Captain. Will Director Pavel Kamenski please report to the officer's dining hall. I repeat. Director Kamenski—please report to the officer's dining hall. That is all."

He looked at Belov, still annoyed, and moved on.

Yet he would sit in the dining hall for the next half hour, picking at a slice of Natalka, a layered Russian cake he was fond of, and lucky enough to find available tonight for dessert. Kamenski never arrived.

"May I join you, sir?"

It was Nikolin, down from the bridge for his meal shift. "Please do," said Fedorov. "Though I must say, I'm not in the best of moods, Mister Nikolin."

"Me neither, sir. I've been feeling very strange of late."

"We all have. These time shifts are very disconcerting. This latest event was uncontrolled, and I think more than the ship was bent and warped when we moved. But you look very glum, Nikolin. Why such a long face?"

"I can't really say, sir. I was at my post an hour ago, and something very strange happened. It's a bit of a riddle, literally."

"What do you mean."

"Well sir, I play with riddles… It has neither eyes nor ears, but it leads the blind. Things like that."

Fedorov smiled. "What's the answer? I thought of a seeing eye dog, but it clearly has both ears and eyes."

"A walking stick," said Nikolin, seeming a little more himself for a moment. Then a squall of what Fedorov might only interpret as sadness seemed to sweep over him, and his eyes had a distant look.

"I play riddles with anyone I can find," he said. "And sometimes I will send them over the ship's private text messaging system," he confessed. "I was checking those file archives as part of the general diagnostic you ordered on all ship's equipment… and I found something."

"What Nikolin? You look upset."

"I am, sir, but it feels like my roof has caved in—*Choknutyj.*" That was an untranslatable Russian word for crazy, and Fedorov could understand how anyone on the ship might feel that way just now. "When Karpov was here—during that last incident on the bridge," said Nikolin, "I caught part of the radio transmission on a recording when the Admiral was ordering the Captain to stand down. I didn't know what to do, but I had been sending riddles to someone on the text messaging system, and I used it to give warning of what was happening. I ran across the very message I sent in my system check, by chance I suppose. It was very upsetting. The station number was listed, and the crew member's code comes right after that for message routing. I had been playing the game, sending riddles to that same code earlier that day, so I looked it up." He gave Fedorov a puzzled look. "There's no one assigned to that code sir. It was void—designated unused."

"Perhaps you got the number wrong," Fedorov suggested.

"No sir. The code was on numerous text messages I sent that day, always the same number, and these are permanent assignments, like a person's email address. Yet when I queried the database the code was unassigned."

"You are certain of this number?"

"001-C-12." Nikolin rattled off the number from memory. "I know it as easily as my old street address. 001 is for main bridge stations. Sub-codes C-10 through C-12 are for personnel serving at the sonar station."

"Velichko?

"No sir, his number is C-11. I double checked that."

"I see… So you say you have messages in the archive sent to C-12, but no one has that number? Then you found a glitch in the system, Nikolin. Good for you! This could be a clue. We will have to give the electronics a deeper look. If this data was not stored properly, or perhaps written wrong by the system, then other things could be amiss as well. I discovered a problem with the Purser's data just a little while ago."

"I suppose so sir, but you don't understand…" Nikolin had a tormented look on his face now. "When I saw that number, it was as though something broke inside me, and I remembered. 001-C-12. The number kept after me. I knew it meant something—someone, but I could not remember who it was. Then this feeling came over me that is hard to describe. I felt so sad, as though I had lost a brother—my best friend. That's when it hit me, Captain. My best friend! Yes, I knew who had that number now—I could see his face, hear his voice, remember. It all came back, and I remembered he had been taken ill—just a little while ago sir. So I went looking for him. I went down to sick bay and asked the Doctor about him, but he had no idea who I was talking about!"

"Well who *are* you talking about?"

"Alexi, sir. Alexi Tasarov! I can't find him! I've looked all over the ship!" There was a pleading look on his face now, very troubled and bothered.

"You can't find him?" Now Fedorov realized he had been sitting there waiting for Director Kamenski for the last 45 minutes. Something about Nikolin's travail suddenly struck him like a hammer."

"You can't find him? Have you gone to his quarters?" His mind offered up the next logical step in solving that simple puzzle, but even as he did so, he had the feeling that the missing piece meant something much, much more than it seemed on the surface. Nikolin was sitting there, telling him he'd lost his best friend—telling him he could not find this man Tasarov...

Fedorov knew every man that served in a main bridge station, with no exceptions, but he had no recollection of this name— Tasarov...

Until that very moment.

Something gurgled and bubbled up from deep within him, not the boiled stew and tomatoes he had for dinner an hour earlier, but from some deep inner place that seemed almost primal, an old, lost memory, emerging to the forefront of his consciousness.

Yes... *Tasarov!* Alexi Tasarov, the man with the best ears in the fleet! His eyes widened with the recollection, and he could see the man even now in his mind, sitting quietly in his chair, the big headphones like ear muffs on his head, sandy hair protruding from the round rim of his cap, lost in the sound field, or perhaps surreptitiously listening to music when the ship was in a situation where no undersea threats might be possible.

"Tasarov!" he exclaimed. "Lieutenant Alexi Tasarov!"

"You know him?" Nikolin beamed. "I thought I was going mad, Captain. Every time I asked about him, no one knew who I was talking about—not even the Admiral! I've looked everywhere, sir—all over the ship, but he's missing."

Missing... Now the P.A. system announcement Fedorov had made concerning Kamenski seemed to resonate in his mind, yet with a forlorn, hollow feeling. *Missing...* Like the eighth man on Mister Gagarin's duty roster... He was up on his feet, with an energy that seemed to drive him with renewed urgency now. All the strangeness he had felt these last hours seemed to suddenly shatter like a glass. It wasn't me, he thought. Something *is* amiss here!

"Mister Nikolin—Eat!" he pointed at the buffet station. "Then come right back to the bridge. I'm going to get to the bottom of this and find out what the hell is going on here."

He rushed away, intending to go to the bridge, his thought being to report this to the Admiral at once. But another voice in his mind seemed to caution him, and he found himself heading back to the reserve officer's cabin, letting himself in with a furtive glance down the hall.

He went immediately to the nightstand, relieve that it was still there where he had left it out of respect to Director Kamenski. Now he reached for it, with more than a little trepidation, and took it in his hand, somewhat tentatively at first. Then he closed his palm around it, and put his hand in his pocket.

Anton Fedorov was now a Keyholder.

Chapter 35

Fedorov's footsteps came hard on the deck as he hastened to the bridge. Behind him came Nikolin, forsaking his meal and instead struggling to keep up with the Captain, who now seemed driven by a tireless energy. They made their way up the final stairway, and in through the hatch, now permanently open, because the subtle warp in the metal would not allow it to close properly. His eye fell on the dimpled spot in the deck, and his boots were still there, as if glued to the metal deck plating, a reminder of how close he had come to suffering grievous harm. Another few feet, and he might have been standing right in the center of that warped deck zone. Who knows what would have happened to him?

The incident concerning Director Kamenski, and now this sudden revelation by Nikolin had jolted something loose in his own mind—he remembered! The thick, oppressive fog that surrounded the ship seemed to befuddle his mind as well as his senses, and now he could see that many other crew members had been affected this same way. He remembered those first hours after the displacement shift, as he walked the ship to survey possible damage. The crew had seemed listless, confused. Chiefs and Petty officers were growling to get the men moving and put them to some useful work. A few seemed dazed, even lost. He had run into one man, a junior *mishman*, who said he had been looking for the radar workshop, but ended up well forward, under the long empty deck where the missile maintenance crews held forth. He was lost!

While the ship's electronics all seemed unaffected, operating without a hitch, the only damage they had found had been to dead space areas, stretches of metal deck, bulkheads, gunwales and ladders. But now he saw that the men had been affected as well, and it had something to do with their memory.

That was why I could not recall who was on the other side of all those arcane discussions about quantum physics! Director Kamenski! I could not even remember the man's name for a time, until that phrase turned over in my mind, leaping from the muddied pool of my recollection—the slippery fish. As soon as I said that to myself, it seemed to set off a chain reaction, and I started to remember. And by god! When Nikolin first started to spin out this tale about his riddle game, I had no idea who he was talking about—Tasarov! He's clear in my mind now, but thirty minutes ago it was as if he never existed.

What was happening? Are we affected now, just as the equipment and radars seemed to be dazed and inoperable after a time displacement? Or was this something darker, more threatening, more final and absolute. He remembered those missing men when the ship had reached Vladivostok—the list of names coaxed out of Doctor Zolkin by that meddlesome intelligence Captain—Ivan Volkov. They were the names of all the men that had died in those first displacements, in battles we fought with the Royal Navy, the Italians, and the Japanese. Yet when he tried to look up their service records, nothing had been found. There was no record of them in any archive or database in the country. It was as if they had never existed.

Is this what is happening to us all now?

He was through the door, hearing the watchstander announce his coming, though he offered no salute, making straight for Admiral Volsky. Nikolin came up behind him, waiting nervously as Fedorov took a moment to catch his breath.

"Ah, Fedorov, I hope the meal did you some good. I did not expect you back so soon."

"Admiral, I believe we have a serious problem."

Volsky suppressed a laugh. "That is quite the understatement, Mister Fedorov. The KA-40 went up, and they simply could not get high enough to break through this fog. Can you believe that? The service ceiling on that helicopter is 5000 meters, but its grey as a whale's back all the way up! Beyond that, they had a hell of a time finding the ship again on the way back down. We had to use lasers. Another equipment malfunction. They say they couldn't see the ship on radar, and Mister Mikoyan there at the comm station was even beginning to lose our link with them. Thankfully, we got them back, but it was a very chancy landing."

"Sir," said Fedorov, not knowing where to begin. "I think we have more than the equipment and helicopter to worry about now. Nikolin says we have a man missing."

"A man overboard? Who? When did it happen?"

"Not a man overboard, sir, its Tasarov. You remember? He was sent down to sick bay on a stretcher, about four hours ago, just before that system malfunction Kalinichev reported. Just before we lost contact with the *Invincible*."

Volsky seemed to hesitate a bit. "The *Invincible*… Oh yes. Admiral Tovey's ship. Who did you say this man was?"

"Tasarov sir, our number one sonar operator. The best ears in the fleet."

At this Velichko looked over with a smile. He had been listening under his headphones and only caught the tail end of what Fedorov had said, recognizing the familiar phrase that people used with him.

Now Volsky was quiet, his head inclined to one side, eyes looking up, as if he was thinking to see something he was looking for on the overhead HD panel. "Tasarov?" he said. "I must be getting old, Fedorov, or you must be needing sleep. Velichko has been at that post since the morning shift."

"No sir, that is not correct. Tasarov was assigned there this morning. We were discussing that sound he had been hearing. Chief Dobrynin too. We even called down to Doctor Zolkin in the sick bay to check on Dobrynin's condition."

"Chief who? Dobrynin? What department?"

Fedorov's eyes widened with alarm. He went directly to the ship's intercom and punched in the code for sick bay. "Doctor Zolkin," he said. "This is the Captain."

"Zolkin here."

"Doctor… Please update me on the condition of Chief Engineer Dobrynin. Has he been released for normal duty, or is he still with you there?"

The interval of silence hit Fedorov with a sinking feeling. Then

Zolkin came back. *"Chief Engineer? You mean Byko? He isn't here, Fedorov. I haven't seen him today."*

"No, Doctor, not Chief Byko. He's Damage Control Chief. I'm speaking of Engineer Dobrynin—Chief of propulsion and reactor operations."

"I'm sorry, Captain. I don't know the man. He must be very healthy. Good for him!" There was Zolkin's inevitable humor, but Fedorov was not happy. My god, he thought. Another man that no one will have heard of, like Tasarov, like the missing man on Mister Gagarin's duty roster, like Kamenski! It isn't just the ship we must worry about now. *It's Paradox Hour!*

Fedorov seemed shaken as he thumbed off the hand microphone, letting it dangle limply from the coiled wire. It shifted back and forth with the movement of the ship, a silent pendulum of disorder, wanting to be cradled again, safe in the overhead intercom station, and not left like that, dangling, loose, forgotten.

"See what I mean sir!" said Nikolin, and Fedorov gave him a quick glance.

Now he looked directly at Admiral Volsky, his voice taut, the tension evident as he spoke. "Admiral, what I am now about to say will seem preposterous, but you must have faith that I have evidence to support every word of it. We're in trouble—extreme danger—at this very moment. Not just the ship, but the crew itself. Men are being reported as missing. That alone is cause enough for alarm, but what I say next is the real problem—no one remembers them, just like Zolkin there with Chief Dobrynin. Are you saying you have no recollection of the man? He was coordinating all our earlier time displacements with those ears of his. And then there is Tasarov, our number one sonar man—Nikolin's best friend. And one more man has gone missing, Director Kamenski is not in his quarters, and does not answer to intercom hails. He's missing too, sir. They're all simply gone."

"Director who? Kamenski…" Volsky lowered his heavy brows, thinking deeply. Fedorov was watching him very closely, waiting, then he spoke, with hasty urgency.

"We met him in Vladivostok, sir, after we returned from the Pacific. Inspector General Kapustin brought him in on his investigation, and he came to your office at Naval Headquarters, at Fokino. He had photographs, Admiral. Remember? Photographs of the ship as it was moving through the Straits of Gibraltar. We asked him to come with us when we boarded *Kazan*, on that mission to try and stop Karpov in 1908! He's been with us ever since. My god, I spent hours and hours with the man in his cabin, right across from your quarters, Admiral. Don't you remember? You told me to ask him about the gophers—in his garden!" He realized that last bit might make him sound like a fool, but it had quite the opposite effect on Volsky.

"Gophers?" His eyes seemed to catch fire, brightening with newfound awareness. Now he looked around, from Samsonov, to Rodenko, and then to Nikolin and the sonar station, where Velichko sat beneath his head set, oblivious.

"Kamenski," he said haltingly. "Yes... Director Kamenski. The Gophers in the Devil's Garden. That man had a knack for colorful metaphors. I've twiddled with that one in my mind for months."

"Then you remember?" Fedorov beamed, a feeling of great relief sweeping over him. He gave Nikolin a nod, smiling. "You remember sir—Tasarov? Chief Dobrynin and Rod-25...?" He waited, almost breathlessly.

"Tasarov, Tasarov," said Volsky. "Yes... Lieutenant Alexei Tasarov." He looked at Nikolin now. "What have you two been up to, Mister Nikolin? Sending more riddles over the ships messaging system? Don't think I don't know about it."

"That's it, sir!" said Nikolin. "That's how I remembered. I was just telling Mister Fedorov about it, and he remembers too, but no one else, Admiral. No one on the ship knows anything about him— not even Doctor Zolkin. I went down there first thing, but the Doctor says he never heard of him. What's happening? Where is he?" Nikolin seemed at the edge of tears, and Volsky raised a hand, father-like, as if to calm him and offer comfort."

Now the Admiral looked to Fedorov, a grave expression on his face. "Any others?" he said, thinking first of the crew. The instant Fedorov had said that about the gophers in the garden, it was as if a bell had rung in Volsky's mind. That single thread of memory had rippled with fire, the energy leaping through one synapse after another in his tired brain, and the soft glow of recollection rekindled as it went. Places in his mind that had been stilled, as though misted over with that same heavy fog that now surrounded the ship, were now suddenly awake again, remembering... remembering...

"Director Kamenski is missing? You are certain of this?"

"I've been to his quarters, sir. No one is there, and the room itself looks as though it was never used! The Ship's Purser has no record of any visitor quartered there, and no recollection of the man either. And by god, I nearly forgot he was here myself, until a phrase he used came to mind—slippery fish. He always said that about the way the ship seemed to move in time. Then it all came back!"

"And Tasarov? He is missing as well?"

"Nikolin put me on to that," said Fedorov. "You know those two are inseparable. I think that attachment, a long, deep attachment of friendship, was simply too strong a bond between them to be easily forgotten. Nikolin came to me just now in the officer's dining hall. He said he felt like he had lost his brother, but could not explain the sadness he was experiencing. Then he remembered, though no one else remembered Tasarov. Their friendship was simply too strong to be easily broken."

That was the only way Fedorov could explain it, a bond of friendship that was so strong that not even time and fate could break it. For some unfathomable reason, Tasarov had vanished, just like Kamenski. Nikolin had felt that loss on some level, that terrible emptiness, a god shaped hole in his soul. And just as those colorful phrases the Director had used jogged loose memory in the minds of Fedorov and Volsky, Tasarov's message ID had struck Nikolin through with the light of recollection, and he suddenly knew what he had lost.

"Dear lord, Fedorov. What is happening here? Is this what you have warned of? Are we facing this paradox hour you keep talking about."

"Something has changed, sir. Can you feel it? First it was physical—things in the ship suffered actual physical damage. The ship was pulsing, unstable in time. We could all feel it, and god knows Lenkov got the worst of that. Then we just made an uncontrolled shift in time. Who knows why? Yet here we are... somewhere... and the effects we have uncovered extend beyond the damage to bulkheads, deck plates and hatches. Something has changed. Men are missing—so profoundly missing that no one was even remembering they were ever here. Do you remember Chief Dobrynin now?"

"Yes," said Volsky, a vacant look in his eyes. "We needed the Chief to listen to those time displacements, when we used Rod-25. Chief Dobrynin—Yuri Dobrynin! He is a friend of mine as well, Fedorov. I have shared many a good cigar with that man, and Zolkin will come to his senses as soon as I get down there and rattle the Vodka cabinet. The three of us had a nip or two in Zolkin's office from time to time. He'll remember."

"I remember Tasarov now!" It was the deep voice of Viktor Samsonov. "Yes, sir. How could I forget? He was complaining to me for days—about that strange sound he claimed to hear."

Now Fedorov looked to Rodenko, who had drifted into the conversation, a puzzled expression on his face. "What about you, Rodenko?" asked Fedorov. "Can you remember Tasarov now?"

Something about Samsonov's comment concerning that strange noise had shaken the teacups in Rodenko's cabinet. He blinked, looking a bit bewildered, then spoke. "The sound... Yes sir. Tasarov. He said he was hearing something, and I had him trying to work it like a possible contact. Yes! I remember now. Lieutenant Tasarov!"

"Dobrynin was hearing that same sound as well," said Fedorov quickly. "Now both men turn up missing, and they were also nearly wiped from our memory, as if they never even *existed*, just like the men on that list Doctor Zolkin gave to the Inspector General. But they *do* exist—in our minds." He pointed a stiff finger to his head, where the black Ushanka cap he always wore was tilted at an odd angle. "We can remember them now, just like Kamenski told me."

"Kamenski? What did he tell you, Fedorov?" asked Volsky.

"That he could remember many versions of the history we were living through. He said his books changed, from day to day, right before his eyes, *but not his head*." He pointed again. "He could remember events that everyone else had no recollection of at all—events that history itself denied, as if they had never even happened. Do you recall those discussions, Admiral? Remember? Your Chief of Staff at Fokino knew nothing of Pearl Harbor—because our stupid intervention here changed the American entry date in the war. It was 'Remember the Mississippi,' not 'Remember Pearl Harbor.'"

"Who can forget that?" said Volsky.

"Some on this ship may have," said Fedorov. "Just like we very nearly forgot about Tasarov and the others—my god—might there be more men missing? I was talking with Gagarin in the workshops, and he seemed very troubled, thinking he had a short shift, with a man missing. It was as if his old habits were at odds with the reality around him. I think he was struggling to remember something, just as I was, and Nikolin. Just as you did Admiral."

"Who else?" said Volsky. "Might there be other men missing? What if none of us remembers? We'll have to find a way to go over the entire crew with a fine toothed comb and count our heads."

"Orlov would be the man for that," said Fedorov, fingering the pocket compass the Chief had given him, suddenly remembering the man.

"Orlov?

Now Fedorov gave the Admiral another cautious look. "Gennadi Orlov," he said. "The Chief. He's the one who found that thing I threw over the side—the Devil's Teardrop…"

"He reached for the dangling intercom handset again, grasping it and raising it to speak. "Chief Orlov, please respond immediately. This is Captain Fedorov."

They waited, each man looking from one to the other, wondering, held in suspense, as if they were waiting at the edge of infinity itself. They had all climbed to this place together, and the rope of their recollection and memory was still dangling over that precipice, as they waited for the last man to come up.

But he never came. Fedorov repeated the call, but it went unanswered, his voice echoing plaintively through the ship, hollow, forlorn, lost.

Orlov was gone.

Chapter 36

They stood in a circle around the Admiral in his chair, instinctively closing ranks, as if to guard against some icy wind that might sweep over the bridge and take another man—then another. Any man who ever joined the military, on land or sea, knew there would come moments when they would sit and stare at those empty chairs, the memory of lost comrades, fellow soldiers and sailors, still bright and glowing in their mind. But the men who made those memories would be gone, and that was sometimes an agony worse than a missing arm or leg. Those lost limbs sometimes still tingled with a strange sensation, phantoms, ghostly remnants of the life that was once there. Now they all felt that same prickling recollection of the men who were no longer there—Tasarov, Dobrynin, Kamenski, Orlov…

How many others were gone, forgotten, swept away on the tides of this sea of time, their memories hidden by the thick fog still enfolding the ship? They stood there in that circle, Volsky, Fedorov, Rodenko, Nikolin, Samsonov, five who knew, contemplating those empty chairs.

"Why, Fedorov?" said Volsky, reaching for understanding. "Is it that these men failed to survive our recent displacement? Are they out of phase, stuck somewhere else? Are we going to find them in a storage locker somewhere, like Lenkov's legs?"

"No sir," Fedorov said emphatically. "I know that Dobrynin was here after that shift—right in sick bay. I called on the Doctor to check on him myself when I was walking the ship to see about shift damage. Orlov was here too! I remember he came onto the bridge, complaining as he often does, and he handed me this!" Fedorov showed Volsky the pocket compass, its needle still wildly erratic."

"Yes," said Volsky. "I remember that… we all remember that. Correct? Rodenko?"

"He went over to have some coffee, sir," said Rodenko. "Then he went into the operations room, but I was just in there, and there's no sign of him. Not even his coffee mug."

"So they were here *after* the shift we just made," said Fedorov. "But I think Tasarov went missing *during* the shift. I clearly remember someone saying Velichko had the best ears in the fleet. No offense to Mister Velichko, but we all used to say that about only one man—Lieutenant Alexi Tasarov. Am I correct? It struck me as odd at the moment, but there was too much to worry about just then. After that I walked the ship, and I could see the men were somewhat confused and disoriented. One even reported he thought someone was missing on a work shift, but I took no real notice of that. Yet I know Dobrynin was in sick bay, so he must have vanished some time after that."

He gave them all a wide eyed look. "That means this may not be over yet. These effects could continue."

"Not over? You mean others could go missing—just disappear?"

"Like Dobrynin, Orlov, Kamenski…" Fedorov had made his point clearly enough. "Yes, I think Kamenski may have survived the initial displacement as well, but then he vanished too. We've clearly entered some altered state here, and like ice freezing, it doesn't always happen at once. It takes…. Time…"

The thought that others might soon feel that cold freezing hand of time on the back of their neck gave each man there a shiver. Volsky lowered his voice, seeing other junior members of the bridge crew looking their way now.

"Why these men, and not us?" The Admiral had a scattered look on his face.

The anguish of the question clawed at Fedorov, though he had no real answer. All he could think of were the words Kamenski had spoken to him in their last meeting… *Now you question the choices Death makes… Why do leaves fall in autumn, Fedorov? Who decides which ones go first?*

"Consequences," he said, unknowingly echoing the very same word Orlov had spoken to Karpov when Sergeant Troyak first burst through the bridge hatch when the Captain had tried to take the ship.

That all seemed so very long ago now, another memory, another reality.

"If these men are taken from us, then we may have done something that affected their personal lines of fate. Then again, maybe that thing Orlov found had something to do with all of this. Dobrynin spent a good deal of time around it during his examination of the object. Even my brief handling of the object caused that strange event with my hand, and Orlov, god rest his soul, he was carrying the damn thing around in his pocket!"

"But Tasarov? Kamenski? They had nothing to do with that thing," Volsky protested, inwardly grieving for the missing, like a father who had lost his children.

"It is only one possible explanation," said Fedorov. "Maybe it had nothing to do with these disappearances. Perhaps it was us—the ship and crew—all of us, as I said earlier. We could simply be fated now, fated to face the consequences of the world we have created in the future with our actions in the past. I don't have all the answers. Right now everything is spinning like a mad top. We're somewhere, but we don't know where. It isn't just these three men that have gone missing. From Admiral Tovey's perspective, we've *all* gone missing— right along with the ship itself." Then something occurred to him, that had stood as one of those stubborn unanswered questions in his mind for so long. "Just like Alan Turing's watch," he said.

"What is this you say?" said Volsky.

"You remember how Turing claimed his favorite watch went missing, only to reappear in those file boxes containing evidence of our earlier time displacements? They appeared at the same time we arrived here, in June of 1940, but time had a problem with that. You and I both know that everything in those files was created in the future, mostly in 1942 from the dates on the material. Everything in those boxes then moved to 1940—including the watch. Apparently Turing must have had the watch with him while he was working on those files in 1942. Who knows, perhaps it slipped and fell into one of those file boxes. When they moved here, strangely following in our wake, there would have been a problem. Unlike the files, *that watch was already here.* It existed in June of 1940, and so how could it travel back inside one of those file boxes? It was a paradox, and look at the way time handled it. Turing's watch went missing. It simply vanished, until it turned up later in that file box. *We* vanished the same way, the ship, all of us, because we face the same paradox."

"Yet we thought we would have until July, Fedorov. We first shifted on July 28th, during those damn live fire exercises. You are saying this is not so? This paradox business has already happened?"

"Perhaps. It may have merely been the ship's instability in time that provoked this latest shift. In that case, perhaps Time is just taking advantage of that to sort things out."

Then this is the result?" said Volsky. "Lenkov? That warped deck over there where your boots are still stuck? Men missing?" He shook his head. "I know you cannot know any of this for certain, Fedorov. Forgive me if you hear any blame in my tone. I mean none. If these are the consequences of our actions here, we may never know why some are missing, while we still remain. A pity we don't have Kamenski to weigh in on this."

Now Fedorov remembered what he had found on that nightstand. He reached into his pocket, feeling the key, his mind returning to that piece of this shattered puzzle.

"Kamenski left something behind," he said, drawing out the key. "I found it on the nightstand, just sitting by the lamp."

"That is one of those mysterious keys, is it not?" asked Volsky. "If I understand correctly, one was responsible for moving the *Argos Fire*—displacing it in time, just like Rod-25. Yes?"

"Not exactly, Admiral. I asked Miss Fairchild about this, and she believed it was the box that moved the ship. The key merely activated it. In fact, she said she believed there was a fragment from the Tunguska Event in a hidden compartment of that box. I do not know how she would come to that conclusion, but apparently British intelligence knew about the odd effects surrounding Tunguska, and we both know what Orlov found there…"

"Only too well," said Volsky. "But I don't like this, Fedorov. That thing might be part and parcel with what we are dealing with now. What if you turn up missing next, just like Kamenski?"

"I don't think the key caused his disappearance," said Fedorov. "It was placed on the nightstand, as if he had deliberately left it there to be found. If Kamenski just vanished, and the key was all that remained behind, why wouldn't I have found it in some haphazard place, perhaps on the floor, or chair where he often liked to sit and do his reading. No. I think he meant to leave it behind, and meant for us to find it if that is so. Fairchild seemed to think these keys were very important sir. In fact she claimed to be their keeper, on a mission to recover any known key they could find. That was what this rendezvous with *Rodney* was for, but when I last spoke with Director Kamenski, he told me Fairchild was mistaken. She was not the keeper of those keys—Kamenski said he was!"

"What? You mean he knew about these keys all along?"

"Yes sir, he said he had been a Keyholder for over thirty years. Apparently the KGB found this that long ago, and he's had it in his possession ever since."

"Remember what I said earlier, Fedorov. There's more to that man than we know. But I don't suppose that key will unlock the dilemma we now find ourselves in. We still don't know our position, in space *or* time. What are we going to do about this situation?"

"We should look after the crew first," said Fedorov. "We know men are missing. There may be others we do not know about—others we've forgotten."

"Yes, we must count heads," said Volsky. "Yet a few minutes ago no one here even remembered Tasarov. Taking roll call is going to be a bit of a problem under these circumstances."

"Perhaps we can check all the ship's records," said Fedorov. "I'm beginning to think these changes are still underway, a process that has not reached completion. If that is so, there may be some record or clue that can help us. I suggest we start with the ship's primary roster, and see if Orlov and the other missing men are still listed there. Yes, we might find some evidence—particularly the digital records. All the electronics seemed unphased by this last event… except the Purser's computer. He had no record of any assignment to Kamenski's quarters. I think we must act quickly now. Whatever seems to be happening to the ship and crew might still be underway. Mister Nikolin, see if you can find the ship's roster in a digital file, then compare it to any printed physical roster we have. Check for discrepancies. Check everything."

"Then we will finally have a count on the empty chairs," said Volsky with a somber tone.

"As to where we are, and what happens next," said Fedorov, "I do not think we can just sit here, waiting for the axe to fall. What? Will we watch people disappear, one by one? It feels like we are sitting here with all our heads on the chopping block, waiting for the executioner, or worse. No. I think we must do something. We still have those two control rods. Remember what we discussed? Time to go to Plan B."

"But Fedorov," said the Admiral. "Chief Dobrynin is gone. We have no one who can listen to the event, the reactors—no way to control the outcome."

"We had no control over this the first time we displaced," said Fedorov. "In fact, it wasn't until we reached the Pacific that we put two and two together and figured out Rod-25 was responsible. I say we should just get on with the maintenance procedure, and see where it takes us. Anywhere would be preferable to this nightmare. We must try and take our fate into our own hands."

"Spoken like a good ship's Captain," said Volsky. "If we end up in the Himalayas, sitting on some lonesome peak like Noah's Ark, then we'll all have a good meal, and hike out."

Fedorov nodded, as he could think of no real reason why they should not try—aside from the possibility they might end up *inside* the Himalayas, which he had suggested to Volsky earlier, though he said nothing of that now.

"I think we must hurry sir," said Fedorov, with more urgency. "We've got to take some action before it's too late! These events are still unfolding. The longer we delay, the greater our peril."

"Very well," said Volsky. "Now that I notice all these stripes on my jacket cuff, I think I will start giving some orders. Mister Nikolin, get back to your station and dig up those digital files, but first send a message to the reactor room. Tell whoever is in charge that they are to retrieve the Beta control rod from storage and re-mount it in the number twenty-five reserve rod position. They are to prepare for normal rod cycle maintenance, to be initiated on my order, or that of Captain Fedorov or any senior officer on the bridge. Hopefully, no one else will be leaving soon…"

He gave them all one last look, as if trying to firmly fix the image of each man in his head, seeing the lines on their faces, their eyes, remembering them, loving them all. Then he smiled.

"Let's get to work, gentlemen, before we end up having coffee with Orlov!"

That was life in a nutshell, thought Fedorov. They were all going to disappear one day, in one way or another, and then simply vanish from this world. It was all about the things they could do while they were still here.

* * *

Far away, perhaps in another time and place, the world *Kirov* had vanished from was still raging with the ravages of war at sea. As *Rodney* foundered, her hull rent open by the explosion of her own torpedoes, two ships appeared on the horizon, *Renown* and *Repulse*, rushing to the scene with guns elevated for battle. And off to the southeast, *Argos Fire* was dashing forward into the fray, the missile crews rushing to their stations.

Yet Kapitans Topp and Hoffmann were not to fight alone. Lütjens' task force was also arriving on the scene coming out of the southwest like a sudden squall. There sailed the ship that had once been fated to meet its doom this very month, the *Bismarck*. And behind came another ship, larger, more powerful, looming like a shadow of death, the *Hindenburg*.

Not wanting to miss out on the action, Admiral Tovey had also altered his course to steam north to *Rodney*'s aid. Though he might come late to the party, HMS *Invincible* would soon make its presence felt with the roar of nine more massive 16-inch guns. It was to be the largest naval battle ever to be fought in the Atlantic, a collision of five battleships, three battlecruisers, and one interloper from another era, desperate to save *Rodney*, and not knowing her quest was already foiled.

But time and fate were fickle partners in the mad dance that was now underway. Things gone missing in one era, might be found somewhere else. No one knew just then where the quest for that missing key might now lead, or what the fate of England's embattled new ally might finally be.

Kirov had left the world of the here and now, its sharp bow slipping into the grey shadow of Paradox. The strange effects had started with Lenkov, with that awful unheard sound, but they would not end there. Each moment was now bringing the ship closer and closer to that final tick of Time's unfathomable clock—that final hour when *Kirov* would be held to account for all its many interventions in the history of these events.

As with Alan Turing's watch, the ship had slipped into some sallow purgatory, waiting to be judged, and not knowing whether heaven or hell would greet them with that final tolling of the hour that Fedorov had feared for so long. Their presence in 1941 had been a grave and insoluble problem for Time.

On one side of that equation, the ship and crew were set to pierce the ground of infinity, to be planted in the cold northern seas of World War Two like a darksome seed of doom. On the other hand, that seed had already bloomed, a black rose, its thorny stem scoring the history as it grew, its dark flower a shadow in the Devil's Garden of time. Yet only one of the two could remain when that final bell tolled, and Time would have to choose which side of that equation would balance through to the zero sum it was seeking now. Which would it be, the darksome seed or the black rose?

It was time to decide, because the hour of fate was drawing nigh... *Paradox Hour.*

The Saga Continues...

Season 3 of the *Kirov Series* opens with Volume 17: *Doppelganger*, where the answer to the dilemma that now faces Mother Time will decide the fate of the ship and crew. Battle still rages in the Atlantic, and Elena Fairchild arrives on the scene to discover the crisis aboard *Rodney* has made her quest for the lost key impossible. Yet there she meets one other uninvited guest, an American officer who reveals that he is not the man he seems. Together they consider what they may have lost, and how it might yet be saved.

Meanwhile, Vladimir Karpov has discovered that his own personal fate is also in jeopardy as his dwindling lease on time runs thin. Realizing the dilemma that had plagued Fedorov for so long, he rises in *Tunguska*, intent on seeking the heart of a gathering storm, in a desperate attempt to save his own twisted soul from the ravages of Paradox. As he peers through the shattered glass of history, deep into the mirror of time, he suddenly discovers his own self looking right back at him.

The exciting alternate history of WWII careens forward into 1942, as Germany now makes its great bid to destroy Kirov's Soviet Russia and smash the last of the stubborn British resistance in the Middle East. Yet new weapons of war will appear, strange doppelgangers spawned from the legacy of *Kirov*. Now they darken the battlefields of Europe, when the tempo of technology leaps ahead to produce a new generation of tanks, aircraft and the deadly art of missile warfare arrives years early.

Don't miss the premier of Season 3 of the amazing *Kirov Series— Doppelganger*.

Reading the Kirov Series

The *Kirov Series* is a long chain of linked novels by John Schettler in the Military Alternate History / Time Travel Genre. Like the popular movie "The Final Countdown" which saw the US Carrier *Nimitz* sent back in time to the eve of Pearl Harbor in 1941, in the opening volume, the powerful Russian battlecruiser *Kirov* is sent back to the 1940s in the Norwegian Sea where it subsequently becomes embroiled in the war.

Similar to episodes in the never ending Star Trek series, the saga continues through one episode after another as the ship's position in time remains unstable. It culminates in Book 8 *Armageddon*, then continues the saga in *Altered States*, which begins the second saga in the series, extending through Volume 16.

How To Read the Kirov Series

The best entry point is obviously Book I, *Kirov*, where you will meet all the main characters in the series and learn their inner motivations. The series itself, however, is structured as sets of trilogies linked by what the author calls a "bridge novel." The first three volumes form an exciting trilogy featuring much fast paced naval action as *Kirov* battles the Royal Navy, Regia Marina (Italians) and finally the Japanese after sailing to the Pacific in Book III. The bridge novel *Men Of War* is a second entry point which covers what happened to the ship and crew after it returned home to Vladivostok. As such it serves as both a sequel to the opening trilogy and a prequel to the next trilogy, the three novels beginning with Book V, *9 Days Falling*. Each trilogy in the series is followed by a similar "bridge novel."

The *9 Days Falling* trilogy focuses on the struggle to prevent a great war in 2021 from reaching a terrible nuclear climax that destroys the world. It spans book 5, 6, and 7, featuring the outbreak of the war in 2021 as Japan and China battle over disputed islands, and the action of the Red Banner Pacific Fleet against the modern US Fleet. It then takes a dramatic turn when the ship is again shifted in time to 1945. There they confront the powerful US Pacific Fleet under Admiral Halsey, and so this trilogy focuses much of the action as *Kirov* faces down the US in two eras. This second trilogy also launches several subplots that serve to relate other events in the great war of 2021 and also deepen the mystery of time travel as discovered in the series. The trilogy ends at another crucial point in history where the ship's Captain, Vladimir Karpov, believes he is in a position to decisively change events.

The next bridge novel is *Armageddon*, Book 8 in the series, which concludes the opening 8 volume Kirov Saga, continuing the action as a sequel to Book 7, while also standing as a kind of prologue to the next eight volume saga that begins with the *Altered States* trilogy. In this third trilogy, *Kirov* becomes trapped in the world made by its many interventions in the history, an altered reality beginning in June of 1940. The opening volume sees the ship pitted against the one navy of WWII it has not yet fought, the Kriegsmarine of Germany, which now has new powerful ships from the German Plan Z naval building program as one consequence of *Kirov's* earlier actions.

The *Altered States* saga spans books 9 through 16, initially covering the German attack on the carrier *Glorious*, the British raids on the Vichy French Fleets at Mers-el Kebir and Dakar, and the German Operation Felix against Gibraltar. Other events in Siberia involve the rise of Karpov to power, and his duel with Ivan Volkov of the Orenburg Federation, one of the three fragmented Russian states. (And these involve airship battles!)

The sequel to the *Altered States* Trilogy and the bridge novel leading to the next set is volume 12, *Three Kings*. It covers the action in North Africa, including O'Connor's whirlwind "Operation Compass" and Rommel's riposte with his arrival and first offensive. The main characters from *Kirov* and other plot lines from the opening 8 book saga figure prominently in all this action, with a decisive intervention that arises from a most unexpected plot twist. Book 13, *Grand Alliance* continues the war in the desert as Rommel is suddenly confronted with a powerful new adversary, and Hitler reacts by strongly reinforcing the Afrika Korps. It also presents the struggle for naval supremacy in the Mediterranean as the British face down a combined Axis fleet from three enemy nations.

The *Grand Alliance* Trilogy continues with *Hammer of God*, covering a surprise German airborne attack, and the British the campaigns in Syria, Lebanon and Iraq. It continues in *Crescendo of Doom*, the German response as Rommel begins his second offensive aimed at Tobruk on the eve of Operation Barbarossa. At the same time, the action in Siberia heats up in a growing conflict between Vladimir Karpov and Ivan Volkov.

You can enter any of these trilogies that may interest you by first reading the "bridge novel" that precedes the trilogy. For example, to read the 9 Days Falling Trilogy, begin by first reading book 4, *Men Of War*; and to read the *Grand Alliance* Trilogy, begin by first reading book 12, *Three Kings*. To enter the third saga that begins with Volume 17, *Doppelganger*, we advise you to first read the bridge novel *Paradox Hour*, though your understanding of the characters and plot will be fullest by simply beginning with book one and reading through them all!

More information on each book in the long series is available at www.writingshop.ws

KIROV SERIES - SAGA ONE: *Kirov*

First Trilogy: Kirov
Kirov - Kirov Series - Volume 1
Cauldron Of Fire - Kirov Series - Volume 2
Pacific Storm - Kirov Series - Volume 3
Bridge Novel:
Men Of War - Kirov Series - Volume 4

Second Trilogy: 9 Days Falling
Nine Days Falling - Kirov Series - Volume 5
Fallen Angels - Kirov Series - Volume 6
Devil's Garden - Kirov Series - Volume 7
Bridge Novel:
Armageddon – Kirov Series – Volume 8

KIROV SERIES - SAGA TWO: *Altered States* (1940 – 1941)

Third Trilogy: Altered States
Altered States– Kirov Series – Volume 9
Darkest Hour– Kirov Series – Volume 10
Hinge Of Fate– Kirov Series – Volume 11
Bridge Novel:
Three Kings – Kirov Series – Volume 12

Fourth Trilogy: Grand Alliance
Grand Alliance – Kirov Series - Volume 13
Hammer of God– Kirov Series – Volume 14
Crescendo of Doom– Kirov Series – Volume 15
Bridge Novel:
Paradox Hour – Kirov Series - Volume 16

The series continues into 1942 & 1943 with:
Doppelganger – Volume 17

Discover other titles by John Schettler:

Award Winning Science Fiction:
Meridian - Meridian Series - Volume I
Nexus Point - Meridian Series - Volume II
Touchstone - Meridian Series - Volume III
Anvil of Fate - Meridian Series - Volume IV
Golem 7 - Meridian Series - Volume V

Classic Science Fiction:
Wild Zone - Dharman Series - Volume I
Mother Heart - Dharman Series - Volume II

Historical Fiction:
Taklamakan - Silk Road Series - Volume I
Khan Tengri - Silk Road Series - Volume II

Dream Reaper – Mythic Horror Mystery

You can view information on all these books at:

www.writingshop.ws
or
www.dharma6.com

Mailto: john@writingshop.ws

Made in the USA
Lexington, KY
08 February 2015